# WARLORD!

Kate and Trace had been lucky. The trip in the Trans-atmospheric Vehicle—a hypersonic aerospace plane—had taken days off the usual journey to the Lunar Service Station.

Now the sixteen-hour flight was almost over. Trace sat watching Kate, wondering if they were still on the same team. No matter whose game she was playing, she was still the Kate Brittany he'd known in the original Operation Warlord's heyday. For better or worse, he must remember that. And of all the rough and ready agents from that group, besides himself, she'd been the only one to survive. And it wasn't just because she was on the moon, out of harm's way. It was because she was damned good at what she did.

He resolved to make sure that, in her heart anyway, she was working for and not against him. If they could come through this together, and not end up on opposite sides of the playing field, maybe there was a chance that they could have a future, after all . . .

He was still weighing the matter when the lights in the TAV's ceiling flickered, dimmed, and died . . .

# WARLORD!

## Janet Morris

PUBLISHED BY POCKET BOOKS NEW YORK

Distributed in Canada by PaperJacks Ltd., a Licensee
of the trademarks of Simon & Schuster, Inc.

Another *Original* publication of POCKET BOOKS

**POCKET BOOKS, a division of Simon & Schuster, Inc.**
**1230 Avenue of the Americas, New York, N.Y. 10020**
**In Canada distributed by PaperJacks Ltd.,**
**330 Steelcase Road, Markham, Ontario**

ISBN: 0-671-61923-3

First Pocket Books printing September 1987

10 9 8 7 6 5 4 3 2 1

Printed in Canada

TO ANNE H. FREEMAN, MY MOTHER

# PROLOGUE

Richelson was halfway in love with the lady he'd brought up here for a little show-and-tell skydiving—or else he wouldn't have *brought* her skydiving.

Skydiving was Richelson's private passion. Up here where the clouds were like a fleecy mattress and God calls all the shots. Alone with your body and mind and the force of gravity. You fall until you float and you rate your own record: one screw-up, and you don't float. You just fall.

The Beech droned contentedly, cruising with nary a buck; the wind was going to roar like Judgment Day when the jump door was open, but now there was time for high-voltage reflection, for the obligatory assessment of your life you always made before you put it on the line.

This time it wasn't only Richelson's life he was risking. He'd brought the lady with him, on his kind of date: a date with fate. He'd seen other guys take women skydiving out here, west of Los Alamos; he'd met women skydivers before, too. It wasn't that he was testing the lady, it was that he wanted to share something he'd never wanted to share with any woman.

And this lady, Robin Faragher, hadn't even turned a hair when he'd asked her if she'd come. "Of course," she'd said with a little flick of her shapely right shoulder. "I'd love to, Mac."

As it turned out, she wasn't just game; she knew the ropes. She'd dived before. Like somebody'd made her special for him, Richelson thought as the six skydivers in their chartered Beech went through their equipment check.

If Richelson didn't already have a wife and kid, he'd have proposed to her on the way down, when they joined hands, as they'd agreed—stabilize, lock up, and float together until they had to pull their chutes' ripcords.

But Richelson did have a wife and kid, both of whom he dearly loved. Finding somebody like Robin Faragher was a once-in-a-lifetime thing, but it had come twenty years too late.

Still, you took what you could from life in a business like Richelson's. Any job he did might be his last. Any work that came his way was too high-risk for your average Joe. So his recreation and, on occasion, his love life mirrored his occupation.

His onetime boss and old friend Trace Rand used to accuse him of "pushing life's envelope." It was true, but Richelson didn't know any other way to fly.

And, damn it to hell, neither did this crazy lady beside him.

Robin Faragher was five-foot-eight, statuesque and blond, sexy as your monthly centerfold. In the three weeks they'd known each other, he'd taken her cross-country on dirt bikes, fishing, hunting, and rock climbing. For Richelson, that was dating.

But skydiving, and next week, scuba diving—that was courtship. He was aware, looking at the pert profile of the woman adjusting her helmet next to him, that he might be getting in too deep with her.

Risk taking was what Mac Richelson was all about.

The jump master started talking, and Richelson listened up: he'd arranged for Robin and him to jump first. He couldn't afford a truly private charter, but time and gravity were going to allow them an uninterrupted duet, if the jump master did what Richelson had slipped him an extra fifty to do.

Ladyfriend or no ladyfriend, jumping is serious business, even when it's not over hostile territory with fifty pounds of weapons and pack.

Richelson checked his webbing, his chutes—especially his emergency chute—and stepped into the jump bay as soon as it was opened, hands braced above his head on the plane's metal.

He saw Robin's upraised hand at the same time he got the jump master's signal.

Then reflex took over, training and will overrode the perfectly sensible fear of dropping off into nothingness and falling until you bounced, and Richelson's knees flexed and arms pushed.

A weekend pass to heaven, was what it felt like to his terror-sharpened senses.

All alone at first, he fell away from the plane, volplaning his mass through thin air that began to have palpable thickness: waves and currents, lash and gust. And lift.

Once he was stable, spread-eagled on the air as if it were the ocean's surface, he began really to enjoy himself.

The law of gravity used to have a rule that like objects fell at a like rate, no matter their mass. That was before aerodynamics advanced enough to rephrase it: the rate of fall of like objects depends on their composition.

His composition was flesh, and when Robin Faragher swooped into view in a power dive, it scared the hell out of him. She was crazier than he was!

Or something was wrong! Maybe she'd passed out, frozen up. You fall like a stone, feetfirst or headfirst . . . or tumbling.

Just when he was considering a power dive of his own to catch her receding form, she spread out and slowed her descent.

He angled down, relief coursing through him, and made a beeline for her outstretched arms.

3

When he was almost level with her, he realized that she had something in one hand.

It wasn't until he was drifting over and down to her, his hands reaching for hers, that he realized what it was: a weapon.

The taser she was holding spat wire-conducted needlelike bolts, carrying forty thousand volts of current, at his chest.

His body spasmed reflexively and Richelson was falling, out of control, spinning head over heels toward the ground below.

Richelson didn't know it, any more than he knew that the bolts had gotten him in the heart, going right through his suit, before the woman used the wires to pull them free of his flesh.

If he'd known, if he'd been falling but still conscious, he'd probably have tried to recoup, pull his chute's ripcord, or at least control his landing so that when he hit, it wasn't face-first.

But before Richelson's body struck the desert below, he was stone dead.

He hit face-first and then bounced, hit again, face and chest pulverized from the two impacts that destroyed any evidence of foul play a casual autopsy might reveal.

High above his head, the gaily colored chute that was Robin Faragher's opened, and she swung beneath it like a barnstormer, all red and gold and blue in the sunlight.

Above and behind her, other chutes opened as other skydivers pulled their cords.

From the landing site, a siren began to wail and a four-wheel vehicle sped across the desert toward the corpse that had been Mac Richelson.

It was too late for anything but prayers, once Mac started to fall, Robin Faragher was heard to say after she landed.

Nobody who saw what was left of Richelson could argue with that.

Book One

# GROUND EFFECTS

# Chapter 1

# NICKEL IN
# THE GRASS

The Mexican moon was rising, fat-faced and smug, over the Pacific when the American walked down his little stretch of beach to throw a wad of shredded printout into the sea.

In Puerto Vallarta, a half hour's boatride up the coast and the nearest accessible settlement, the indigs and campesinos called him Señor Rand. The chief of police there, more familiar and conscious of the privilege of rank, called him Trace during their occasional all-night poker games.

He'd gotten used to it—to being Tracey Rand, the reclusive American who lived where the jungle met the beach, on a cove that could be reached only by helicopter, boat, or determined men with machetes and snakebite kits willing to make their own road. But he'd never get used to the kind of message he'd gotten tonight.

He unclenched his fist and let the shreds of printout fall. The wad spread before it hit the water, fanning out in the seabreeze. The moonlight struck the paper as it was caught by the tide and for a moment it looked like a Portuguese man-of-war, deadly tendrils trailing as the currents sucked it away from the shore. Then the paper, soaked and weakened by the weight of the water and the pull of the waves, began to disintegrate as it sank.

When all sign of the printout was gone, Rand knelt down in the surf, oblivious to the froth soaking his cutoffs.

There had been six others like him once—seven Americans, trained at great length and expense by one administration to do a job its successor deemed abhorrent. Now, if the message his satellite dish had relayed could be believed, there were only three left: himself, the sender, and a woman he tried never to think about.

Sitting on his heels in the surf, he stared up at the moon while the tide inched in, lapping his calves and then his buttocks. The man in the moon smirked down at him idly. It was the evening of the American called Tracey Rand's thirty-ninth birthday and one of the few friends he had left in the world had managed to get himself killed skydiving. Hell of a birthday present. *Thanks, Richelson. Happy landings*.

Richelson had been a pilot. Pilots shared a superstition: throw a nickel in the grass before takeoff and touch down safe and sound. Richelson must have been short on pocket change.

Behind Trace, from the house five hundred yards inland, a woman's voice called his name, asking in Spanish if everything was all right.

It wasn't, but he lied and said it was, adding, "I'll be right up, America," when she reminded him that dinner was almost ready. He'd hired her as much because of her Christian name as for her utility: she was trilingual in Spanish, Italian, and English; she had a husband who came with her, part of the package—an electronics specialist, a veteran of the Mexican army—and the pair willingly policed the grounds in exchange for U.S. dollars and room and board. There had been other couples he'd interviewed who were as competent at the right melange of skills and as anxious for the job, with work so scarce and the peso devalued to the toilet-paper level—but he'd hired America and her husband, Jesus, because he liked the idea that God

8

and Country were taking care of him. One way or another, Trace wanted to be able to say that.

He heard her go back into the house; the slap of the screen door was testy. The home he'd built here was minimal, a collection of supports and screens under a roof that wouldn't leak. He didn't mind the snakes or the scorpions and the jungle was gentle, even beneficent. He'd been in jungles that hadn't been, and it was very like him, Davies had said on the single occasion when any of the others had visited, to settle in a place that would put him nose to nose with so many unpleasant memories.

But Davies didn't understand him—never had, or Davies wouldn't have sent the message, not worded like that: RI-CHELSON TAKEN OUT SKYDIVING. SUGGEST MEET. COME ON IN WHILE YOU STILL CAN. I DID. D.

So Davies was playing with the big boys . . . again. Hadn't learned a damn thing.

Tracey Rand raised his head to the moon and squinted, trying to see beyond its supercilious smile to what must be going on up there. He hadn't heard a damned thing about the project since he'd left it, but if Davies had "come on in," it meant that there was more than one man in the moon—more to the U.S. moonbase than a "scientific, automated research installation," and a "minimum lunar base, temporarily occupied, supplied from earth during the construction phases of a lunar oxygen production pilot plant."

Of course, there had to be, with the Soviets up there too.

With his naked eye, Rand couldn't see the orbital GEO or LEO stations, or the orbital transfer vehicles (OTVs) shuttling between them. But his mind's eye remembered everything he'd promised never to reveal when he'd signed his SCI (Sensitive Compartmented Information) secrecy oath/clearance form. Most especially, he remembered one line of bureaucratese: *Lunar Growth Phases—lunar self-sufficiency research base scenario.* And he remembered the tables that followed, especially those under the TOP SE-

CRET/NOFORN stamp indicating that this particular batch of Sensitive Compartmented Information was considered a matter for the U.S. intelligence community only. That was what NOFORN always meant: "No Foreign Nationals" privy to whatever was in the designated jacket.

You could have an SCI clearance without having a Top Secret, but the seven of them had had both. And when they were beached, scrubbed before action, some people had tried very hard not to view them as potential time bombs, walking national security risks, or targets for early retirement.

No foreign nationals, Rand was certain, could be proved to have taken the trouble to thin the seven of his group down to three. But somebody had. That was what Davies was telling him, and Davies had been the most naive of the group.

Rand had known it would be like this. He was living a painstakingly quiet life in Mexico, on a cove inaccessible to anything but chopper, boat, or SEAL team, because of it.

He hadn't tried to market unclassified pockets of his expertise the way Davies had; Davies was willing to play politics, to consult in the intelligence community, to walk a thin line Rand hadn't the patience to tread. Trace Rand had just picked up, lock, stock, and pain, and limped down here to live on his disability pension.

Down here where the jungle made lots of noise if you tried to hack your way through it and where his electronic countermeasures could be interfaced with the protective features of this handy little cove to afford him as much security as a reasonable man might demand.

He didn't like Davies telling him it wasn't enough. And that was what the printout was saying, in no uncertain terms. Davies had called Richelson's death the way he'd seen it: as a "takeout."

And Davies hadn't mentioned a single word about Kate, up there with the U.S. lunar base contingent, who was sure that she, a woman and a diplomat of sorts, was safe from any reprisals: she was still a team player in good standing with the United States government.

Rand lay back in the surf, rubbing an old scar on his left hip and letting the mild discomfort of the chilly tide on his torso sharpen his mind as he stared at the moon. He wondered if she knew, if she'd heard, if they'd let her hear: the three of them were an endangered species; Richelson's death proved it beyond a doubt.

He'd thought it would come to this from the stand-down, but none of the others had believed him. They hadn't wanted to. On the surface of it, there hadn't been any reason to—classified projects were scuttled every day. A dead project didn't necessarily make for dead people.

A revived agenda, however, had entirely different implications.

He sat up on his elbows, squinting now at the moon as if the project guidelines were laser-printed on its craggy face.

Maybe that was what Davies meant by "Come on in." Maybe some fool on the Intelligence Advisory Board wanted to start things up again. Maybe, if the foregoing were true, it was the only sensible thing to do.

Trace didn't want to think so. He'd signed enough paper and taken enough polygraphs to last him the rest of his life. If his erstwhile superiors wanted to, they could demand to review his every grocery list for thirty days before he could send his Mexican couple to the store for supplies. They could put cryppies—cryptographers—in his bathroom and Defense Security personnel on his roof.

He'd been very careful to give them no reason to do any such. He'd refused commissions to train personnel for various "friendly" governments; he'd let his membership in AFIO (Association of Former Intelligence Officers) lapse. He'd done everything, at thirty-five, he might have been expected to do at fifty if he was as disgusted and heartsick and melancholy as his kind tended to get.

Rand didn't want to get angry, get mobilized, get to thinking about alternatives or scores left unsettled or dead friends who never made the sort of mistakes that killed skydivers. He especially didn't want anyone to think he was remotely concerned with national security or global policy as purveyed by American interests.

Tracey Rand wasn't even his real name (he'd been re-settled by something akin to the FBI's witness program) but he was determinedly limiting his activities to those that would serve Trace Rand's interests: staying alive, out of harm's way, out of anybody's spotlight.

Damn Davies, for writing forcefully between the lines that Rand's only hope of doing that was bound up with what was left of his group: with Nathan Davies and Kate Brittany.

The mellifluous voice of America, summoning him to dinner, made him sit up abruptly in the surf.

Maybe he'd go to Richelson's funeral. He hadn't gone to any of the others. Davies would be there, certainly, but Kate Brittany probably wouldn't. Even the newest crop of U.S. intelligence advisers ought to know you didn't spend all that time and money to insert a "special activities" agent like Kate into as circumscribed and sensitive a venue as the lunar base and risk blowing everything over a groundside funeral.

Getting to his feet, he took one long last look at the rising moon before turning toward the house. He really liked it here; he wasn't bored, he wasn't restless. He'd managed to put that part of him to sleep.

That was what he risked if he followed through on Davies' suggestion: waking up.

And he wasn't sure he wanted to do that. But he owed Richelson something, and if Kate wasn't standing around the coffin, dressed in black and evoking too many of his ghosts, it didn't have to be *his* funeral. He could probably walk in, show himself to be harmless, tractable, even in-consequential, walk out without so much as a polygraph, and be back to the serious business of beachcombing by the following evening.

He was whistling an old rock tune as he walked up toward the dining table set with candles on his veranda, a sure sign that he didn't believe a word of what he was telling himself but that it wasn't going to matter: he'd made up his mind.

# Chapter 2

# LOW
# EARTH ORBIT

Kate Brittany was dreaming she was back on Earth. She had on her black pressure suit and she was sitting at one of those white-painted, wrought-iron patio tables that have glass tops.

The glass was translucent, wavy-surfaced as if it were a miniature, frozen ocean. On it was the debris of a long wait: crumpled cigarette butts in an overflowing ashtray, white Styrofoam coffee cups through which brown beads of liquid had sweated, highball glasses drained to their dregs, and the tools of her onetime trade—small arms, plastique and det cord, miniaturized black boxes with variously configured LEDs waiting to be lit and quartz timers waiting to be activated.

In the dream she knew her real life had taken her past those days; but it seemed reasonable, even pleasurable to be there. Beneath her metal chair, the floor rocked gently, as if the surface on which their table rested was a float at a Miami marina, a barge, a pleasure boat. On her wrist was a graphite composite chronometer with a second hand sweeping in analogue on its left, a time-elapsed/time-to-go correlate on its right, and a digital display window below, reading out 13:20 hours.

She could see her watch quite clearly, every sun-bleached

hair disturbed by the rubber watchband on her tanned wrist, each tooth in the zipper that snugged her suit to her fore-arm. And she could feel how her body pulsed in those days; it was good to be at her physical peak, even in a dream. There was a salt mist all around, an early morning fog that would burn off with the rising of the sun and the taste of it with her coffee was part of the old excitement.

So was the fact that, in her field of view as she licked the coffee beads from the outside of her Styrofoam cup, she could see other wrists bearing other watches identical in type to her own. Larger wrists, to her right and to her left, opposite her and in between around the table: enough of them, and each recognizable by some specific ring or scar (or, in one case, the team leader's red stripe up his suit's black arm) that she knew they were all together again.

In the dream, Kate was conscious that her eyes were tearing with happiness as she reached out to touch the wrist on her left, the one with the thin red stripe on the suit, when Richelson leaned across the table toward her and said with his lopsided grin, "C'mon, Katydid, just one time, throw a little of that my way."

When she met his eyes to answer, they dissolved into empty sockets punctuating bleached bone and she was looking at a skeleton in ops gear who had the Latin motto of Richelson's special-forces alma mater written in blood on its forehead.

She tried to push her chair back and run, but she was bound in it. She tried to scream, but couldn't even manage a whisper. On her right and left, Davies and Rand still looked normal, but all the others around the table were animated skeletons in combat gear.

When she woke, tears were leaking from her eyes, her arms were thrown up to her face, and she was straining against her safety harness.

Three of the other space shuttle passengers were looking at her askance, and the NASA flight attendant was leaning over her, his brow furrowed: the passenger module that filled the shuttle's bay wasn't meant to accommodate passengers having psychotic episodes. The attendant already had a syringe prepared. Nobody talked much about this sort of thing, but it happened. . . .

Kate waved the attendant's hand away, saying clearly and precisely in her most professional voice, "Kate Brittany. Science attaché from Cop One. I don't need to claim diplomatic immunity for a bad dream, do I?"

The attendant hesitated, frowned, then answered her ultra-sane smile with one of his own. "No ma'am. Sorry, ma'am. If you need anything"—he offered the syringe as if it were a cocktail—"just ask." And he backed off, toward the hatch leading forward to the flight deck.

There was a certain camaraderie between the shuttle crews and the space station/lunar base personnel, even if the males tended to refer, in private, to their distaff counterparts as "astronettes."

Kate had used that camaraderie to good effect several times during what would be, by touchdown in Florida, her eight-day journey home from Copernicus One, nestled south of the Central Peak in the lunar crater's midsection. It took nearly as long by shuttle (though there were quicker ways) to make the Luna/Earth journey as it had taken Apollo, America's first moon mission. Then, the technology had been in its infancy; now, there were stopovers to make: at the Lunar Orbit Service Station waiting for an Orbital Transfer Vehicle (OTV) to take her to the Low Earth Orbit (LEO) station where the shuttles docked; another wait on the Low Earth Orbit station until the shuttle was ready.

It was during her time on LEO that she'd received the news of Richelson's death and the permission—if not the order—to detour on her way to Langley for her scheduled briefing long enough to show up at Richelson's funeral.

The cold, bureaucratic wording of the message telling her of Richelson's death had sparked the dream, surely—that, and the lack of sleep, endemic in her profession, plus the varying G-forces that wreaked havoc with human biology. That was *all* it was.

She stretched in her harness, trying to avoid the covert glances of the others onboard—maintenance types due for groundside vacation, aerospace community functionaries: a dozen in all—and rubbed her puffy cheeks with her hands. Less than ninety minutes, or one full rotation, out of LEO and she was swelling up like a toad all over again.

By the time she got to the funeral service, she was going to look like hell.

She tried not to think about it—not about Richelson or about any living ZR/SEAL alumni she might meet there.

She couldn't afford to be distracted. The briefing she was attending at Langley had been the most important thing on her calendar for the last three months. It was a briefing she could only receive face-to-face: there were some things too sensitive to discuss any other way.

# Chapter 3

# MOON
# SEALS

The situation report that confirmed Tracey Rand's arrival in Washington was slugged with the designation HILEV and hand-delivered to Nathan Davies's peach-and-rust Embassy Row hotel room.

The hotel was one of the finest in Washington, heavily starred and set amid the missions of foreign governments, one in which Davies never would have stayed unless he was here on expense account business, even though it was within walking distance of the West German embassy where he'd had dinner tonight and the British embassy where he'd have dinner tomorrow night. Of course, one didn't walk, in one's tuxedo: limousines were provided.

A string of them came and went below him, at street level, collecting and delivering dignitaries, some of whom, like Davies himself, were preparing for the space talks soon to start in Geneva, being briefed and coached; all of whom, also like Davies, waddled about in "full penguin suit," determined to look as if they were enjoying themselves while on their nations' business even though it *was* business, business of the sort that made pâté tasteless and filet take on the consistency of inner tube.

He'd come back from the German dinner honoring the accomplishments of the European Space Agency determined to shed his tux and his upset stomach and, after a shower, find some feminine companionship—no reflection on his wife, just the only remedy Davies knew for the icy feeling that had settled in his stomach.

But he sat now, wrapped in a terry courtesy robe, beside the tux laid out neatly on his bed, staring at the HILEV envelope unopened in his hands.

By the time it had arrived, Davies had already read Rand's own note, slipped under the door when Davies had come out of the steamy bathroom: *And ye shall know the truth and the truth shall get you killed. Trace VIII–XXXII.*

It was a trifle disconcerting, to say the least—not only because Rand had found and contacted Davies before the combined resources of the FBI, Defense Security, and CIA's Staff D could even verify the recluse's whereabouts, but also because of the message itself.

Was it a threat—a death threat? Was Tracey Rand telling Davies to back off, or else? Was the former Q-group leader involved, somehow, in the high attrition rate among ZR/ SEAL alumni?

It was hard to think clearly with so much adrenaline pumping. Davies sat on his hotel bed tearing Rand's message into thumbnail-size pieces, then placed them carefully in the ashtray on the nightstand. Looking around, he noticed the smoke detector (too close to the bed not to go off if he burned the pieces where he sat), and carried the ashtray to the bathroom, where he flushed the contents and stood staring into the bowl as the blue water returned.

There was a chance, Davies thought, leaning on the pseudo-marble vanity, that Trace was just delivering tit for tat: the message was a paraphrase of the biblical verse etched into the Georgia marble of the south wall of CIA's central lobby at Langley. Davies had no doubt that it *was* Trace's message—the sardonic black humor, the macho facade, the deft send-up of intelligence-community posturing . . . all had his signature—but the ex-ZR/SEAL group leader might simply have taken umbrage at being disturbed during his meditations, or whatever he did down there among the Third Worlders and the parrots.

With a sigh, Davies turned on the "cold" tap and leaned on the vanity's top with both elbows to splash water on his face. When he'd done that, he stared at the image confronting him, its skin mottled red and white from the chill and shiny with droplets.

The most foolish thing he'd done in an otherwise sterling career was to sign on to ZR/SEAL in the first place. The escapade sat in his file, sandwiched between promotions and citations, squat and ugly, out of character, his single failure.

Not that it had been his fault. A scrubbed project was seldom the manager's fault—it was a matter of budgetary constraints and the change in philosophy that accompanies any change in administrations.

Five years had aged Davies perceptibly: his small-featured face was thickening in the jowls, every line under his bright blue eyes had deepened, the parentheses around his mouth were more pronounced, his lips had learned a contemplative set that some might call sullen. His brown hair had thinned, too, retreating from his forehead. But these changes were cosmetic. It was the rest of him, gone to flab under his calm Brooks Brothers exterior, that was sure to evoke that aura of disapproval Rand could summon like a plague.

Now that Trace was here, Davies realized he really didn't want to see the bastard. Even if the man was his only hope of not going the way of Richelson, Blake, Kendall, and Frank. Trace Rand was probably tanned like a surfer and in better shape than most twenty-year-olds, despite his "disability" pension. He didn't sit at a desk all day and get cramps in his arm from talking on the phone, or lie awake at night wishing he dared take a pill to get some sleep because he'd better be sharp in the morning. Paper wars, those were Davies' province.

And he was good at it, too. A fine administrator, he'd likely make supergrade at his next performance review.

If he lived that long. If whoever was taking out ZR/SEAL assets reasoned that a desk jockey like Davies wasn't a threat.

The water on his face, evaporating, gave him goose-flesh. He smiled at his reflection professionally. He was due at a trilateral Space Talks conference in Geneva in three days—trilateral because the European Space Agency and the consortium it represented were considered one ne-gotiating body, the U.S. the second, the USSR the third. There were other interests, of course, but these were client states, UN blocs and lesser-developed countries (LDCs) who wanted rights they'd never be able to afford to exercise without the helping hands and open checkbooks of the su-perpowers or the European Economic Community.

He really wanted to survive to present his proposals at Geneva. The amount of security coverage he'd been given since Richelson's death spoke resoundingly of the intelli-gence community's concern that he might not.

Of course, they didn't like losing their own in question-able circumstances, and paranoia was the community's work ethic. But everyone was being too careful to make sure that Davies wasn't "disturbed or distracted" and to see that his aides knew as much as possible of his agenda for the Space Talks. It was enough to give anyone the shivers.

Perhaps that was why there had been so much concern when it was learned he'd contacted Rand in Mexico.

Not that anyone would admit to having doubts as to Rand's loyalties. Living in the Third World didn't make the man an opposition player. Rand's loyalties ought to be above question, Davies snapped when a usually polite, heavy-set fellow from CIA's Staff D broke protocol and cover and upbraided Davies for "muddying everybody's water . . . sir."

Staff D handled communications intelligence, supported

the secret service when the president was offshore or the FBI when a foreign leader was in the continental U.S. It had once housed CIA's executive action capability, ZR/RIFLE; until five years ago it had included ZR/SEAL. ZR/SEAL alumni, especially dead ones, were its province.

As ex-ZR/SEAL personnel, Davies supposed he ought to be grateful for CIA's concern. But he wasn't. It frightened him like nothing since his days in Trace Rand's Q-group had frightened him.

SEAL had been a designation reserved for the U.S. Navy's sea, air, and land special operations teams until a space-happy U.S. president who was also a Soviophobe had revitalized Staff D's ZR capability. When the acronym SEAL followed the digraph ZR, those letters meant Special Element Aerospace Lunar and represented a team of intelligence polymaths whose combined abilities should have been able to "counter Soviet espionage or technology-transfer activities from Low Earth Orbit outward which involve human collection on-site."

A subsequent policy wielded by a new, more liberal administration had made ZR/SEAL obsolete before any of its members had settled into the space shuttle's passenger module, but not before Tracey Rand's Working Group had acquired a James Bondian reputation in circles with need-to-know and been dubbed "Q-group" by the hardballers, the "Moon Seals" by the community in general.

Now, for reasons known only to policymakers on both sides, somebody was methodically and deniably eliminating the entire erstwhile line unit.

It made Davies, who was under commercial cover, the franchise holder on a proprietary company of CIA's that "free-lanced," consulting on international and especially space affairs, very uncomfortable when he thought about it. But the pragmatic reality of four deaths in the last six months wasn't arguable. Neither was the fact that, of the three remaining ZR/SEAL members, Tracey Rand was the most expendable. Kate was next, of course, from Davies' solipsistic perspective.

And he'd been able to convince those concerned with the Space Talks to share his view. Thus, the message to Rand and Kate's orders to attend Richelson's funeral.

All Staff D had to do was protect Davies long enough and well enough to let the dangled bait flush the killers: if Trace was too tough a target, there was Kate, a woman.

Meantime, it was business as usual—or as close a facsimile as Davies could manage to project.

He was certain enough of his own survival, that night before the funeral, to hope that the actors, when brought to light, would be from KGB's Illegals Directorate, not from somewhere in the voluminous and polarized ranks of the American intelligence and military-industrial complexes.

Because there was something going on up there on the moon. Some black project in the works at the Copernicus crater mining site had triggered the killings, and not even Davies could find out what it was.

Quitting the bathroom as if it were the source of all his troubles, Davies headed for the suite's king-size bed, stripping off his robe and grabbing pajamas as he went. He'd changed his mind. He wouldn't go out—it wasn't wise, wouldn't be fun with some Staff D member tagging along, albeit unobtrusively, in his wake. He'd have room service send up a bottle to help him sleep, call his wife, watch a pay-movie until he dozed off.

He had no intention of picking up the HILEV surveillance report on Rand that the agency had sent over, or of dialing the Tyson's Corner Marriott and asking for Rand's extension. But he did.

When he got no answer, he sighed and took out his reading glasses. He should have expected a dead end. The man who'd sent him that note wouldn't be sitting by the phone at 2000 hours on a Friday night, not in a location so insecure that routine surveillance could pinpoint it—not when it was open season on Moon Seals.

The report was at least ten pages thick—somebody demonstrating efficiency—and Davies settled his reading glasses on his nose, curling up with the sheaf of papers in a comforting parody of normalcy.

Perhaps, since the report contained deep background on the subject, he'd come across Tracey Rand's true name. But he didn't.

# Chapter 4

# POST MORTEM

The funeral service was held in a hangar at Langley Field and the guest list was exceedingly short.

The marines with the closed casket were the only ones in uniform, although at least half of the guests had the erect, at-ease posture of current or former military personnel and dark suits that managed to convey the same martial air that a sea of braid and shoulderboards would have.

So it seemed to Catherine Brittany that the hangar was a microcosm of the District: if military personnel were required to wear their uniforms in D.C., the nation's capital would look like the war college; if they'd worn them here, the hangar would have looked like a bivouac for the joint chiefs of staff.

But everyone was in civvies, making it that much harder to tell the players without a scorecard.

Kate Brittany's one debit as a special activities operative doubling as a moon-based diplomat was that she stood out in a crowd; no matter how short she cut her hair or how unobtrusive her dress, no one ever needed a scorecard or a hint to notice her. She could wear a bag over her head, and if she ventured onto an airliner, into a hotel lobby, or out on a street by herself, any number of gentlemanly strangers would offer to ''help'' her—not from any projected vulnerability (or at least she didn't think so), but some subtler reaction men experienced when in her presence. It had always been that way. Short of growing a beard or becoming a bodybuilder, she'd thought of no remedies.

It had been worse when she was younger, because she hadn't yet proved herself and still had that desperate desire of the intelligent-yet-attractive female to be taken "seriously." Now, in her midthirties, she was only occasionally devalued because of her appearance. And, too, her youthfulness and inherent sensuality had become, over time, an asset. Somewhere in her deep brown eyes, or in her vaguely exotic cheekbones and finely aquiline nose, or in the softly generous curve of her lower lip, lay the reason men warmed to her and women cooled; she didn't worry about it, any more than she cared that her chestnut hair was cut short for convenience or that her body was still puffy from spaceflight—at least, she didn't worry often.

Today, she must remain unobtrusive. So she sat in the rear row on a metal folding chair throughout the ceremony: Richelson had a wife and son, up front, to shed tears and receive the folded flag from the casket and condolences from the chaplain, presidential aide, and special-forces brigadier in attendance.

Kate wondered, watching her own white fingers twist a handkerchief in her linen-skirted lap, what the bereaved widow was making of all this; what she'd been told and what would be left a mystery; whether the National Reconnaissance Office or the air force or CIA would dare give Richelson a medal, with all the attendant questions, or let matters lie.

She hadn't met anyone she knew, which was understandable: she'd come in late, having missed her first connecting flight from the Cape, and slipped into a vacant rear seat while Richelson's fourteen-year-old son was valiantly struggling through his portion of the eulogy.

Almost immediately upon taking her place in the empty back row, Kate had wished she'd never come. Earth gravity felt heavy and restraining, despite all the calisthenics required of Copernicus One personnel; her cheeks felt puffy even though the fluid bloat from her shuttle flight was draining; her eyes burned and her ears ached and her limbs threatened to behave like overcooked spaghetti. It wasn't simply a reaction from so long spent in lunar gravity: it was more psychological than physical, she told herself— the traumatic necessity of behaving like a diplomat when she wanted to cry.

She ought not to, had no right to display emotion, not here, where Richelson's wife, whom she'd never met, might jump to awkward conclusions. And there were so many awkward conclusions.

She saw the honor guard with their rifles and was thankful that there'd be no gun salute here—that was for Arlington and she wasn't going to the interment. The fact that Richelson was being buried at all was odd—he'd always said he wanted his ashes scattered over Bragg. The damnedest thing about this whole funeral was that Richelson hadn't wanted one. You ought to be able to get your last wish granted, even in the District. But the system, inertia-bound and cumbersome, ground on and on, oblivious, and Richelson wasn't going to be able to waft on the breeze, particles of him here and there forever. . . .

She craned her neck, looking for familiar faces in the crowd, and saw none.

In the front row, Richelson's blond wife hugged the folded flag and broke down, sobbing softly. Her son, fair and slight like his father, tried to comfort her, and people all around stood politely, talking and shaking hands with their neighbors so the woman wouldn't feel she was a spectacle.

Then a limo with little flags on its front fenders came purring through the hangar doors, the hearse right behind it: someone had decided they'd better get the wife away before they loaded the corpse.

It was *odd*, Kate thought as she rose to her feet and

sidled leftward toward the aisle without glancing away from the woman being helped into the limo. Behind her, marines began to heft the casket. It was damned odd that an inter-agency event was being made of Richelson's death, and that she'd been requested to attend through channels, yet ignored when she arrived. Odd but not out of character—the system was too big, too unwieldy; Murphy's Law was firmly at America's helm.

For an instant, rebellion coursed through her: she'd go to the grave site, tell Richelson's wife and son some of the reasons they had to be proud of the husband and father they'd lost.

She'd be willing to bet that no one else had. Or would. At best, Richelson might get an Exceptional Service Medallion, and that must be accepted without explanation. . . .

*They were fifty fathoms down in murky water and the satellite was beeping encouragingly. All she could hear was her own heart and her oxygenator until Richelson's helmet came in contact with hers and his southern drawl promised her, "Trace'll be okay. The suits are up to it. There, see? He's waving."*

*And she could see their team leader gesticulating, trapped under the satellite that had rolled onto his thigh and hip.*

*The pressure suits were new, experimental, designed for the fluctuating G-forces of transatmospheric flight, not for deep water. The leader's communications gear had failed, taking the entire team's link with it, when the Soviet satellite rolled onto him.*

*In the light from her helmet (a murky cone that bobbled before her as she swam) she could see dark swirls that might be blood. There was no way of telling if the pinned man was signaling them, or just limp, unconscious, his limbs waving in the current. . . .*

Kate Brittany let out a shuddering breath and blinked back into the present. Clutching her overnighter/briefcase before her, eyes on the pale woman in the black limo pulling away, out the hangar's doors, she bumped into someone sitting in the aisle seat of her row.

"Pardon me, I didn't see . . ." Then Kate looked around at the man, now rising, who'd put his hand on her hip to steady her. "You!" She took a step backward, away from his hand, still on her hip now that he was standing.

Tracey Rand looked virtually unchanged. A shade under six feet, his compact, wiry frame and slightly slouching posture still made him seem bigger: she'd always thought of him as a smallish large person; although only two inches taller than she, he tucked in his chin and bent his head to meet her eyes. His black-haired head hadn't a hint of gray, he was tanned so that the white shirt under his charcoal suit coat seemed phosphorescent, and his eyes were faded from the sun to a pale gray-green the way they always got when he was outdoors a lot.

She stared openly, with increasing consternation, and he stared back with the high-voltage combination of complete attention, calm receptivity, and frank amusement that had always left her speechless.

"Miss me?" he said sassily, restoring the pecking order and breaking the spell that kept her frozen. "You never wrote, never dropped by." A slight smile took the sting from his accusations; his low voice always meant that things were under control. His suit coat was open; his hands slipped to his belt line, one on each hip.

It was a posture she remembered from countless field briefings, and it was a reason not to fall into his arms.

She couldn't start things up again. Messing around with him had nearly ruined her life once. She thought she'd kill the desk jockey who'd so cavalierly decided she ought to be at Richelson's funeral.

"Dropped by?" she echoed, meaning to lace her words with acid but managing only a plaintive wistfulness. "I don't even know which ocean Puerto Vallarta's *on*. And you know how I hate choppers."

"And boats." He grinned, while behind him the crowd began to drift, headed for the hangar's rear doors.

Her glance went to his left hip—she couldn't help it. His presence brought the memories evoked by Richelson's death into a focus so clear they might have been the subject of yesterday's situation report.

When she raised her eyes from his hip, his hand was outstretched to take her by the elbow. "It's fine, good as new . . . almost. Good enough for what I ask of it, anyway. Shall we?"

He took her case and she let him guide her out into the aisle by the elbow, as if they'd both planned it. The accident off Sakhalin Island had left him with no perceptible limp, but five years ago it had had more negative consequences than anyone could ever have imagined.

They were sauntering among the guests like some local couple from Georgetown and it seemed so natural to Kate, following his lead once again, no questions asked, that she was out in the bright May sunlight, headed across the tarmac to the parking lot, before she could summon the strength to object.

"I can't . . . I don't want to go to Arlington. He wouldn't have wanted it . . . Rich wanted to be cremat—"

"I thought we'd go get a drink and catch up with them at the reception, after." He steered her toward a Mercedes with a rental plate parked among the dark G-12 sedans and she caught sight of their combined reflection in a shiny paint job: the tall woman with the space-bobbed hair who met her gaze was half leaning upon her companion for support—her feet weren't used to high heels, her legs shaky in Earth gravity—but her pale jaw was clenched and her head held high.

She squeezed her eyes closed to shut out the reflection with all its connotations of might-have-beens and shifted her weight so that he took his arm away and said, "Unless I'm interrupting something . . . ?"

30

"Yes. No. I don't know. Since when do you drink? And before noon?"

"The drink's for you. You look like you need—uh-oh." Then: "In. Quick. Watch your head."

Sharp, clearly enunciated orders. She was in the car, sliding over toward the passenger side, before she asked what the problem was.

Then she saw it and didn't have to ask: Nathan Davies, who'd been project manager on ZR/SEAL, was hurrying toward them, tie flapping. The harsh light was as unflattering to his thinning pate as it was to his thickened form. With him were two men from the Pentagon, managers of the National Reconnaissance Program whose faces she knew from trade publications and news broadcasts, and a third man, taller than the others, with a white shock of hair, a long jaw, and a blue suit so perfectly tailored it had to be in lieu of a uniform.

"What do I call you?" she whispered, leaning across the seat toward Rand as he slid behind the wheel. "Still Trace?" She tossed her case into the back seat.

"You bet. Keeps it simple."

"Maybe for you," she muttered. It had been his work name on ZR/SEAL. She'd called him that the night she'd lost all control with him and nearly everything she cared about. She didn't want there to be another night like that. She had her life too well ordered.

He cranked the starter. She heard the blown engine thrum, saw him touch buttons. The doors around her locked, the sun roof opened, and the car began to roll backward out of its parking slot.

He was watching his rearview mirror narrowly. Then he sighed, "Shit," under his breath and tapped a toggle.

The car stopped, purring, as the driver-side window rolled down. He put an arm on the sill, a motion that included a desultory wave of acknowledgment, then inclined his head toward the approaching men and said, "Hey there, Davies. Thought I'd see you here." And waited.

31

"Dr. Rand, this is General—"

Trace interrupted the introduction of the blue-suited man with the shock of white hair. "I know, Defense Security. Don't do this to me, Davies. No business—not for me, not with you. Didn't you get my note? Gentlemen, this is a sad day for all of us, and my ladyfriend here needs a good stiff drink. I'm sure you all know how to reach me if you must." As he spoke the last words, he took his foot off the brake and the Mercedes, in reverse, rolled obediently backward.

From somewhere, a man in a sports jacket and wearing sunglasses stepped unhesitatingly into the path of the car's bumper.

Trace Rand shook his head and stopped the car, said to Kate under his breath, "Some things never change," and, when she didn't reply, looked at her sharply. "You up for this? Little powwow with the community about the vulnerability of our precious hides?"

Kate ran a hand up the back of her neck and through her short chestnut hair, an unconscious gesture of frustration. She was due at CIA for her briefing in an hour. She felt distinctly uncomfortable as she replied, "I still work in the community, Trace. You know that."

"Yeah, all right." He leaned away from her, his shoulder and head out of the car now: "Where and when?"

"An hour," replied the white-haired general who couldn't have been more than fifty. "At Langley, Dr. Rand."

Kate slid toward Trace on the seat, touching his arm. "You don't have to, not because of me. I'll just get out and—" And she meant it: no one had said anything to her about shanghaiing Tracey Rand back into harness; if anyone had, her answer would have been a resounding negative—Rand was dangerous to her health. But so was whoever was greasing former Moon Seals. He would know that. And he'd soon know a great deal more if the briefing in question was the one for which she'd been brought down from Cop One. Too much for anybody but designated hitters. Feeling like a traitor, she added very low, "It's *my* briefing, Trace—five'll get you ten."

He ignored her (she remembered how many other times he'd done so), responding to the white-haired man instead. "You'll leave word with the gate guard? I couldn't get the citizens' tour on my own."

"That goes without saying." The general smiled, while beside him Davies was gesturing, first at the car and then at the cloudless sky above, deep in whispered conversation with the two men from National Reconnaissance.

"An hour? Okay. You want to tell that guy to move out of my way?"

The general signaled and the security type stepped smartly aside.

"Wave at the nice men, Katydid," Trace suggested as he spun the car out at speed so that its tires squealed and the gathered brass jumped back in a body.

"Jesus God, Trace, now I really *do* want that drink," she said, trying not to giggle.

"You'll get it," he promised, negotiating the car past the patient stream of funeral-goers in line for the procession to Arlington by taking the Mercedes up on the grass meridian. "You know I always deliver."

"I remember. But you should remember—so do we."

He was cowboying the car out of the air base, looking for his chance to swing onto the access road that would take them to the Beltway.

He found an opening and G-force pushed her back into her seat as the Mercedes squealed into a U-turn across three lanes of traffic and accelerated away from Langley.

"Where are we going?" she objected. "We've only got an hour. Trace, look . . . are *you* worried? About our lives, I mean?"

"One question at a time. We're going to my hotel—for your drink."

"Your hotel," she repeated dumbly, sorting furiously

33

through her own confused reactions for a reason to object that wouldn't sound childish and vulnerable. She was no teenager; she ought to be able to handle an hour with Tracey Rand and not panic.

She was still trying to come up with a good excuse when he said, "As for your second question, that's where the rubber meets the road, isn't it? We'll talk about it."

*We'll talk about it:* another echo from her past. She tried to remember one time when they had. She couldn't. So she said, "You haven't asked me what it's like, working on the moon. Everybody else does. . . ."

"Maybe I don't want to know." He was more relaxed now; his voice had lost its sharp edge. "You haven't asked me what it's like to be a Mexican beach bum."

"It makes sense, what I'm doing," she said defensively. "If you were cleared for . . . if I could explain, you'd agree."

"Talk to me, then."

"You know better. Maybe they will at Langley." The Langley in question wasn't Langley Field or Old Langley, but an exit off the Beltway marked by a green-and-white road sign with an arrow pointing right, at the end of which was the Central Intelligence Agency.

"They'll tell me my life's at risk. I know that. I came here anyway."

"Why *did* you come? You didn't go near Richelson's widow; I'd have seen you."

They were heading toward McLean; the divided highway was lined with high-tech architecture, the lairs of the Beltway Bandits who raided federal budgets and used the loot to raise these towers of mirrored glass and granite.

"Why? To see you."

"Oh, sure." The man was dangerous, there was no doubt about it.

"And because Davies sent me a weird-ass note. And because Richelson deserved to have somebody there—besides Davies . . . somebody who knows what it all meant."

She couldn't help the bitterness that snuck into her voice. "Okay, Q-leader, maybe you'd like to tell me: What did it all mean? Something? Anything? You had plenty of time to think about it, learning to walk all over again."

His eyes left the road to meet hers for only an instant, but she felt a perceptible spark at the contact. "It meant more than what you're doing now—exporting all this mess"—one hand indicated the acronym-labeled corporate headquarters on either roadside—"all the superpower rivalry and parochial European partisanship and commie/capitalist hatreds to the fucking *moon*. And beyond. Haven't you stopped to think that there might be something wrong in perpetuating a system that's tearing one planet apart so that we can *keep doing it* up there in case we screw up so bad down here there's nothing left?"

She was so startled at the last thing he'd said that she didn't even bother to object to what preceded it.

"So you *do* know about Cop One—Copernicus One . . . the real story, I mean."

"Honey," he said wearily, "I helped draw up the game plan."

"But now you've had a change of heart?" They were going to have a fight, a knock-down-drag-out verbal war, just like they used to have, from which both of them would emerge with bloody memories and no answers. And she couldn't stop it.

"Like you said, I had *lots* of time to think about it."

"Things are different now, Trace. Truly. Or I wouldn't be doing it . . . I don't have to, you know." She didn't care what she said, she just wanted to derail the argument before momentum took over.

"That's something, anyway. Well, go with God, then."

"Go? Where? To Langley? You said you'd go too . . . meet them, talk to—"

He flashed her a quick, bad-boy grin. "That was before I realized I could force you to all sorts of lengths to convince me to listen."

# Chapter 5
# THE BRIEFING

Walking through Langley's central lobby with Kate Brittany, Tracey Rand had felt as ersatz as his identity, as misconstrued as the mosaic eagle's-head-and-shield crest underfoot, and as temporary as the borrowed abstract art lining the white walls of the first floor.

Only Kate's proximity, the linen and perfume of her, had made any sense of his presence here. She was one good reason to endure what was to come: he didn't want to find himself back up here in a week or a month for her funeral—she was too much alive, and so were his feelings.

Not that such feelings made sense to him. She confused him, attracted him, and repelled him; she was a willing part of the community from which he'd resigned, full of battle fatigue and despairing; she was too smart to fool and too dangerous to fool around with. His body reacted to her with such concentration that he was preoccupied; he'd been so before and made a mistake that had cost him a great deal of pain and left him with a prosthetic hip joint.

But it wasn't her fault, any more than the intransigence of the bureaucracy she served.

From the north wall, the bas relief of Allen Dulles snubbed him even before he'd reached the elevator. Kate had gotten him smoothly past the visitors' parking lot on the right side of an otherwise untenanted street, past the gate house and its mechanized barrier, and beyond the reception desk where credentials were checked.

Now, she pressed the elevator button for the seventh floor and shook her head when he opened his mouth to comment.

Like the half hour they'd spent in his hotel's bar, this interval would pass without any exchange of relevant information. He respected her for it, but it irked him.

The seventh floor was the domain of supergrades and she'd come up in the world, to be able to access it so casually.

As she led him down a corridor and into a government-style sterile, blue briefing room where rows of orange movie-theater seats faced a dais behind which was a projection screen, he covertly studied the swinging hips and stockinged legs before him, looking for something he wouldn't like—some change that would make a difference in the way he perceived her, a chink in her armor that would allow his mind to override his body.

He'd tried in the hotel bar to do the same and failed there as he failed here. He'd known back in Puerto Vallarta that seeing her would be the worst of what was to come. Trace Rand could leave—*had* left government, because it disappointed him, because it was lacking in ideals commensurate with his own, because it just didn't *work* right, couldn't subscribe to his maxim, "If it ain't broke, don't fix it." But he'd never left Kate.

She remained in his sandbagged emotions, hovering there like a taunting ghost slugged "unfinished business." Probably, he told himself, because she kept letting him know they were incompatible, that he'd never have her, and he didn't know how to take no for an answer.

Probably he would have come up here even if she wasn't involved. It was his own ass he was trying to save, if Davies was right.

Alone together in the briefing room, they sat side by side

in the front row and he said, for the sake of small talk and a chance to meet her wide-set brown eyes, "Back at the bar, you asked me if it was more than my accident . . . why I left."

"Qualified personnel are at a premium," she said guardedly, knowing him well enough to know that he was going on the record with whatever he was about to say, not for her, but for whomever would later review the briefing tape. A wary expression drew a deep, habitual group of furrows between her brows, like the Cyrillic character for *P*.

"There's a story that's probably true, since the briefing officer involved told it to me: he went up to the Hill with his graphs and charts"—unconsciously, Rand gestured to the projector on the dais—"in the late fifties to get funding for the black project that began CIA's satellite program. He explained in detail, for hours, while the old senator whose committee could make or break the budget snored intermittently.

"When the briefing officer had finished, he thought he'd blown it, but the old senator leaned forward and said, 'Okay, you've got your money, son. Just tell me one thing: what keeps them things from falling down?' "

Kate's brow was smooth now; a smile threatened to invade the corners of her mouth; her eyes said, *Incorrigible*, but her lips replied only, "And that's why you left? Because some things never change? It's not true, you know—we're changing things. For the better. In spite of everything you—"

The swinging doors opened and men's voices preceded three people into the room: the white-haired general, Andresson, who had invited Rand to the briefing; Davies, waddling along beside him; and Bates, from Staff D, who had briefing slides under his arm.

Finally, Rand's adrenaline level rose sufficiently to take his mind off the woman beside him.

Bates meant trouble, hardballers, serious business—Staff D didn't screw around; they were the ultimate security force. Trace ought to know; when he'd cared about who was who in the community, his Staff D affiliation had been a matter of pride. Back then, he'd thought reasons were best left to wiser heads; being among the best of the best had been enough. When he'd been young and impatient, the ability to *act*, unequivocally and nearly unilaterally, which Staff D possessed, had overshadowed all questions of propriety or consequences.

That was then. Then, Bates had been an occasional problem—a dissenting opinion voiced with parallel rank behind it. Now, if Rand was reading the signs, Bates was in charge of protecting the lives of what remained of ZR/SEAL—of the three of them in this room.

And Andresson, the general, was here to throw a cloak of respectability, of official sanction and of nearly limitless clout, over the proceedings.

"Hi, Bates," said Rand with a desultory wave. "Davies, I should have known you'd be the one holding things up. Can we get rolling?"

Kate's hand touched his knee, rested there. *Okay, okay, I'll be good.* For her, he'd try to be.

Andresson reached in his pocket and pulled out a telescoping chromed rod much like an old-fashioned car-radio antenna. In the trade, it was called a spook-gooser.

Alternately collapsing and extending the pointer between his palms in a habitual nervous gesture, Andresson said, "Let's save the small talk, gentlemen and lady. Mr. Davies assures me that you know, Dr. Rand, all the deep background you need to about Cop One; Mr. Bates has had you cleared to your former level."

Andresson's gaze caught Rand's and held: Trace was being told that he'd been investigated thoroughly, that his own "deep background" had been combed for the merest hint of shifting loyalties, and that he'd come through clean. He wouldn't have if they'd polygraphed him and asked about drug use—if they still worried about that.

What they were worried about, he knew, was that he'd

object to being run through the mill without notice or that he'd tell them to take their clearances and shove them. He just nodded: if they were this worried, he wanted to know why. Even the knowledge that they were counting on just this reaction didn't bother him. It was his ass, after all.

When Rand broke eye contact, Andresson pulled his pointer to full extension, and added, "So if you don't want to go any further with this, say so now. You can go back home and play with your pet snakes. Sit through this, and you're on board for the duration."

"Or till death do us part?" Rand quipped. Kate's hand finally left his knee. "Go ahead, General," he added. "Anything that'll get Bates up here in broad daylight has got to be worth hearing."

The woman beside him sighed deeply, shaking her head, and slid down in her seat. He remembered her reaction from other briefings: if they glimpsed each other now, laughing out loud was a real—and inappropriate—possibility.

Davies, who had been standing near the door all this time, sighed deeply and lumbered toward a seat behind him. Taking it, he said, "Off to a great start, Rand."

Rand ignored him; the words had come to him on that particularly pungent halitosis that fear imparts to human breath.

Davies had plenty of reason to be nervous, Rand found out as Bates slipped large, custom-made slides on the opaque projector and Andresson, with his spook-gooser, pointed out the changes in the wiring diagrams associated with the administration of Cop One since Rand had defected to a Mexican beach.

The project objective was still the same: set up a self-sufficient colony with a credit base of liquid oxygen fuel, refined from the Copernicus crater's central peak and shunted into orbit to supply the manned station and space transportation systems at a lower cost than fuel could be boosted from Earth. The various cover missions—scientific, commercial, research and development—were ongoing, including a dark-side radiotelescope station, agricultural and mining ventures. But the real mission was still the same: military command, control, communications, and intelligence (C3I); surveillance and monitoring of Soviet activities on earth and in near space; and supremacy in strategic defense—laser battle stations, preemptive strike capability from space on Soviet space weapons. And, of course, containment of Soviet expansionism in orbit, on the moon, and beyond.

There was something else, he realized as the wiring diagrams (charts showing command structures reaching from the Pentagon's Tank, in which the joint chiefs held forth, to the diplomatic modules buried two meters deep in the lunar regolith) went by and he began noticing that there were components missing.

The missing components of those charts begged a question of memory: how much did Rand recall of the Mars mission, a project so black that it couldn't appear on wiring diagrams shown to three people on Langley's seventh floor? The omission, he was certain, was a confirmation—they knew he knew, and they were telling him that (a) the project was on line and (b) they were concerned that it might be in some way connected with the deaths of ZR/SEAL alumni: Blake, Kendall, Frank, and most recently Richelson.

What the general told him, once Bates had removed the final slide from the projector and the wall screen behind Andresson went blank, was, "We need to reactivate ZR/SEAL, after a fashion. We want you to join Ms. Brittany at the Cop One U.S. mission, under nondiplomatic cover, if possible."

"What?" He didn't believe it and turned in his seat so that he could see Bates, tall and broad, now at technical ease against the wall.

Bates had a moon face and close-cropped graying hair. He shrugged and affected a paternal, concerned smile so foreign to his features that the result resembled a man who'd unexpectedly found himself sucking on a lemon.

"Rand—we'll call you that, if you don't mind. . . ."

It was a reminder, unsubtle and clear, that the man called Tracey Rand long had been and still was under the tacit protection of the government he'd served. He sensed Kate's discomfort as she shifted in her seat beside him so that her thigh rested against his. He kept his eyes on Bates.

"We don't want," Bates cautioned, "to educate too many people . . . not about Cop One, or its extensions; not about the ZR personnel attrition—not until we can determine who's picking you people off. You ought to be able to see that."

"I see it. I just don't think I belong on the moon—I'm not—"

"You don't belong in a box, like Richelson," Kate interjected, her voice tense and low.

"In such a constrained environment, where movements of hostiles and possible hostiles can be easily monitored, we have a chance of determining—" Bates started to continue, as if instructing a child.

Rand interrupted: "You have a chance of flushing whoever it is, with us as bait." He shifted again, this time to face Davies, and said, "Tell me, Bates, is Davies here going too?"

"*Me?*" Davies's outrage showed; his face fluoresced red. "I've got Space Talks to attend."

Decoys, then. They couldn't risk the embarrassment of having Davies greased at their damned Space Talks.

He watched Davies silently for a long moment, until the little consultant/diplomatic troubleshooter began to sweat. At least he could still elicit the same reactions he'd been able to in the old days.

But, the moon?

Kate was staring at him, he could feel her. When he turned that way, he saw something very unusual: on a face that never showed emotion that was spontaneous, except in his dreams, a battle for composure raged.

Rand leaned toward her and said, in an intimate voice better suited for private conversation, "What say, Katydid? You want me up there? And if so, in what capacity?"

"I . . . that is, whatever the staff decides, of course. But Trace," she added, fully in control once more, "I'd love to show you what we're doing up there—the progress, the interlunar community. The way the Russians, the Europeans, and we—"

That was the party line, and he knew it. What he'd seen earlier had been truer: shock, that matters were estimated to be so desperate to have counseled such a move; distress that she hadn't been warned; fear for her position; doubts that this did not in some way reflect on her own job performance. If they were bringing him on board, was she demoted? And personal qualms.

Well, he had them, too.

Then Bates took over the briefing and began cataloging and collating the circumstances of the various "accidental" deaths of the other ZR/SEAL members, and Trace's adrenaline level shot higher.

Sitting there, faced with unequivocal evidence that none of the four ZR/SEAL deaths had been accidental and that one at least—Kendall's—could be sourced to a foreign government (sourced, but not confirmed), Rand's heart began to pound.

Back on his beach, he'd worried that the part of himself he'd lulled to sleep and kept asleep for so long would wake. But that awakening was so abrupt and so complete that now, as he cursed under his breath and his hackles rose and anger lent him a strength he hadn't felt in years, he realized it wouldn't have made any difference to the outcome of this briefing if Kate Brittany weren't on hand.

He wasn't about to sit around waiting for somebody to kill him, and he wasn't about to sit back and let somebody kill a project to which he'd given so much.

His hip twinged, a phantom pain reminding him just how much he'd given. He cared about nothing but how much support and how much control they'd give him.

If he was going to play hide-and-seek with agents of a hostile government on the moon, they'd better be willing to give him everything he asked for—all the help they could.

And that included Kate. There would have to be a restoration of the old pecking order, he realized, as he realized that they'd better get Davies out of here soon (Davies shouldn't know specifics and they were right up to his clearance ceiling) and that the briefing would probably last all night, if they wanted Rand ready to lift off with Kate the day after tomorrow.

He didn't have any doubts that he could do the job and survive it, until he looked at her face when they broke for dinner and saw stony betrayal there.

# Chapter 6

# REDOUNDING

"You bastard," Kate accused Rand through gritted teeth as, four hours later, they got into the limo pulled up at Langley's main entrance, waiting to take them to the British embassy party. "You arranged this whole thing somehow, finessed it—didn't you? You want to tell me how?" *And why, Q-leader? I was doing fine, thank you very much, without your so-called "guidance and co-ordination."*

"How?" he echoed quizzically as he slid into the gray plush of the limo after her and their driver shut the door. "Just in the right place at the right time, I guess. The hows and whys that matter are all tied up in the casualty rate . . . something's wrong with Bates and Company's assessment, you can bet. Zip up those bodies in a bag called Soviet sabotage and *presto,* problem solved, case closed but for verifica—"

"Don't you *dare* throw up a shop-talk smokescreen, Tracey Rand. I want to know why you had to leverage your way into my poor little project, what the big attraction is—" *Why you had to pick my desk to sit at, just because you decided to come out of retirement.*

The limo pulled away from the curb, heading for the gate house on its way to the Beltway. Rand slid sideways in his seat and peered at her gravely, his eyes shifting minutely like some motor-driven camera lens as he studied her face, her throat, then what lay below, calculating body language and tension levels and she-didn't-know-what-else. Taking his time about it, letting her know he was thinking about the question and the person posing it.

Just like old times, again. Like the way everyone at Langley, including Bates, had hopped to once Rand started asking his blunt questions and making his outrageous suggestions: What, exactly, were the factors common to the four deaths in question? On what was the assumption of Soviet foul play based? Who had sourced the single poisoning death—Kendall's—to EastBloc, and who, if anyone, had independently confirmed the investigating officer's data? What kind of legend did the Central Cover Staff propose to give him for his trip to the moon?

And, when the summoned cover-staff officer was finished making Tracey Rand into the CEO of a private security firm going after the business of American companies with branch offices at Cop One, his final, non-negotiable demands, phrased as questions: How much working capital did he have? How much authority? Did Bates have hot-line procedures worked out that would grant Rand instant access to Bates, any time of day or night, without going through intermediaries?

Kate had watched Rand tweak the system from its intractably compartmentalized norm into something verging upon autonomy with a mixture of jealousy and awe.

The awe had worn off now and all that was left was dull anger. *They'd never let a woman hack through all their carefully placed red tape like that. They wouldn't dare.*

Maybe it was true, but it wasn't comforting: she'd just seen a man walk in and create a position for himself above and beyond hers, grabbing more power in a few hours than she'd been able to accrue in a lifetime of effort, while letting all and sundry know that *he* was doing *them* the favor. It might be simply a matter of balls, but it galled her.

When Rand finally answered her question, she'd forgotten that she'd asked it and the limo was long past the gate house, speeding toward Embassy Row and the British party that Bates had decreed she couldn't miss and Rand should attend. "Great place to start you and your cover off, with everybody who's anybody in the European Space Agency present and accounted for," Bates had insisted, and sent a gopher to both of their hotel rooms to pick up their party clothes.

"The 'great attraction,' as you call it," Rand said now, after five miles of deliberation, "is pretty basic—survival. Yours. Mine. The project's."

He wouldn't name the project, oh no, not here, where the Langley-cleared chauffeur might not be secure enough to suit Trace Rand. *WARLORD, you paranoid bastard. Say it: Project WARLORD, in pursuit of which the U.S. is going to use nukes against an unsuspecting planet in violation of every existing space treaty and in preemption of those to come. Go ahead, Trace, I dare you: say Black Project AN305 663, code name WARLORD. Say it in caps. It's cost you enough—your hip, your career, our—*

But he wouldn't say any of that. She was supposed to be grateful that he was looking out for her safety, that he'd come selflessly out of retirement on his damned Mexican beach because he worried about her. "Come on, Trace, you didn't do this for any sterling, heroic reasons. You certainly didn't do it for me—not waltz right in and roll over me like some kind of road grader—I went from project director to glorified secretary in less than four hours. . . ."

He frowned and sat back, eyes averted, staring out at Massachusetts Avenue's bright lights. "I missed you, Kate. I know how it looks, but there's only one way to get anything done in this government. You asked me how and why. I told you. I have a real fondness for staying alive. You know me well enough to know that hasn't changed. And next to my own funeral, yours is my greatest preemptive priority." He shrugged. "No use pretending you weren't a factor in my decision." He faced her abruptly.

"Because you were. You want to quit now and come back to Mexico with me, I'll toss all these perks back in their faces."

She didn't know what to say. He was playing bait and switch. He must be. *You throw me a bone and I'm supposed to climb right into bed with you? Good planning, mister—waste not, want not, and I'll be the closest thing to a willing female you'll be able to find on the moon.* One part of her wanted to say *Come on Rand, cut the crap.* The other part, the part that remembered how good it had been with them before it all went bad, won.

"I missed you, too. But what difference did it make—does it make? We did without each other well enough for five years. We'll handle this as a strictly business venture and then not see each other for another—"

"Let's not limit our options, okay, Katydid? Both of us hate to be wrong, or out of control. Speaking of control, as far as I'm concerned—no matter what Staff D thinks or Bates thinks—you're my briefing officer on everything lunar. I just wanted to get you the muscle you're going to need. Think of me as a handy, versatile tool. . . ." He grinned and, despite herself, she laughed explosively.

He reached out and touched her hand, turned it, and brought her palm to his lips.

"Jesus, Trace, lay off, will you?" *Bastard. Seducer.* But she'd known he was both of those. It was her own reaction to him, uncontrollable and inarguable, that made her so angry.

She jerked her hand away and said, "You wanted more briefing, here it comes. The British embassy party is hosting every ESA rep in Washington, and the newbies getting ready for their first lunar shift. The talk will be mostly about overcoming the difficulties—and U.S. resistance—inherent in the transfer of American space technology . . . everything from SDI elements to moon mining . . . to our NATO allies. So you'll need to know the players."

She spent the rest of the ride briefing him as best she

could on the political animals he'd meet in tuxedos and Lagerfeld gowns at the British embassy.

At least they'd be late. When they got there, many of the truly heavyweight luminaries would have left: Washington shuts down early; the workday starts at eight in the morning and ends at four in the afternoon.

As they pulled into the embassy's drive, Rand said, "It looks different, or am I wrong?"

"Different? Oh, yes . . . I forget you've been living in some Mexican cave. Terrorists bombed the old embassy; this new one's only been officially open for three weeks." How could he not hear these things? How could he not care enough to keep tabs on what was going on at home? Unless he truly didn't give a damn anymore. Unless he'd really come up here only to protect himself—and her?— from what he perceived as a personal threat. Her head spun briefly. For her sake most of all, then; because from what she'd heard, his Mexican home was as safe as a Libyan fortress. *Damn you, Trace, we can't start this up again, you ought to know it. Look what happened the last time. . . .*

The chauffeur opened the limo's door and offered her his hand. The Staff D gopher had brought the wrong "little black dress" but it was close enough, with pearls, for government work, especially with her Siberian lynx jacket over it.

Rand jackknifed out of the car, as casually elegant in his dark blue suit and camel-hair coat as any of the dips they'd meet inside.

The winter air chilled her—or maybe it was that, in all the time they'd spent together, they'd never done anything like this. When she'd thought she was in love with him, she'd dreamed of going out in public together, to a function like this . . . the perfect couple.

Now that they were really going to do it, they were an ex-couple and far from perfect, but it still took her breath away to walk up those stairs with him, present her invitation (a "plus one") and have the British staffer announce their names as they ran a gauntlet of official greeters under Waterford chandeliers.

Kate had to remind herself forcefully that the man with his hand decorously on her elbow had just usurped every command aspect of her position, undermining her authority more thoroughly than it would be if the *Post* ran an exposé about her having a KGB lover. Otherwise, she'd start living the fantasy—believing in him and his Mexican beach. If he'd wanted her, he'd had plenty of time to let her know. He'd had five years. She resolved to make him wait another five. It was the least he deserved, now that he was Q-leader again.

As they were descended upon by waiters and waitresses with Mumm's and canapés, and then by British representatives who knew Kate Brittany as the science attaché at Copernicus One's American embassy, Kate made smooth, if numb, introductions: "Tracey Rand of Cislunar Security, a private firm looking for Cop One contracts."

Meanwhile, she was thinking that it was a good thing that "Q-Leader" was just a figure of speech. Technically there'd been no Q-section since Kate Brittany was in kindergarten; but then, technically there was no ZR-capable unit in Staff D or anywhere else in CIA. Q-section had been the first designation for what couldn't be designated—dirty tricks beyond the government's ability to own to, a unit whose mission description was only a cover for what it really did.

Trace was and would always be a Q-leader to anyone who worked with, or against, him. His CIA-generated cover was barely better than going naked.

She thought she caught a flicker of recognition in the eyes of an Indian they encountered named Chandra, who had a British accent and affiliation. Chandra was about fifty and would be on the shuttle with them, he said with assurance. "I'm the new co-director of the joint British–Indian metallurgy venture."

More than that, Chandra wasn't saying. The woman with him, a tall blonde with a tiny waist in a red beaded dress, gazed at Rand like she was moon-struck.

Somebody or other, Kate couldn't remember her name. It didn't matter; she'd see her again, on the shuttle or thereafter, where she'd be wearing a nametag on her flightsuit and have an affiliation patch on her arm.

Kate tugged on Rand's sleeve subtly and said, when she had his attention, "Look, there's the U.S. mission director, Harper. Excuse us, I must introduce Dr. Rand before the director leaves."

Director Harper's wife was also tall, also blond, and very charming. She hadn't gone to the moon on her husband's last tour, and she was at pains to let Kate know that this time she'd "be going up there, too. Isn't it exciting?"

*Just great, Mrs. Harper. But we don't have many tea parties. Of course, with your clout you can probably remedy that. . . .*

The director himself was as tall as General Andresson, whom Kate saw in a corner and tossed a smile, but heavier set, with the same puffiness to his rough-hewn features that Kate still saw in her own when she looked in the mirror.

She wondered how Harper had gotten down here—he hadn't been on Kate's shuttle—and when and why, then shelved it. Once you start suspecting, it's easy to suspect everyone and everything. Conspiracy is a state of mind.

"Excuse me, Director, I didn't hear you?" She smiled to cover her lapse.

Harper said, taking his velvet-collared coat from an aide who came scurrying to hold it out, "I said, 'With you to show both Dr. Rand and my wife the ropes at Cop One, I won't have a thing to worry about, beyond introducing Dr. Rand to the Right People and making sure his calendar's full and his trip profitable.' "

"It's a deal," Kate replied bluntly, and smiled again to make a joke of what she'd said.

But it was no joke: she and Harper had just come to terms.

"Mission accomplished?" Trace guessed when the Harpers had left.

"Part of it, anyway," she said, steering him away from Andresson, who was closeted with Bates by the fireplace. Probably rating their performance.

"Those two didn't tell me they'd be here," Rand said, pointedly not looking at the two men who'd briefed them earlier. His tone was mildly accusatory.

"They didn't tell me either. What do you think, they're in league with me to run some game on *you?*" Bates and Andresson were here, but Davies wasn't? What did it mean? Something? Anything beyond the fact that it was late, Davies probably left early, and this reception was as much a part of Andresson and Bates' job as it was hers? She rubbed her arms, suddenly rough with gooseflesh. "Cut it out, Trace, you're giving me the creeps."

"I'm sorry." Rand spread his hands. "Just antsy. But you're right—we can't talk here. The olives are probably bugged. Anybody else we've just got to see? I need some time alone with you. We've got plans to make."

There was no arguing with the way he'd put it. She hurried him through the rest of those introductions she deemed absolutely necessary and then let him call for their car.

She was caught in some dream where events proceeded, involving her without her consent, as if some scenario had been set up beforehand. He needs some time with me alone. Oh, and it's just business.

"Your place or mine?" was the next question, and when he posed it, she said "Mine," as sullenly and coldly as she could manage.

It might as well be on her turf.

But when they got to her hotel, the Madison, she nearly panicked. Only the quiet, conservative elegance of the lobby saved her. Nothing bad ever happened here. No one ever got out of control here. Central American dictators and Filipino opposition leaders had stayed here and emerged, unscathed, well fed, pampered, and happy.

Nothing was going to happen with Trace Rand that she couldn't handle—unless she let it happen.

She was a big girl, in control of her own life, a GS-15 with good prospects. What was he? *A Q-leader,* her mind answered.

In the elevator she said, "I can't wait to get back to the moon."

"Where you'll be calling the shots? Suits me, too." He was leaning back against the elevator wall, his coat over one arm, his suit jacket open. "You're very good at the social whirl, you know. I've been out of circulation a long while and even in the old days I was always uncomfortable at one of those parties. With you, I didn't even have time to get nervous."

"Nervous? You?"

Eye contact like a spray of cold water in the face: "Me. Nervous. Kate, I'm really going to need you on this. You've made tremendous strides while I was learning how to take a few steps. So has the technology. So has the country."

The elevator stopped at her floor. Its door opened, revealing an empty, quiet corridor. "Come on, Trace, you're really making me uncomfortable." She stepped out, onto the thick, patterned carpet.

"Don't let me. We're going to need our combined expertise and then some. The only thing that's making *me* uncomfortable," he said, following her, "is the autopsy on Kendall, and on Richelson."

She was already fumbling in her evening purse for her hotel key card. She found it, inserted it too fast; the lock's LED stayed red. She had to extract the card and reinsert it. This time the lock blinked green and she grabbed the latch to open it before the light turned red again.

"Kendall and Richelson? You think Kendall's death

wasn't a heart attack, induced by some untraceable Soviet chemical? Richelson's was heart-related too, if I read the data right, so they're making the same assumption. What's wrong with that?''

''Why wouldn't the Soviets bother to vary the method like they did with Frank and Blake—if it was the Soviets? Richelson wasn't a good heart-attack candidate; he'd just had a physical that proved it. And what was the delivery system used? What's this handy-dandy time-release substance and how do we avoid it if nobody'll tell us what to watch out for—or who? Everybody on the plane with Richelson checked out with flying colors. It's a damned shame Richelson's corpse was so smashed up, organs jellied and so forth. But as it stands, Staff D is grasping at straws, in my opinion.''

Inside now, he closed the door behind him.

Her clothes were strewn over the king-size bed and the antique chair and even askew on the real oriental throw rug.

''Damn that gopher!'' It wasn't her mess, but somebody had to pick it up. Doing so, she said, ''But Bates said . . . Why would anybody bother grasping at straws?'' She straightened up. ''The other two deaths were a car accident and a self-inflicted—Frank ate his own gun. What are you getting at, Rand? I'm not a homicide detective and neither are you.''

''Somebody wanted to make damned sure that these deaths couldn't be written off as accidents, or coincidences, or anything less than Soviet wet work. Hitters don't tend to advertise, unless they're terrorists.'' He shrugged. ''And this isn't terrorism, but it's damned sloppy for KGB or GRU.''

''You're saying you don't believe it was . . . what Bates and Andresson think?'' She bent again and furiously grabbed the rest of her clothes, wadding them into a ball and throwing them into a corner. She'd send Bates the cleaning bill.

"I'm saying I don't know, is all. Something's funny. Big bad superpower rivalry. Somebody from the opposition taking out ZR/SEAL, lock, stock, and clearances. . . . Could be a warning to somebody. Could be a Soviet warning to the U.S. to back off. Could be internecine. Hell, our side could have wasted Kendall, Frank, and Richelson just to make sure you and I would get together for this little tête-à-tête, for all I know."

"Let's call room service"—she sighed—"before it closes or I get as paranoid as you are and I'm afraid to. What do you want? I'm getting espresso and 'assorted pastry.' "

"You," he said from very close behind her, where she was reaching for the phone on the Chippendale table. His arms went around her waist.

"Rand . . . Trace . . . we don't—"

"Yes we do," he said, nuzzling her hair.

And despite everything, or because of it, she didn't have the strength to argue. Or the inclination. She continued her motion, leaning forward as if for the phone, but her attention was riveted on his hands, one sliding up from her waist, the other down.

Her mouth said, "Bastard. Don't confuse me," but her body wanted to stretch out under his hands. She arched like a cat when he cupped her breasts.

He said into her ear, "You're not confused, and neither am I. We know just what we want. It's only a matter of time, anyway. . . ."

She was willing to let him convince her, or unable to stop him. It summed the same.

When he'd slid her skirt up over her hips and pulled her back against him, she gave up completely and heard herself saying, "God, Trace, I want to lie down with you."

Then his fingers were at the zipper on her dress and hers, behind her, at the buckle of his belt. "We will," he promised as he pushed her dress off her shoulders.

"Wait until you try this in moon gravity," she murmured to the top of his head, leaning against him with her hands in his hair and his face pressed against her belly.

He pulled her down to him, on the Madison's little oriental throw rug. "Wait, my ass. I've waited five years for you, Katydid. We've got lots of lost time to make up for."

They didn't make it to the bed until much, much later.

# Chapter 7

# SCRATCH
# ONE SEAL

Davies had no idea why he'd agreed to meet the Brit functionary at the American Cafe in Tyson's Corner, unless it was the desperation in the man's dark eyes.

It had meant leaving the party early, and leaving the pretty women he'd met there, with one of whom, if he'd stayed, he probably could have scored.

It also meant leaving the limo at his hotel and getting a rental car, a move his three security aides would have refused if he'd told them.

So Davies hadn't told them. Whatever this meet was about, the Brit who'd approached him was acting as if it was a matter of national importance—as if British security matters would be discussed. Davies wasn't averse to the occasional intelligence coup.

But he knew very well what would have happened if he'd gone over to Bates or Andressson at the gala and told them, or even sent his Staff D boy off with a message: Davies would be refused permission to make the meeting, or be covered so thickly with backup that the nervous Brit would have been scared off.

Davies certainly wouldn't have been allowed to sneak out the back door of his hotel into the waiting rental car and drive off into the night, alone. Which was the only way the Brit was going to have it.

It was a very naughty thing to do, and it was dangerous. If the Brit were trying to compromise Davies somehow, drum up some faked scandal just before the Space Talks, Davies might be walking into a trap. So, he decided, heading his rental car along increasingly deserted streets toward Virginia, if anything seemed the tiniest bit suspicious—if the Brit asked for one iota of information or even hinted at some covert arrangement that might be read as espionage on Davies' part, he'd just drive away.

Just like that.

He wasn't sure that the American Cafe—or anything in Tyson's Corner but the hotel bars, would be open this late. And that gave the whole enterprise an air of verisimilitude: spies don't lure you to a closed restaurant so that you can't have the "supper and sensitive bit of chat" that the Brit promised.

Outside of protecting his own security, Davies wasn't too worried. And he was feeling like a truant—slipping surveillance like this would put him one up on his overweening bodyguards, over whose heads he could hold this escape eternally. They'd give him more space, after this, or he'd report their lack of performance to their superiors— to Bates himself.

One way or another, he was master of his hounds now. Even if the meet turned out to be no more than a Brit wanting to feel out the possibilities of picking up a little extra money as a U.S. intelligence stringer—even if the Brit didn't show, in fact—Davies was still winning by having managed to slip his nation's best and most friendly surveillance.

After all, Davies was ex-ZR/SEAL, too. He'd learned a thing or two, managing that project. They didn't have to treat him like a valuable but nutty professor. The way security was sticking to him, he couldn't even get laid unless he had the Agency send up an "escort" from the ranks, duly cleared through channels. Bates had made that clear to him tonight, at the reception, in front of Andresson himself.

*Well, screw you, Bates.* It had been embarrassing to have his behavior critiqued by some security type with more brass than brains, and in front of Andresson. Davies' private life was his own, thank you very much.

The lights were less bright and less frequent once he'd left Mass Ave. He watched the rearview mirror for signs that his boys were on to him, following discreetly behind, ready to pick him up again at the American Cafe.

Talk about embarrassment! That would be intolerable: driving into the parking lot and having Staff D appear at his table, tapping its collective foot and probably scaring his Brit contact half to death.

If they did, Davies would show the proper amount of outrage, make sure no attempt was made to compromise him or his companion. The thought nagged him, and his foot bore down on the gas pedal. It wasn't beyond Bates and his boys to take a perfectly innocent meeting of two professionals like this was going to be and read into it any amount of covert nastiness. Even to jump to conclusions, assuming that Davies was the one looking for extra pocket change from the Brits, instead of the other way around.

Spying wasn't restricted to hostile governments, oh no. Even in special relationships like those between America and Great Britain, or America and Israel, there was always money for corroborative sources, so that one's government was certain that the information it received from a so-called friendly nation was as comprehensive as possible. It wasn't espionage on a grand scale, like that mounted by the two superpowers against one another, but it was espionage nevertheless.

Davies belatedly wished he'd brought his pocket dictation tape deck, with which he could have recorded the specifics of the Brit's approach. But he hadn't. It wasn't really his field, he admitted as he negotiated the sensible but obscure maneuvers necessary to get him off the Beltway and onto the divided highway he'd have to take until he'd passed the restaurant, where he'd turn across multiple lanes of traffic in order to access the parking lot, across the meridian strip of the divided highway, where all the one-way traffic was headed back toward Washington.

There were a few cars behind him, among the night traffic of semis and vans, but none of the smaller cars had been with him since Mass Ave., he was reasonably certain, and the big stuff was hauling massive loads to government subcontractors out here.

Not much longer, now. He was doing a good job. A great job. He wondered if, should the coup be juicy enough, he'd find a way to let Tracey Rand know that he, Davies, had personally recruited a corroborative source among the British moon-based contingent. Or should he keep the agent to himself? Tell no one, if he truly hadn't been followed, and have his own man to spy on Tracey Rand and Kate Brittany—and everything else going on up there, where Cop One was deployed on one side of Copernicus's central peak, opposite Sveboda, the Soviet "mining and scientific" installation?

With the two superpowers digging toward an eventual collision, miles under the lunar regolith, things were becoming increasingly tense. There was a game of chicken going on up there, and neither superpower was willing to be first to blink in the lunar staring match under way.

It was foolish. There was plenty of lunar oxygen and "green cheese" rock for both nation's emp-hardening purposes. There was no need, with the entire moon there for the taking, to have developed confrontational postures. That was, in part, what the Space Talks were all about. It was what Davies was concentrating on, at any rate: a proposal that suggested a two-degree outward correction to the course of both superpowers' mining ventures. Just two degrees. Without that shift, eventually the Soviet and American mining operations were going to collide.

Neither international law such as pertained in Antarctica nor space law as it was currently written had provisions for adjudicating such a situation. The "first come, first served" basis for international zones was obviously insufficient. All hell was going to break loose up there if nobody stopped it well before critical mass—and close proximity—was reached. Davies had devoted four of his last five years to the problem; he was his country's leading expert.

And his expert opinion was that (even without whatever America, through Project WARLORD, was doing on the dark side) the delicate doctrinal stalemate, buttressed by armed belligerence and currently called Mutually Assured Survival, that kept America and the USSR from open confrontation—this balance of power on which civilization teetered was in danger of collapse.

When a situation has reached such an impasse, delicate diplomacy is the necessary solution, not the sort of wild-ass hijinks of men like Tracey Rand.

Seeing Rand at the briefing had been unpleasant; thinking of Rand on the moon was more so. Davies understood the reasons behind Bates's decision—in fact had agreed—but Rand always made Davies want to prove that brains were worth more than brawn and brute instinct in the modern world.

So developing his own source among the Brit contingent working at Copernicus One was the perfect balm to Davies's abraded ego. Tracey Rand might be in better physical shape—might even be capable of melting the iceberg that was Kate Brittany, as rumor had it he'd done once before—but time would show that Davies was the better man.

Beating Rand at his own game was, Davies admitted, the most alluring part of this midnight escapade—perhaps the only reason compelling enough to cause Davies to shake his own security coverage at a time like this, when his ZR/ SEAL affiliation was proving to be such a liability.

For Blake, Kendall, Frank, and Richelson, it had been deadly. . . .

About to make his turn across the meridian, Davies didn't notice that the eighteen-wheeler barreling down on him wasn't slowing. His eyes were on the dark parking lot and two-story front of the American Cafe, searching for a man who ought to be leaning on the trunk of his car, waiting. . . .

The eighteen-wheeler's horn blared at the last moment, but not soon enough for Davies.

The sound of rent metal and squealing brakes and shattering glass buried Davies's final scream as the huge truck bore down, the deformed rental sedan demolished by its bumper.

The two wedded vehicles skidded sideways across the meridian until the cab of the truck jackknifed. The momentum of the trailer behind it, combined with the jammed front wheels of the truck, which were fouled by the twisted metal of the rental car, caused the truck to flip over on its side in a majestic shudder reminiscent of a gray whale at play.

It landed with the cab on top of what remained of Davies's car in a symphony of squealing brakes and blaring horns from the traffic behind.

Just before the truck's gas tank exploded, sending out a shock wave that broke every window in the American Cafe, the truck's driver scrambled out of his overturned cab, down to the macadam scarred with rubber from the crash.

Then he jumped over a slick of puddling gas leaking from the truck, took a few steps backward, and lit a cigarette before he ran like hell to safety on the far side of the road.

# Chapter 8

# AND THEN
# THERE WERE TWO

Rand reached over Kate's white shoulder to get the bedside phone. It wasn't yet dawn outside her hotel-room window, but the phone had a red light that blinked with every ring, making it impossible for him to ignore.

"What, damn it? I didn't order a wake-up call . . ."

Kate sat up, the sheet clutched to her throat, her face impassive, her thick short hair tousled.

The caller, Bates, was saying, ". . . Davies got it while you two were cozying up, about oh-one-fifteen hours—a semi rolled right over him, then the whole mess exploded. The truck driver's been with us since the event, and he's clean so far as we can see."

"Why the fuck couldn't you have waited until the damned sun came up, if you waited this long?" Rand looked at his wristwatch, which told him it was a little past five in the morning. Pincering the phone between his ear and shoulder, he grabbed a notepad and pen from the nightstand and wrote: *It's Bates. Davies dead. Pick up john phone.*

She slid out from between the sheets, naked, and ran into the bathroom. He could hear the click as she picked up the receiver and punched the lit button on the bathroom's wall phone. He didn't care whether Bates heard it or not.

Bates was telling him that items of national security didn't restrict themselves to "anybody's working hours. You're lucky we didn't call you sooner. You're lucky we knew you were with Brittany and not at your own hotel, or we'd be breaking down her door right now. Is she—"

"I'm right here," Kate said laconically.

"Good," said Bates with an invisible nod. "We want to get you people out of there, and somewhere secure, ASAP. Here's the drill: you're on the seventh floor, which is lucky—the circuit breaker panel's opposite the elevators there, I'm assured. Rand, you get out there and trip every circuit on that panel, taking out the elevator and the lights. Brittany, you cover him from inside your room—this is no dry run. Then you both pack up what you can carry and stay inside, no room service, no visitors, until my people come to get you up the backstairs. The leader will ID himself—scar over right eyebrow back into hairline, a picture of my dog . . . Brittany, you know what that dog looks like. They'll have a special weapons case for each of you, with wrist manacles. Three guys in all: the one with the scar is blond, one-eighty-five; two blacks accompanying. Go right down the back stairs. They lead to the garage. Blue van there—blond drives you both to someplace safe. Secure car phone if you need it. Questions?"

"Nope," said Rand.

"No sir," Kate chorused.

"Over and out," said Bates, and the connection went dead.

"Over and *out?*" Kate groaned into the mouthpiece of the bathroom phone. "Give me a break."

"He's trying to," Rand said. And, louder as he hung up the phone: "Let's get a move on. This sort of thing happens fast."

Amazingly, on the heels of his admonition, he heard her turn on the shower.

If she was playing cooler than thou with him, he'd be glad to let her win by default.

He grabbed his jockey shorts and stumbled into them on his way to the bathroom.

At least she hadn't locked the door.

Inside, it was already steamy and she was a blur behind the translucent shower curtain.

"Kate, Jesus, what do think this is, a UN field trip?"

From behind the shower curtain, she replied: "I don't know about you, but I'm betting this might be the last shower I get until we reach the shuttle's decontamination bay."

"Fine, I guess another couple minutes won't matter." But he didn't believe it. He turned on the sink tap to fill a glass with cold water—the steam was making him lazy, or else he was as crazy as Kate Brittany. "You're supposed to cover me. What with?"

They should be doing what Bates had suggested, *now*, damn it, not after she'd done her morning toilette. Exasperating female.

She slid back the shower curtain abruptly and stood there, the water still running down her soapy body, hands in her short wet hair: "With the forty-four magnum gas-powered mini-Wildey in my briefcase. Any objections?"

She'd been armed all along. He remembered her tossing that case cavalierly into his rental car's backseat. He didn't know why it bothered him, but it did. He didn't know what was bothering her, either, but something sure was.

He took a step toward her. With the shower curtain open, water was spilling onto the tile floor. "Kate—" One hand outstretched.

"Back off, Dr. Rand. Last night was . . . probably a mistake. Whatever it was, don't count on it happening again." Her eyes were burning under the skullcap of sopping hair.

"Gee, and I thought you had a good time. But don't worry, I don't count on anything. Ever."

He got the hell out of there and started to pack—her bag, because he hadn't brought one.

She came out a few moments later, wrapped in a terry towel, combing wet hair straight back. "Don't pack my stuff—you don't know . . ."

"Sorry." Palms toward her, he retreated. Maybe he shouldn't have rushed her but, God, he hadn't thought he was forcing the issue. His sort of simplification was obviously complicating things for her. He had no idea what she was trying to tell him, and no time to find out.

"Where's my damned gun?" she muttered, and caught her lower lip between white teeth, bending over to root through her combination-locked briefcase, which he'd thrown on the bed but not attempted to open.

What he wanted to do probably wasn't the right thing, but he had to do something. "Katydid . . . come on, last night was—"

She whirled on him. "I told you, forget last night."

"Forget the best sleep I've had in five years? No way. Come on, Kate. Davies is dead, okay; it's scary, yeah. I'm here. I'll take care of—"

She backed away as he moved toward her until the backs of her knees hit the bed on which her briefcase now lay open. "You? You can't even take care of yourself. I've got to cover you, remember? Poor Davies . . ."

Now he saw the glitter of incipient tears in her eyes.

"Kate, damn it, I'm sorry if last night's a problem. But it shouldn't be. As for Davies . . . it's not going to happen to us. Trust me, okay? You used to." And he closed in on her as inexorably as he could manage, trying not to resent her incredibly bad timing. This wasn't the moment for recriminations or morning-after regrets; this was the moment to get their asses the hell out of harm's way.

When he was nose to nose with her, he put his hands on her shoulders, careful not to be overly suggestive or overly brusque. "You and me, okay? We'll do just like we're told and we'll work the rest of it out in the time we'll have—and we will have it. Later. Okay?''

As if somebody had deflated her tires, she crumpled against him momentarily.

He let his arms slide down around hers, and she immediately straightened up.

At least she didn't pull away. In the circle of his arms she said, ''I'm okay, Trace. Really. Just Davies—they put everything they had into protecting him.''

''No they didn't; the results prove that. And anyway, the only person who can protect you is yourself. It's that simple. You do your job, I'll do mine, and we'll keep ourselves alive long enough to worry about what last night did or didn't mean. I promise.''

Her eyes searched his and he let go of her. Hands at his sides, he kissed her chastely on the forehead, stifling the impulse to ruffle her wet hair.

She looked at him for another instant, shook her head as if at an intractable child, and then began unpacking and repacking with quick, jerky movements.

He dressed too, running over Bates's instructions in his mind, and didn't look at her again until he'd finished. She was pulling a second pair of pants on over her jeans, and tucking in three layers of shirt.

''In case,'' she said to his questioning look, ''we end up not taking any of this.'' Her hand indicated the chaos of her baggage that he'd tried in vain to order.

She took the gun from her open briefcase and jacked the slide, the self-suppressed, vented muzzle of the gas-powered magnum aimed at the ceiling as she did so.

He saw the trick she used to compensate for her physical slightness: instead of pulling the slide toward her, she held the slide steady and pushed the gun away. Whatever worked, with a big piece like that in such small, delicate hands.

It was just like her to carry the biggest caliber she could manage; the gas-powered Wildey had dial-a-recoil, so he had no doubt she could hit what she was aiming at, not just the first time, but every time. She'd always worked hard at her shooting.

"Okay? Ready?" he said. "If the bogeymen come, don't worry about me—I'll be on the floor with my head covered. Shoot if it's just a couple and you think you've got a chance. Otherwise, slam the damned door shut and shoot through it—God knows you've got the slugs for that—if you have to. It matters more that one of us is here for Bates's pickup crew than that we both earn medals following orders."

He needed her to know—to believe—that his expectations had limits. But she didn't answer, another bad sign. So he added: "Probably be fine, you know. And you're worth more to this project than I am—you've got some idea what's going on up there."

"Yes, all right," she admitted, brightening somewhat.

He wasn't sure he liked that, but it was time to go see if Bates's paranoia had any basis in reality.

He didn't look at her again, just went to the door, opened it a crack while he stood against the jamb, and peeked out. A nice, empty, civilized hallway.

But his heart was pounding in his ears as he opened the door farther, slipped through, and hugged the wall, heading toward the elevator.

The double-doored cabinet that held the circuit breakers was right where Bates had said it would be, at hip height, set into the wall. It wasn't even locked. He bent the gooseneck aviator's penlight in his shirt pocket to the proper angle, anticipating the darkness that would descend on the windowless corridor when the lights went out, took one apologetic look behind at the elevator, whose indicator told him it was descending toward the lobby, and started flipping switches.

Somewhere an alarm bell rang, just as the lights in the corridor went out.

His fingers flew down the parallel rows of the panel and,

not bothering to close the cabinet's doors, he half bolted for Kate's room, the light from the penlight bobbling before him.

There she was silhouetted by the daylight of her room's window, the wide, suppressed muzzle of her gas gun staring at him.

She ought to have closed the damn door. He'd have to teach her better tactics.

But inside, when she hugged him wordlessly, he began to think that he was just overreacting to the anticlimax of it all.

They sat on the bed and talked about the poor souls trapped in the elevator, their door locked, listening for sounds of running feet.

There was lots of traffic in the corridor by the time the knock came on the door.

Without thought, Rand picked up the gun between them on the bed and went to peer through the peephole.

A blond man, the right size and weight and with the requisite scar, was training a flashlight on himself and the picture of a basset hound he was holding up to the peephole.

"Kate? Make the ID?"

She came up beside him and peeked over his shoulder, careful not to stand directly before the peephole where a shot could tear through wood and any flesh behind it. "That's Bates's dog." She nodded. "Looks good to me."

She stepped away from the door and, when he motioned to her, opened it.

The big blond with the basset-hound photo and his two black companions entered. The two blacks had bulletproof aluminum attaché cases with manacles bolted into the metal next to their handles. The blond motioned that the two cases be given to Brittany and Rand.

"Aren't you going to open them?" said the blond when Rand simply shrugged into his camel-hair coat and then clasped the cuff about his left wrist, with Kate following suit.

"You're the cavalry, fellas. We're just the passengers."

The two blacks exchanged looks while their commanding officer said, "Right, then. Let's go. We'll send somebody back for the lady's things."

"See?" Kate whispered to him under her breath as she followed the blond out the door once the two blacks had entered the hallway and pronounced it clear.

It spooked Rand something fierce to be descending endless flights in the dark stairwell lit only by red emergency bulbs whose batteries had seen better days.

Nobody talked, and the sounds of heels on metal resounded until they were deafening enough to blot out the harsh noise of his breathing and his pulse in his ears. He was out of practice. Cloak and dagger hadn't gotten any better, or any more pleasant, since he'd given it all up.

The blond in the lead pulled out a miniature transceiver and muttered into it when they reached the second-floor landing.

By the time they came out into the garage, the blue van that Bates had told Rand to expect was waiting, belching carbon monoxide, its engine revving loudly.

Everything sounded preternaturally loud: the echoes of their feet and the engine noise and, somewhere, a car door slamming, all reverberating off the garage's concrete walls.

From within the van, someone slid the side door back, and he reached for Kate's arm to help her up into it.

"I can manage," she said, her face pale and her lips quirked.

Putting his foot wrong one more time. He scrambled in after her, his free hand in his overcoat pocket where the Wildey was. Maybe it was the gun that bothered her—that he'd taken it. Belatedly, he offered it out to her and, behind him, both black men stopped in their tracks, the door half closed.

"I guess you'd better have this back," Rand said to Kate.

"Thank you," she said primly, taking it by the butt as he held it out.

The slider slammed shut, the blacks settled in, the blond up front said, "Seat belts, everyone. It's going to be one hell of a ride," and gunned the motor so that the van burst out into Washington traffic, picking up a police motorcycle escort waiting in front of the Madison.

Rand blew out a noisy breath and said, "Somebody want to tell us where we're going?"

"Canaveral, when we're sure it's safe," said the blond up front.

"See?" Kate grabbed the three layers of shirt she'd put on and eyed him with satisfaction. "I told you so."

"Yeah, I wish I'd planned ahead," he said, and reached out an arm to slide it behind her head, along the seat back.

Wherever Bates was going to stash them for the next twenty-four hours, he'd have plenty of time alone with Kate, to set things straight.

And, after that, they'd have all the time on the moon together. On the moon, where it was probably safe. Or safer.

Damn, Davies. ZR/SEAL was down to two. After all the time Rand had put into it, he was going to do his best not to let the Moon Seals become extinct. Maybe there was just the two of them left, but they were male and female. He'd never been more glad of that.

# Chapter 9
# LIFT-OFF

"Somewhere safe" turned out to be a seamy, pink-and-green hotel near Canaveral. It was humid and moldy and their bodyguards were getting on Kate's nerves. The ride down here, with only occasional stops at fast-food joints, hadn't been what she'd expected.

She'd expected a private jet and VIP treatment, but either Bates thought it was too dangerous to fly them and add to their already high profile, or the budget for the care and feeding of ZR/SEAL had just been cut.

Rand had the adjoining room to the right of hers, the three men who'd escorted them down here had the one to her left, and the four who'd met their van at the Florida line had an additional room on the far side of Trace's.

"The seven dwarfs," Rand had taken to calling them, once it was clear that the whole entourage was checking into the motel together.

That was last night, and she'd slept restlessly, if at all, expecting him to slip through the connecting door at any moment, rehearsing what she'd say and do when he did.

But he hadn't, and now the sky was lightening as it only did in these latitudes, creating a sunrise as spectacular as marigolds strewn on black velvet.

She could hear him moving around in there. He hadn't

had any hesitation about popping in and out of the connecting door last evening, when they dined on takeout fried chicken and little plastic containers of slaw, washed down with Maccabee beer one of the bodyguards had found in a liquor store.

It was just as well he'd taken her at her word, she told herself. When he'd come into the bathroom while she was taking a shower in the Madison, all she could think about was her flaccid muscle tone, legacy of the moon's one-tenth gravity that no amount of lunar calisthenics could prevent.

She felt like a cow; she smelled like a pig; she didn't want him crawling into her bed, sneaking around like they used to do when they didn't have enough sense to realize that the excitement they felt was primarily due to the illicit nature of their affair.

God, if she'd known she was going to see him, she'd have shaved her body hair, she thought as she stretched and turned her head, noticing shiny beads of sweat sparkling on the tuft under her arm.

She threw off the covers and made her way through the sunrise-gilded motel room to take her shower, a luxury the earthbound took for granted.

Door open so that the steam wouldn't make her groggy, she stepped in and let the free water pummel her. When she'd first seen Tracey Rand at Richelson's funeral, she'd been swept up in the old game again. She told herself, as she soaped her body, that it had to stop. Now. Before they got to the moon and things became really complicated.

She had her nicely ordered life to protect. Her work. Her position, which he'd set teetering without so much as an apology. As if it didn't matter that he was usurping her position. And anyway, when he found out about the way things worked up there—about what she was doing up there—about Ilya . . . he was going to be exceedingly pissed.

She had a right to have a boyfriend. A lover. Two lovers. Ten lovers, if she chose. Still, the idea of explaining about Ilya—or not explaining—distressed her.

Tracey Rand wasn't the sort of man to be understanding about such things. And she shouldn't give a damn what he thought. Let him concern himself with his briefing material on the dark-side radio telescope, shielded from the background noise generated by terrestrial sources—a parabolic dish in a convenient crater, supported by a science complex dug down into the regolith.

The briefing book on it had been in his attaché case, along with some very special weapons. They'd gone through their cases together, fingers greasy from chicken, and found that he'd been issued a bit more hardware than she; otherwise, the cases' contents were identical.

Which meant that, by omission, everything he really needed to know about WARLORD and Cop One and the dark-side science base, she'd have to tell him.

But what she told him about her personal life was up to her. She finished soaping and rinsed, turning the tap slowly and inexorably to cold. She gasped when the spray turned so icy that the cold water burned, slapped the tap off, and reached, eyes still closed, for a towel.

Rand handed it to her. "Thought you were up."

"Christ, Trace, what are you, a bathroom fetishist? What right have you got to—"

"The seven dwarfs are gone. Thought you'd better know as soon as I did."

"What?" She looked at him over the towel. He was fully dressed in a Florida shirt and khaki pants one of the dwarfs had brought him with last night's dinner. There was nothing even remotely sexually suggestive about the look on his face. She'd seen that look before, in too many memories and dreams—his face squared off; his jaw corded; the hollows under his cheeks pronounced. Like he'd been the first day she'd gone to visit him in the hospital after the Sakhalin accident and he'd told her to get on with her life, that he was opting out of the project. "You look grim as death."

"They're gone, I said." Crossing his arms, he leaned against the powder-blue vanity. "Pulled off by Bates. No explanation beyond us not needing them anymore. I just checked with Bates from a phone booth—it *was* his order. No explanation there, either."

She stepped out of the shower, ignoring her nakedness, wanting only to be dressed to meet her fate, whatever it was. Brushing by him out of the bathroom, she grabbed her underwear and jeans. "So now what?" she said as she wriggled into them.

"Now," he replied, "we make it to the launch pad however you're used to doing it. That's all Bates said—you'd know how to take it from here. They left us a car, anyway. That white one."

"It's okay, really." She pulled her tank top over her head and it hit her shoulders damp from her wet hair. "We'll attract less attention without bodyguards."

"Yeah, I bet Davies thought that, too."

Was he frightened? She turned to scan his face for signs of panic. He'd been hurt, really hurt, and then he'd quit, not even interested enough in whether his accident was purely that, or somehow sabotage, to hang in long enough to find out.

Maybe the Tracey Rand she remembered wasn't the Tracey Rand she was dealing with. People change, and she'd never been able to read him—that was what made him so fascinating.

Kate's professional life was dedicated in large measure to crisis preemption, to calming people and situations, to making the extraordinary seem unremarkable. She began rattling off the procedure that would get them aboard the shuttle, careful that her words came out in a soothing, measured rhythm meant to communicate calm.

". . . and that's it," she said as they walked out the motel room's door toward the white sedan the dwarfs had

75

left for them, "if all goes well. If it doesn't, Bates's head will roll for pulling the dwarfs off us at just the wrong moment. Believe me, he doesn't want that."

"Yeah, well, maybe. But I'm not taking that car."

They were standing before it, each with their aluminum cases manacled to their wrists, looking like any couple arguing about where to have breakfast—any couple with dip-courier attaché cases fastened on them. "Fine," she said. "What do you think, the car's going to blow up?"

"Don't want to find out, okay? Now, let's get a cab."

"A cab." *You find one, buddy. It isn't even breakfast time yet, and this isn't exactly Main Street.* But he did find one, after she'd followed his fast, stiff-legged walk to the motel office. She hadn't noticed the limp before; it gave her heart pause to see it.

*He was lifting her effortlessly onto him, hands under her buttocks, a half smile of pleasure on his face. In the next room, the rest of the team was waiting for its briefing, for the order to get their wet gear and head for the staging area. . . .*

The cab he found was yellow; its driver Jamaican, with Rastafarian dreadlocks. Kate gave him the gate at Canaveral she wanted and settled back in her seat. Rand was staring out the rear window at the white car as if he was waiting for it to explode.

Something was going to, if not down here, then up there, she was certain.

But it wasn't the white car. That would be too easy. She wished she'd thought about Ilya and how she was going to deal with both of them up there, then told herself it wouldn't have made any difference. She had the right to sleep wherever she chose. She was sure Rand hadn't been celibate for five years.

It was business, not just pleasure, with Ilya, but suddenly it seemed not only promiscuous but worse—as if she was whoring. Well, maybe she could keep it from Trace, or convince herself it wouldn't matter if he found out.

After all, they'd both had a "good night's sleep" in separate rooms. When he turned to her, she began explaining to him what he might expect at Canaveral.

When she'd gone through the whole standard drill for space-shuttle passengers, so that if anything was out of the ordinary he'd know it as it happened, he asked only, "What about a spacesuit? They still have to be custom made, right?"

"Your old measurements, your old gear from . . . the last time. The technology hasn't come any further." Fifteen years' time lag from government-classified to general usage was still the rule of thumb as far as technology went. His glance flickered away from her when she mentioned the old suit, though. It hadn't protected his hip, and what had happened to his hip had hurt his mind, some way. She was almost certain of that now. "You have trouble with that, Trace? It'll be a new suit—just mocked up from what they had. Anyway, you probably won't be strolling around in vacuum much."

"Don't count on it. You aren't reading between the lines. Whatever they want us up there for, they wouldn't include me in that 'us' unless there was some hands-on."

"Everybody gets a suit, Dr. Rand. In case of emergencies."

"Emergencies are my specialty—or they used to be."

He was just impossible. She didn't mind so much that he was resentful; it was the superiority in his tone, as if she'd forgotten how to read the writing on the wall and it was a good thing that he was along to remind her.

"I'm your 'briefing officer on everything lunar,' remember?"

"I remember."

"Dat be it, missus?" said the Jamaican cabbie, slowing the car just short of the turnoff to the OFFICIAL USE ONLY ramp that would take them to the military floor of NASA's newest building.

"Yes. Take this off-ramp, drop us, and keep going

around. You'll come out right there." She pointed across the meridian at an off-ramp.

The squat seven-story building before them had just been completed; it gleamed postmodern-white in the morning sun. At the ramp's head, she told the cabbie to stop, opened her door, and got out, bumping her knees on her aluminum attaché. The uniformed guard waved familiarly from his kiosk. Behind her, Rand was paying the fare.

Relief overswept her as the cab drew away and turned out of sight without incident. Here, she knew the ropes. She'd been back and forth a dozen times, three from this new facility. She knew everybody she needed to know, and the ones that mattered knew her—on sight.

And it was a good thing, because Tracey Rand was as taut as piano wire, preoccupied, fumbling with the ID card hanging around his neck on its chain of connecting metal balls so that the Hispanic NASA guard looked at him and asked: "Are you all right, sir? Preflight jitters? We haven't lost a second-generation shuttle yet. And it's two today, so the odds are even better."

"Thanks for the pep talk," he told the guard, who lowered hurt eyes.

"You didn't need to be nasty to him," Kate objected as they toted their cases in through the glass-and-concrete lobby, across a hangar-size floor of polished granite peppered with information desks, waiting-room seats, walled cubicles, and unobtrusive, plainclothed guards. When they were funneled by the building's design into a narrow corridor where a desk blocked access, they handed their credentials to a man in the gray-blue of the U.S. Space Command and were allowed to pass under a sign reading MILITARY PERSONNEL ONLY.

Which they weren't, but there was no special access terminal to the shuttle for CIA or Staff D or ZR/SEAL. The security was so obvious, so concerted, and so impressive once beyond that checkpoint that Kate could feel Rand, beside her, relax. She didn't have to look at him to know that his face had lost its squared-off appearance; she could hear the soft edge come back in his voice as he made occasional comments.

He tensed up again in the decontamination bay, which made her feel suddenly protective. He hadn't asked for this assignment; it wasn't his fault. He'd just walked into a bad situation. And she really did believe Bates—they'd be safer on the moon. Safer than Richelson had been, and safer than Davies, with all his security coverage.

She resolved, watching Tracey Rand's impassive face as technicians fitted him into his spacesuit and his skin lost all color, to stop worrying about what he thought of her and start trying to do her job. Rand, out of his element now and for what could be months hereafter, was going to need all the help she could give him. Whatever their relative rank and relative clout, on the moon, Kate was the field expert—the expert in survival, which was the only expertise that counted. Whatever they had to do to get WARLORD off the drawing board and into space, while trying to flush out whoever was eradicating their team, they'd have to survive to do it. Rand had helped create the timetable for WARLORD, and perhaps the mission objectives, but it had been Kate, these last five years, who'd been making things run, day to day.

And if he couldn't understand about Ilya, then that was his problem, not hers. She'd had her reasons. She still had them. Tracey Rand was a big boy. She was a big girl. It ought not to matter who slept where.

But God, it did, to her. And she couldn't just cut Ilya loose. She had too much time put in. Nor was she certain that Trace would ask her to. But she wanted that. The least he could do was be jealous, even if it caused complications.

Or she wanted him not to find out. Which, on the moon, was nearly impossible. There wasn't enough of a crowd to hide in. She raised her hand to put it to her forehead and received an admonition: "Don't move yet, Ms. Brittany."

They were checking the seals on her suit. She was so used to it, she'd hardly noticed. She'd been too busy watching Trace's pale face, on which every whisker stood out, and the sweat on his brow not even NASA air conditioning could avert.

Well, he'd have to handle it. Nobody'd thought to wonder if he could. Did he dive anymore, or was that a problem, too? She couldn't ask. She just went through her check, stood in the decontamination bay with film glasses over her eyes, and then got into the waiting blue coveralls that said BRITTANY over one breast and had her Cop One diplomatic patch on one arm.

His flightsuit was identical, except for his nametag and his affiliation patch, which had a red stripe through it declaring to the initiated that he was a civilian attached to her mission. They couldn't do any better for him until he was on the moon, when they'd land him a contract with one of the big space industrialists, an extension of his cover.

There was a period of waiting in which she tried not to drink too much coffee, and he slumped in the seat opposite the window, out which could be seen two shuttles on their pads.

Then someone came to get them, and they were escorted through a tunnel, outside to a waiting van, empty but for its driver, who took them and their aluminum cases to the shuttle gantry's elevator.

Not until they were entering the shuttle's hatchway and making their way back into the Spacehab passenger module did she realize they hadn't exchanged a word since he'd gone through his suit's test.

She said, "Trace, you're not worried, are you?"

He replied, "What good would it do? Like the guard said, there's two of these. We got a fifty-fifty chance that ours won't blow up."

"Bite your tongue," she said, and ducked through the hatch in front of her to see Mission Director Harper and his blond wife in the first pair of seats, calmly reading

80

magazines while the NASA steward mixed them a drink from a portable cart.

"Like a damned airplane," she heard Trace mutter, before Mrs. Harper saw them and insisted they "sit down and have a chat."

The woman didn't seem to understand how much thrust they were about to endure, riding a disposable rocket into space.

They had orange juice with the director, to be polite, and then headed toward their seats, three rows back. The steward said the flight wouldn't be full.

That was something, anyway. It occurred to her that there was no need for two shuttles if this one was only taking a few passengers, unless passengers weren't the primary payload.

Then more people came aboard, Chandra and select Europeans from the joint projects, and she and Rand stowed their cases in the lockers under their seats.

Just before takeoff, Trace ran his finger down her arm and, when she didn't pull away, closed his hand over hers on the arm rest. "Thanks," he said.

"For what? I didn't do anything, say anything."

"That's right." He brought her hand up to his lips and kissed it, then nodded. "Like I said, thanks."

She wished he wouldn't do things like that in public; she could see one of the ESA men, someone she and Ilya both knew casually, peeking at them. But then she didn't care.

The intercom was telling them to prepare for lift-off, and she was fighting the adrenaline that was attempting to push her stomach up into her throat.

This time, when he took her hand, she squeezed his fingers.

Then the countdown began. For once, it went flawlessly, with no interrupts, and at the end of it was the gigantic, shuddering roar and impossible heaviness that was the only sign, in their pressurized, windowless module, that the shuttle was leaping toward space on gouts of flame.

**Book Two**

# SKY HIGH

# Chapter 1
# TRANSIT

Intellectually, Tracey Rand understood that there was nothing magical or even remarkable about his eight-day flight to the moon. You climbed out of earth's gravity well and then slid into the moon's. You changed horses, of course, at the LEO station, because the shuttle went no farther than two hundred and fifty miles above the earth; from there, you and the Spacehab module you inhabited were ferried by OTV to the Lunar Service Station, and from the LSS by "moon truck" down to the surface and Cop One.

Anytime during that trip when your acceleration or rotation equaled thirty-two feet per second per second, you experienced Earth-normal gravity; only during lift-off was the G-force considerably more; sometimes during transit you were weightless.

Like now. It was just physics. It was nothing special. Yet Tracey Rand was glued to his seat's monitor like a kid on his first plane ride. The monitors took the place of airplane windows, helping passengers to avoid claustrophobia. With a flick of the four switches below, Trace could alter the telemetry he was receiving: he could look up, down, backward, and forward.

Right now he was looking "up," at a starscape dominated by the moon as he'd never seen it. He'd seen satellite-bounced telemetry, down on Earth, and still photos and tape, but "live" from space meant something entirely different when you were live *in* space.

For Trace Rand, who'd sacrificed so much to WAR-LORD, who'd eaten and slept and, in sleep, dreamed of this moment, only to have given it all up, the view out his monitor was like redemption. Or resurrection. Or Judgment Day. It was as close to a religious experience as he was capable of having, just sitting there in the shuttle while the positive and negative responses of his battered body and mind wrestled with the sensory input he was receiving.

The moon was more battered than he was—a target, scored by thousands of meteor hits, pocked by its own internal and violent reactions. The moon was where mankind would make or break its future. The moon was not the same moon that had smirked down at Rand in the surf on his Mexican beach.

This moon was different. This moon was a venue. This moon was where Tracey Rand was going to find out if he still had what it took—if, somewhere below the scaffolding he'd built over his past, the same imperatives that had almost killed him once still applied.

He liked the hell out of it, now that his body had stopped demanding that he flee or fight the might-be sarcophagus of his customized spacesuit and the multi-G pressure of lift-off. There was a child in him, a boy he hadn't encountered for ages, someone he'd caged in his mind for being too dangerous, too cavalier with life and limb, who'd always wanted only this: to go to the goddamned moon.

To walk on it. To burrow into it. To make a home of it and an ally of it. It smiled at him, didn't it? Beckoned. Promised.

Now it was going to deliver, one way or the other, on all the facile promises of life and love and adventure it had made to all the generations of men who'd trekked by its light, made love under its spell, or gazed at it through crude instruments until their sight dimmed. It was going to give mankind back its future, a new frontier, become a staging area for the conquest of the solar system and beyond, delimiting the options of a race determined to breed and squander itself out of existence.

Or it was going to be the final frontier, the fire base from which the last weapons a warlike race would ever make blasted Earth back to the stone age.

One or the other result was inevitable, even when Trace left WARLORD. Perhaps before. Cooperation had never meant so much to man as it did entering the twenty-first century. The stakes were higher now than ever in history: learn to live together, to channel aggression outward, toward the planets and then the stars, or turn on each other like too many tigers in a circus cage.

Sitting with Brittany beside him, floating nearly imperceptibly in their harnesses during a zero-G interval, Rand felt as if, for that one moment, all the stresses of the race were contained in him. Work it out—the fears, the hostility, the deadly superpower gamesmanship—and live to fight or flee another day, because a man, no matter his ideals or intentions, couldn't totally override his genetic imperatives.

Trace had seen action in two Middle East shooting wars during his military service, joined CIA on discharge, been a hostage negotiator, a technology-transfer troubleshooter, a peacekeeper, and later, a technical means specialist. He'd fought in the appropriations wars before Senate intelligence committees and in the grant wars undertaken by major universities, so the ethical wars of the scientific community were as familiar to him as the covert wars of classified-program development.

But it wasn't until, one day on a field trip with British friends, he'd seen two mud skippers fighting over their muddy territorial boundaries that his experience had integrated into knowledge. The mud skippers, slimy little creatures with nail-head-size brains, fought to the death on their tidal flats while he watched. A naturalist with the party had explained in technical terms what Trace hadn't needed explained: mud-skipper males bit each other's heads off over females, over trespass of the mud walls they built in accordance with their programming, and basic male-confronts-male hostility. It wasn't learned behavior. It wasn't sane behavior. But it was unavoidable behavior. Not just the gaping of jaws and the thrashing of tails in warfare, but the whole series of events, including the urge to create mud-skipper architecture, were genetically predetermined.

He'd thought then that, without room to expand, the human race was doomed. He could see it in the thrashing bodies of the nearly mindless mud skippers. Like he could see it in his own memories, where it was impossible to argue that intellectual ability or sophistication or moral fiber were sufficient to override the mandates of his genetic inheritance.

WARLORD owed its genesis to that field trip, to an accident of proximity that had allowed Trace Rand to see himself and his race in lower forms of life. The intervening years, the struggle to sell the idea, get the funding and the muscle to ensure continued funding, the sacrifices, and finally, the accident that should have sidelined Rand as a player, had made him feel that his race *was* a lower form of life.

And yet now, staring out his monitor at the moon, he was unreasonably optimistic. Sure, there were casualties—Richelson, Davies, the rest. There always were, in a war. There were probably casualties he didn't know about, too.

But there was hope. WARLORD had survived—distorted, misunderstood, but it had survived. If Rand could survive on the moon long enough to implement operational goals, it would thrive. The superpower rivalry might kill him in the process, but it was that very rivalry he'd used to drive the project, power the funding, and push the envelope of credibility in the minds of space managers and legislators alike.

When he'd gotten himself crushed under that satellite,

he'd written off WARLORD along with himself. Maybe it didn't have to be that way.

He'd been having a tough time in the suit, yeah. Kate had seen it, okay. Lift-off had broken the perpetual-motion device that was his chemical reaction to bad memories and lack of faith in his own performance.

He'd gotten this far. It was going to take more than the covert bogeymen who always haunt the closets of black projects to stop him. He was on his way to the moon.

It was so damned amazing that he wanted to cuddle the woman beside him. Kate was a part of all that past pain, but also a part of the first real optimism he'd felt in years. He'd take her back when this was over and introduce her to Jesus and America . . . to the jungle, to the beach.

When it was over, and he had WARLORD back on course, Bates's enemy agents caught or neutralized, ZR/SEAL's score settled. Sure he would. It was as likely as him having made it into a civilian shuttle berth under commercial cover.

He'd been relieved that they hadn't sent him via the Consolidated Space Command Center in Colorado Springs, from where all purely military shuttle missions launched. They were giving him a good chance to win. And it was a game whose rules he understood, a game he was as able to play as the next guy.

But maybe not as able as the next girl. He studied Kate Brittany surreptitiously out of one corner of his eye. She was giving her dinner order to the steward; he'd have to give his next.

All this time, Kate had stayed in the game, telling herself that what she was doing was worth any price. That was what you had to tell yourself. Trace knew how it was; he'd left when he didn't believe that anymore. You can't save the world all by yourself, but you can look after your little piece of it. One of these days, she'd probably find out it wasn't enough, like he had.

And yet, tonight, it seemed like enough. He'd had his

five years off. He was glad now he hadn't said no when Bates had asked him to come aboard. Not because he thought that whoever had killed the other Seals couldn't find him and scratch him on the moon, but because, damn it, he'd left something behind when the shuttle lifted off: as if it were a concomitant of gravity, he'd shaken off the burden of failure that had been weighing him down since the accident.

He hadn't felt so good since before he'd fucked up his life in a moment of inattention and watched all his dreams drift away like the oxygen bubbles from his rent suit.

"Same as she ordered," he told the steward when the man asked about his choice for dinner, and turned to Kate: "What's our ETA at LEO?"

"Another three hours, given docking traffic and the way they handle things with dips on board." She inclined her head forward where, beyond the facing seats, the ESA types, Chandra animated at their center, were drawing the U.S. mission director, Harper, into some sort of political debate. Beyond them, the two blond women were out of their harnesses; with the shuttle in burn, they had enough weight to keep them from floating from their feet.

"Want to join them?" Rand asked her. She'd been quiet, and he wasn't sure if it was a disapproving quiet.

"We should," she said, locking her hands in front of her and stretching in her seat like a cat, "but I don't want to. Let's pretend we're immersed in technical details." She tossed him a wicked grin. "When we get to LEO, we'll have stopover quarters—time and privacy for serious talk. Right now, I don't know what you need to know, so ask me anything that comes into your head."

"You don't want me to do that," he shot back.

Her coffee came and she cracked the seal of her straw and sucked with expert ease. "It's my job, Trace."

"Okay. Spend the night with me on LEO? I'm just not oriented enough to be able to do without you. . . ."

"Right." She nodded gravely. "We're here to serve,

Dr. Rand. In the meantime''—she leaned across him and her breast brushed his knee as she stretched to flip toggles on the monitor panel—''let's give you your LEO orientation. Hit that button there when I say 'next.' ''

He found the button and fingered it questioningly.

"That's it. Okay, next."

He pressed the button and the screen advanced from black to star-studded black with a close-up of the LEO station in the foreground.

They went through the on-board orientation tape, Kate giving him all the frills. She showed him the docking areas for shuttles, and the extruded ring that housed Spacehab modules and OTVs to carry the passenger modules, rather like large torpedoes, from LEO to the Lunar Service Station and beyond. She showed him a schematic of the erector-set LEO station, and then close-ups of the "corridors" that universities and corporations added to the U.S. government superstructure that made the LEO station United States territory. That was the rule up here: if it was your superstructure, it was your turf.

Then their dinner came, and with it, the two blond women, who asked Kate politely if they could sit in on the rest of Rand's briefing, after dinner.

"We couldn't help overhearing," said the first blond, who was Harper's wife, "and you're just so knowledgeable, my dear, that we thought we'd try and convince you. My husband hasn't told me anything near what you're telling . . . Dr. Rand." She squinted at Rand's nametag. "And Dr. Chandra has kept Robin equally in the dark. Oh, I'm sorry," said Alicia Harper. "Have you met Robin?"

"At the British embassy party," Kate answered quickly. "Hello, again."

The second, younger and prettier blond woman nodded. Rand remembered her now and wondered how he'd even fleetingly imagined that the two fair women looked alike. The director's wife was soft and plump; this woman was in exceptional physical shape.

"Well?" said the woman whose nametape said Robin Faragher. "What do you say? It's easier to absorb all this from an expert—especially a woman expert." All the while, her eyes never left Rand.

"Fine with me," Rand said, feeling he ought to say something. "But Kate and I are going on to classified matters, I believe, after we eat."

It wasn't polite, but it was an easy out. Up here classifications were status symbols. The women would either now proclaim their clearances in haughty good fellowship, or go back to swapping recipes. He didn't care which. He just wasn't ready to have the diplomatic exigencies of station life intrude on him quite yet.

Kate thought otherwise, evidently. "Not for another hour's worth of work, we're not. Sure, ladies. As soon as you've eaten, we'll be glad to read you in."

Both women thanked Kate and drifted away, Harper to her husband, the other woman to Chandra.

"Did you see her patch?" Kate asked, frowning.

"Uh . . . no, I didn't notice." The lady's arms hadn't been what caught Rand's attention.

"Chandra's executive assistant, I believe. From the ESA metallurgy project, anyway." Her tone had a brittle edge.

"A problem?"

"Only if you catch the pitch she's so obviously throwing," Kate retorted, eyes on her lap tray, where she was determinedly quartering her entrée.

"Katydid? Look at me."

She did and he said very solemnly, "Don't worry about me. I'm with you until you say otherwise."

"It's not you I'm worried about, Trace. It's her. I don't like her."

He couldn't say that jealousy wasn't a clear indicator of anything but functioning hormones; she'd have strangled him on the spot. The promise in the blond woman's eyes had been unmistakable. So was Kate's reaction.

"Look," he said, exasperation showing, "let's eat, be

nice to 'em, then get rid of 'em, okay? I don't know about you, but I don't need any complications, not here, not now, not later.''

''End of discussion,'' she told her dinner, letting him know that he'd slipped back into his old habit of laying things out for her unequivocally.

Damned women were so complicated. On the moon, he was beginning to think, two pretty women were going to be one too many.

# Chapter 2

# LOW
# EARTH ORBIT

Of course, with Director Harper and his ditsy wife aboard, there had to be a cocktail party scheduled for their "evening" stopover. Kate was cursing herself for her bad luck, the system for being distorted by ego-related perks, and Rand for simply existing as the shuttle docked flawlessly in the VIP bay and the pressurized lock in the forward section sighed open.

Waiting for Harper and his wife were LEO station functionaries in their white dress coveralls and ESA officials along to make sure Chandra's party received no hierarchical slights.

With any luck, she and Trace Rand could just slip away quietly in the wake of so much converging brass. But her luck stayed bad: both Mrs. Harper and Chandra's sloe-eyed assistant made special pilgrimages back through the crowd to them, pressing their invitations to tonight's event.

"Nineteen hundred hours, remember," said Robin Faragher, with a flutter of eyelids just short of flirtation, while her ESA party watched.

"My dear, you must come and bring Dr. Rand," Alicia Harper said through freshly reddened, craggy lips. "We'll have a chance to make sure he meets *everyone*. . . ."

Everyone who was anyone, Kate thought, bristling even

more. Everyone who wouldn't pay attention to either of us on our own merits. *Everyone I can damn well do without, Mrs. High-and-mighty. Why don't you take your diplomatic spotlight and shove it the dark recesses of your person, before you get us killed. . . .*

And that stopped Kate with one hand already reaching for the attaché case in the locker under her seat. Had she thought that? Was she worried about that? Up here?

She told herself it was just overreaction to Richelson's funeral and then, right on its heels, Davies's accident. Death. Murder. Execution. Whatever the hell it was. Just overreaction, and yet there was no reason to assume that foul play was limited to Earth. Neither foul play nor bad luck had any correlation with Earth's gravity well.

There were as many ways to kill a Seal up here as there had been down there. Maybe more. The only real benefit to being here was a benefit to the investigators of any incident that might take place: the pool of possible perpetrators was smaller. And even Rand wasn't arguing that Davies's death hadn't precluded speculation that, somehow, the loss of ZR/SEAL members was just a run of phenomenal coincidence.

This was no time to be feeling that her luck had gone bad. She jerked the aluminum case out of its locker and stood up abruptly, not realizing how close behind her Trace was standing. Her buttocks connected with his pelvis. His hands went around her waist to steady her.

"Sorry," she said with an embarrassed toss of her head. "I guess I don't have to explain that it takes a little time to adjust your muscles to the gravity differential. Even after just a few days groundside, I'm overperforming again."

"Excuse me?" came his amused voice. His hands were still resting lightly on her waist. This time, she didn't care if any of their fellow passengers saw. In fact, it would suit her if both the blondes were watching.

But they weren't; they'd left with their surrogate entourages, she found when she looked. They were the only two still in the shuttle's passenger module.

"Overperforming—that's what we call it when your muscles still think they need to deliver the same amount of torque they did on Earth. We've got four-fifths Earth normal out here on the rim of LEO most of the time, but your body takes a while to realize it."

"And by then we'll be gone," he said, still holding her. "It's going to be an interesting night. I don't know about you, but I'm determined to turn in early. Dip parties aren't my idea of a fruitful use of our valuable time."

*Some serious innuendo, Dr. Rand.* "Check," she said, and he did let go of her, stooping to retrieve his own attaché case. When he straightened up, he was fingering the manacle bolted to his case. "I don't think these are necessary here, do you?"

"No, but it's SOP. Anyway, who knows what's necessary in these circumstances? Richelson didn't. Davies sure as hell didn't."

"You're really spooked, aren't you?" He closed the manacle around his left wrist.

"I'm really careful." *God, don't take it personally, Trace. It's got nothing to do with your manhood. You're barely competent up here. You don't know the ropes. You didn't see your face when they checked your suit. Bates was out of his mind, or willing to take chances I'm not, with both our lives.* "Careful is what life up here is all about." She headed forward, toward the open lock.

He paced her, his first few steps overleveraged in the light gravity so that he drew ahead and had to wait for her to catch up.

When she did, his grin was sheepish. "Let's see how you do that."

She demonstrated: "Drag your feet. Think of shuffling and you'll be just about right."

He tried it while she waited and watched as he strode down the aisle and back. Although she was careful to be clinical about her observations, the jerkiness in his returning gait was more from self-consciousness than any attempt at adjustment.

He said, rubbing his neck with his free hand, "I'll do, I guess. What about the party? From the way you handled it, I assume we've got to go, but I don't have clothes and I don't think you do—"

"It's not like that up here. Not formal, I mean. I've got good credit, we'll get you something." *And me, too.* She had some things in the locker she kept here, but with the two blond barracudas at the party, she'd want better. No skirts or dresses, of course, but the stations had their own fashions, tailored for lower gravity. She'd play show and tell with either of those women and not worry who'd win.

"*I'll* get *you* something—the least I can do."

"Fine, Trace. First things first, okay? Let's go find our rooms and put in for a secure terminal so we can check in with groundside." And read what's on the media in the briefing book packets. And find out from Bates who the hell this Robin Faragher is.

She led him out of the shuttle, down the "corridor," which was no more than a plastic docking tube, and into the reception area. There she skirted the little knot of white-clad functionaries around Harper's party and went straight to the reception desk against the far wall.

Trace was gawking at the various information and routing counters, at the signs indicating the major multinational corporations who kept blocked rooms and their own passenger modules at LEO.

The woman behind the reception desk took Kate's card and punched up her room assignment, complete with accreditation and preferences, and found her a room in the government staff section.

"I'll want one adjoining for my friend, here. We've got to work all night," she said, and asked Trace for his credit card.

It should have been smooth as silk, but it wasn't: Trace's

card matched his cover. They wanted to put him in a commercial corridor and they couldn't give him a secure terminal on this short notice.

She started to argue and the woman behind the desk went ramrod straight and stiff-lipped, telling her with body language and a disapproving scowl that registration wasn't going to cut her a bit of slack, that Kate Brittany's personal preferences had no bearing on LEO policy: government types in one corridor, corporate creatures in another, and he was lucky he had a room at all, with no current affiliation.

Trace's hand squeezed her arm and she broke off the argument. "All right, put him wherever you want, but route any incoming calls to my quarters." *That blatant enough for you, bitch?*

The woman's disapproval heightened, and she began to recite rules Kate knew better than she. "Look," Kate said, reading the woman's tag and pronouncing her name with all the potent threat of her diplomatic rank behind it, "this man is a guest of the Cop One mission, and I know the SOP here better than you do. Punch the damn card. I'm in a hurry."

She stalked away from the reception desk with too much fervor, so that she bounded three ungainly steps and swore under her breath.

Trace was right behind, and then beside her. "Bureaucracy isn't anything new. Forget it."

"God, I hate this. Every little thing is going wrong. It's a terrible sign."

"Don't get superstitious, Katydid. I'll show you my room, then you'll show me yours, and Bates'll pick up the bill for a bed I'm not going to sleep in."

Still, there was too much hassle in what should have been a routine process. She wanted to chalk it up to an officious woman in a low-clout job, but she couldn't.

As they headed toward the escalators that would take them "down" to the elevator banks, she couldn't shake the feeling of foreboding she felt. Seeing Chandra staring after them didn't help any.

Tracey Rand's room was in a corridor halfway around the outer rim; they had to pass the shopping quadrant to get there. She was still so angry that she grabbed a bodysuit Trace commented on, without concern for price, and slapped her Cop One credit card down on the counter. When she signed the bill, her stomach lurched; but Trace had good taste and ZR/SEAL still had a contingency fund.

At least it was something she could use on the moon, not the simulated Earth-style floppy clothing some people wore here. She tried not to be resentful that, in the midst of all this trouble, Tracey Rand's mere proximity had her worrying more about what she was going to wear to some stupid party than what she was going to find when they got Bates's media into a secure terminal. Or whether someone up here was waiting for the right moment to relegate Kate Brittany's concerns to academic history.

It doesn't matter how you look if you're dead, but all the way along the commercial corridor to his room, she kept seeing phantom visions of herself with her lungs blown out her mouth and her eyes burst from depressurization.

When he said, "Katydid, why so quiet?" she actually flinched.

"Trying to find your damn cube, is all."

"Cube?"

"Cubicle. One single-occupancy module, cylindrical, toilet and refrigerator/cookstove under the sleeper, fourteen feet long, task chair and work area foldouts on the other side. But don't try to get your sleeper down when the desk's up and running." She flashed him a sour smile. "People have had to be cut out of their cubes from trying that— stuck like flies in amber."

He didn't laugh; he had a professionally concerned look on his face. She could have punched him. She could have cried. Poor Davies. Who was at his funeral? What were they telling his wife? Maybe she and Richelson's wife would put the pieces together at a widows' coffee klatch; they had as good a chance as she and Rand of figuring out what the hell was going on.

When he saw the single-occupancy module, no more than a cylinder screwed into the corridor, he grunted. "You weren't kidding. Is yours any better?"

"USG? You bet," she said, hearing the sarcasm in her voice and wishing it wasn't there. They punched the lock and left the cubicle with its DO NOT DISTURB LCD display enabled and a forwarding patch on his phone, and hiked all the way back to the commercial hub because every elevator was in use and waits, on LEO, could be interminable.

There she could get a government express elevator. She was about to slap her priority card into its slot when he said, "Wait a sec," and disappeared into one of the gauntlet of expensive shops which, before today, she'd never even entered.

She slumped against the prefab wall, waiting for him, eyes on her feet, wishing she could keep her mind on business with him around. It had been all she could do not to show him how to unfold his sleeper from his cube's wall, as if there wasn't going to be either the time or the inclination later.

She was giving herself a lecture on being too easy, too proprietary, and too preoccupied with Tracey Rand even to survive, when he came back, his gait well under control now, even to her critical eye. Under one arm he had a box in fancy gift wrap.

"God, Trace, what's that? We're not supposed to be spending mission credit on—" Then she remembered the shopping bag she was carrying.

He was already responding, "Part of my commercial cover. Come on, let's call in."

"Yessir," she said, jamming her card into the U.S. GOV'T ACCESS ONLY elevator slot so that it bleeped in distress before it opened to admit them.

Empty, thank God. They stepped in, she entered the code for her room and leaned against the wall, eyes closed because she wanted to cry, suddenly, for no reason but frustration. With him. With herself. With the dead Seals and Bates and everything.

Somewhere along the way, he kissed the top of her head and she leaned against him, not caring if he thought she was weak. She was. And even through their clothing, the physical pressure of his presence was welcome.

When the elevator bleeped again and opened onto the government corridor, he whistled: he'd seen the stark, minimal commercial zone and appreciated the difference here—the carpeted floor, the wider spaces between cube doors, the occasional simulated wood-and-brass of VIP suites.

She wished she rated one of those, but she didn't. Still, her cube was twice the size of his, with a permanent desk, two track chairs, a secure terminal, and three telephones, one of them with video capability.

Inside, with the door shut, she pulled down the sleeper irritably, unclasped her wrist from the case, and tossed the case and her package onto the bed before she sat on the edge of it, head in her hands.

She could hear him moving around, but she didn't look up. If she did she was going to cry. She wanted him to stay. She wanted him to leave. She was never going to survive the remainder of their eight-day journey to Cop One, not in such close proximity to him, not when she was so confused.

She didn't raise her head until she heard the soft, tonal beeps of the vid-terminal phone and the louder whirr of the computer as he turned it on.

He already had the scrambler engaged and the modem transmitting their call request when she reached him.

"Bates's office?" she guessed, and he nodded absently, still hunt-and-pecking on the keyboard, his eyes on his codebook. "Ask for a complete bio and security check on Chandra and Robin Faragher."

That brought his head up out of the book. His eyes searched her face and she thought, *If you make one crack, I'm going to strangle you with wet panty hose and say Faragher did it.*

He said, "Good idea," and went back to watching his fingers on the keyboard.

She wished she was angry that he'd usurped her prerogative by initiating the call, but she was relieved. If he wanted to take some of the burden, fine. He was getting paid for it. And she wasn't his secretary.

He hunted-and-pecked and waited and decoded and hunted-and-pecked again. It was all standard stuff and Kate left him to it: they were here, alive but trapped in the many-tentacled red-tape octopus, and unless Bates had something more to say to them, it was all routine.

She unpacked the bodysuit she'd bought for the party and shook it once to watch its nacreous shimmer. Feeling better, she punched some coffee out of the "kitchen" and sat back on the bed, sipping it and watching his shoulders hunch over his work.

Damned domestic, the two of them, and she wished she knew whether she liked that, whether it meant any more to him than an effective way to do the job. But even if she asked, she couldn't be sure she'd find out.

He sat back finally, one hand massaging the nape of his neck, and the screen before him started to fill with data. "Want hard copy on Chandra and Faragher?" he asked without looking at her. "It's lots more than one page."

"Yes, if we're still going to the party. We won't have time to read it now."

He nodded and punched up the printout. "We'll run the rest of the media later too, then?" He was asking her. "Most of it so far has just been secure com procedures."

"If you think it can wait." Part of her wanted him to suggest that they skip the party after all. They still had to run the entire code briefing on the dark-side project. Of course, they could do that at Cop One. . . .

He powered down everything as soon as the printer stopped spewing sheets and came over to the sleeper. "Got you something in that store," he said almost shyly.

"What? You were supposed to get a change of clothes for the party."

"I did, but I got you something too." He slit the wrapping and opened his parcel, then pulled out a little plastic box with an orchid in it.

A real orchid. On LEO it would have cost a week's pay.

She didn't know what to do, or what to say, and there was nowhere to run in her cube—not even a bathroom big enough to turn around in with your arms outstretched.

So she said, "You're crazy, you know that?"

He said, "I'm certain of it. That's a bribe so you won't tell anybody." He leaned down on a stiff arm to kiss her.

"We're going to be late to Harper's party," she protested mildly.

"Yeah, ain't it a shame?"

"Trace, this is serious."

"You're damned right it's serious. I'm going to need lots of practice in reduced gravity before we try this on the moon."


"So glad you could make it," said Director Harper with a shadow of disapproval in his voice when they arrived, an hour late, at the reception. "Let me introduce you to some people, Dr. Rand."

The paunchy director had looked more dignified in his shuttle flightsuit coveralls than he did in his Cop One dress suit, with its body-hugging curves. Most of these dips and corporate types, Trace realized, looked flabby and unhealthy.

Except for Kate, who, sporting her orchid, looked as good as she felt, and Robin Faragher, who was making no attempt to hide her interest in him.

Cut loose from Kate by what seemed to be executive order, chaperoned by the mission director or his wife, Rand

103

played account executive and talked about Cislunar's security expertise and its hunger for orbital and lunar business, and tried to remember the names of the men he met.

About two hours into the affair, he saw Kate with Chandra and wished he'd taken time to read the deep background that Bates's office had sent up. If it was a mistake not to have read it, it was too late now to rectify it.

He was getting the distinct impression that Robin Faragher thought Tracey Rand was part of her job, which meant that she was part of his, somehow or other.

"Let's get out of here for a bit," Robin Faragher said to him, contriving to look up under her froth of naturally blond hair although she was nearly as tall as he. "Surely you have not seen enough of LEO yet."

"I'm working," he reminded her. "I've got to land a few of these accounts or I won't be worth the fuel expended to get me up here."

Faragher laughed throatily. "Payload and payback, yes. That is the equation. I can help you with ESA, you know. Really I can."

"I don't doubt that you can." He didn't back up as she moved in. It would have been offensive and, anyway, she was more than just attractive.

If he couldn't feel Kate's eyes boring into his back, he'd have brushed against Faragher's hips in their tight blue bodysuit before this.

The moon-style clothing suited her; she had nothing to hide. At first, in his snug low-G tuxedo, he'd felt like he was in some high-tech wet suit, but now he wasn't uncomfortable. And the lady obviously found him acceptable.

So there was only the judgment call: rebuff her advances for Kate's sake, or play along because it was his job—or might be, or could be said to be.

Just as he was getting ready to try putting his hand on the small of Faragher's back, he heard Kate's voice.

She was arm in arm with Director Harper, and both were

headed their way. Faragher said, "Here comes your keeper."

Perceptive. Or deceptive. He said, "Come on, Kate's an old friend, showing me the ropes. Up here I'm going to need all the friends I can get."

"That's nice to hear," said Robin Faragher, and turned her dazzling smile on him at full power for the first time. Without it, she was merely an attractive, European-looking blond woman; with it, she was a movie star, a temptress, a repository of delights.

He blinked away an instant, technicolor fantasy involving that mouth in graphic activity, and took a deep breath as Kate said, a trifle too loudly, "Guess what, Trace? Director Harper and his wife aren't going the rest of the way by OTV and moon truck—they're taking a Transatmospheric. And they say we can come along, if we'd like."

Kate's eyes were sparkling with excitement. Going from LEO to the Lunar Service Station by Transatmospheric Vehicle would take days off their trip—the hypersonic aerospace plane was capable of Mach 25. "That would be much appreciated, Director Harper—the sooner I get to Cop One, the better."

Beside him, Faragher pouted visibly. Then her features smoothed as Kate and Harper drifted away to finalize their schedule.

He never did get a chance to let Robin Faragher show him LEO, but when they parted, she kissed him on the lips and promised that "we'll be seeing lots more of each other on the moon." She even gave him her lunar phone number.

And when Kate and he got back to their quarters and she started leafing through Faragher's background, they learned something.

"Trace, she was on the skydiving flight with Richelson! She was *there* when he was killed!"

"What?" he said, and then: "Doesn't prove anything." He took the background check from her, scanning quickly. "Staff D gives Faragher a clean bill of health."

"Why wouldn't she have said something, though?"

"To us? Why would she? There's no overt connection between us and Richelson. If she *had,* that would have meant something—it would have meant that she knew we were ZR."

"And the way she was climbing all over you proves she doesn't?"

He had no answer for that, so he said, "Look, let's go through the rest of this stuff Bates sent, before we get caught flat-footed." He almost added *again* but he didn't want to admit that he half believed the conclusion Kate was jumping to.

Proximity isn't guilt. Coincidence does exist. And the fact that Robin Faragher might be more than she appeared didn't answer Rand's most burning questions about what was going on up there on the dark side, and why. He needed some connection to become apparent, some reason or method or thesis that connected ZR/SEAL deaths to WARLORD. If sabotage of WARLORD was truly at the heart of the matter, then the question was one he'd asked himself before he signed on to this mission: who was doing it, and why?

# Chapter 3

# BLACK PROJECT

Rand had dreamed about Richelson and he woke in a cold sweat, his stomach churning and Kate snoring softly beside him in the bed of her LEO cubicle.

Normally in the wake of a bad dream he'd have gotten up and gone down to the shore, walked it off. For a moment, before he realized who was beside him and why his stomach felt light and his equilibrium disturbed, he'd been going to do just that.

Now he froze, bare feet on the floor, the covers thrown back, praying she wouldn't wake up. There was no place to walk here but through endless corridors, and that wasn't going to help. He leaned his elbows on his knees and put his head in his hands, letting the dream cycle. At least he hadn't talked in his sleep. The last thing he wanted was to answer Kate's questions about his bad dream or see that look in her eyes, like he'd seen it during his suit fitting at Canaveral.

The same look that he'd seen on her face when she'd come to see him in the Tokyo hospital after the accident, when he'd been lying there doped out of his mind with drip needles in his arm. He wasn't a sick puppy. He wasn't a vet back from Central America or the Middle East minus a limb and shell-shocked. He wasn't a mental case or a retarded child for her to nurse. He hadn't been then and he was lots better now.

Palms pressing his eyes, he went searching for the dream. And found it: he'd been floating between the stars with Richelson, both of them in spacesuits. Okay, maybe that was the lesser gravity here; he was reacting to the four-fifths G, trying to make sense out of it with his subconscious.

Richelson had been trying to tell him something though, waving signs like some living semaphore because their com units were down. He felt guilty about Richelson, okay—that wasn't anything unusual: he was alive and Richelson was dead and Richelson had been one of his men—one of his responsibilities—for nearly three years. And ZR/SEAL, or WARLORD, or some combination of the two, had gotten Richelson killed. So *he* had, Trace Rand told himself savagely, playing his ace against unmetabolized guilt: you faced it and went on to new business.

He didn't feel guilty about Davies; Davies hadn't been in the dream. He rubbed his palms slowly against his closed eyes in circular motions. Who had, then? There are two other spacesuited figures with their cyclopean, golden eyes, swimming toward him and Richelson, gesturing to them. . . . And Richelson had been signing to him to use caution, to come away, take cover.

But there hadn't been any cover, not in empty space . . . only whatever they were building, a bristly ball of antennae and delivery systems . . . WARLORD!

He sat bolt upright in the bed and Kate scissored her legs, moving restlessly beside him in sleep. His hands balled into fists around the edge of the mattress and his eyes glared into the dark of the confining LEO cubicle, as if the dream were running on a video screen before him.

The two approaching had been women; in the way of dreams he'd known that. Kate and the blond girl he'd just met, Faragher. Okay, that was just his mind telling him he was going to have woman trouble; nothing spectacularly insightful about that. And yet, there was more there—Kate had had a briefing book under one arm. Faragher had had . . . something in her hand. Something Richelson was sure was dangerous.

Richelson had been trying to warn him off, for certain. Richelson was playing the part of his analytical subconscious, then. Warning him off the mission, he told himself. Warning him off because, when Tracey Rand had read the final briefing material that Bates had sent up on encrypted media, he'd realized that WARLORD had mutated, in five years, into a travesty of the original project.

WARLORD, in simplest terms, was a terraforming project. It would introduce into the atmosphere of Mars certain catalytic chemicals that would create a bio-active atmosphere on Mars. It had been a "black project" because, if it hadn't been secret, the U.S. Congress would never have approved its funding—the results were too far in the future to enhance any legislator's bid for reelection; the international repercussions of a unilateral attempt by the U.S. to alter conditions on Mars were bound to be controversial.

That was then, when Rand had left the project. WARLORD was slugged with high-level security flags now because it involved nuclear warheads. The Soviets were doing something on Mars, too. WARLORD in its present incarnation involved the covert assembly, on the moon's dark side, from apparent space junk and seemingly peaceful satellites, of a nuclear-powered *planetismal*—a heavy-mass projectile that would strike Mars at its equator. The impact would, in conjunction with subsequently delivered chlorofluorocarbons, begin the terraforming process. It would also wipe out whatever the Russians were doing there. In its present form, WARLORD would be nearly undetectable: its early effects would resemble Martian dust storms; the emp and impact shock waves would destroy whatever equipment the Soviets had on the Martian surface that

109

might have been able to transmit through the dust and high-velocity wind. There would be no trace of U.S. involvement, interference, or foul play for the Soviets to bring to the UN or the World Court.

But whatever the USSR was doing on the Martian surface would be blown to hell. And if that was, as an NRO analysis among Rand's briefing materials suggested, a project to set up a Mars base or Mars colony, the only thing that was going to keep the superpowers from going to war because of WARLORD was secrecy: the Soviets weren't admitting they were doing anything on Mars beyond "peaceful scientific unmanned missions."

The encrypted briefing had made Rand so angry that he hadn't gone to bed until well after Kate was asleep. She'd been hurt, he knew, by his disinterest; she'd been defensive and angry, even voicing the peculiarly feminine surmise that "It's Robin Faragher, isn't it?"

He'd just waved a hand at her and gone back to his work. She was free to think what she chose; all he'd been able to think of then was WARLORD. If they'd managed to field the team and get the project up and running five years ago, or even three, it wouldn't have involved nuclear means; it wouldn't have involved destroying what might well be a major Soviet base; it wouldn't have gotten Richelson, Frank, Kendall, Blake, and Davies killed—at least not by covert means.

And he was sure of that, now. Someone wanted to stop WARLORD. Someone was sure that ZR/SEAL was necessary to WARLORD's implementation. He couldn't argue that: according to the data he had, Richelson, Blake, and Kendall had been reassigned to the mission. That would have been enough to spook whoever didn't want WARLORD to go on line. The deaths were a message in no uncertain terms: back off or face the consequences.

But whose message? Richelson kept waving to him in his mind's eye, signing things he couldn't quite make out.

Was it internal opposition to the project from within the defense or intelligence community? Was it the Soviets? Or was it even simpler? Was it a decision taken somewhere in the U.S. security establishment to erase all knowledge of WARLORD from the minds of any but current program participants?

The last postulate might be flawed, he told himself: Davies was pretty current, pretty useful, and assigned to a very sensitive berth on the Space Talks team—a berth in no way concerned with WARLORD. And yet Davies could easily have been considered a security risk. Rand had made enough similarly tough calls to know that given enough at stake and sufficient paranoia, Davies could have been deemed expendable.

His hands were aching, digging into the mattress. He uncurled his fingers and flexed them, peering into the dark. His instinct was sometimes the only thing he trusted; his dreams were infrequent enough that he considered them channels from his correlative subconscious.

And in his dream, Richelson had been telling him in no uncertain terms to run like hell, to hide. Hiding from women wasn't Rand's idea of a workable strategy at any time; hiding from Kate was something you had to do in plain sight. Hiding from Robin Faragher went against his job description—he was moon-bound to do a job. That job included finding out who was operating against WARLORD and stopping that someone, as well as overseeing the project's final phase.

He'd have help once he got to the moon, help from Bates's people. And he'd have Kate with him, every step of the way. He shifted in bed to look at her and saw nothing but grainy darkness. Was he actually considering her as a potentially hostile player?

The only answer he could give himself was Richelson, waving him away from the two women in spacesuits. Was he confusing his personal feelings with his job?

He'd botched everything that mattered to him the last time he'd worked with her.

He held his breath and listened to her breathing, probing for any sign that she was faking sleep. She sounded as if she were in a perfectly normal sleep cycle. He raised his legs and slowly drew the covers up to his chest and she sighed and rolled over, her back to him, curling up against the wall.

Even if everything to do with WARLORD went perfectly, even if there were no bellicose repercussions over America's unilateral seizure of Martian exploration rights and redefinition of space law, it would take decades for Mars to be transformed. *Mere* decades, he'd said in the initial proposal.

So one way or the other, he probably wasn't going to live to see the end of it. That didn't mean, however, that he wouldn't give it his best shot.

He'd paid in advance for the privilege. And if the woman beside him was part of the problem, he'd deal with that. When the time came.

In a way it was easier to consider her as a possible opposition player. Falling in love with Kate Brittany had nearly ruined his life once. He couldn't let it happen again. He couldn't afford a mistake. He couldn't afford to be less than perfect, and that wasn't as easy as it used to be. He couldn't afford to care about anybody the way he'd cared about her. He had to keep his eye on the ball, and that meant WARLORD.

He was almost hoping, as he slid his arm across her waist and pulled her buttocks against him, that she was one of the bad guys. If he could treat her like part of the game, like he'd treat Robin Faragher, the risk factor would be much lower.

But in five years, he'd never managed entirely to forget her. Kate and WARLORD, inextricably bound up with one another, in a category he couldn't convince himself, all that time, to forget. Unfinished business. Failures he couldn't rectify and couldn't justify.

As her breathing quickened and her buttocks snuggled against his groin and he realized she was no longer asleep, he was telling himself that, this time, he'd be more careful.

Kate and WARLORD were the only two things he'd ever let himself love. And love, as Richelson had told him one night over too many beers, could get you killed.

# Chapter 4

# FAST
# TRACK

The aerospace plane looked like a cad/cam acid dream. It was a wedge with curves, a spearhead with three kinds of engines to thrust it from Earth to deep space: a turbo-ramjet to move the plane from a groundside runway to Mach 4; a scramjet to swallow the shock—pass air and fuel through the engine at supersonic speeds while moving the shock wave aft of the combustion area—at speeds above Mach 4 in atmosphere; rocket engines to turn the air breather into a vacuum-capable spaceplane.

She was heat resistant and hypersonic, the cornerstone of the Strategic Defense Initiative program: the thousands of SDI space-based platforms that maintained the superpower stalemate could never have been emplaced on time, on budget, and with the requisite security constraints without her.

She was one of a fleet of fifty maintained by the Consolidated Space Command, and using her for passenger transit was, in Kate Brittany's experience, unheard of. But she was no longer wondering how Harper had gotten groundside in time for the British embassy party.

The answer was right before her eyes, in a shrouded landing bay: the U.S. military didn't leave its TAVs floating at external dock where other nations might have a

114

chance to steal its secrets by electronic snooping or any other means.

She'd never been in this high-security docking bay before, and she had Trace to look after, so she couldn't gawk through the double-thick armored window separating the waiting area from the pressurized bay where a dozen men crawled over the spaceplane, readying it for the next leg of its flight.

Turn-around time on the spaceplanes was still classified, but then, so was this entire area. Despite extensive entry procedures, guards armed with electropulse stunners and conventional kinetic kill rifles stood at intervals along the corridor and in the small waiting room itself.

It bothered her, sometimes, to realize how militarized space was, but she knew that there would be—could be— no manned presence in space without military objectives. Space wasn't cost effective for anything but strategic development.

Something was bothering Trace, too, she was sure. He'd been cold and distant when they got back from Harper's party, then waked her an hour before her alarm went off to make love to her.

She kept telling herself that she was imagining the change in him, that it came from one of their insoluble differences: he was an early bird, cranky and tired in the evening, and she was a night owl. She should have let him go off with Robin Faragher and let nature take its course: trying to get Rand interested in anything but his work after twenty-two hundred hours was a waste of time.

Still, he was different. Something in what Bates had sent up, he'd said when she broached the subject: "Read that stuff again, and we'll talk about it where we know the room's been swept."

Swept for bugs, he'd meant. If she had a dime for every time he'd promised that they'd talk about something and broken that promise, she wouldn't need her government pension. When he said that, it usually meant the subject was a personal one. Trace didn't talk about personal matters; he kept you guessing.

It was driving her crazy already. She found herself stiff and holding her breath when the door to the waiting area sighed open and Harper's party came in—because she was afraid Robin Faragher would be coming with them. You can give yourself a lecture when your emotions are out of control, but it doesn't help.

Tracey Rand had insinuated himself into her life again and, like the last time, Kate was losing control. Her mind still functioned, but it was no longer autonomous. The dichotomies inside her were infuriating. It was tough enough being an intelligent woman in government, where everything she did was scrutinized by males with bias, but being lovesick was simply unacceptable.

She was irritable, so perhaps it wasn't Rand who'd changed. He was beginning to seem like a threat to more than just her job description: he was driving her to distraction and she was letting it happen. *Again.* And she was willing to bet the same thing wasn't happening to him.

For the first time since she'd realized that she'd have to tell Rand about Ilya, she wasn't dreading it. Watching him transfixed and fascinated by the TAV, his eyes locked on the men tending the plane in its bay and his mind a million miles away from her, she thought, *Good, you arrogant bastard. We'll see what happens when you find out that you're not the only one who can play things "business before pleasure."* Because Ilya was more business than pleasure, although he was all the pleasure she was built to handle.

"Hello, Director Harper, Mrs. Harper." She nodded primly when the Harper's four-person entourage arrived. Rand turned away from the window at the sound of her voice and approached the converging group, looking right at home in his coveralls and a shoulder-slung gearbag, his movements easy in gravity that had given him problems only the night before.

"Greetings, my dear," Harper said and, with a twinkle in his eye, took her cheeks between his hands and bestowed on her a continental greeting, kissing both sides of her face while his wife smiled patronizingly.

Director Harper was Kate's height, a short bull of a man who could have passed for a picture-book Santa Claus who'd had his beard shaved. The determined kiss in front of his staff was meant to convey status, she knew, but the twinkle in his eye and his wife's attitude conveyed something else.

Flustered, she took a step backward, listening to Rand say, "I hope I don't have to kiss you too, sir, to thank you for this." He motioned toward the plane behind the window. "The sooner we get up and running, the better. And I've always wanted to ride in one of those."

"You'll like it," said Harper, his broad, white-haired head bobbing. "We know you need all the help you can get, Dr. Rand, and now that we have you, the task at hand is to integrate you into our organization as quickly and painlessly as possible."

*Jesus God, Harper's been talking to Bates.* She was shocked, although she couldn't have said why, exactly. As mission director, Harper's job was much like that of an ambassador on Earth; he had a right to know what was going on in his organization. And they did need help. But until now, Harper had never paid any attention to her, or her project.

Mrs. Harper was staring at her.

"Excuse me, ma'am? I didn't hear you. . . ." *Lame, lame. Pay attention to what's going on, Brittany. Get yourself together.*

"Dear, are you feeling all right? You seem awfully pale."

"No, no, I'm fine. Have you been on a TAV before, Mrs. Harper?" Beside her, Harper was engaged in low conversation with Trace, and the two men were drifting off where neither the women nor the two male aides would overhear. Her hackles rose. She shouldn't be cut out of whatever was going on between Trace and Harper. It was her project, not his. . . .

"Mrs. Harper, I have to . . ." What was she going to say? *Go talk to your husband, you silly twit?—reassert my position?—kick Trace in the balls and demand that your husband not treat me as your baby sitter?* ". . . make sure that Dr. Rand has everything he needs," she finished weakly.

"Don't worry, dear." The director's wife smiled. She was as well preserved as modern medicine could make her, but still had three brackets around the corners of her mouth when she smiled. "My husband will see that Dr. Rand has everything he needs. And you'll tell me about the social scene up there." Her eyes lifted momentarily, as if the moon were above their heads.

It wasn't. Helping Alicia Harper with the protocols she'd face on the moon should have been the job of her husband's social secretary, but Kate began, miserably, to do as she'd been asked. Somebody was going to pay for this, when she found out who to blame.

When the boarding door opened to admit them to the docking bay, Kate was still explaining to Alicia Harper how "one gets along with the various ESA and ComBloc representatives in station. It's so small, everyone knows everyone else." *And everyone knows everyone else's business. Do you know mine? Are you a player, privy to your husband's innermost thoughts, or just the bored wife, and they're throwing you a bone, letting you go lunar?*

No answer for that, and no real way to ask the question. With Alicia Harper by her side, she followed Trace and Director Harper into the docking bay and up the steps into the TAV, trying not to be rude but wishing the woman would just shut her mouth.

It wasn't every day you were ferried to LSS by spaceplane. If Mrs. Harper hadn't latched on to her, she might have gotten a peek into the cockpit. As it was, she was shown to her seat by a polite man in Space Command coveralls, a seat beside Alicia Harper.

Director Harper and Trace Rand were seated behind them, where a small bank of monitors were set flush into the wall by a sign that said REST ROOM. The two aides stowed baggage and then took the seats opposite Kate and Mrs. Harper.

That left six empty seats in the passenger module. An expensive trip, if passengers were all the spaceplane was carrying. Behind the passenger module in the long cargo bay, military payload was doubtlessly stored. So perhaps, she told herself, they'd leave dock without additional passengers.

Just when she was sure that would be the case, three men with military haircuts and security patches on their arms came aboard, saluted the general direction of Harper's seat, and scattered themselves among the remaining seats, talking in low voices.

One of them kept looking at her, but that didn't mean anything: she was the prettier of the two women and the security men were young and healthy.

Thoroughly uncomfortable now, she got out of her seat and went back to Rand's, feeling the men watching her. "Trace," she said when she got there, "let me have that background material on Chandra and Faragher. I want to go over it before we make LSS."

That brought Harper's head up and a calculating glitter into the mission director's eye. But that was what she'd wanted, wasn't it? To assert her position, make it clear she wasn't here to baby-sit Harper's wife?

Trace said, "Hold on a sec," and pulled his gearbag out of the locker under his seat to remove their attaché cases.

Before he could give her hers, Director Harper said, "My dear, you'll have plenty of time for that. I'll consider it a personal favor if you'll keep my wife in good spirits. She needs a firsthand orientation that only another woman can give."

Kate straightened up and crossed her arms. "Fine," she said coldly. "What's her clearance level?"

Trace shook his head minutely, one eyebrow raised, but said nothing.

Harper smiled patiently and told Kate that his wife had been cleared for anything Kate might want to tell her. At the same time, the flight attendant came toward her, asking her to "Please take your seat and fasten your belt, ma'am."

She did, feeling better, not worse. One of the security men watched her frankly. She ignored him, fastening herself into her harness.

Then a voice from the cockpit welcomed them aboard and told them they'd be docking at the LSS station for refueling in sixteen hours, where they'd have a ninety-minute layover before continuing on to lunar dock.

"Oh Kate, dear, isn't this exciting?" said Alicia Harper.

"Yes ma'am," Kate replied. Harper did have some serious clout, getting spaceplane service all the way to the lunar surface. Or else, whatever was in the cargo bay that was so sensitive it needed three on-board security guards was headed for Cop One, too.

Mrs. Harper said plaintively, "But it's such a shame we can't see what's happening . . . these things should have windows."

"Yes ma'am," Kate agreed, waiting for the thrust of engine burn to shut the woman up when it tried to grind them into their hydraulically cushioned seats.

Once they were under way, she'd have plenty of time to decide how to tell Tracey Rand about Ilya, and when.

If she knew Ilya, despite all considerations of security, he'd wangle a way to be there to meet her when the aerospace plane landed on the moon.

# Chapter 5

# SPACEPLANE

Sixteen hours is a long time to be cooped up with strangers in a cylinder sixty feet long and fifteen feet wide.

By the time "brunch" was served by the flight attendant and one of Harper's aides, Rand had had enough of Harper's probing helpfulness to last him the rest of his life. And they were only four hours into the flight.

Kate had drifted away from Harper's wife and was sitting with the Space Command security contingent. Laughter floated back to him from their seats, and that made him even more restless.

Still, he was making progress with Harper. Although Rand had been careful to volunteer nothing that Harper might not already know until he'd checked with Bates, the mission director was determined to be of assistance.

"It seems to me," said Harper once the flight attendant had lowered the seatback tray and placed his food in front of him, "that the arrangement best suited to your needs would be this: you'll come to the mission and begin a security study of the premises for us. It'll give you good credibility with the contractors, and give you continual access to me, my office, Ms. Brittany, and any equipment you might want to use."

"Whoa," Rand said cautiously. Harper shouldn't know

this much, and this little. "I want to build up a real clientele here; a direct connection with the U.S. Mission might discourage some independents—I'm not government. I don't want to give that impression."

"Dr. Rand," Harper said, fixing Trace with his glittery eyes, "*no one* works on the moon without an interface with a major power. I'm offering you a chance to bid for a government contract—I'll have a Request for Procurement drawn up with the specs. You'll have a copy of the RFP in hand within twenty-four hours of lunar dock." The Santa Claus eyes narrowed. "It'll make your comings and goings—and Ms. Brittany's—easier."

"That's very kind of you, sir." *And you're right, I can use the cover story initially, a reason to bop in and out of the Cop One diplomatic mission buildings. But I probably won't give you a bid you can accept—in case anyone infers, or wants others to infer, something from that. Tag me as CIA, and I'm useless there. Commercial cover means just that, buddy. And you know it.* "But Ms. Brittany—Secretary Brittany—and I are old friends, that's all. Without her encouragement, I wouldn't have taken a flyer up here in the first place."

"I didn't mean to suggest otherwise," said the mission director. "Kate is one of my best people."

*Proprietary bastard.* Rand pushed his seatback tray away so that he could slip out from under it. "So I noticed. And since she's finished with your wife for the moment, I'm going to join her for brunch." He slid from his seat and picked up his tray. "I'd appreciate it, sir, if you'd let Kate and me use these seats—we've got some data to look over. After brunch, if it's not an inconvenience?" He hated mollycoddling the brass, but he wasn't going cards down with Harper until he was damned sure somebody else had. Bates should have warned Rand, and all the innuendo in the world wasn't going to make Rand give up one iota of data that Harper didn't already have. Information was the only power worth having up here.

Or anywhere, for that matter. You didn't give it away, you traded for it. And Harper's offer of a government contract to Cislunar Security, Rand's imaginary company, wasn't worth anything but a hard look at the man who'd made it.

"It's no inconvenicnce," Harper said as Rand, balancing his tray, made his way forward to where Kate was lounging with the security types.

As he reached Kate, he saw Harper take his own tray and rejoin his wife in the forward seat that Kate had vacated.

"Hiya, Trace," Kate said a trifle too brightly. "Meet the guys—Crane, Marshall, and Foster. Dr. Tracey Rand. He's in your orientation."

Crane, the ranking security officer, stuck out his hand. "Sir. Been looking forward to this." Under the bullet head and military haircut were sharp blue eyes. "Captain Bates says we're to give you both all the help we can, once we've delivered our payload."

The support Bates had promised him, then. "Glad to know you. We're going to need all the help we can get." Rand shook Crane's proffered hand and looked the other two over: early thirties, fit and seasoned, all with multiple mission patches down the arms of their coveralls—ZR/SEAL recruits. He made eye contact with each in turn and found there only steadiness, readiness, and mild curiosity. Wondering if they knew what had happened to the men they were replacing, and how long and how well they'd been trained and briefed for this, he regretted for an instant that he couldn't tell them they were mistaken, he didn't know what they were talking about.

Worst case, they were last-minute add-ons, cannon fodder Bates had drafted as an afterthought, once Rand agreed to take the job.

Now that he knew what was going on up here, he wished he hadn't come forward. Eating their bacon-and-egg omelets with a relish that let Rand know this wasn't typical

TAV fare, the security men swapped stories with each other and Kate about people he didn't know and missions he wasn't privy to.

Kate settled down beside Rand halfway through the meal and said: "They're good guys; loosen up."

"They know the attrition rate in this outfit?"

"Life sucks and then you die." She shrugged. Then through nearly unmoving lips she added, "Crane says this cargo's for you—for us, on dark side. Drivers."

Nuclear cargo, she meant. For WARLORD. "Let's not talk about it here," he admonished sternly.

She turned to him then, hurt in her expression. "Then where? If we can't talk about it here, we can't talk about it, period. We'll have to learn sign language and dig a hole in a deserted crater."

He put a hand up to fend her off, conscious of the security men close by. "Easy, Katydid. How long have you known this bunch?"

"Oh, four hours, give or take. Seen 'em come in and out of Cop One, though. Don't worry so much, Trace." She frowned and scanned his face, then his tray. "You haven't touched your food and it's the good stuff. Did something happen back there? With Harper?"

Before he could answer, Crane flopped down into the facing seat. "Harper? We've got paperwork for Harper, ma'am, reassigning us to you once we've completed the drop. You want it now?" He reached out a hand without looking and one of the other men gave him a folded document, which he then held out to Kate.

She took it without turning a hair and said, "Because of the way things work on Cop One, Rand, they'll be assigned to me. Any problem with that?"

"Just that you look so damned happy about it. Come on, girls, give us a couple minutes. Your boss and I have got to talk."

Grumbling good-naturedly, the three men picked up their things and moved down the aisle.

"Something *did* happen with Harper, didn't it?" Kate demanded.

"Yeah. He offered me an RFP for the Cop One government station—the mission buildings. So I could come and go without raising any eyebrows, he just about said. Did you know he'd been briefed? Did anybody *tell* you he was put in the picture? How far?"

"Jesus . . . no. Look, you don't want to be too closely associated with the mission, not the USG facility. The obvious logic jump from there is Agency personnel. . . ."

"Don't you think I know that? Still, it'll make the first few days simpler, I guess. I can get to you, or the secure com equipment, easier. But I'm not going to win the contract. I didn't tell him that."

"That's fine if there are other bidders." Her brows knit. "Maybe Bates did read him in, I don't know. Maybe he's assuming a . . . personal reason you might want access to the buildings."

"I'm assuming that myself," he said softly, and took her hand."

"Don't," she said.

"Say it again, like you mean it, and I won't. Come on, Katydid, give me a break. We need each other on this one. It's tough sledding for me too. I just can't help worrying about everything and everybody. You especially. I don't want anything to happen to you."

"To either of us," she corrected, her hand quiet under his. "Oh, damn, Trace . . . you get me so confused. It might be okay, with Harper. Give you good credibility with the contractors and the ESA types, especially if you lose the bid: USG wants everything low bidder, and you'll lose it because the low-ball job isn't up to your specs. Costs more to do things right, especially at Cop One."

"And your security boys? Were you waiting for the right time to tell me?"

"I was as surprised as you were," she said honestly,

and then her hand did move in his: it overturned and grasped his fingers. "Let's start over, okay? I'm not good at wanting anything as much as I want it to work with us. It throws me off my stride."

"Yeah," he said. "Know what you mean," and laid his head back against the seat. "When you're ready, we can use that seat row with the monitors and I'll go over the encrypted brief with you. And we'll look Chandra and Faragher over together, with a fine-tooth comb. I don't like the way this thing's coming together. Either Bates is flying by the seat of his pants, or he doesn't trust us—me—enough to tell us what we've got to know to do a good job."

He'd meant to say *to survive*.

"I don't think," Kate said slowly, her eyes on the three security officers, "that anyone—not even Bates—was certain enough that you'd take this on to prepare for it. Might be that's all you're feeling: this government doesn't get off the dime fast, or at least not very well, and nobody was prepared for you. I know I wasn't."

Watching her, he kept wondering if she was telling him the truth. One way or another, she was telling him what he ought to be telling himself. Sometimes, he forgot how perceptive, and how competent, she was. It was her femininity, her softness, that did that; but he was glad she hadn't developed a hard shell to mask it.

No matter whose game she was playing, she was still the Kate Brittany he'd known during ZR/SEAL's heyday. For better or worse, he must remember that. And of all the rough-and-ready polymaths from the original group, besides himself, she'd been the only one to survive. And it wasn't just because she was on the moon, out of harm's way. It was because she was damned good at what she did.

He resolved to make sure that, in her heart anyway, she was working for, and not against, him. If they could come through this together, and not end up on opposite sides of the playing field, maybe there was a chance that he could show her his beach, after all. . . .

He was still weighing the matter when the lights in the TAV's ceiling flickered, dimmed, and died.

She grabbed him in the dark. "Trace!" It was a strangled little cry, a muffled bleat for help from someone who wasn't constitutionally able to ask for it.

He put an arm around her and squeezed. "It's okay." If it wasn't what the hell was he going to do about it?

He could hear the other passengers, the mission director demanding that his aides find out what was going on, his wife begging for reassurance, the three security guards cursing.

Then lights came on—small, hand-held lights. One came bobbing toward them.

"You all right, ma'am? Dr. Rand?"

It was Crane's voice, and Rand said, "Yeah, but there's a gearbag under my last-row seat. I've got to—"

"Marshall, get Rand's gearbag."

Rand didn't know why he'd asked for it, beyond the fact that he had flashlight in it. The weapons there wouldn't help against a power failure.

"I'm going forward," Rand said, "to talk to the pilots."

"I'll do that, sir," Crane replied. "You stay with Ms. Brittany. There're escape pods in the cargo bay, so don't sweat it."

"Hell of a long way home," said someone behind the second light.

"Shut up, Foster," said Crane. "Stay with them." His light disappeared forward.

By the time Marshall came up with Rand's bag, Kate had ceased shivering and he stopped rubbing her arm. As he reached out to take his bag from Marshall, the lights came on, flickering before they steadied.

Blinking in the sudden glare, Rand saw Harper, both

aides huddled around him as if they could protect the director with their bodies, and his wife with her knuckles jammed in her mouth.

The two security men were perched on either side of the hatchway forward to the flight deck, holding their flashlights tight to side arms.

Rand shook his head at the guards and the weapons disappeared. He hoped to hell those were rubber bullets; there was nothing in here worth shooting everybody's air into space for.

Crane came back from the cockpit and said, "Little electrical trouble, folks. We're on emergency power till they trace it. Won't be more than an hour or two's delay, nothing to worry about, they say."

"He means we're dead in the water," Kate said under her breath, but straightened her shoulders and arched away from him.

Harper's aides were making lots of noise now, demanding answers from Crane that he either couldn't or wouldn't give. Harper himself was wiping his face with a pocket handkerchief and his wife was dabbing at tears.

"Anything like this ever happen before?" Rand asked Kate.

"Not that anyone's admitting to, sir," Crane said before Kate could respond. "But they're sure they can bring her home even on emergency power—just take a little longer. What I want to see is the guts of this baby once they tear her down to see what triggered this fuck-up."

Then Crane added, " 'Scuse me, got to go cool them out," and headed down to where Harper's aides were demanding "an explanation and a full investigation."

Marshall shook his head and followed; Foster leaned against the flight-deck hatchway with his side arm once again in evidence.

"Home?" Rand echoed Crane's word quizzically, looking at Kate for enlightenment.

"LSS—that's their base station. Or was."

"Fuck-up?"

"You know what he's saying as well as I do. What with the sensitivity of the cargo—not us, just the stuff in the hold—sabotage is a real possibility."

"That's comforting. At least, when things don't work well, there's a reason."

"Or an excuse." She sighed. "God, I hate feeling helpless."

She didn't have to say it. He could see it in her pale face and pinched lips. He could feel it in his own reaction to what had happened—and to Kate herself. Chips went down, and no matter his doubts about her, he'd tried to physically protect her. He hoped to hell she wasn't playing him. His gut instincts were going to kick in, if she were, exactly the wrong way at exactly the wrong time.

Until then, they had their hands full without doubting one another. Anyway, he had too many other people to worry about, too many doubts and too many fears to become estranged from his single putative ally.

He said, "I know it's not politic, but I'm so damned glad we're both still alive, I really want to kiss you and the hell with all these people watching."

She smiled bleakly. "You know, I haven't necked in public since we . . . since . . . what the hell." She reached over, put her hand on the back of his neck, and guided his lips to hers.

When they disengaged, Crane was standing over them, expressionless: "Sir," he said crisply. "Pilots say to tell you give them half an hour and they'll make up the lost time on the other end."

"Crisis over, Crane?"

"Just till we find out where things screwed up, sir. But that's life, isn't it? If you want, pilots say we've got enough juice that you two can use the aft terminal."

"Let's do that, Kate. It'll take our minds off it, at any

rate." *Take our minds off the fact that, if the pilots are wrong, we can't hitch home from here, honey, and escape pods aren't any way to fly.*

But the pilots weren't wrong and by the time the lights flickered back to normal power and the TAV got under way, they had their heads together before the aft terminal, trying to find something in Chandra's background, or Robin Faragher's, that didn't jibe.

# Chapter 6

# LUNAR SERVICE STATION

Kate didn't realize how much danger they'd actually been in aboard the crippled TAV until the spaceplane limped into the Lunar Service Station's emergency dock, where every light was flashing and a Code Red team stood by with fire fighting gear and paramedics.

The whole LSS bay had been foamed as soon as it pressurized. Men in red fireproof coveralls with dangling respirators came slogging through the foam and up the ramp to whisk Harper, his wife, and their aides safely away.

Throughout it all, Crane stood impassively by the forward hatchway, arms folded, eye-locked with Kate. She was so angry she almost forgot about Tracey Rand, beside her, watching everything without comment.

Once Harper's party had debarked, she exploded: "You want to keep your job, *Mister* Crane, you get a lot better at communicating priority information, and *fast.*"

"Yes ma'am," Crane said curtly. "It won't happen again, ma'am." Marshall and Foster, his two subordinates, slid by him, headed for the flight deck, intent on ignoring the incident.

Or with more important things to do. Crane, too, unwound from his post and began to follow.

"Not so fucking fast!" she blurted. "You haven't told my why."

"Ma'am?" Crane faced her again, this time at technical ease.

Beside her in his seat, Tracey Rand shifted restlessly.

"I said, I want an explanation. Why weren't we told how difficult the situation was? How dangerous?"

If Crane looked to Rand for help, she was going to strangle both of them with her bare hands, even though those hands were shaking with fury and—might as well admit it—retroactive terror.

"Ma'am, aboard this vehicle, the pilots call the shots. It's a military transport and my group isn't officially assigned to you until our cargo's delivered. Which it almost wasn't."

"That's an excuse, not a reason," she retorted.

"Pilots didn't want to risk letting Harper know how bad it was—wasn't nothin' any of you could do to help, and nobody wants an official investigation that would shut down TAV flights for weeks—maybe months. Offend these embassy types"—there was honesty and a plea for understanding in Crane's voice—"and you risk project shutdown, especially when it's a military vehicle and we're carrying civilian brass."

Rand, beside her, shifted slightly closer. If he put his hand on her knee or opened his mouth, she was going to bite his head off. He didn't. He cupped his chin in one hand and kept silent.

"Investigation of what, Lieutenant? Sabotage? What's going on here?"

"That's what we'd like to find out, ma'am. Now we've got enough stopover time to be asking rhetorical questions. With your permission . . ."

"Permission, shit. I want a full report when you're done. Come to my quarters with it personally, no matter what time it is," she said, and waved Crane away.

As he disappeared forward, Rand busied himself stowing both their cases in the gearbag that concealed them.

"You think I was too hard on him?"

Trace looked around at her. "I didn't say anything."

Great. "But you think so."

"Kate, I'd like to know what happened out there just as much as you would. Especially how close a call it was—if it wasn't an accident or a pure and sloppy malfunction, then the question's got to be, was it an attempt to scare us or kill us?" He shouldered the bag and jutted his chin forward. "Come on, let 'em work. Show me LSS before we have to rendezvous with Harper."

They'd promised to have dinner with the Harpers when they were told their stopover had been extended from ninety minutes to twelve hours. She regretted it now. "I might get a headache," she said, preceding him up the aisle toward the exit hatch.

"That's good for you, but then I'd have to go it alone. I want to check with Bates about Harper first—how deeply he's been briefed. Can you arrange it?"

She paused in the hatchway, scanning the foamed ramp and the men scurrying around. "Of course. Right away."

A big-wheeled flatbed with electronic equipment on its carrier was pulled up to the TAV; the designator on its side said CSCS—Consolidated Space Command Security—under the same solar-system insignia that Crane's group wore. Crane was talking to one of the men on the flatbed; both of them were wearing com mikes. Close by, Marshall and Foster were shrugging into radiation suits.

Rand saw too and took her by the elbow. "Let's get out of here." He nodded toward a man waiting in a standard LSS transport that looked like a cross between a jeep and a golf cart. "That must be ours."

It was and they drove off alone, after Kate dismissed the driver with a wave of her credentials, toward the automated access door.

When it opened, revealing LSS in all its multistrutted

warrenlike profusion, Rand whistled softly. From the docking hub, the Lunar Service Station stretched out in all directions, a tubular maze.

"You don't see it like this from any other place," she told him. "We're equidistant from everything—solar collectors, high gravity quarters, production bays. From the moon, fifty percent of lift-off mass can be payload, compared to the one-point-five percent of the shuttle's mass leaving Earth—that's a twenty- to thirty-fold advantage in launching from the moon to here for distribution instead of from Earth to LEO—" She broke off.

He was grinning at her fondly. "I know," he reminded her.

"Sorry," she said, flustered. "Sound like a lobbyist, I guess. But I care—"

"Don't apologize. So do I."

In silence, she drove into the cargo routing corridor and on until she reached the outer rim, past the huge equipment maintenance and pressurized storage bays and all the modules necessary to enable LSS to service the needs of the human colony on the moon and facilitate transshipment of lunar products and data to LEO as well as conduct zero-G and vacuum experimentation and manufacture.

They drove past areas assigned to multinational corporations and those restricted to American national interests, past ESA bloc corridors that supported the European Space Agency's lunar consortium, and by a huge observation lounge open to the stars. Occasionally she'd sneak a look at Rand's face and see there an almost childlike excitement, laced with approval and pride, that she understood all too well.

Maybe they'd exported all their human foibles with them, but they were here—man was making a go of it in cislunar space. Somehow, the quiet ride through the man-made satellite of the moon calmed her.

Even if they found out that the incident aboard the TAV was, as Crane obviously believed, a concerted attempt at sabotage, it wasn't really surprising—just human nature. There would always be greed, jealousy, violence, and treachery, wherever there were men. Somehow that seemed a small price to pay for the privilege of being here—part of the leading edge, wrestling the real enemy, the unknown.

Taming the universe wasn't too grandiose a term for what was happening here. One bit at a time, man was learning how to make any environment his environment. Maybe when all that was done, humans would learn to live in peace with each other. But if they'd done so by now, there would be no outward push to the stars, no thirst for elbow room, no need to turn aggressions against Nature, humanity's first and constant opponent.

With mere ingenuity and determination, with the modest weapons of technology and genius, human beings were beginning to bring the solar system under control. LSS was the only place Kate ever seemed to sense the larger picture. It was why she liked to come here. On the moon, the risks were still too pressing, man's hold too tenuous, the installations too small and impermanent, to think about the future. Down there, you felt like you were holding on for dear life—in one-sixth gravity, you bit down on the dream between your teeth and fought like hell for another six months' worth of funding.

The moon could still be lost by the fainthearted, the stay-at-homes, the dullards, and the fearful. LSS was what made the moon colony dream that it might be self-sustaining, someday.

And since those dreams were still classified, the colony was technically no more than a lunar looting party digging out iron-rich olivine and processing lunar silicates and oxide minerals for the liquid oxygen that could be extracted from them. Without the extraction plant that reduced raw soil by flourine or iron-titanium oxide by hydrogen, the moon colony wouldn't have a chance of permanence. The military would have roboticized a plant to boost up all

135

the "green cheese"—a mineral useful in "hardening" defense satellites against emp—and left the moon with a few newly deepened craters.

But the technology and the resources were there to make the moon a cost-effective and therefore self-sufficient base. The Russians knew it and the U.S. knew it and ESA knew it.

Nobody was admitting, of course, that each nation was hunkering down for a long stay. Nobody except the dreamers, and they only in their sleep. Partitioning of the moon was an inevitability, and one no one looked forward to. With ESA and the U.S. and the Soviet Union all presently dug into Copernicus crater, that partitioning was becoming a prickly international issue.

The sabotage of a U.S. Space Command transport by a hostile power would have ugly, dangerous repercussions, intensifying an already volatile situation. Crane had been right.

Suddenly, wheeling the LSS "car" into a U.S.-only drop-off station, she felt badly about the way she'd upbraided the security officer. "Trace," she said as she pulled the car to a stop, "*do* you think I was out of line with Crane? Came down on him too hard?" She turned off the electric car and swung one leg over the side, then paused. "Well?"

"I . . . wouldn't have done it that way. But you have different problems. I'm sure he's had surly COs before."

"Surly?" she said archly, then caught herself. She'd asked him; he'd told her. Not patronizingly, candidly. "I guess I asked for that. Maybe we will beg off with Harper and have dinner with Crane and his ConSecs instead—take them someplace nice." *Take them to the exec dining room, where they can't go on their own.*

"Let's see what they come up with," Trace replied as he got their gearbag and hefted it. "Maybe that would be a good idea. After we've checked with Bates on Harper, though. Same drill, here? Separate areas? Rooming hassles?'' He came around to her side of the car and she struck off toward the kiosk where she'd drop its key into the automated lot attendant's hopper and punch in her credit number for Cop One billing.

"No rooming hassles here; as the science and some-time-cultural attaché from Cop One, I've got a permanent berth . . .''

He gave her a sidelong glance and a wry headshake.

"And guest quarters,'' she added defensively.

"Katydid, I wish you'd relax.''

"I wish I could. Maybe after we find out whether somebody tried to turn us into space junk.'' He didn't answer so she let it ride, wondering why she cared so much what he thought. He wasn't her boss anymore, not really.

The layout on LSS wasn't much different from LEO's, on the rim. The government section was more extensive, big enough to be an embassy compound in an earthly Middle East nation. Her rank put her rooms a corridor away from Director Harper's, so they didn't have to worry about running into him in the halls. At the corridors' juncture was a diplomatic mess that served twenty-four-hour food on three tiers.

She stopped there and got takeout, telling Trace to wait outside. When she came out, carrying a poly-pack of coffee, beer, milk, and assorted snacks, he said, "It's like a damned hotel.''

"Yeah''—she grinned—"a no-star,'' wrinkled her nose, and let him follow her to her rooms.

A little plastic plate bearing her name and title was set into the door; inside, he muttered, "It *is* like a damned hotel,'' and she realized that he'd expected something as spartan as LEO.

"Don't get used to it,'' she said, putting the takeout food on the table in the suite's central room: "Conference table cum dining nook; the obligatory Secure Telephone Units, including permanent down-links—red for moon, blue for Earth—and I can tell you those were hard to get. Comfort station in between, but don't expect a bathtub. We're not that civilized yet. Your sleeper's the door on your left. I'll give you your own key to the corridor door and you can close off the connecting door if you want privacy."

"I don't," he said with patient reassurance.

"Well, whatever. Look, I'll get this call in to Bates, you unpack that stuff." It came out in a rush. She didn't look up, just went to the down-link and began punching in access codes. "You want to tell me how you'd like to phrase this request?"

"Sure." He came over and stood behind her. "Send it encrypted, use whatever code name Harper's got. Ask for his briefing class number and a confirm or deny on his involvement. And say that I said I don't want any more surprises: if there's anybody who's privy or ought to be, I want a list, now, or everything's going through Staff D's groundside office. The cost alone ought to make them think twice."

She nodded. It was what she would have done on her own. When she'd typed in the request and sent the message, she stood up.

He was right behind her. "I thought you were going to unpack that stuff. There's nothing in my storage locker . . ."

"Hey, come on. If you're nervous because of what's happened, that's one thing. If it's me . . . I can go take a nap or something—"

"I just want to know whether somebody tried to kill us." She moved past him, to the simulated wood table, and began pulling the poly-packs out of the bag, slamming them on the table.

"Want a guess, unsubstantiated speculation?" His voice came from right behind her.

"Yes. Sure." She took the last pack of black coffee out of the bag, crushed the bag in her hands, and threw it with practiced ease into the iris of the trash bin.

"You bet somebody tried something. And you know it, too. That's not usual, coming in on a bed of foam with paramedics for a reception committee. My guess is we'll find out that if those pilots hadn't been all they ought to be, we'd still be floating out there waiting for search and rescue. That emergency-power interval wasn't to make us comfy, it was so they could do some inspired jury rigging. And we ought to find a way to thank them for being better—and cooler—than they had any right to be."

"You're right," she admitted. "We'll send up a letter of commendation even though we'll probably see the Con-Sec staff officer at dinner."

"You mean this isn't dinner?" Mocking, trying to tease her out of the mood that must be showing on her face. "Katy, what the fuck is it?"

"It's easy to kill somebody in space, Dr. Rand. It's easy here, it's easy on the moon, and it's twice as easy in transit. Maybe we ought to be asking ourselves how come, if somebody was really trying, it didn't work."

"I've been wondering that myself. Warning shots are real infrequent in this kind of game, though." His face relaxed, though she hadn't realized until it did that he'd been tense also. Infinitesimal changes in musculature ran over his frame and, in their wake, she began feeling physically attracted to him again.

Until that moment, when her body began tingling slightly in proximity to his, she hadn't realized that, for some time, she hadn't felt it. She looked at him narrowly. "You've been awfully quiet, yourself. Wired. Like somebody else. Want to tell me why, or was it just the close call?"

He laughed and it had been a long time since she'd heard him do that. "Caught me. I guess I wanted to hear you asking those questions—the right questions. Because I'm asking them, and if you weren't, I ought to be wondering why not." There was a hint of apology mixed with the relief in his tone. He moved a few steps closer and hugged her to him, so unexpectedly that the container of hot coffee was pressed between them.

She said, against his chest, "I ought to be furious at you for the implications."

"Don't be," he said into her hair. "I'm just doing my job. But it's going to be lots easier now."

"My coffee," she protested, and he let her go, but didn't step back.

"What's the percentage of earth gravity here?" he teased. "Do I need more practice?"

"You'll get it," she promised haughtily. "When I say so."

"Okay, lady," he agreed, and started examining the containers she'd bought. "Want to talk about Chandra and Faragher then? Did you see anything in their background checks that I didn't? Anything that rang false?"

"Nope. Chandra's just what he should be: an Oxford-educated Indian who can trace his lineage back to Nehru. She's probably smarter than I am, judging by the string of initials after her name, but there's no crime in that. ESA people are in a funny position up here, trying to walk a line between the superpowers, keep up their relations with both, get as much as they can from each side . . . no different from groundside politics. Still, I don't like that woman."

"I don't really, either, you know. But I think she's someone I ought to cultivate." He caught her gaze and held it with his, unblinking. "Business only, Katy. She was coming on so strong, there's got to be more to it than meets the eye. Can you handle that?"

*Here's my chance. Oh, Trace, I don't want to screw this up. Please understand.* "If you can handle the fact that I've got a similar situation with somebody on the moon," she said breezily.

"Only one somebody? That's hard to believe."

"Only one that concerns you—that might concern you if I don't explain. I'm having—"

Just then the modem bleated and the data feed came through from Bates's office, telling them that Harper had

had a "Class Five" briefing and any data the mission director had beyond that was "unsubstantiated through this office."

"So?" Kate asked Rand.

"So maybe it's fine, and we do need somebody with Harper's kind of clout up here." He rubbed his jaw. "But if Bates is telling us the truth, Harper's got one hell of an organization, to have put everything together so fast."

She flashed him a smile. "I'll take that as a compliment."

"I'm not sure it's meant that way. If you agree, I'd like to keep Harper as much in the dark as possible."

"Fine. That's another reason to cancel dinner." She shut off the down-link and told him to shred the document. "Just put it in the trash, there. I'll call ConSec and see if the boys would like to join us."

"Wait a minute, Kate. What was it you were going to tell me about this guy on the moon?"

Her face went stiff. Her neck flushed; she could feel the heat creeping up into her cheeks. Staring at the phone in her hand, she said to him: "Right. Ilya Palladin, Soviet second secretary assigned to Sveboda. I'm having an affair with him. He'll probably wangle a way to be in the arrival lounge waiting for me."

She didn't look around. She didn't want to see his face. She waited for the inevitable response. She didn't have to wait long.

After a three-beat pause, Trace said in a flat voice, "Second secretary? Kate, second secretary at a mission like the Soviet moon station? Have you thought about the possibility that this guy's KGB?"

"I'm sure of it. That's why I'm sleeping with him." She punched up the security desk and began the task of finding Crane's detail and inviting them to dinner.

# Chapter 7
# CONSEC

Lieutenant Lincoln Crane of ConSec—Consolidated Space
Command Security—didn't like pissing away two of his
remaining precious hours of layover having dinner with the
brass, but there was no way around it.

His two specialists, Marshall and Foster, were neat and
scrubbed and in their seats in the exec dining room precisely on time. They'd still have been waiting at the door,
being ogled by the doubtful hostess, if Crane hadn't scoped
the situation and told the woman they'd wait at Secretary
Brittany's table.

Now they were doing that, all three pretending not to be
uncomfortable there, surrounded by every dip and dip/
spook with a grade level high enough to get them in here.
Director Harper was here, and Brittany was supposed to
have dinner with Harper and his wife. It was Brittany's
problem, and if Crane wasn't overloaded with his own, it
might have been interesting to see how she dealt with it.

Marshall, toying with a matchbox-size white noise generator that protected them from the kind of electronic
eavesdropping that could be mounted here, was talking
about the TAV's in-flight failure ruefully.

"Lucky it wasn't the master CPU that had that hairline
crack, or there wouldn't have been time to pull the circuit

142

board, let alone get out a soldering gun.'' Marshall shook his head. "That's as close as I ever want to come to breathing vacuum.''

"Who do you think they were after, sir?'' asked Foster bluntly. "Us? The cargo? Harper? Those intelligence types—the Seals?''

"Beats me. Thing to do is watch and wait till whoever it was tries again.'' The Central Processing Unit with the cracked circuit board had been one of seven on board. Indications of its malfunction had been so subtle before the pilots shut it down that, if they hadn't done so, the fuel-regulation system might well have blown up the next time rocket power was called for, incinerating everything and everyone—Harper, the Seals, and WARLORD's crucial nuclear components. It was enough to give you the shakes.

And subsequent examination of the circuit board had proved only that the cracks were there. They shouldn't have been. The TAV's seven CPUs were torn down and examined every two hundred hours of flight time. This board had been changed at its last major servicing—during the turnaround on LEO. The damage was such that no malfunction would read on the instruments until the whole package went blooey. A nervous pilot with a sixth sense had saved everybody's ass, a human computer who "felt" a certain sluggishness in his throttle had made an on-the-spot decision to shut down the TAV and start looking for a problem there and then. If he hadn't, or hadn't been able to convince himself and the other pilot it was worth the risk of looking bad, none of them would be sitting around here wondering who to tell how much.

The ConSec trio had no doubt that it was sabotage. As its leader, Crane had jurisdiction over dissemination of that information; the pilots would do as he asked. And the only people Crane was sure weren't guilty were those who would have died if the threat became reality.

In a way, it was nice not to worry about Harper, or the two Seals who'd be cutting his orders for the next few weeks. But that left the rest of the Consolidated Space Command, as well as all of ESA, the Soviet Sveboda and the U.S. Cop One missions. Not exactly a finite list of suspects.

Crane had let his boys order drinks; he turned his own wineglass in his hands. Wine. Dress clothes. Fancy dinners when he should be sucking soup, lying on his back under the TAV's console with those pilots.

The spaceplane's crew weren't afraid, but they weren't flying that sucker again until they could give it a clean bill of health. And Crane damn well agreed with them.

What he wasn't sure he agreed with was ConSec's dispatching officer, who'd assigned him to Staff D's ZR/SEAL for the duration.

He'd heard about the dead Seals; he didn't want to be one. And he'd heard about the Seal leader, through channels, off and on over the years. The man was out of circulation, so far as anybody knew, until the beginning of this week. The whole mission command structure wasn't real confidence building: a woman and a cripple.

So when, fashionably late, Rand came escorting the woman who was Crane's CO until WARLORD went operational, Crane still hadn't decided how much and what to tell the two Agency types who'd booked the table. His job was to protect them and support their mission, not educate them.

The very sight of Brittany made his spine stiffen. She had a big mouth and she threw her weight around. On the moon, that weight was a fraction of what it was here, technically, but there were other kinds of weight. ConSec was a fledgling service; Crane wasn't about to let anybody treat his men as expendable grunts; Agency catechism read that anybody, especially bodies like Crane, Marshall, and Foster—military bodies—was expendable.

Some stuff to get straight, then, without seeming insubordinate. He rose like he'd been taught to do when greeting a lady, and the woman in the sparkly jumpsuit frowned at him. "As you were, Lieutenant; gentlemen."

Rand pulled her chair out, noticed the white noise generator, and leaned forward once he'd taken a seat beside the woman. "Okay, guys, what's the story on the TAV?"

Marshall lowered his head and fingered the generator. Foster's muscular neck tensed. Crane looked at Rand and said, "We don't know yet, sir. We're still checking it out."

"No you're not," said Trace Rand levelly, flicking one corner of his menu with a steady finger. "You wouldn't be here if that were true. And we wouldn't have invited you here if we didn't know that. This is a working dinner. Let's work." His glance flickered to the white noise generator. "Ms. Brittany and I can't cut you any slack unless you help us."

"You're the targets, best as we can figure, so who's cutting who slack?" Foster burst out resentfully, then sat back, one finger laid across his lips.

"That's what I thought," Rand said easily, and smiled for the first time. "Look, let's clear the air: this is your venue, girls, but it's not scaring me to death. Kate and I have worked together before—"

"We heard—" Marshall said.

Crane was content to let the string play itself out; he didn't like a tight rein on men like Foster and Marshall, and right now it was important that Brittany and Rand realize how savvy and how special Crane's specialists were. The five people at this table were going to launch the most sensitive and seminal American space project since the first moon shot. They had to trust their assessment of each other's limitations to be able to fill the gaps.

And Crane hadn't much faith in men who walked away from jobs before they were finished. Brittany was a team player, a pro—women were touchy, sometimes, in positions like hers, but touchy was something Crane understood. His fuse was short too, especially when it did him some good to let it be.

Brittany spoke for the first time. "That's what we need to know, gentlemen, exactly what you've heard. What you surmise. What the betting pool is."

Then Crane took a shot. "On your survivability as an individual, or as part of this group? As part of the group, no sweat, no odds. We always get the job done. The two of you aren't going to become statistics on our watch, that we can promise." Crane's record was perfect: he could baby-sit Christ in a lion's den and come out clean. They probably knew that, but he wanted them to *believe* it; there was a distinct difference.

He studied Tracey Rand's face and saw only control, maybe a touch of assessment. These two were shacking up and didn't care who knew it. They'd been hot and heavy before. Tended to be a negative, but it was their business. As the only two of their kind left, they had plenty of reason to huddle together at night.

"There isn't any betting pool—we win 'em all." Crane bared his teeth. "You tend to go clean until you get dead, up here. And we're not bored with living. You tell us what you want, that's what you'll get. You go sneakin' around like the spooks you are, with no backup and nobody informed—" He spread his hands and dropped them to the table. "Well then, we can't help that. We got everything Staff D thought we needed to make us capable of replacing what your team lost—plus new stuff you've never heard of. It's up to you two how you use us; technically, it's up to you, ma'am."

"Then stop calling me 'ma'am.' I'm Kate. Trace and I don't stand on formality—we'll need and want equal access to you."

*In other words, lady, he's your boyfriend and you don't want to pull rank on him; or he's your boss and you're feeding us what he cuts you for orders. Fine with me, either way, as long as it's smooth.*

"Somebody or other—only the passengers and crew of the TAV excluded—wants equal access to both of you."

146

Crane decided to throw them a bone. "Definite tampering in that problem we had. Fixed now; lift-off on schedule unless Harper slows us up."

Rand seemed to relax in some subliminal way. He opened his menu and, as if that were a cue, a waiter arrived.

They ordered, the lady first, so that by the time the waiter got around to him, Crane was no longer trying not to see the menu prices. Their treat, their perks, their attempt to be friendly.

Working relationships weren't optional on something like this; whether he liked or hated these two, he was assigned to get them through WARLORD alive. He just wanted Tracey Rand to give him one sign that that was what Rand wanted, too.

When, after the waiter had left, Rand began asking gently probing questions about the possibility of Brittany's permanent quarters here being bugged or insecure, and then about ways Harper might have learned more than Staff D meant to tell him, Crane finally admitted to himself that the big guy with the long, stellar file was all right.

Was *still* all right, even after what had happened to him, a year of surgical reconstruction, and four years sitting around on some Third World hacienda's beach.

It was when the two officers began explaining their game plan that Crane began, once again, to have doubts about what ConSec had gotten him into. But then, doubts or no doubts, once the TAV boosted toward Cop One and the dark side five hours from now, it was time to stop worrying.

One way or another, the good times were about to roll.

# Chapter 8

# HUNTER'S MOON

Boarding the same TAV again—this time in full spacesuit because of what had happened the last time—wasn't the easiest thing Tracey Rand had ever done.

Still, you got back on the horse that threw you. He'd done lots of diving after the accident, as soon as he was fit enough to handle it—or before he was, according to his doctors.

He was sweating in his helmet the way he'd been sweating under Kate an hour before they'd vacated her LSS quarters. It was an old superstition of hers, an old custom of theirs—one for the road. She was never unresponsive, but facing the unknown, her passion was monumental.

"God, Trace," she'd panted, laying her cheek against his shoulder, "I'm going to miss you so. How are we ever going to manage it?"

"I don't know," he told her, and he didn't: on the moon, they'd both have other priorities, and hers—the Russian named Palladin—was bothering him already and he hadn't even met the man. Leave it to Kate to go to bed with the enemy—literally.

Since he was attempting to do the same thing himself—would do it, if his guess was right and his luck good—he couldn't say anything to her.

148

They'd be living separately, like they'd lived all these long years. Maybe she'd been fishing, looking for some declaration of his feelings or some promises he might not be able to keep, but he couldn't take the bait. They both needed all the professionalism they could muster.

He kept trying to wipe his brow through his space helmet and he kept trying to get the pilots to give him real-time telemetry of the moon. And he kept trying to ignore the jealousy he felt: give it another name, another connotation, tell himself it was just professional concern for her safety, for the mission's security, for the kind of trouble she could be in if later it could be said that her relationship with Palladin had helped compromise ZR/SEAL or WARLORD.

He couldn't say any of that to her. It would sound too much like what it was—bias. He just wished she hadn't told him, even though he'd surely have found out.

Waiting for the TAV to blow up under him as it left the emergency dock headed for the moon, he had enough on his mind without worrying about who Brittany was screwing.

Five hours ago, in the restaurant, they'd encountered Harper. The diplomat had ignored what he obviously perceived as a snub, but let Rand know he did so perceive it. Coming slowly and somehow laboriously to Rand's table, Harper had said, "Good evening, gentlemen and lady. I won't take but a moment of your time. Since the emergency you're dealing with obviously has to do with the one we just survived in transit, I've decided to take Alicia the rest of the way by priority moon truck—this evening. As soon as you reach Cop One, Dr. Rand, come and see me. Assuming you *do* get there, of course." Harper flashed white, perfect teeth. "Best of luck, and all. Take good care of your charges, Lieutenant Crane."

Everyone had murmured politely as Harper waddled back to his waiting wife and aides. Among Crane's group, knowing looks had flashed that Rand wasn't sure he understood at the time.

He still wasn't sure if those covert glances were meant as anything more than a comment on the intestinal fortitude of diplomats and diplomatic personnel, although Crane had admitted later that there *was* a betting pool—over whether or not Harper would fly the rest of the way in the suspect TAV.

Crane's explicated position was that "every spacecraft needs a little tuning up now and again. We're comfortable with the risk of flying her—it beats the risk of transferring her cargo where we don't know who's watching."

Rand hadn't argued; he'd flown enough to understand the risk, and understand that you could get killed stepping off a curb in Centerville, USA. Crane's ConSecs were watching for any flinch of discomfort, any sign that Rand was losing his nerve.

It was a good thing they couldn't see him sweat, that his suit's temperature regulator was equal to the workout his physiology was giving it now that he was aboard the TAV. He wouldn't explain to Crane or anyone else that it wasn't the aerospace plane's performance as much as it was the suit's that had him so nervous. Dead in a fireball was dead before you knew it; dying slowly, trapped in a malfunctioning piece of body armor—that was an experience he didn't want to repeat.

The TAV shivered on its track. The station crew was in position to wheel it out of the emergency bay, tow it to space dock, where if it exploded on engine burn, nothing more than the single vehicle would be destroyed, and let events take their course.

The spaceplane had been tuned up and checked out and rechecked. Only a flight test would prove whether those precautions had been sufficient. If the plane blew under them, it would prove that the sabotage was concerted—that someone aboard LSS as well as someone back on LEO was in the pay of a faction hostile to WARLORD . . . and to the remaining Seals.

Through his seat, Rand could feel the motion as the tow

"truck" began to maneuver the plane into position. He kept wishing he could see what was going on out there.

Because he couldn't, he turned his attention to what was going on in the cabin. Crane and Kate had their com sets off, their helmets together—one of the best security procedures available when you wanted to talk privately. Behind them, Foster and Marshall were busy looking busy.

Probably as jumpy as Rand, and trying like hell not to show it. Men trained to handle conflict don't do well in situations where the only acceptable response to danger is a passive one. Crane's group was going to need some tweaking—not an easy thing to do on the moon, when Rand would be posing as a civilian contractor fishing for clients.

But he'd work it out; it was just logistics and start-up glitches. Somehow, from his base among the civilian modules dug into the lunar regolith, utilizing his purported invitation to bid on a government contract, he'd make the whole thing play. Harper's offer was probably going to save his ass.

Kate's fine pale body kept interrupting his concentration. Once she and Crane broke their huddle, she came toward him and took the seat on his left.

"Here we go," she said, her voice scratchy through the com system in their helmets.

Crane and his boys strapped in too, and a pilot's laconic voice in his ear said, "Thirty seconds to engine burn and counting."

Rand's stomach did a flip and he realized that he was suddenly weightless, held in his seat only by his safety harness.

Then the same pilot's voice began counting down to zero.

Kate's gloved hand sought his. He took it without turning his head. Maybe he should have sent her with the Harpers. He'd had the chance. But she would have been insulted beyond measure, and he couldn't bring himself to treat her that way, even if it saved her life.

151

During those final seconds, freeze-frame moments he'd spent with her, especially their last "night" in her LSS quarters, kept kaleidoscoping his thoughts.

Then the pilot's voice said, "zero," and weight returned to Tracey Rand's body abruptly as the rocket engines ignited.

He thought he could hear the roar through his suit and the TAV's skin, but it was probably his pulse. He forced his eyes not to close and he counted his breaths, holding Kate's hand.

"Burn nominal," said the voice from the flight deck, the voice of a man he'd never met who held all their lives in his hands and acknowledged it on this one flight by letting them listen in on what, customarily, was secret ritual.

As soon as they'd throttled up and out of LSS orbit and the ship didn't blow, there were his phantom recollections of Kate again—Kate as she'd been in her LSS quarters: a seductive apparition; a sprite he could touch but couldn't hold; an end result when he was still at midgame.

Maybe he could find some way to take this Ilya Palladin out of the picture—permanently. He shook his head at what he'd just thought and spoke into his helmet's com mike: "Come on, guys, give me the moon on my minitor." *To take my mind off my troubles*.

"Roger. Coming up," came the response in his ears, from the flight deck where there was probably as much palpable relief as in Rand's own skull.

They weren't dead yet. And all the troubles to come were seeming like privileges. The moon blossomed on the monitor to his right and he turned from the waist, as if he were in a fighter jet, to look at it.

And the sight did help. Full, from the telemetry angle he was being shunted, it grinned at him. You never saw it from Earth the way it looked from space; the stars were undimmed by atmosphere, glittering for thousands of years, a temporal backdrop.

The moon itself was even more the ravaged target—no man's face here, just pocks and bumps and jagged rims. But beautiful, so beautiful, full of every promise and dream that had made the man called Tracey Rand willing to risk everything, repeatedly.

It was almost beautiful enough to make him forget the woman in the seat beside him, her face inscrutable in her helmet, her gloved hand clenched in his. Almost, but not quite.

He squeezed the hand he held, a gesture part triumph, part comfort. He didn't say anything on the open circuit. She'd been here before. She was used to the magic of it, the adventure of it. And the danger of it wasn't news to either of them.

The way he felt, though, was new to him. If someone said to him, "Go get your hip crushed underwater, spend a year in the hospital, and four getting yourself back in shape and then you can go to the moon," he'd have volunteered in full knowledge of all to come.

All, perhaps, except Richelson's death. If Richelson were aboard, he'd have wangled his way onto the flight deck. . . . Rand shook his head to clear it and felt Kate let go of his hand.

"Pretty," she said. "Awesome. You never get used to it, you know."

He hadn't known, though he should have guessed. He didn't take his eyes away from the telemetry, where the moon seemed to be growing perceptibly larger. He didn't say more than "Yeah, I bet."

After all, they were on an open com circuit, and once they debarked below, at Copernicus One, there'd be someone named Ilya Palladin, waiting.

He'd have five days to get his moon legs before the ESA party arrived and, Palladin or no Palladin, Kate Brittany was going to be very busy helping him.

Now that he was reasonably sure that the TAV wasn't

153

going to blow them to hell before they made it to the moon, he could concentrate on just how busy he *could* keep her.

Tracey Rand from Cislunar Security was going to have his hands full evaluating the U.S. Mission. He just hoped he didn't have to do it in a spacesuit, or that his body would get used to wearing this kind of gear again. Otherwise, the enemy, whoever it was, wouldn't have to kill him: he'd drown in his own sweat.

# Book Three

# MAN IN
# THE MOON

# Chapter 1

# COPERNICUS
# ONE

Kate Brittany had never before traveled to Cop One by spaceplane. She'd always taken a moon truck—the passenger version of the lunar lander—down from LSS to the manned installation nestled on the "south" slope of Cop One's central peak.

Nestled on and in the mountain, Cop One burrowed deep into the lunar regolith; like an iceberg, what could be seen from the surface was only a fraction of its total expanse.

Coming by moon truck, one wasn't struck by the precariousness, the impermanence, of the lunar installation, because one didn't see it. The moon-truck landing pad was very much like a freight elevator; the truck's driver put the pods down on the pad and the entire pad descended into the interior of Cop One, where the lunar dock was pressurized before any passengers debarked.

Coming by moon truck, Kate had never glimpsed the outside world—never moon-walked, never even had to rely on her suit's oxygen as more than a precaution.

The TAV's lunar landing was very different, however, and she hadn't considered how those differences might affect Tracey Rand. The spaceplane made its landing on a surface "runway" Kate had never realized was there, over at the military-access-only part of Cop One, shielded from

157

Soviet eyes by the double blind of Copernicus's central peak and the intervening bulk of the Cop One installation itself.

Once the spaceplane came to a stop, its passengers were expected to moon-walk over the surface in one-sixth G to a series of locks that began with one exterior door marked AUTHORIZED PERSONNEL ONLY—CONSOLIDATED SPACE COMMAND.

Since the people using this entryway were commonly military, no special care had been taken to make the procedure civilian-safe or civilian-simple. Kate kept stifling the impulse to take Trace's gloved hand as they trekked the hundred yards to the lock, over open lunar terrain in vacuum, and his steps kept lifting him into ungainly hops that put him ahead of the others in their party.

It was tense and she was sorry, listening to the breathing of the two pilots, Crane's Q-group, and especially Trace's in her helmet. She kept resisting the urge to vocally coach him, knowing it could only make matters worse.

Looking for something besides the floundering Rand to fix on, she turned to get a last look at the TAV. It seemed, sitting on its runway, to be indigenous to its environment, at home here, as if it had been designed for the moon. Around it were Cop One techs, preparing to hook it to a tow truck that would secret it in a low-profile hangar camouflaged to look like the crater floor into which the station was built.

Though she'd never needed to know this much about the military's access to Cop One, she felt somehow that she'd been hoodwinked, tricked—all this, and she'd never seen it before.

The lock system, once they reached the complex of exterior hatches and elevators, was more complicated than that at the general-access lunar dock she was accustomed to—and more basic.

They rode down in a "lift" whose sides were open to lunar regolith, rough-hewn and cold. When the cage stopped, lights changed colors on the plate by its doors, gasketed pressure locks came together above their heads with a smack she could feel through the soles of her boots, and then the lights on the panel turned green as "one atmosphere" was reached.

It was now safe to take off their helmets, to breathe, and to debark. It startled Kate immensely when, as the panels in front of them drew back, she realized she was in an area she recognized: the government transit lounge.

They all stepped out, the two pilots heading for a corridor marked CREW as they lifted their helmets from their heads. Kate was disengaging her own and helping Trace with his when she spotted Ilya Palladin in the reception area, his hands pressed to the separating glass and a welcoming smile on his face.

"Trace," she said as soon as his helmet was off and he could hear her, "there's Ilya. I've got to go. Shake hands for the audience. Crane will take good care of you until tomorrow morning, when you can find me in my office— won't you, Lieutenant?"

"That's right," Crane affirmed, his helmet already under his arm, his two subordinates behind him.

Trace stared unabashedly at the glass partition behind which Palladin waited, then at Kate. Then he took her extended hand and, unsatisfied with that, pulled her close for what she hoped appeared to be a chaste, Washington kiss.

"I'll bring your case to your office in the morning, then. I don't think he should see me giving it to you here."

"Yes, all right, fine." She was flustered. She'd forgotten how it might look; she'd failed to reclaim the case in sufficient time to avoid the awkwardness; Tracey Rand had just covered what could have been a glaring error on her part. She reminded herself that she mustn't underestimate him and left the former Q-group leader in Crane's care without an apology or a backward look.

From here on in, they were up to their ears in the game

and she had to play her part perfectly. Both their lives were at stake.

Ilya Palladin was tall and sturdy, a broad-faced Slav with sharp features. As handsome as he was, she never failed to be startled by his good looks when she hadn't seen him for a while: Ilya's peaches-and-cream complexion, his two-meter solidity, and his Adriatic eyes all had a magnetism about them that memory, somehow, could not hold.

Nothing about his person, not even the fact that he religiously kept in shape despite the lunar gravity, could prepare an observer for the formidable intelligence lurking behind his narrow eyes.

"Kate, darling," he said as she approached with a smile on her face and returned his perfunctory, diplomat's embrace. It was all they ever risked in public—the upper-class familiarity of a Soviet second secretary and an American of parallel rank—but it allowed them a moment of privacy and a reestablishment of their priority relationship.

"A new friend, made on the trip?" he asked, his gaze on Rand and the ConSecs—and probably on the military lift from which they'd just emerged, that she'd like to believe was as new to Ilya as it had been to her.

Although it probably wasn't. She wouldn't be surprised if Ilya Palladin knew all about the TAV's landing, the aboveground hangars shielded with moon rock, and things she'd not yet learned about her own nation's installation.

But none of that precluded their friendship. Rather it encouraged it: one needed one's friends in every port, especially friends of high rank in their government like Ilya. "Yes," she responded to his question. "A Dr. Rand, from a private security company named Cislunar. He's trying to get some contracts up here—military, diplomatic, civilian, whatever he can manage."

"Security?" Ilya released her from his embrace and stepped back a discreet distance, a naughty smile playing ⁀he corners of his mouth. "*We* would hire him, but then no one else would, so I suppose you don't want my help in this.''

"No, not with that. But I'm starving and I've lots to talk to you about. Have you plans for dinner?'' No mention of what he'd gone through to get in here; they never remarked upon one another's work directly; politics in general, however, and ESA in particular, were subjects where no holds were barred.

"Only to buy it for you, if you'll allow me—in Cop One, where the food is so much better.'' His eyes twinkled. Bad Russian food was something he wished his nation hadn't exported to the moon; with her as his "guest,'' he could charge the most expensive cuisine Cop One had to offer on his expense account. They did it all the time. "But the real question is, do your plans for after dinner include me?''

"Ilya,'' she laughed, hoping that, when she turned, Trace Rand wasn't still watching her, "you'll have to wait and see. Dinner, of course. I'll tell you all about ESA's maneuvering in Washington and you'll tell me what I should know that's been going on up here while I've been gone.''

"A deal.'' He nodded and held out his elbow like some giant, Slavic duck. "Let us go. I am famished.''

As she took his arm and let him escort her, he inclined his head and said very softly, "We've heard of the death of your friend, Dr. Davies, and you have our official condolences. He was a loss to the Geneva commission, and thus a loss to us as well.''

What the hell did he mean? For an instant, she'd thought he meant Richelson; then she'd realized that it was Davies, that Davies's death was hardly classified, and that the Russians probably did consider Davies a loss. But still, Ilya had brought up a ZR/SEAL death and it shook her.

"Thank you,'' she said primly. "I'll convey the message to the appropriate parties.''

"Kate?'' Her Soviet lover stared at her probingly, guid-

161

ing her as he did so toward an elevator that would take them deeper into Cop One, where the restaurants were. "Is there something wrong?"

Ilya knew her well; sometimes it was a blessing; for the next few weeks, it was going to be a problem.

"Wrong? With ESA, you mean—with Chandra and that bunch coming up here at the end of the week? I was going to ask you . . ."

He clucked disapprovingly. "Not business, not now, not yet. This man's death really troubles you, yes? We have heard that you worked closely with him, years ago."

This was the time to say it, she realized, before Ilya caught her trying to withhold information or in an outright lie. "I've worked closely with lots of people, over the years. I worked with that man you just saw, Dr. Rand, at one time, too. It's not that I was personally fond of Davies, it's the loss of what he represents. He had a proposal to present at the Space Talks that might have lessened tensions considerably, I heard. But I didn't hear the specifics."

That was the way the evening was going to go. The two of them would quote generic sources, and fence and trade innuendo and occasionally hard fact, carefully keeping count of the bits of data being acquired by both sides.

They would do it over dinner in Cop One's most expensive restaurant, she realized when Ilya asked her in the elevator if she wanted to change first. And then, afterward, they would go to her quarters and reaffirm the fragile personal peace in force between them, a peace that might be difficult to maintain now that Tracey Rand was on the scene.

# Chapter 2

# DIPLOMATIC COVER

Cop One was all grays and muted tones—blue and taupe and green; colors meant to soothe, to reduce stress and fatigue. Rand's stress had been reduced as soon as he stepped into the first lock; it had nearly evaporated when he stepped out of it in the lunar reception lounge and was able to take off his helmet.

Since then, he'd been feeling incrementally worse, but not as bad as he had trekking over the exposed lunar surface with only his suit between him and a very messy death in vacuum.

It was a damned shame that he had this pathological fear of malfunctioning life-support equipment, but he knew the only way to conquer it was to endure it. Lots of things in life were like that. You toughed out what you couldn't ignore.

Like his first sight of Ilya Palladin taking Kate in his arms, and the macho cracks among the ConSecs thereafter as they escorted him to his cubicle and left him with numbers he could call in an "emergency"; like the mediocre food and the trouble he had guiding it to his mouth in one-sixth G; like his inability to sleep, despite the restraining straps, meant to be comforting, that held him to his bed in the civilian quarters he'd been assigned.

Sleeping on the moon was something he hadn't expected to be difficult. But with his eyes closed, his body kept thinking it was underwater, and that triggered nightmares he hadn't had for years. After one of the longest nights of his life, he was glad to fumble around in the low gravity and the strange environment, his orientation map in hand, looking for a place to get breakfast.

In the coffee shop, he managed not to spill food all over himself, the table, or the air in his immediate vicinity, and that pleased him. It was easier to walk without bounding this morning, too. Give him a week, he told himself, and he'd be negotiating Cop One's physical pitfalls as if he'd been doing it all his life.

Right now, he had to find his way to Harper's office, establish the bona fides of his cover, and then, that done, he could drop Kate's briefcase at her office: something he was looking forward to with emotions more mixed and more intense than he might have liked.

Harper's office was corridors away from the civilian one in which his twelve-foot-long cubicle was situated; the diplomatic section of Copernicus One was equidistant from the commercial and military areas. It boasted a few wood-grained doors hosting the occasional departmental insignia on bright colored plaques, but otherwise seemed identical to his civilian corridor.

Waiting in Harper's anteroom, watching a curly-headed female receptionist peck at her computer keyboard, he turned his orientation map in his hands and tried to get a sense of Cop One's layout. From that document, it was impossible. Certain things, like the military entrance lock through which he'd come, weren't depicted on the diagram at all; certain others, he must assume, would be misrepresented. The occasional automated walkway, like a lateral escalator, was well marked; so were the "lifts" and the restaurants and the shops and the contractors' offices and manufacturing facilities.

Other things, things Trace had to see, such as the Con-

Sec headquarters and CIA station, might as well have been nonexistent.

Oh well, some things never changed. That was what he had—or would have—Crane and the ConSecs for. As soon as was prudent, Crane and his two specialists would take Rand to the dark side. Right now, the three were delivering their classified cargo to the top-secret installation there, somewhere under the scientific station housing the radio telescope.

Until they returned to Cop One, Rand had only his cover and his orientation to be concerned with—and Kate. He'd made up his mind last night that, whatever the putative value of Ilya Palladin, his own mission had to take precedence. Telling Kate that wasn't going to be easy. Forcing the issue through channels, however, was something he'd prefer not to do.

So he waited for Harper and studied his map and, eventually, the receptionist eased fluidly from her chair. "Director Harper will see you now, Dr. Rand."

He followed the woman into the mission director's office and mouthed pleasantries until the door closed behind her and the two men were alone. Then he said without preamble, "I'm going to need more orientation assistance than I thought; you were right."

"Didn't sleep well?" Harper guessed. Behind the mission director's desk were pictures of him with various politicians; the smile on his face matched the smile in those photos—impersonally friendly, practiced, like a department store Santa's.

"Not real well, no. It's nice to know the problem's common, but not nice to know it's so obvious."

"Relax, Dr. Rand. Until your ConSec people get back to extend your orientation, you've got nothing more pressing than learning how to do just that."

How the hell did Harper get his information? Or was he just fishing? A Class Five briefing would have entitled him only to mission parameters, not specifics. But then, Rand cautioned himself there were so few people here that, given certain information, it wouldn't be too hard to figure specifics—not for Harper, or for others of his rank who had an interest in keeping abreast.

"I've got plenty pressing: I've got to find a way to keep ESA and the Soviets from seeing through me like you do. Lives might depend on it."

"One of them yours?" Harper sat on one corner of his desk, seeming more fit in this environment than he had in higher gravity; here his belly didn't roll flabbily; here his motions seemed perfectly controlled and perfectly attuned; here he knew he was calling all the shots and it showed in everything he said and did.

"That's right, one of 'em's mine." Cautiously, Rand sought one of two chairs bolted to tracks before the desk and sat down. Chairs were an Earth invention; here they might, someday, be superfluous; and yet, one-sixth gravity was still gravity. And humans, as humans will, brought their customs with them. Locking one ankle around a chair leg, Rand continued: "I'll need lots of Kate's time. Can we clear her decks somewhat? I want to be up and running by the time that ESA contingent gets here."

"I've never seen a man so anxious to draw fire," said Harper with uncharacteristic candor that left Rand momentarily speechless. "But then," the director added, "I suppose that's what you're here for, though I don't approve. We don't want any trouble here, Dr. Rand. We've never had a serious incident of violence on Cop One—not anywhere on the moon—and I'm going on record: I don't want to have to write one up while I'm mission director. I know your plan in general; I can guess the rest." He held up a hand when Rand started to object that he'd misunderstood. "Don't humor me, Dr. Rand. I'm neither misguided nor misconstruing. I realize the necessity of what you're doing—at least of the thinking groundside that decided that necessity—but I want you to understand: we're a very small community. It's one thing for you to come up here as a civilian; it's another for you to be closely aligned with our diplomatic personnel . . . or ConSec personnel." Owlishly, Harper peered at him.

Rand said, "I understand, sir. I'm used to assessing risks. I'm going to be very careful—and very busy selling Cislunar's services to the contractors. So if you'll just give me the Request for Procurement you promised, I'll be on my—"

"What I'm saying, Dr. Rand, is that we're very small here; everyone has a reason to be here, and everyone knows everyone else's reason. If there is an element hostile to your mission up here, as well as groundside, I'll do all I can to protect you. But I have to know what you're doing—what to protect you from."

*This guy wants reports!* The realization gave Rand a start. "Well, sir, so far it's seat of the pants. I'll keep you apprised. I can use all the help I can get."

"Good." Harper nodded. "In that case, now that we've reached a meeting of the minds, my wife has suggested we invite you to a cocktail party, such as one can have on the moon. This evening at five, at my residence. My girl has your packet ready." Harper slid off the desk and extended his hand in a smooth gesture.

Rand bolted out of his chair, chuckled self-deprecatingly, and shook Harper's hand. "Thank you, sir. I appreciate it."

He wasn't sure if that was true, but the Harpers' friends were as good a place as any to start.

At the door, he asked over his shoulder, "Would it be appropriate if I brought Kate Brittany?"

"I believe she's already coming, with a Soviet functionary, Ilya Palladin, as her escort. Good-bye, Dr. Rand."

# Chapter 3

# SECOND SECRETARY

Ilya Palladin of the Soviet moonbase, Sveboda, was the ranking KGB officer on the moon. A colonel in the Soviet army, he was responsible not only for security matters, the entire GRU contingent of the Soviet military, but also for all "anticosmic defense" matters and technology-transfer gambits: in other words, part of his job was to steal as much Western technology as possible, while about his primary job of intelligence collection.

Palladin's many hats—diplomat, army officer, KGB and GRU and PKO functionary, as well as industrial spy—all sat comfortably on his broad, intelligent head. The hat of lover to Kate Brittany, however, wobbled occasionally, sometimes precariously.

Tonight was one of those times. As he escorted Kate into the scandalously elegant residence of the U.S. diplomatic mission director, Harper, Palladin was finding it difficult to keep his mind on the business of lunar espionage. Kate Brittany had come back from her earthly sojourn to Washington subtly changed. She was preoccupied and nervous and, in some indefinable way, more vulnerable than Palladin had ever seen her.

Some men might not have noticed this, but Palladin was trained to notice everything. And where Kate Brittany was concerned, noticing everything was not a mere duty, but a pleasure. Last night when they'd retired to her quarters, she had been athletically demonstrative, determined to prove how glad she was to be back in his arms. This was not like Kate. Kate was secure, competent, professional; she never felt the need to prove anything. Not, at least, with him.

They had discussed the pending arrival of new ESA personnel at length. This was nothing new. They continually compared notes on their mutual competitor, the European Space Agency. Early in their relationship, they had agreed that intelligence sharing, where it related to ESA, was the most effective way to do their jobs.

It was a secret that they did this, of course; such intelligence sharing was irregular; it would be difficult to explain and more difficult to approve through channels that were earthbound and thus myopic, and also paranoid by nature.

Those men and women who were stationed on the moon experienced a certain commonality of interest: survival here was a prime concern; one planned for contingencies such as environmental failure. One looked out at the stars without their softening blanket of atmosphere and the stars looked back, whispering to a man's mind about the precious gift of intelligent life and the foolishness of internecine squabbles between the nations of humankind.

Once man in profusion left his earthly womb, Palladin was certain, his feeling toward his fellow man would change. In the meantime, Palladin was a good Soviet citizen. His sexual intimacy with Kate Brittany had been duly cleared through the appropriate offices in Moscow; he was on record as cultivating Brittany, a potential "agent of influence" and thus free to do as he pleased in the matter of the American woman.

It bothered him tremendously that, tonight, she seemed so different. It was not just the new and expensive jumpsuit she had bought on her trip—an overt piece of glistening, body-hugging fluff that was unlike anything he'd seen her wear previously. It was not just the way she'd gasped under him last night in an overt display of pleasure when usually she was reticent. It was not just the degree of her interest in one Robin Faragher, the assistant of a man named Chandra, an Indian assigned to ESA's new metallurgy project. It was, Palladin was certain without knowing why, something deeper, something systemically different in her that he sensed.

As she slid away from him in the carpeted reception hall of the Harpers' residence, he could have sworn it was a difference of some much simpler sort. Kate Brittany was behaving as if she had a new lover, some illicit affair of the heart that put distance between them by its very existence.

If this were true, Palladin had no doubt as to her partner: the man she'd kissed farewell in the military lounge yesterday, Tracey Rand. Palladin's sources told him that Rand had been to her office this morning. He had gone in carrying more in his amorphous bag than he'd had when he'd left. More than this, Palladin's silicon and flesh-and-blood spies could not determine.

He'd sent a request groundside, asking for background on the man in question. Now he must wait. If Rand checked out, then Palladin would suppress his feelings. Simple jealousy was no reason to put a person under hard surveillance, nor to designate a target. Kate Brittany was an opposition player, and players often found themselves caught up in webs of expediency.

Perhaps this Rand, to whom she now gravitated while Palladin watched, ignoring the buffet by which he stood, was merely what he professed: a private security contractor. Perhaps Kate's familiarity came from prior acquaintance, as she'd said. Perhaps there was nothing deeper, nothing more sinister, no reason to treat this Dr. Rand as a KGB target of opportunity.

If this was so, then Ilya Palladin would deal with his

jealousy as he dealt daily with the fact that Kate and he could never have an uncompromised relationship—that the draconian nature of their affair was what kept it so interesting.

Ilya Palladin would not arrange an accident for Tracey Rand simply because Rand was sleeping with Kate Brittany—*if* that were true, as rumors carefully collected by all means suggested. Nor would he attempt to compromise the integrity of the man, bring him under Soviet control, for personal reasons.

Watching the two of them together, Palladin found himself hoping fervently that the man Kate was bringing over to meet him would turn out to be a political, ideological, and active adversary. It would support the urge that Palladin felt to get his hands around the other man's neck and squeeze.

When Kate and her companion reached him at the buffet, Kate said brightly, "Ilya, this is Dr. Rand—Trace. Ilya Palladin, the one man you'll need to know from Sveboda."

Introductions made, Kate stepped back a pace.

Rand's eyes were opaque and steady on him. "Hello, Secretary Palladin. Kate tells me good things about you." Rand's voice matched his eyes but carried an undercurrent of hostility that Palladin understood.

Definitely, these two were more than friends. He said, "Remember, Dr. Rand, our dear Kate is a diplomat. What can she say but good things?"

Rand bared his teeth in appreciation of the joke and made as if to drift away.

"Russians, you know," said Palladin, casting his net to draw the fish back in, "place little store by Western pleasantries; the truth suits us better."

Rand hesitated, seemed to weigh his response, and then said, "No kidding? And I thought deception was the Soviet state religion. Learn something new every day."

"You'll learn much new here, Dr. Rand, in the next few

days." Voice a bit louder now, to keep Rand from breaking off the conversation, Palladin closed the distance between them. Off to his right, he could see Kate, a sour look
on her face, shaking her head nearly imperceptibly at him.
"Kate has told me you are in the private sector—commercial security."

"Yeah, that's right. I'm also trying to get the government contract for the diplomatic mission. If I do—"

"If you do, you and I will then be professional cohorts,
perhaps occasional opponents. In the meantime, if there is
anything I can do to help you—if you would like a tour of
Sveboda, some vodka, or a candid exchange of views on
some subject or other, do let me know. You can usually
reach me through the central Sveboda switchboard, or
through Kate's office." He stepped back, point made, signaling an end to the conversation.

"I'll keep that in mind," Rand said, just as Alicia Harper, all well-preserved charm and bounteous blond beauty,
came up to take him by the hand and guide him "into the
thick of things, doctor. It's no fair, you hiding out here
with your own kind."

Rand went meekly but Ilya saw Kate, still off to the side
fingering a slice of gravlax on her styrene plate, wince. *His
own kind.* Ilya Palladin mentally thanked the diplomatic
matron for the hint, or slip of the tongue, or assumption
that had made her state the obvious.

Alicia Harper's words were not sufficient to form a determination, but they were sufficient to allow him to con-
front Kate with his suspicions.

"Catherine," Palladin said, once he had a plate of his
own to fill from the buffet before which she stood, "what
do you think Alicia meant by that: 'your own kind'?"

Kate's face seemed pinched and her eyes were full of
shadows as she glanced at him, then back at her food. To
the plate in her hand, she responded, "He's from Cislunar
Security. He's got a similar background, I guess, if it's
Alicia Harper who's determining the equation."

172

"I did not think she meant he was a diplomat."

Kate broke a tine of her plastic fork and made a grab for the fragment. "Ilya, I'm in no mood for an argument over semantics, not when the speaker's that bubble-headed twit. You want to know about Trace's background, just ask me."

"Good." Palladin grinned. "Tell me, then, about Dr. Rand's background."

"Later," Kate replied. "When the party's over and we're back at my cube. If we don't end up having a fight first."

"So? A threat or a promise?"

"God, Ilya, will you get off it? I've never seen you like this before. He's just one more newcomer as far as I'm concerned."

It didn't play, and she knew it. Miserably, she slapped her food down on the buffet table and went looking for "somebody who can offer me a drink and some civil conversation."

He followed after her, suddenly having more at risk than he was willing to lose. His relationship with Kate Brittany was one of his most valuable assets. And she was the only woman on the moon who truly attracted him. Sometimes, he knew, women chose to pick fights because of hormonal imbalances, or to test love, or merely for the pleasure of making up afterward.

Palladin fervently hoped Kate's reasons were one of the above. He really didn't want to credit the notion that she was picking a fight with him to be able to spend more time with Tracey Rand. If that were the case, she would be acting under orders, in her government's interest, he told himself.

The woman he'd bedded the night before could not, this next evening, have lost all interest where passion had been so recently and fervently displayed. Therefore, her reasons must be official, if reasons there were. From that assumption—more acceptable than the simpler one of a fickle woman's changing tastes in partners—one could jump to a supportable conclusion: Dr. Rand was here on subterranean business, the business of the United States.

Even as he grasped Kate's arm and began to apologize, Palladin found himself anxious to prove his thesis. Then he could act on it. If Tracey Rand was a player, then the game was about to become very interesting, indeed.

Three hours later, in Kate's cubicle, she was trying to quell the suspicions an unfortunate interchange had raised in Ilya Palladin's mind.

Angry and anguished, she made love to the wrong man and cursed herself, her job, Alicia Harper, Trace's obdurateness in particular, and the diplomatic/intelligence corps in general.

This wasn't what she'd expected to do with her talents when she'd become a civil servant. With Ilya on top of her and her legs wrapped around his waist, she did her best to react as she ought to—as she would have, until Rand came back into her life.

But it was no good, in her heart. That made the rest a matter of play acting. She did the best she could, but Ilya was a sensitive lover. He wasn't fooled.

And that made this agonizing personal failure a possible professional calamity. She'd never even guessed that her body would try to reject her customary lover.

But it did. And Ilya's feelings were hurt, although he tried not to show it. This led to an equipment failure of the most embarrassing sort and at length they lay, panting and despondent, side by side on her narrow bed, a silence full of barbs between them.

"Well," he said, at last in English—he'd said some things in Russian she was pretending not to have understood. "Where do we go from here?"

"Nothing's changed," she lied in a trembling voice. "It's just that I'm tired from the trip and my body's holding water. . . . We'll be fine tomorrow, maybe even in an hour or two. I'm upset; you're upset. We just need to get used to each other again.''

"Da," he sighed. Then, politely, he put a hand on one of her breasts. "All will be well in the morning, after a good night's sleep."

He got up and started to dress. She didn't try to stop him, even though it was a long way to Sveboda and she knew how difficult—not to say embarrassing—it would be for him to arrange transit this late in the sleep cycle.

There wasn't any use in trying to pretend she wouldn't be glad to see him go. But so much was at stake, she did. And he did: they needed each other, professionally; they cared about each other, personally; neither of them knew how to admit failure of any sort, sexual failure least of all.

When he kissed her softly on the forehead and she closed the door after him, unwilling to watch the big, forlorn man trudge down the corridor, she slapped the door and leaned against it.

*Goddamn you, Trace. You're going to ruin everything.*

She just hoped that Ilya didn't take it into his head to make things difficult for her—or for Rand.

Standing there, with the possible repercussions of this abortive evening crashing in on her, she began to tremble.

She'd have to find some way to get Ilya firmly back on her side, smooth things out. Palladin was a hardballer; both the Soviets and the Americans up here were playing for keeps. Accidents on the moon were easy to arrange.

And ZR/SEAL personnel were accident prone.

Then she did open the door, ready to run down the hall after Ilya, to bring him back, to soothe his suspicions, to make sure that there were no repercussions from tonight that she'd regret.

*God, Trace, if we're not careful—if we're not a whole lot more careful—we're going to get ourselves killed.*

But Palladin had disappeared, into an elevator or around

175

the corridor's turning. And Trace Rand was the last person she was going to call for solace.

As alone in her room as she'd been in the hall, Kate straightened the rumpled sheets that smelled of fear and aborted lovemaking and spent hours trying unsuccessfully to get to sleep.

# Chapter 4

# DARK-SIDE GAMBIT

Crane and his boys were alone in the otherwise empty moon crawler when they noticed a Soviet "truckski" following in their wake. Thirty degrees starboard, it lumbered along, keeping its distance, invisible to everything but the electromagnetic sensors in the ConSec crawler's countermeasures console.

If this ConSec moon crawler had been as innocuous as it looked, Crane wouldn't have had the slightest notion that his vehicle was being tailed. Utilizing hand signals, he alerted Marshall, beside him in the front seat, to duck through into the cargo bay and warn Foster that there might be trouble.

When Marshall came forward again, Crane shot his subordinate a questioning look and received a thumbs-up in answer. They couldn't risk talking about the problem, not with the kind of snooping equipment that might be trained on them. Anyway, they didn't know if they were really going to *have* a problem, or just an escort.

The escort, of course, was trouble enough on a high-security delivery run like this one. "Want to run the old tape?" Crane said casually.

Marshall understood what he meant: run the multifunction surveillance recordings of their trip to the dark-side radio telescope installation, and check to see if the Soviets had been on the crawler's tail the whole way. The crawler made constant recordings; Marshall's task now was to find out when the Russians had first picked them up.

It was going to take a while. Crane concentrated on his driving, one eye on the little red display grid that, now zeroed on the following truckski, told him where it was and what it was doing.

Damn shame they couldn't have gotten the WARLORD cargo deployed without making waves. Maybe, just maybe, the Soviet vehicle was simply curious. It might have picked them up routinely, like ships passing in the night, and decided to follow because it had nothing better to do.

But Crane's crawler, having hauled nuclear cargo, was going to be hot in various signature bandwidths. There was no way to avoid a certain amount of trace heat, not when you had nukes on board; nukes, like infrared, left a telltale behind for a significant amount of time. That telltale was as clear to the right equipment as the grimace on Marshall's face behind his helmet's faceplate as he said, " 'Bout two hours, I make it."

Two hours out of the dark-side installation, the Soviet vehicle had picked them up. Damn and all, caught with their hands in the cookie jar.

They weren't supposed to be transporting nukes out here. It was against all the conventions, and once the Soviets verified that the crawler Crane was driving was a U.S. vehicle—which they could do by recording its destination, the U.S. military garage at Cop One—diplomatic protests would be lodged.

The whole project was now in danger. Any inquiry, or demand for one, threatened WARLORD. There wasn't anything on the dark side that needed nuclear fuel—not in the quantities the Russian vehicle might be able to establish that Crane's crawler had been carrying.

The solution was obvious to Crane, but he was hesitant to implement it. If there was some way to determine that the Soviet vehicle on their trail wasn't enhanced, didn't carry spy equipment, then he wouldn't have to blow it to bits.

But the chances of a truckski out here not being equipped to avail itself of surveillance opportunities were pretty slim. The chances that the truckski was following them precisely because it had detected a trace of lingering nuclear signature and wanted to verify the provenance of the cargo hauler, were much greater.

Crane leaned forward, his gloved hand picking up a stylus attached by a string to a clipboard on the Consec crawler's dashboard, and wrote, *Let's blow it*.

His was a considered decision. The repercussions of a lost Soviet spy truck were, in his estimation, less than letting that truckski get back to Sveboda with hard evidence. Of course, some data might already have been sent to Sveboda from the truckski, but electronic data could be argued to be fake; video tape with real-time designators on every frame couldn't be disputed successfully.

It was a question of weighing the negative impact of various unsavory scenarios. And Crane was sitting in the seat where the buck invariably stopped. He couldn't call in for a conference or boot the decision to higher authority — any call would alert the truckski.

And he couldn't let the truckski waddle on home with enough on-board data to prompt an official accusation that might shred WARLORD's veil of secrecy.

Too many had given WARLORD too much over too long for him to let the project be surfaced by a piece of bad luck. *If* that was all it was. Crane was well aware that the Soviets would learn something if he blew their truckski to hell. But they'd learn less than if he let the truckski follow him back to base, or tried to warn it off. So it was damage limitation, pure and simple.

Marshall, beside him, was already preparing to launch a kinetic-kill missile carrying conventional explosives. He'd snapped down a panel and brought up a targeting array.

179

That array controlled a missile launcher camouflaged into the sidewall of Crane's ConSec crawler. Crane glanced at the cross hairs and varied his vehicle's attitude sufficiently to center the target.

When he got into position, a red circle appeared automatically on the LED targeting screen before him. But it was Marshall who had to push the button.

Marshall's eyes met his, querying.

Crane nodded decisively, hoping that the truckski was robotic. He couldn't know for sure without asking for a signature sweep that might alert any personnel behind him: counter-countermeasures weren't undetectable.

Marshall pushed the button and both men watched the computer display before them. The crawler shivered, then lurched, as the rocket launched: every action has an equal and opposite reaction, even on the moon.

The specially devised lunar hunter-killer took only seconds to reach its target, but for those seconds the dark side around it was lit as bright as day.

Then the targeting array recorded a kill. Marshall got out of his seat and headed back into the body of the transport to get an eyeball on the damage.

If the missile had done its job, there wouldn't be a piece of truckski left that was large enough to determine the cause of the explosion.

If it wasn't a good hit, they were going to have to go back there and pick up the pieces manually, load them into the back of the crawler, and then find some way to get rid of them.

In any event, the whole situation had just escalated. WARLORD was in danger of exposure; Crane's group was in danger of disciplinary action; relations between the superpowers were in danger of deteriorating further.

Crane sweated it out in silence until Marshall came back, then held up a gloved hand to forestall any imprudent comments over their suits' com frequency. But he needn't have worried.

"Nothin' out there, boss. Must have been my imagination," drawled Marshall with a spreading grin on his face.

It was a damned good thing that sound waves didn't propagate in vacuum, or they'd have had the whole Soviet contingent down on them before they got out of the area. The shock wave, of course, would be noticeable, but shock waves could come from lots of things. And on the cratered moon, one more crater wasn't anything to write home about.

Without conspicuous fragments of the truck to analyze for signs of foul play, the Soviets might hesitate to mention this little event. They'd have to admit they were out on the dark side with a surveillance vehicle, and following a U.S. vehicle for purposes of intelligence collection. . . . Even if the Russians knew exactly what had happened, and had a pinpoint location on the truckski they'd just lost, they might think twice about lodging a formal complaint.

Not that a formal complaint was the worst thing Crane had to worry about. Behind him was the radio telescope installation, putatively peaceful and scientific and pure. Under it was a storage cavern they'd hacked out of moon rock, and in that cavern were the painstakingly accreted bits and pieces of what was going to be WARLORD, sooner than anybody thought.

Now all Crane had to do was get back to Cop One and report to Brittany, before somebody else told her what had happened. He thought about that for a moment, and about his urge to bypass Brittany and go straight to Rand with this one. He knew what Rand, a former Q-group leader like himself, would say and do.

Brittany was an unknown quantity, a female, a diplomat, a negotiator.

Taking stylus in hand once more, Crane wrote, *Watch for bogeys,* and Marshall nodded: to report to anyone at all, Crane and his boys would have to make it back to base in one piece.

If it began to look like that wasn't likely, Crane would call in on an open channel. But he'd hate to do that. That would blow everything wide open, maybe even precipitate open hostilities. So far, the lid was still on.

Part of his job was to keep it that way until Rand got his ass in gear and Crane could get the good doctor dark side, where they'd start putting the pieces together for WARLORD's launch.

Crane hoped to hell Brittany wouldn't decide that, in the wake of this destabilizing incident, the whole project would have to be put on hold until suspicions could be allayed, tensions reduced, and tempers calmed. That was what she might say, all right.

His hands so tight on the wheel that they ached, Crane decided how he was going to play it: if he lived long enough; if no Soviet missile came flying over the cratered landscape to even the score.

He'd go to Rand and Brittany simultaneously or, failing that, route to Brittany through Rand. It wasn't that he didn't trust Brittany, it was just that he wanted to do a minimum of explaining.

And, more than that, he wanted the best odds he could muster that what he'd done here didn't delay the project he was trying to put on line. He'd hauled hot cargo, risking his life and his genetic potency, to the dark side because, after the sabotage aboard the TAV, he was beginning to take WARLORD very personally.

Somebody had tried to kill him, and his boys, and everybody aboard the TAV to stop the delivery of something—Rand, the cargo . . . something. And for Crane, being designated a target was about as personal as it got.

They drove for fifty kilometers in silence and then fifty more, bantering neutrally in order to keep their spirits up.

Then they crossed over a ridge and saw the demarcation line—the place where the dark side ended.

Technically, the two hemispheres of the moon were called the "near" and "far" sides, but nobody used that nomenclature anymore. Once he got past the dark-side boundary, he could relax. It wasn't that far then to Einstein crater, where they could leave the incriminatingly hot crawler and fly back to Copernicus. With any luck, Crane would be visiting Tracey Rand by 1600 hours, getting the sort of help he needed to cover his tracks.

# Chapter 5
# SVEBODA

The news of the lost surveillance drone rocked Sveboda's KGB station as if the lunar regolith were still quaking with shock waves from the explosion on the dark side.

Ilya Palladin's hot line rang off the hook as various components of his organization reported in, determined to shirk responsibility as best they could.

The drones were expensive; this drone had been sending curious information, readings indicating that nuclear material had been recently transported by the manned moon crawler it was tracking. That vehicle's most recent port of call, best intelligence affirmed, had been the U.S. dark-side radio telescope installation.

Palladin told his secretary to hold the rest of his calls and stared unseeingly at the blotter covered with doodles on his desk. Then he picked up the background check on Tracey Rand that had just come up from Earth on his ground link and began to read.

When, in Rand's background file, the designation ZR/SEAL came up, Palladin's shoulders hunched. He'd seen that acronym before. An hour later, having cross-referenced and come up with Kate Brittany's dossier and another incidence of the designator ZR/SEAL, he sent two requests earthside.

One was to Moscow, for everything KGB headquarters had on ZR/SEAL missions and personnel, active or inactive.

The other went by shielded ground link to somewhere in the Western hemisphere, asking the same questions.

Both replies came back within half an hour, and from both sources Palladin learned something.

Moscow Center told him that the recently deceased Space Talks negotiator, Nathan Davies, had once been a member of the same ZR/SEAL unit as Rand and Brittany, and that Davies was not the only recent casualty with Seal designators after his name: four others from the unit had died within the last six months. And it gave him one other, much more important, piece of information: at the end of the terse encoded document was a KGB cautionary flag, the equivalent of a padlock, which told Ilya Palladin that there was more information on file but that it was locked up, unavailable even to an officer of Palladin's rank without special dispensation.

The other request for information on Rand and ZR/SEAL yielded a surprising degree of correlation, even to the equivalent of a jacket flag at the end of the document: this source, too, had more information but was unwilling to share it.

Ilya Palladin sat back in his ergochair and pondered what he had learned. Coincidence was, in his business, sometimes the equivalent of corroboration. As he fed the two documents languorously into his desktop shredder, he considered the obvious conclusions: something was afoot and that something had a great deal to do with ZR/SEAL, living and dead. He'd seen the Seal designator in Kate's file previously, of course, but out of context, in among the string of acronyms that defined her career, it had meant nothing of consequence.

Now, with Rand on the moon, it meant considerably more. Kate had not tried to hide the fact that Rand and she had worked together before, Palladin reminded himself.

Sometimes the best place to hide is in plain sight. By itself, the coincidence of assignment would not have been incriminating, but followed by security flags, it took on new meaning.

The flag from KGB told Palladin that someone at the center, someone of power and influence, had decided that whatever information comprised the rest of the file Palladin had requested was too sensitive for even the ranking KGB officer on the moon to access at will. Which probably meant that some operation was under way about which Palladin purposely had been kept in the dark.

He sat forward, powered up his encrypted ground link, and began typing out data requests with priority clearances, requests that would go to the chief operations officers in KGB and PKO simultaneously. Anything taking place on the surface of the moon was Palladin's business. Now that he knew something was up, he was damned if he was going to tolerate being kept ignorant of what that something might be.

The corroborating report he'd gotten from the West, from a special contact of his, was even more confounding. To that source he sent a strong protest that, if he were to be effective, he would have to have all relevant data on the operation and personnel the source was withholding.

In this last communiqué, he could and did let his pique show. Palladin's job was to gather and evaluate intelligence; he would not tolerate being told there was information crucial to his tasks that he could not have.

Then again the KGB colonel sat back, for the first time letting his personal feelings cycle. Kate was involved in something important, perhaps even dangerous, that she had not told him about. Within her security restrictions, they'd always been honest with one another. How could he help her if she would not tell him she needed help?

It occurred to him that the only circumstance in which Kate would be forced to behave in such a manner was a circumstance in which she was actively working against the best interests of the USSR's Svoboda station. It was a personal betrayal of the same magnitude as the KGB flag on his request for Rand/Seal data.

For some reason, his own organization and the woman who was his most intimate companion both had decided that what they knew was too sensitive to share with him.

Which meant, obviously, that some operation was taking place, or would soon take place, on the moon and that this operation was of the highest volatility.

He didn't know which he resented more: Kate's behavior, or his organization's. The corroborating Western source might feel the need for caution where Palladin was concerned, but Kate and KGB both knew him well enough to know that he could be trusted.

This obvious lack of trust troubled him greatly. There was no situation he could envision in which his help was not sufficiently valuable to be worth the risk of putting him in the picture.

His secretary's voice came over the intercom, gently reminding him that he'd lost a surveillance drone and this, to many on the moon and on Earth as well, was an event of the highest priority. He shelved his private speculations, preparing to deal with the exigencies before him. If proof could be found that the drone had been taken out by the Americans it was following, then a back-channel protest could be lodged—nothing formal, because the drone shouldn't exist, shouldn't have been on the dark side with all that spy equipment, shouldn't have been following a U.S. vehicle or monitoring the goings and comings around the U.S. radio telescope installation.

As a matter of fact, Palladin realized, he wasn't sure quite why the drone had been out there doing that, or on whose orders it had tailed the American crawler.

With an infuriating and growing suspicion that someone in his station was acting under orders that Palladin, the duly appointed KGB resident at Svoboda, knew nothing about, he depressed the toggle that allowed him to speak to his secretary.

"Send Oleg Ruskin in here, as soon as possible," he said in a voice so controlled that it sounded flat and nearly mechanical.

Then he sat back to wait. Ruskin was the only other man at Sveboda with the clearances and connections to have ordered the surveillance drone into action—the only man who could have done it without Palladin's approval.

Waiting for the younger KGB agent to arrive, Palladin rehearsed what he would say. He would tell Ruskin that he knew that Ruskin was to blame for the loss of the drone, and demand a full explanation. If he must, Palladin was willing to suspend the agent and co-opt Ruskin's files.

That would flush the wolves. If Moscow Center was running an operation up here, through Ruskin, without Palladin's knowledge, then Palladin must put a stop to it. Put Ruskin and his scheme at risk. Make it clear to KGB on Earth that Palladin was less of a risk than the ambitious fool they'd tapped in his stead.

If Ruskin knew anything of consequence, Palladin would hear every bit of that information before Ruskin left his office. If it became clear that Ruskin was merely playing for personal advantage, perhaps Palladin could make use of that. If it turned out that Ruskin was not acting under orders, then Palladin's course of action was clear: silence and deport the criminal to Earth, where any wrongdoing on Ruskin's part could be slowly and painstakingly drawn from him by experts.

In his heart, Palladin did not believe that he had found a Western mole or even an independent play for power by Ruskin. In his heart Palladin believed that KGB, in its finite wisdom, had decided on an operation concerning the American woman, Kate Brittany; and that to run such an operation, Ilya Palladin was not the appropriate choice.

And since that determination (if it had been made) by groundside authorities reflected on Palladin's loyalty and his ability to perform, he was willing to ram it all the way up the chain of command until he received profuse apologies and regained the complete trust of KGB's highest functionaries.

Kate Brittany was a woman about whom he cared passionately, true. But she was just a woman. Ilya Palladin cared, most passionately and most of all, about his career. About his job and his ability to do that job. No personal considerations could be allowed to interfere.

If he must, once he'd reduced Ruskin to quivering tractability, he would convince Moscow Center of that.

Before he sent an official communiqué to Earth, however, he'd need to know everything there was to know about the U.S. dark-side radio telescope installation, about the transfer of nuclear material there, and about anything else that might, in any way, be connected to the flag on the file before him—the file that both explicated and implied some operational connection between Tracey Rand and Kate Brittany.

With a pencil, on the file folder, as he waited for Ruskin to arrive, he traced and retraced the letters ZR/SEAL.

# Chapter 6

# CISLUNAR SECURITY

Tracey Rand had been in the newly constituted office of Cislunar Security for exactly two hours and fifteen minutes when the doorbell beeped for the first time.

It couldn't possibly be a client. He hadn't even gotten his com equipment up and running yet. The twenty-four-by-twelve-foot cubicle he'd secured among the contractors in the commercial corridor of Cop One wasn't ready for business, not by a long shot—not even if he'd intended to do any business while he was here.

On top of that, he had an appointment to meet the incoming moon truck carrying the ESA contingent in forty-five minutes. It hadn't been easy to wangle a slot in the party greeting Chandra, Faragher, and the other newcomers of the ESA contingent, but he'd managed to talk Harper into it. Rand needed the orientation lecture and tour of ESA as much as Chandra or any of his people did.

So he was harried when he straightened up from the carton he was unloading and hit the button that drew back the door, a pile of colored file binders in his other hand.

In trooped Crane, Marshall, and Foster, all pumped up over something. You could see it in the energy that jumped between the two subordinates, in the lazy movements of Crane, their commander, as the door shut behind them and

Crane, with annoying familiarity, hit the security block on its panel beside the door.

Eyeing the little red *armed* light that told Rand his office was now as immune to surveillance as technology allowed, he said, "To what do I owe the pleasure?"

There were only two visitors' chairs, set into tracks in the floor. Crane took one, Marshall the other; Foster stood by the door at technical ease.

"We thought we'd better tell you what happened out there before things get garbled, especially since we couldn't find Brittany."

"Okay." Rand nodded cautiously, thinking that the ConSecs probably hadn't looked very hard for Kate: he'd talked to her in her office less than twenty minutes ago. "Shoot."

Crane shot. "Sir, on the way back from a routine trip to RTI—the radio telescope installation dark side—we ran into a Soviet vehicle in trouble. We went to investigate, of course, but it blew up before we could get to it. There isn't much of anything left." Crane grinned bleakly.

"I see," said Rand, playing along. "Well, it's good that you answered their SOS, but I'm not the one to tell. Secretary Brittany—"

"There wasn't one," Crane interrupted, making things clearer. Marshall beside him, looked over at Foster, who was studying the security plate on the door for any flicker of attempted interference.

"What?" Rand asked, then caught himself. The ConSecs had taken out a Russian vehicle, then, and were concerned enough about it to have come straight to him—for corroboration, for protection, for help with Kate because they'd exceeded their authority. Just what he needed: another reason for her to resent him. He scrubbed his jaw with one hand, put down the data files he was holding in the other, and sat on the edge of his desk, studying the ConSecs.

Crane's every muscle was intent on telling Rand that

what had happened couldn't be helped, that he and his two men weren't going to accept less than direct orders from Rand as to how to proceed, and that those orders ought to have the highest priority.

"All right, let's go find Kate and tell her," he said, picking up his key card from the desk. "I've got to catch up with her before the ESA moon truck docks, anyhow."

Watching the three ConSecs, Rand cataloged their reactions. Crane's square, open face smoothed as he stood up; his eyes telegraphed relief and approval. Marshall, beside him, stood a fraction of a second later, his heavier frame drained of tension. Foster ran a hand through pale hair and disengaged the security block on the door before he was told to. They were a very well-trained working unit; Rand resisted the tendency to think of them as one entity— once he got to know them, their individual strengths and weaknesses would become clear. He'd already noted that Foster occasionally blurted his emotions, and that Marshall was the most suspicious of the three.

Moving toward the men waiting at the door, Rand cautioned himself not to assume anything, or to take them for granted. Crane was their team leader and that bond was implicit. They'd come to Rand with this in order to make sure they got the response they wanted, not out of any implicit loyalty or professional judgment of ability. And yet, it felt good to have men like these under him again; he'd have to watch the natural urge to trust them.

There wasn't anybody on this one that he could trust, not even Kate. She'd proved that yesterday, when he'd told her flat out that his mission had to take precedence over whatever she was doing with Palladin, and she'd flown into a rage.

He didn't know enough yet about lunar loyalties or exigencies to be able to anticipate the reactions of any of the players to stimulus, especially the kind of stimulus Crane had just laid in his lap.

So he paused and said very softly, "Foster, when I want

that block down, I'll tell you. When we're finished talking, I'll tell you that. When we're ready to go hunt up Brittany, I'll give you an order. Don't anticipate me.''

It had to start sometime. He had to bring these men into line or Crane was going to manipulate him for ConSec purposes. Since he had no idea what those purposes might be, he didn't want to start guessing.

All three men snapped to and Rand nodded. ''That's better. As you were, then. You want to tell me what really happened out there and why you didn't go to Kate with it—clear and off the record?''

Out came the white noise generator that Marshall carried with him and Crane started to explain.

When the ConSec lieutenant had finished, Rand grimaced. ''Thanks for the vote of confidence, guys, but Brittany's going to be rip-shit you didn't go through channels—I suppose you know that?''

When Crane was absolutely certain that Rand was waiting for a reply, he said, ''Yes, sir, we know that. But under the circumstances, we didn't want to risk any result but the one we need: complete cooperation.''

''What sort of cooperation, Crane? You want to pretend this never happened? It's not likely to go unremarked.''

Foster, still by the door, was tensing up. Marshall noticed and went to the younger man, whispered something. Crane responded to Rand's question: ''Sir, we don't think the Soviets will go public with this. If they do, we'd like to make sure you're the one who determines what the U.S. response ought to be.''

*Gee, thanks, buddy. Just what I need—a reason to have a knock-down-drag-out with Harper.* ''I like your accident scenario, if it'll play. Now, before we take our united front to Kate's office, I think I'd better tell you that I want to get dark side as soon as possible.''

''We expected that.'' Crane nodded. ''We're about ready for you over there—if this doesn't screw things up.''

''You set it up. Let's go fix this little problem of yours.

And for Christ's sake, let me handle Kate; it's bad enough that we're doing this, going behind her back." *It's bad enough that I'm doing what I'm doing to her, without you guys making it clear that I'm doing it publicly.* "She's the one that's got to take this mess to Harper, you know. I don't have the guts or the clout to do that."

The three ConSecs chuckled and Rand racked up one point for himself: they'd be okay, they were reacting just right in all the clinches.

"All right. Now, the door, Foster, if you please."

And into the corridor they went, while Rand broached the subject of the three "doing a little moonlighting for my company on this downtime you've got coming, gentlemen." It might cover their visit, and he'd already cleared their participation through channels: he had to establish a staff up here, and a reason to be seen with these men. The paperwork for their "leave" and the funds for him to pay them were on the way.

He just wondered if it was still a valid cover: blowing away a Soviet vehicle wasn't the best way to keep your profile low, not on the moon. He wished, not for the first time as he walked the commercial corridor with the uniformed ConSecs beside him, that there were more people up here, more confusion, more room to hide.

But there wasn't. Rand had almost told Kate last night that attempts at keeping their mission covert were bound to fail. He still thought that was so. He might as well put a sign on his back that said AGENT AT WORK.

The ConSecs knew some tricks he didn't: they found a government-only elevator and cut out half the corridor walking between the commercial zone and the embassy offices in the government sector.

There Crane flashed his humorless smile and got them past three checkpoints without so much as a document being offered. It should have been comforting, but it wasn't. The question nobody had asked, even in Rand's office, was bothering him tremendously: what had precipitated the dark-side event?

Either it was coincidence that the truckski had locked on to Crane's crawler, or somebody was monitoring WAR-LORD every step of the way, somebody inimical to its completion. Crane's sabotage theory was looking better and better, although yesterday Rand had been willing to discount it, as Harper kept suggesting he do.

Kate's office had an anteroom and a human receptionist, a pleasant young man who recognized him with a cheery "Hello, Dr. Rand," before catching sight of the three uniforms trailing in Rand's wake.

He'd have to get these men into civilian clothes if this kept up, he realized. But first things first. He leaned both hands on the receptionist's desk and said very quietly, "We've got an emergency, for Brittany only. Can you get us in there right away?"

The receptionist frowned, chewing his stylus, and looked at the computer screen set into his desktop. "She's not with anyone right now, sir. . . . Take a seat and I'll check."

Foster said something uncomplimentary under his breath about having to wait. Rand ignored it: Foster was still Crane's to discipline and probably would remain so. The three ConSecs sat, but Rand didn't. Sitting was one of the most difficult moon maneuvers for him to get used to. It was easier to stand. Whenever he sat he wanted to hold on to something or strap himself in. So he hovered by the desk until the receptionist showed them into Kate's office.

"Well," she said, her face flushed, "this is an unpleasant surprise. All three of them? Was this absolutely necessary, Trace? How do you think we're going to cover the four of you roaming the corridors like some gang of—"

"Kate, they blew up a Soviet surveillance truck on the dark side," Rand said. "If you're worried about covering something, worry about that."

She didn't even bother to act surprised. She sat back in her chair, running a stylus through the short hair at her temple. "I know. Ilya called me. He was . . . unhappy. There's nothing to cover—at least not yet. He says it was a drone—no one on board. Do you understand?"

"No," said Rand.

"That's something," said Crane, while behind him the two ConSecs exchanged loaded looks.

"Well, for your benefit then, Trace: with no human casualties, there's no need to admit the incident, Ilya thinks. At least until he can find out more about it himself."

"What's that supposed to mean?" said Rand, forgetting the ConSecs in his audience.

"What it means, Dr. Rand, is that I don't want to talk about it until I know what I'm talking about. For the moment, there'll be no official inquiry." She shifted her gaze to Crane. "I assume you didn't log this?"

"No ma'am."

Rand winced at Crane's choice of address but had to let it ride.

"Good. Don't do anything until I tell you. Is that clear? Until *I* tell you. And put in for your ground leaves, the three of you—we can't have you following Trace around like a pack of hounds in uniform. It's too hard to explain. Now, if you'll excuse us, soldiers, Dr. Rand and I have private matters to discuss."

"Yes ma'am," said Crane, all ice. "Sir, we'll leave word where we'll be, if you need us later." He motioned his people and with peremptory farewells, all three left the room.

When the door sighed shut, Kate leaned forward, elbows on her desk, and said, "How dare you? Under whose authority do you—"

"I'm sorry, Kate, but they showed up at my office. Let's not sweat the protocol, okay? I brought them right to you. All they want is to know they didn't screw up. They don't trust dips; it's the military mindset, that's all."

Her face was still stony and he wanted to take her in his arms and soothe her. But this was neither the time nor the place. "Look, I was coming over here anyway; I think I need help with this ESA tour business." What he really wanted to talk about was Ilya Palladin: what she and Palladin had agreed about the shoot on the dark side, what she thought the Soviets would do.

But it wasn't the time for that, either.

"Fine, Trace. I'll take you over there now. But in return, you'll do me a favor."

"Anything, Katy—" He didn't finish enunciating her nickname. Somehow, it wasn't appropriate anymore, not the way things were between them. He wanted to say that anything was fine with him, as long as it got them back on track. But that wasn't appropriate here and now, either.

"Good. You stay out of my personal life. You stay out of my command structure except where your security or mission security is involved. From now on, it's just business."

"However you want it," he replied, hoping that she didn't really mean it, that her anger was simply a reaction to the crisis Crane's people had precipitated. What he really hoped was that he'd misunderstood what she'd meant when she'd said that she was reserving judgment until Ilya Palladin could "find out more about it."

You didn't go to the opposition for help in deciding how you were going to respond to an incident of open hostility between the superpowers. At least, Tracey Rand didn't.

# Chapter 7

# EUROPEAN SPACE AGENCY

Coming into the ESA arrival lounge, Kate could feel the tension jumping between her body and Trace Rand's as if it were as physical and visible as lightning jumping from pole to pole. Things were just as bad as she'd feared they'd become, with him up here.

Possibly worse. Ilya was caught up in some sort of internal wrangle. He couldn't tell her exactly what, of course, but his voice and his words spoke volumes. And all because of Rand's trigger-happy ConSecs—damned Q-group that wouldn't even have been on the scene (and certainly not on her conscience) if it weren't for Tracey Rand.

Coming on the heels of the abortive night she and Ilya had spent together on her arrival, the incident involving the Soviet drone was just too much. It was straining her relationship with the single most important contact she had on the moon. And Ilya deserved better—better from her than she'd managed, at any rate. She resolved that, as soon as she saw Trace safely integrated into the ESA tour group, she'd call Ilya, offer dinner and whatever—make amends, at least personally.

Trace didn't understand, couldn't understand, that Ilya Palladin was one of the most valuable allies she had here— that the U.S. had, even though he wasn't her spy. In

Trace's world, there were no shades of gray. You were on his side, or you weren't; you gave one hundred percent, or nothing at all. He'd never make a diplomat, and his presence in what was increasingly a diplomatic situation could lead only to more trouble.

She should have known; she should have listened to her instinct. She should have said something to Bates when she'd had the chance, submitted a formal dissenting opinion. She should have done something. Now it was too late.

She'd failed to act because she'd assumed that her doubts and fears about him stemmed from purely personal qualms. She'd forgotten that wherever Trace went, chaos was sure to follow.

Chaos was the last thing they needed here on the moon, so close to the opening of the Space Talks. She and Ilya would brainstorm all night, trying to find a way to keep the dark-side shoot from becoming a diplomatic hot potato. Then she'd see what she could do to get Tracey Rand sent groundside and to hell with WARLORD.

She snorted aloud and Rand looked over at her questioningly. Involuntarily, she closed her eyes as she said, "Nothing. Just a frog in my throat." Why was it, when she looked at this man, every sensible thought she had flew out the window? For everyone's health and well-being, she'd have to get away from him. Or else she was going to be useless in the difficult days ahead.

When she opened her eyes again, he was still watching her with mild curiosity. Behind him, the ESA contingent was beginning to emerge from the corridor leading from the dock. There were half a dozen newbies, Chandra and his assistant, Robin Faragher, in the midst of them. The newcomers were clumsy, gawking, flushed with excitement.

Like Trace had so recently been. He'd adjusted well, and fast. As if reading her mind, he reached out a tentative hand to her and said, "You know, we still haven't given my sixth-G performance its final rating."

Sexual innuendo, personal charm, all the right moves at just the wrong time. She said, "And we're not going to, at least not until I get this mess your goons made straightened out."

"Kate, I had nothing to do with that. I didn't even know about it. . . ." Spread hands, innocent look.

"Like you don't even know about the repercussions, or the consequences? The trail of destruction in your wake isn't your business, is it? Better ask yourself, Trace, how much WARLORD's worth."

His mouth tightened into a thin line. He said, "*You,* you mean? Come on, Kate, get off my case. You know, I wouldn't even be up here if you hadn't seconded Bates and Andresson's motion."

*Checkmate, you bastard.* "Even I can make a mistake. I'm going to be spending the evening with Ilya, trying to undo what you've done," she declared defiantly.

"I don't see how you read it that way, but you're entitled to your own opinion." He gazed beyond her, at the new arrivals. "I'd like you to tell me that you and your Soviet friend aren't compromising one another—and both your missions—for personal reasons. I'd like you to explain how come you're waiting for a KGB man to tell you what you need to know and what you ought to think about that truckski incident. But I don't think you will and I'm not going to force the issue. I'm not going to write a memo or lose any sleep over it. I'm just going to do my job."

"And the devil take the hindmost," she replied bitterly. "Just like old times."

"That's right," he said. "Now you do yours. Introduce me into that party and go about your business. If you want me, you know where to find me."

*God, I hate it when we fight. I hate you, sometimes. I'd like to slap your sanctimonious face.* But she couldn't do that, not here, not now. And he *was* just doing his job. Only this time, she was in a position where that job was one that was threatening hers—maintaining equilibrium and information flow between the various embassy stations.

"Let's go then," she answered him, shifting the folio under her arm, and led the way toward Chandra, deftly cutting through lesser functionaries and a babble of French, German, and Italian to reach him.

There were more than twenty-five people clustered around Chandra, his assistant, and their group—ESA maintained a presence in space not only for the European Economic Community, but for its once-colonial allies. Thus Chandra, the half-Indian diplomat who headed the new metallurgy project, was a favorite son not only of the Brits, but of the nonwhites from Sri Lanka to Gabon.

On the moon, little matters like religious affiliation and regional grudges tended to melt away, leaving larger issues to stand clearly defined. The LDCs—Lesser Developed Countries—had no foothold here except the largess of the great powers. Yet they were here, mostly on ESA money and ESA sufferance. Hence, India had satellites and satellite link stations with computer-imaging capability, even though on Earth they were still drawing on whitewashed walls.

It was the only way, Kate Brittany had come to believe, to redress the disparities and balance the inequities between the lesser and more developed countries: give those nations a stake in space, in technology, in the future. Raise the hopes and opportunities of all by raising the ceiling of available dreams, and trust that eventually even the most impoverished would benefit.

Everything else had been tried. There was no way to eliminate poverty, suffering, and primitivism in a few generations, let alone in a chosen year or single lifetime. Somewhere on Earth, in the Congo or along the Amazon or in the Australian outback, remnants of Stone Age man still lived tribally, even while Trace Rand and Kate Brittany argued on the moon. In a way, it didn't bother her— the range of civilization could only be expanded from its

201

farthest frontier. The lunar contingent was the newest link of an unbroken chain comprising every phase of mankind's development since he'd become a toolmaker. It wasn't fair, but it was encouraging, that every interim step from the nomad to the astronaut was represented somewhere, at this moment, among the teeming billions of humans that the Earth supported.

Someday the poorest would be less poor, the uneducated educated, the primitive civilized. For now, all people like Kate Brittany could do was push the envelope, strive for excellence, make the first strides that would beat a path to the unexplored future. Once that future was available, those on Earth could decide whether to take part in it. You had to start somewhere.

Today, that somewhere was in the ESA lounge, where Chandra's black eyes were shining and his purple lips stretched over white teeth in a broad *chatoyant* smile. "Excuse me, Dr. Chandra," she said as the crowd bumped her toward him. "I'm Secretary Kate Brittany, from the U.S. Mission, perhaps you remember me. We met at—"

"Of course," said Chandra, his long lashes fluttering over slightly bulgy eyes. "From Washington. And your companion . . . ?"

"Dr. Rand, yes. Dr. Rand would like to join your party for the orientation tour, if that would be acceptable? I've cleared it through channels, all I need is your okay."

"Ah," said Chandra, making a show of deliberation. "So we shall trade favors? In return then, you must"—he pursed his lips gravely, then widened his eyes as if a brilliant idea had just occurred to him—"join my little family for dinner at the ESA facility this evening. Tut, tut; I will brook no argument. Eight o'clock, then?"

Out of the corner of her eye, Kate saw Rand striking up a conversation with Robin Faragher. *Go ahead, Trace. Get yourself messed up with Ms. Unknown Quantity. Her tits'll make it worth your while.* She didn't care what he did anymore. She didn't care if he shacked up with Chandra himself. She had to get back to her office and find a way to meet Ilya somewhere secure so that they could implement some damage control, and do it before the dinner she'd just been roped into attending.

"Twenty hundred hours, then, Dr. Chandra," she said lightly. "Take good care of my friend." That was all she had to say; Chandra was aware of her cautioning undertone. Hopefully, he'd not have to work too hard at it: for a man who couldn't yet remember that they were on twenty-four hour time—Greenwich Mean—Chandra was doing pretty well. By the end of his orientation, the Indian wasn't likely to be so blithe or so cocky. There was lots to learn about Cop One, not the least of that being the degree to which the ESA contingent depended upon the U.S. for its survival.

They didn't have their own lunar station, even. And Chandra was putting conditions on what should have been a simple diplomatic courtesy. Angry at both the Indian for demanding hours of her precious time at a dinner bound to be boring and full of verbal snipers, and at Rand for cozying up to Faragher when Kate had nearly managed to forget the woman, she handed Chandra his official letter of welcome from the U.S. Mission and worked her way out of the crowd.

By the time Rand caught her eye, there were a dozen people between them. She waved desultorily and called, "Have a nice trip," as she hurried toward one of the government access corridors.

What Trace did with his time was his business. Hers, for the foreseeable future—at least until dinner—was going to be taken up with Ilya and joint damage control.

Thinking of how Rand would have reacted if he'd known what she had in mind, she grinned wickedly to herself as she began searching for a likely excuse to go over to Sveboda in person.

Even if it did nothing more, her presence there would convince Ilya that she was still on his side, wholeheartedly.

And that might be the most important thing she could do right now.

Robin Faragher was saying, "All this is really much more splendid than I'd imagined," in an undertone as the ESA tour guide shepherded the eleven people in his party into the metallurgy facility that would be project director Chandra's new home.

"Pretty fancy," Rand agreed, "from what I've seen elsewhere, at least." The woman was spectacular in an athletic way; her blond hair swung freely about her head in the lesser gravity with every overpowered step she took. The hips that propelled her kept snagging his attention; he wanted to put his hand on her waist but it really wasn't appropriate.

Anyway, she'd invited him to the welcoming dinner and wasn't shutting down any of his careful advances. What happened after the dinner was probably going to depend on how far he pushed things.

It troubled him only a little that Faragher—that Robin— was making sure he understood that. It might be simple physical attraction. She was a healthy animal. It was probably something much more sinister. She was in all likelihood an intelligence collector for someone. He'd thought so since she'd tried to snag him at the Low Earth Orbit party; it hadn't scared him then; it didn't scare him now.

For her to do her job and for him to do his job, they had to interact with one another. It gave their meetings an extra spice. It wasn't so much whether he could get into her pants as what he might be trading to do it.

In her face he thought he saw questions mirroring his own—and answers. Her eyes were full of challenge; her steps were too steady to be the reason her breast brushed his arm so often. It was a boy-girl game, one he was playing with all he had.

Maybe harder than he would have played if it weren't for Kate. Damned woman was impossible to please. But he'd always known that. They had ideological differences that were fucking insurmountable. You could bridge them temporarily, to work together. But you couldn't eradicate them.

And Kate was dangerous. Even now, when she wasn't on the scene, she was getting him into trouble. "Excuse me, I didn't hear?" he said to Faragher, who deserved his full attention and wasn't getting it.

"I said, Dr. Rand, that you've adjusted so quickly to all this, I'll have my work cut out for me trying to do as well."

"Trace. And don't sweat it—the first couple nights you think you're falling out of bed, but find something to hold on to, and you'll sleep okay."

"Something like another person?"

Bingo. "You bet," he replied, deadpan. "Need a volunteer?"

"Perhaps. I'll keep it in mind." She smiled like heaven.

They were filing through ESA's twelve-by-thirty-four-foot metallurgy lab, toward the new offices that Chandra and his staff would occupy. He followed in Robin's wake through the hall, past banks of hardware, into the softly carpeted office complex. From what he'd seen of the U.S. commercial corridor, he hadn't been expecting this much luxury.

But then, ESA subsidized its manufacturing ventures, like the EEC subsidized its manufacturers on Earth. It wasn't fair but it made the European firms viciously competitive with the American independent contractors.

Beyond the three adjoining ESA-METALLE office suites was a small corridor containing living quarters. Rand stopped at the access hatch. "I'll wait here. There's no reason for me to go—"

"Come. Come on, don't be shy," said Robin, a temptress with a wickedly incipient pout.

Great. He went, wondering if what he was wondering could possibly happen, here and now.

Somehow, she managed to keep opening and closing the doors of her cubicle's cabinets until everyone but Rand had filed out and along the corridor. He stood in the doorway, arms crossed. "If we lose the party, I can't be much help finding them again. I'm new here myself, remember?"

Her butt was fetchingly displayed as she rooted under the counters in her "kitchenette." When she straightened up, she pushed her mass of hair out of her eyes and said, "We'll find them, sometime between now and dinner-time."

Her eyes met his and locked on like a targeting array and he couldn't quite believe that he was going to get this lucky.

But then her fingers went to the zipper on her jumpsuit, between her breasts, and she said, "In or out, Trace?"

He stepped in and the door closed behind him.

# Chapter 8

# FILES

Palladin still had Ruskin in his office when his assistant buzzed him to say that "Secretary Brittany is on her way to see you. A priority matter, she claims."

Ruskin, who was sweating visibly in his seat but still pugnacious, allowed a sneer to settle on his doughy, pugnosed face.

"Thank you. When she enters Svoboda, you will inform me, so that I can dispense with this other matter in good time," Palladin told the voice at the other end of his desktop terminal. "Meanwhile, have two security guards sent here, prepared to take a person into custody, a person whom they will place under close arrest."

He snapped the toggle down and looked up to see if the sneer was still on Ruskin's face. It was. This was very troubling.

Palladin came around his desk and towered over the seated KGB major. "Ruskin—Oleg, be reasonable. Explain to me your motives for dispatching this drone without my approval, and upon whose orders you have been acting. Give me the code names for any operations such as this one that has just gone so badly, and things will go easier with you. Surely there is *someone* at Moscow Center who can verify that you are not acting on your own, out of perfidious reasons, or in order to sell the information you have gathered?'' He paused.

Ruskin stared at him, unblinking.

Palladin continued. ''Surely telling me the name of your contact is better than letting me—and my superiors—assume that you are collecting information that you then sell on the open market. You know how we deal with such spies.''

Ruskin merely shook his head as if Palladin was some deluded child. And this was most distressing. If Ruskin had been afraid, it would have been less frightening. The agent's silence suggested that Ruskin had nothing to be afraid of, and Palladin did not want to believe this was the case.

Even if the agent was certain that whatever faction he worked for would support him—go so far as to save him—Ruskin still should be concerned about his safety in the interim. Palladin could, without recourse to Moscow Center, order Ruskin shot. Beneath Sveboda, in the miles of tunnels boring toward Cop One through the lunar bedrock, guns posed no safety hazard except to their target; no precious oxygen would be lost, except from the pressure suit of the victim.

Something must have showed in Palladin's face as he considered this alternative, for Ruskin shifted in his seat and said, *"Sekretar,* you are meddling where you do not belong. In things you do not understand, *tovarishch.''*

*Tovarishch:* comrade. Was Ruskin warning him off? Palladin's spine stiffened. "Then, for your own sake, *'tovarishch,'* you had better tell me in what I am meddling.''

Ruskin's face paled further. ''You do not want to know these things, *Sekretar*—Moscow Center does not want you to know them. I suggest you forget what you think you have learned and go about your business.''

Fury began rising in Palladin's throat. ''The lost drone *is* my business. One cannot ignore this. The Americans will not; we cannot. You will explain, *now!''*

Ruskin shook his head. "You are asking for troubles, you know this? Ask your Western contact, whom you call Khimik, to explain your situation. Or ask the KGB *Predsedated* personally." With a smirk, Ruskin stretched out in his chair and crossed his ankles.

Palladin's heart was a block of ice, had been since the mention of Khimik, the code name of his Western source. He'd asked Ruskin for code names, and now he had one. If that were not enough to frighten him, the invocation of KGB's chairman, the *Predsedated,* should have been. But Palladin was in too deep for fright. Fright came when a man outstripped his capabilities, when his subconscious knew he could not prevail. Palladin could—no, must—prevail. It was the only way to save himself.

"I will indeed ask Moscow Center," he said. "And my other sources. None of this avails you. I want to know about the drone—on whose orders it was dispatched, and what other—"

"You want to *know,*" Ruskin said acidly, "more than you are trusted to know. We have kept you ignorant, you and your American slut. If you want to know things, ask her. Ask her about WARLORD. Ask her about her assault group, the ZR/SEALs. Ask her about a man named Davies, who would have proposed, at the Space Talks, that the Soviet Union deflect the course of its tunnels. . . ." Triumphantly, Ruskin sat up straight. "Deflect them from the course on which they now are bent, deflect them from their path, right under the American Cop One Station. You must realize, Palladin, that it is long since you have been trusted to know such things. And that, if any harm comes to me, it will be clear that you are the traitor we suspect you to be. So you are in your own trap, *Sekretar!* And I dare you to call Moscow Center! I wait with anticipation; once you do, I will be sitting in your seat!" Spittle flew from Ruskin's mouth with his last words.

Palladin nodded his head stiffly. "I see. I'm sorry, Oleg Ruskin. You have brought this upon yourself. Now give me the names of those in Moscow Center whom you think will validate you.''

Palladin didn't really care to hear those names, but he took them down as Ruskin boldly named three men high in the Moscow power structure, including the KGB chairman himself.

By that time, his assistant had informed him that the security guards were waiting. When she sent them in, Palladin looked at the two guards who now flanked the prisoner and said flatly, ''Take this traitor into the tunnels and shoot him.''

Ruskin had not been expecting that. He jumped up from his chair, his face a mask of horror, protesting loudly. He bolted for the door, but the two guards caught him.

When one guard had covered Ruskin's mouth with his hand and there was silence in which to speak, Palladin addressed the huge eyes staring at him over the guard's hand.

''Your mistake, Ruskin, was in assuming that anyone on Earth could protect a traitor on the moon.'' He turned to the guards. ''Keep this man's mouth closed. It spews treachery. Bring me back proof that he is dead.''

One of the guards smiled thinly. Proof would be provided: an ear, a hand, a more private part, for this guard was of Mongol extraction. ''You may go,'' Palladin said calmly, and the guards dragged the struggling Ruskin away.

When the door had closed behind them, Palladin sat at his desk and put his head in his hands. A mess, a dangerous mess. He had no doubt that Ruskin was telling the truth: there were factions in KGB; every man of Palladin's stature had enemies. He would trump up some suitable story, backtracking from the result—Ruskin's execution—to the cause—the destruction of the drone—making it seem to be clear proof of Ruskin's espionage. He would then send the entire report down to Moscow Center, to the chairman's own office.

This would show that Palladin was not to be trifled with;

that neither intimidation nor blackmail would avail any person attempting to deal with him. That Ruskin knew the name of Palladin's Western source proved nothing. The source, Palladin would maintain under any degree of pressure, was a collector of his; there was no treason in that relationship, at least not on Palladin's part.

The most likely conclusion to be drawn from what he'd learned from Ruskin was only that there was a move under way in certain quarters to replace Palladin. Palladin, too, had friends at the center. He had faith in his own ability to undo whatever damage Ruskin and his cronies had done to Palladin's position and reputation.

If Palladin discovered that there were more like Ruskin at Sveboda, he would proceed as if he had unearthed a nest of vipers; he would stamp them out. He was station chief; he would wield his power. What bothered him was the quality of Ruskin's information—especially about Kate's ZR/SEAL connections.

He began composing a priority request for data on the upcoming Space Talks, on the recently deceased Nathan Davies, and on something called WARLORD, about which he had heard nothing from anyone until Ruskin invoked it like a curse.

When he'd written the request, he read it over carefully. Certain now that it would serve as a tacit warning to whomever groundside might be acting against him, and that it would go up the wires to the chairman's very office, he sent it by hand from his desktop encryption system.

Just as the system beeped its verification that his message had been received in good order, his assistant buzzed him again: Kate Brittany had arrived.

Palming his eyes, Palladin waited a full minute before he told his assistant to send Kate in. He didn't want her to see any uncertainty, any fear, any doubt in his face, even though he was now aware that he was fighting for his professional—and perhaps his physical—life.

Somewhere down there, on the beautiful blue planet below, a determination had been made that Ilya Palladin could not be trusted with certain data. At best, those who had made that determination were of the hardliners, men who would as soon precipitate an open confrontation with the U.S. as maintain the stalemate.

There were such men in both governments. Palladin was not one of them. It seemed to him, going back over what he'd learned from Ruskin, that the mention of the tunnels suggested that Ruskin's orders were coming from that quarter, and not from KGB's general tasking staff.

It was possible, in an organization so labyrinthine and polarized, that even the chairman might be involved in a provocation scheme without daring to admit to the politburo that this was so. If such was the case, Palladin had his trump in hand—if he dared to use it. If Ruskin was correct in inferring that the routing of the tunnels toward Cop One was a deliberate attempt to raise tensions and/or a covert attempt to begin a subterranean surveillance operation, then there were many reasons that Palladin might not have been informed.

There were also many reasons that no one in the general staff would have been informed. Once the principals knew that Ruskin had been executed by Sveboda's commanding officer, they would pull in their horns, go to ground, or launch a counterattack. It remained only to wait and see which course of action his enemies chose.

For they were enemies. His authority had been subverted; his loyalty had been called into question. Ruskin had assumed that Palladin would believe that any steps taken against Ruskin would prove to those enemies that Palladin was a traitor, and thus Ruskin was safe from Palladin. Ruskin had even attempted, in his clumsy way, to force Palladin to silent complicity by mentioning Palladin's Western contact, Khimik. If Palladin had not been so certain of his source, he might have been frightened into agreement. The source could be used against him, he'd always known that. The source, like Kate Brittany, was a calculated risk, one that could be touted as treachery in certain quarters.

Again, like Kate. He took his hands from his eyes and told his assistant to send her in.

When she entered, her forehead furrowed and her face pale, he met her halfway, exuding calm and capability.

"What is it, my dear?" he asked innocently, putting his arms around her for a chastely diplomatic embrace.

"What is it? I rushed all the way over here because I'm afraid the drone shoot is going to blow up in our faces, and I end up cooling my heels in your antechamber. Aren't you even a little bit worried?" She pulled back in his arms and peered at him harshly. "Ilya, what's going on here? We've got to do some quick thinking, or else I don't understand what's happening."

She was trembling. It warmed his heart that she was so concerned; more, that she understood enough to be so concerned. But he was not willing to be indiscreet, not yet. He was still Sveboda's KGB resident.

He escorted her to the chair before his desk and as she seated herself, still looking up at him inquisitively, he said, "Kate, this incident has brought up many questions. Questions that should be discussed by you and me, privately, before they become public."

"I knew it," she muttered. "Ilya, I'll do the best I can to help you. We're sorry. It was unilateral action taken by a trigger-happy security man. We've got to convince your people of that."

He nodded, going around the desk to take his own seat. "We will, if you and I can act in concert and in full knowledge of the situation."

She blew out a tremulous breath. "Good. I guess that means you haven't had any orders from groundside to make a mountain out of this molehill. Did you find out anything about why the drone was there or who dispatched it?"

"I found . . . questions, as I said. Questions about Nathan Davies. Questions about a combat unit called ZR/

SEAL, of which, unless my sources are in error, not only Davies, but yourself and Dr. Rand were once members."

Kate winced but said nothing, twisting her hands in her lap.

"Questions, Catherine, about something called WARLORD." He was studying her carefully as he spoke the word. Her face was completely impassive, totally controlled.

She stared at him silently for a lengthy interval. "WARLORD?" she repeated finally, her brows knitting. "Ilya, I don't know what you mean . . . WARLORD is our darkside radio telescope, nothing sinister. I'll take you to see it if you like. I came over here to talk about the dark-side shoot. If you don't think we need to close ranks on this, I'll be on my way."

"No, please, I'm glad you came. And you were right to come—we have much to do."

# Chapter 9
# PLAYERS

Seeing all the players in one place made Tracey Rand nervous. Harper's luxurious lunar residence ought to have been reassuring, but crowded with ESA dignitaries, U.S. embassy types, and commercial corridor mavens, the mauve-and-ivory dining hall reminded him of a well-appointed coffin.

One well-placed incendiary and the whole party would become past tense, a statistic, an unavoidable accident. Rand's back was crawling and the sight of Crane, Marshall, and Foster in their full-dress ConSec grays didn't relax him one bit. Crane nodded to him and began making his way toward Rand, alone by the open bar, through a confusion of women and saris and chadors.

Rand looked around for Kate and didn't see her, finding Robin Faragher arm in arm with Harper instead. He didn't see anyone from Sveboda, either, and that bothered him: ComBloc had been invited, should have sent someone. Unless, as Rand's jangled nerves were whispering, this oversized cubicle was populated with sitting ducks.

His eyes lingered on Faragher, on the glistening hair (naturally pale, he'd found out), on the scintillating smile. With her, interrogation had led to infatuation. He wasn't sure which of them had won the sparring match in her cube, but he'd had one hell of a good time. He couldn't imagine not continuing to suspect her, as close at hand as he could manage.

"Hey, boss," said Crane casually.

"Not until tomorrow, when your paperwork kicks in, I'm not," Rand reminded the slit-eyed operator before him. Beyond the ConSec lieutenant's head, Rand could see Crane's men, interspersed between their leader's back and the entryway, their eyes raking the crowd for ringers. Sabotage tended to make you paranoid. "Heard from Bates?"

Rand had detailed Crane to cross-check Faragher, Chandra, and anything else he could think of while filing his report on the truckski incident.

Crane shrugged. "Sort of. Those ESA types are squeaky clean, we're told." Crane's mouth hardly moved; around it were stress lines. Crane was here because he was making damned sure nobody could construe his absence, or his team's, as a sign of guilt or reprimand. As far as Crane was concerned, he hadn't screwed up when he'd attacked the truckski. That determination was broadcast by every line of his body and the jut of his chin. "We're to proceed with caution." His lip curled at the last word.

If they'd been somewhere else, Rand would have squeezed the younger man's shoulder or said something candid and revealing. Here, the little Crane had told him was risky enough. "This place is making me nervous," Rand offered instead, noticing a small box on Crane's belt, beeper-sized, with a red light indicating that its counter-surveillance function was engaged.

"Shows you're awake." Crane shrugged again, an irritable gesture from a man to whom affairs such as this were punishment. "Sveboda ought to send somebody over, you know? Doesn't look right, not to."

"I was thinking that. Unless there's a reason."

"Your girlfr— Brittany was still over there, last I checked. That bother you?"

"I— Not professionally." Rand's turn to make a dis-

216

missive gesture. "Been busy myself, with the newbies. Faragher told me ESA's getting a tour of the radio telescope installation tomorrow—the whole bunch of them. That good or bad for us?"

Behind Crane, Marshall shifted his stance, ostensibly to take a canapé from a tray, and Rand saw Kate and Ilya Palladin enter, arms interlocked.

Crane was saying, "Good, if you want to go over there with them and stay behind. Bad only if they're covering for somebody with the equipment to check for nuke signatures. Might as well use 'em as camouflage, though—if you're ready to go?"

"I'm as ready as I'm going to get," Rand said. The nuclear material for WARLORD's launch couldn't be stashed in orbit, as the rest of the components had been; shielding nukes sufficiently to guarantee that they could pass for space junk was impossible. So the nuke drivers were under meters of lunar regolith beneath the radio telescope installation. Crane, Marshall, and Foster would help him with the final assembly, which included boosting the nukes into orbit without the Soviets getting a whiff of their spoor. It wasn't going to be easy, but it was all planned for long ago.

WARLORD could have been enabled without nukes, if the two-plus years' wait necessary to slingshot non-nuke drivers around Jupiter was acceptable to this administration. It hadn't been. Rand had argued heatedly against nuke components before leaving the project. By the time he was brought back in, that consideration was moot. No one seemed to care that nuclear components tainted the mission beyond what was acceptable in the case of discovery or even postoperation revelation. Nukes equaled warmaking in too many minds at home; nukes equaled "weapons of mass destruction" in every space treaty. Nuking Mars wasn't going to go down well with civilians, let alone hostile governments who wanted to make WARLORD a further example of American imperialism, especially since the nukes would knock out functioning Soviet equipment already emplaced on Martian soil.

But Rand hadn't been brought in to make policy, only to implement some distorted operational goals. By the time he'd realized the degree of WARLORD's perversion, it had been too late to turn back. Now, the only thing to do was win, and win big: launch WARLORD, and make sure that nobody knew enough to start screaming until the payload package impacted Mars, took out the Soviet drone explorers, and the U.S. could calmly blame the whole impact scenario on sunspots and Martian dust storms.

God, it was thin. It was so thin that Rand had been wondering whether that very thinness hadn't been what killed Richelson, Davies, Blake, Kendall, and Frank. He'd wondered that until the attempted sabotage of the TAV gave him grounds to stop suspecting Harper, and (if truth be known) Bates and Andresson and everybody else in his own government who were savvy enough to have the same qualms about WARLORD's impact on cislunar politics that Rand himself did.

Now, he was just wondering—about everything and everybody. Harper was probably expendable, if U.S. interests were nervous enough about WARLORD's repercussions. Or Harper could have been part of an attempt to scare Rand and the ConSecs off; the whole sabotage incident in the TAV could have been played for effect, never meant to succeed in the first place. Bates and Andresson could be burying WARLORD forever while seeming to sanction it by neutralizing all capable field personnel. Rand couldn't count the number of times in recent history that it had happened before: stack the deck, sabotage your own outfit; satisfy the politicians that the situation had degenerated sufficiently that indoctrinating new personnel wasn't worth the risk when the casualty rate of the previous teams had been so high and their effectiveness so low.

Or it could well be that Soviet intelligence had been tracking WARLORD all along. Knowledge was power to act; knowledge of a project like WARLORD would impel any cognizant intelligence service like KGB, too adversarial to consider complaining through channels and too conserving of its assets to risk losing them by admitting to having such sensitive information, to do everything in its power to force the U.S. to shut down WARLORD before launch.

And then there was Kate, coming toward him with her Soviet boyfriend, the two of them thick as thieves. Who could know what ZR/SEAL's last aborted mission and the intervening years had done to her? Sometimes people decided that the only way to help their country might be through actions perceived as treasonous by that nation; it came from working against the intractable inertia of huge bureaucratic systems in which all right action was neutralized by personal bias among bureaucrats.

He'd given a lot of thought to Kate and Ilya Palladin. He was going to shake the truth out of her and, if it wasn't dangerous to his health, accept whatever she told him. He owed her that much. But he didn't owe her any more than that. Robin Faragher had asked him bluntly, during that magical interval in her quarters, if Kate had something against him.

The implications had rocked him to his soul, even though Faragher had blithely gone on to other, more pressing matters of personal gratification. Kate was as likely a culprit as any more distant player in the matter of ZR/SEAL deaths. He hadn't looked squarely at the possibility previously because he didn't want to think about it. Unequivocal exoneration could come only with Kate's death. And he didn't want to find out that way. He wanted to keep her alive; it had been part of the reason he'd taken this mission. But she'd been the only Seal vet who'd been continuously on board since the unit's dissolution.

He shook his head and muttered, "Say again, Crane?"

Crane's gaze was on Faragher, Rand realized when he followed it; off to one side, Alicia Harper had intercepted

Kate and Palladin and was introducing them to someone from ESA.

"I said," Crane repeated, "that I heard you and that Faragher woman got separated from her group for a while. Anything you want to tell me?"

"I'm still doing research. She's very forthcoming, some sort of spook, I think, no matter how clean what you got from Bates was. A real pro."

"Have fun, then. We'll be around if you need us, and ready in the morning; we'll provide you a safe vehicle. Can't have you going with ESA, in case it's too tempting."

*If somebody's bent on taking me out in a crowd where the target can't be determined, yeah. Thanks, Crane. I thought of that, too.* And then, because it was starting to matter and these men had to know just where Rand's weight was going to come down in any crisis, he said aloud: "Thanks, I wanted to ask but thought maybe I was getting old and chicken."

"You?" Crane's face broke into a millisecond of honest grin. "Don't sweat it, sir. Ask whatever you want. We'll do our best to get it for you." With a minimal and covert salute, Crane eased away—not far enough to be out of sight or earshot, but far enough that anyone wanting Rand wouldn't feel he was interrupting.

And that was when Kate broke away from Alicia Harper, who was guiding Ilya toward Chandra and Faragher, and made a beeline for him.

"Trace, we've got to talk." Her face was pinched, her diction clipped. She had on a night-blue jumpsuit that hugged every curve.

Suddenly Robin Faragher seemed like a cardboard cutout, a slightly dangerous hand of poker. "What is it?" He knew Kate—something was really wrong. "Can you tell me here?"

"Give me a hug," she suggested.

"With pleasure."

Her lips to his ear, she blurted, "The cat's out of the bag. Ilya knows about WARLORD—I don't know how much, but the code name, anyway. Something heavy's going on at Sveboda. While I was there he took a message he couldn't have me in the room for, and some guard came in with a . . . piece . . . of something—some*one*—in a box."

"Jesus, I wish I had the rank to forbid you to go over there, or to see that guy." He couldn't help it; he had to tell her what he thought or risk wishing forever that he had, if something happened to her. "Things are too hot for you to be messing around with somebody from the other side."

Their embrace was too long for propriety. He felt her try to step back. He locked his arms at her spine and arched back just enough to see her face.

She said, "Ilya's in some sort of trouble; he so much as told me. He wants to see the radio telescope installation. I told him that was what WARLORD was—just the installation's code name. Nothing classified. It won't play long, I know." She bit her lip miserably. "But I had to say something. These ESA people are going over there, I can take him with them. He's being pushed hard, Trace. He might turn for me, now, if we play him right."

Her eyes were very bright, desperate. But he had to be straight with her. "You're not thinking clearly. You can't trust this guy. Not while you're fucking him. For all you know, he's playing you. Compromise you enough, then . . ."

Furious, she pulled back once again and, when he didn't let go, brought her heel down hard on his toe. "Don't give me that crap about how he doesn't respect me because he got into my pants. It says more about you than it does about him."

With the pain of his stomped toe, he'd released her. Now he held out a hand placatingly. "Okay, Kate. Okay. I was out of line, personally—maybe. Bring him along.

221

We've got the whole damn ESA to wet-nurse, one more won't matter. Or better, send him; I don't think you should make the trip. Even Crane thinks it might be accident prone. Look at—''

"Like you? Trace, you're impossible," she gritted through an emotionless, polite smile as she stepped back three paces. "We'll see you in the morning." She turned on her heel and headed back to the Soviet resident, who was gesturing in animated conversation, sandwiched be- tween Chandra and Alicia Harper. Behind them, unobtru- sively doing his job, was Marshall. Rand was willing to bet that Marshall's equipment tonight included directional and highly selective tape-recording equipment.

A good team, Crane's. If Kate were willing to be part of it—or of Rand's—then maybe this thing would go like it should. There was nothing he could say to her. Anything he said, she read as jealousy. Maybe she was right: maybe Ilya Palladin was about to defect, for reasons related or unrelated to the truckski incident or WARLORD. Maybe it mattered.

Rand didn't think so. It felt like misdirection, lateral escalation, or a host of other Soviet tactics meant to con- fuse or demoralize his mission personnel.

If it wasn't any or all of those, it was just luck—bad luck. Feeling like he needed a port in this storm, Rand looked around and saw Robin Faragher watching him pen- sively.

Maybe she was part of what was beginning to seem like a Soviet-directed counterplot. Maybe she was independent. Whatever she was, she was here and she was interesting and she would take his mind off his most pressing problem: Kate Brittany.

The last thing he would have expected was that, now that chips were going down, Kate was either unwilling or unable to believe anything he said, let alone take his ad- vice. The only recourse left to him was to pull rank, give her a direct order to stay away from Palladin, an order she might well disobey. Even though giving that order might save her life, if matters continued to deteriorate, he couldn't bring himself to do it.

Thinking over what Kate had said, he tried to tell himself that the Soviets, at least, weren't going to stage another "accident" on the dark side that would kill ESA personnel and whoever happened to be with them—not with their own KGB resident along. But he couldn't make himself believe it. If Kate's assessment that Palladin was in trouble at Svoboda was accurate, the man's presence tomorrow on the junket to the dark-side radio telescope installation wasn't any kind of protection. It was a downright debit.

Reminding himself to tell Crane to find a way to watch out for Kate—if possible to make sure she was in the team moon truck, even if that meant bringing Palladin along too—he smiled at Faragher and bent to kiss her.

For some reason known only to his gonads, he bestowed that kiss directly under her ear, instead of on her cheek, and said, "We've got an early turnout tomorrow for the ride dark side. Let's make sure you've met everybody you've got to meet, and get out of here."

Robin Faragher met his eyes boldly. "I was afraid you'd never ask."

It wasn't difficult to get out of there, with the beautiful ESA rep on his arm. It made waves, of course—where he wanted it to: Kate looked past him unseeingly while Ilya Palladin frankly stared; Director Harper broke away from his guests to bid them farewell while Alicia Harper tried not to frown; Chandra stopped in midword, his mouth a purple oval for too long before he snapped his jaws shut and waved politely.

And the three ConSecs, together by the door as they approached, broke their knot. Foster swung out the door just before them and, as Rand escorted the tall blond lady through, said, "Hey, sir, goin' to your cube? I left that package there. Maybe I could tag along?"

"You bet, Sergeant." There wasn't any package, but he

was grateful for Crane's quick thinking. Whatever Faragher's provenance, showing a little concerned muscle couldn't hurt. While his mind sorted through the contents of his attaché case for something to give Foster when the three of them arrived at Rand's cubicle, he said, "Sergeant Foster, this is Robin Faragher, Dr. Chandra's mainstay."

"Yessir, I know." The young ConSec grinned ingenuously at Faragher. "Got to admit—I asked."

Foster, bless his unpredictable heart, flushed.

Faragher didn't. She extended one fine hand gravely and murmured, "It's a pleasure, Sergeant. Now I know someone to call if I need help."

The ConSec paced them along the corridor, telling Faragher where to reach him "if you need anything at all, ma'am."

"Until tomorrow, Robin," Rand interrupted, having made up his mind. "Then you call me. Foster and a couple of his friends are signing on to Cislunar Security's team for a while—good for them, since they've got downtime coming; good for me, since I need to demonstrate that Cislunar has personnel on site already familiar with the moon." Sheepdipping was what you called it, if you understood what was happening. He had to trust that Faragher didn't, or that she'd play along.

He never expected her to toss her head mischievously and say, "Tracey, I suppose this is as good a time as any to let you know: Dr. Chandra and I have been talking about hiring your company to see to our security needs here . . . someone more independent than what the U.S. provides would make us all more comfortable. This metallurgy project is a perfect target for high-tech espionage; we're working on processes that may be priceless, if they succeed."

Shining eyes in a porcelain face; acumen behind them that made him shiver. *So why am I trying so hard with you, honey? Maybe I'll sit back and let you do the seducing—and even get you to pay me for it.* "You're offering me the contract for ESA-METALLE?" He controlled his

224

voice rigidly; he avoided any glimpse at Foster's face, keeping his attention on Faragher. And he found himself wishing that Crane was here, instead—someone he could bounce suppositions around with, later, about Faragher's motives.

"That's right." She nodded as they came to a "lift" and pushed the call button. "Assuming we come to financial terms. And, of course, that taking us on won't compromise your chances of getting the U.S. government account you're so obviously trying for."

"It won't," Foster offered hastily, and Rand could have strangled him. "I mean—I know the ropes better than Rand, and I don't mind telling you, ma'am, the betting pool's against old Harper giving that contract out to anybody his wife hasn't vetted." Foster winked and Rand let out a long slow breath as the lift chimed and opened.

"Ah, politics of personal advantage." Faragher nodded sagely. "Well, then, your superior and I will attempt to come to terms, and by tomorrow, if we're lucky, protecting myself, Dr. Chandra, and the rest of the METALLE team will be one of your priorities, Sergeant Foster."

Foster grinned again, broadly. "Great, ma'am. Our pleasure. Now, you and Doc Rand go about your business like I'm not here—like it'll be if everything works out for tomorrow."

"What? And lose this opportunity to glimpse the future? Heaven forbid. Tell me, Sergeant, about the trip dark side—what to expect . . ."

Rand had never been gladder to get out of a lunar lift. Foster couldn't keep this up, he was certain. The youngest, lowest-ranking ConSec was stretching himself, going for brownie points in Rand's eyes. It was too damned risky, especially because Faragher was a totally unknown quantity.

An unknown quantity who wanted to hire him and his to protect her. It didn't make sense with any of his assumptions or preconceptions. He was so disoriented that, for the first time in a couple days, the moon's lower gravity was making him light-headed.

Or maybe it was the wine he'd drunk at Harper's reception. Whatever it was, when they reached the commercial corridor and Rand's cubicle, he signaled Foster to wait by the door. "I'll get that folder for you and be right back, Sergeant."

He escorted Faragher inside and then realized what he'd backed himself into: he had to get out his case and open it with her watching, or else there was nothing to give Foster. And he couldn't risk even implying sham at any level, not yet.

Well, security was what he was supposed to be. "Just take a sec," he promised the woman who was standing uncertainly by the fold-down table, her evening bag clutched in her hand.

The locker he wanted was behind the foldout bed; he had to lower the bed to get at it. He hadn't even bothered to make the bed, and down it came in a tumble of straps and covers. Feeling ludicrous, he reached up and fingered the combination lock, then slipped out the attaché case and opened it.

She wasn't so far behind him that the array of special weapons in custom-cut foam wasn't apparent to her as he grabbed one of the manila envelopes from the organizer in the case's lid.

"My, Tracey," she said as he closed it, locked it, and shoved the case back in the storage compartment. "I'm impressed. But surely you aren't expecting the sort of trouble those—"

"Look, Robin," he said, thoroughly rattled, slamming the locker door shut. "Don't ask those kinds of questions. I'm in business up here—providing extra support for unlikely eventualities." He'd left the bed down and now, sliding past her to Foster, impassive by the door, realized his error as she sat on it.

"Here you go, Foster. Read in and get it back to me by

oh-six-hundred hours." It was the background on ESA personnel; under the circumstances, the whole ConSec team should read it. "Make sure Crane sees it, and have him give me a call if he's got any questions or suggestions—no matter what time."

He almost added, *dismissed,* but it wasn't necessary. Foster understood exactly what he'd seen and what he'd heard. The young ConSec might on occasion be blunt, but he wasn't stupid. "Yessir, we'll take care of it, sir. Have a nice night, sir. Ma'am." Foster stepped out of the doorway and the motion sensor there closed the door automatically.

Rand smothered the impulse to slump against the door and faced Faragher squarely. "Care to tell me what's going—"

She was taking her shoes off. She looked up from under blond hair flopped over one eye and said, "I thought you'd be pleased. It wasn't so simple to talk Chandra into buying extra security when he would like to believe the project's security is guaranteed by the sanctity of pure research." White teeth flashed. Barefoot, she approached him.

He realized he hadn't noticed her clothes until now, while she took them off, a blouk trail she left in her wake as she bore down on him.

"So?" she said, three feet away from him where he was still leaning against the door. "You are angry? I am misconstruing? If you wish just to discuss the business I concocted in order to . . . ."

No need to let her flounder. He reached out and took her hand. She didn't resist as he guided it to his belt. "What do you think?" he said wryly.

Sometimes, you just didn't know what to do with these high-powered professional women. But this wasn't one of those times. She knew exactly what she wanted and the most trouble he had, once his flesh touched hers and her risen nipples brushed his thighs, was reminding himself

227

that it didn't matter what she really wanted, or what she really stood to gain.

Not then, it didn't.

When she lay in the crook of his arm, her chest heaving despite the lower gravity in which they'd performed acrobatic feats of her devising, he said, "You've never been in moon gravity before?"

She replied, "You're asking if I've ever made love in low gravity before? Only once, with you, this afternoon." She rubbed her cheek against his arm, then stretched to nip his neck. "I think it was good, no?" she said with a trace of the Belgian accent her file said must be there.

"Oh, yeah."

"May I ask . . . never mind."

"Come on, don't do that." He came up on one elbow.

She squinted as if in bright light. "What is it, with Ms. Brittany? I see her with the Sveboda liaison. I see the way she looks at you. She has been . . . standoffish, with us. Are you here in some way because of her? Is she . . . under suspicion of something? Or suspecting you of something? Or us?"

The defiant look in Faragher's eyes was consistent with a woman who wanted to know the score for personal reasons.

He answered her that way. "Nothing for you to worry about, whatever the truth of it." *Careful.* "Everybody makes the rounds up here; it's a small community." Like he'd been here long enough to know that. He wanted to defend Kate, to make some excuse for Ilya Palladin, but he couldn't without telling this woman that Kate was intelligence personnel. And he'd been asking himself the same questions, knowing that, so her purported job wasn't any answer. It was barely an excuse.

"What we are doing—this is making the rounds for you?" A scowl came and went above her high-bridged nose.

"It's not, for you?" Defensive. He wasn't good at this.

228

Next Robin Faragher was going to tell him she fell in love with him at first sight.

Instead, she sat up, her movements stiff, scrambling for her clothes as if he'd insulted her.

She was half dressed before he decided it wasn't an act and said, "Hey, come on—I'm sorry."

"You think," she said, her voice muffled because she was trying to buckle her belt with trembling hands, "that I do this as a matter of course. It is fine that you think so, but it is not true. I assumed too much."

He slid off the bed. "Look, I'm sorry, I said. I'm just not used to . . . things moving so fast. I don't want you to go." *Lighten up, fool.* "At least, not until we get the specifics of our deal worked out."

She froze and then she chuckled, her head raised. She nodded. "Apology accepted. Since it is the best you can do." Barefoot but fully clothed, she sat on the bed again, legs dangling, watching him expectantly.

And now he had to play security expert. He considered telling her that Kate's doubts and any subsequent hostility sprang from the data that placed Robin Faragher with Richelson on the skydiving flight that had killed him, but he couldn't bring himself to do it.

Instead, he took a lesser risk. "Okay, Robin. If you want security coverage, you're going to have to tell me what I'm covering. Who and what you are and what you're really doing here."

Robin Faragher ducked her head and then held out her hand. "I am here because my body impelled me, foolish as that sounds. Hiring you was just an excuse to have time together, but there is reason enough. I am no expert, but something is going on up here, something dangerous. There are rumors that your TAV was sabotaged. I am in charge of the day-to-day running of my project—"

"The staff security officer?" It was the only thing that made sense, unless she was more deadly than a woman so vulnerable ought to be. "Is that why you were skydiving with Richelson?'' It just came out. He couldn't help it. ''Picking up tips?''

She looked away from him and her whole body shivered. When she met his eyes again, hers were swimming with tears.

Somehow, she never answered the question. He was holding her and she was telling him about how awful it had been that day when Richelson died.

Somewhere in their long night she admitted that she'd been seconded by ESA security to Richelson for some private training, and been pulled out after the disaster. The relief he felt was palpable.

When he got back from dark side with her, he'd check her story, which wouldn't have come up with regular backgrounding. But he was satisfied.

She'd been hurt. Traumatized. She found the scar that marked the prosthetic that served him for a hip joint and he found himself telling her something about all that.

Which made them fellows, of a sort, and gave him a reason to admit how good her skin felt against his.

When Crane called him at 0600 hours, he was going to regret the lack of sleep, but somehow it didn't matter now. He was nearly convinced that Robin wasn't a threat, that she was simply as bereft of anyone to trust as was he. Her questions about Kate weren't that different from his own; she apologized for asking them and he replied that ''Up here, even a scorecard won't tell you the players.''

''I will trust you,'' she declared, one finger over his lips and the other running down the line of hair descending from his navel. ''Bodies, unlike mouths, do not lie.''

And that was enough to make them allies, stranded on the moon with so much at stake and everything to lose.

# Book Four

# DARK SIDE

# Chapter 1

# SUNSPOTS

In the white room where too many unfamiliar people milled as harried staffers tried to make sure that every ESA guest was properly suited up for the dark-side trip, Kate Brittany was having an anxiety attack, or a crisis of confidence; she couldn't have said which.

But the results were unpleasantly pressing: her mouth was dry, her heart thudding in her temples and her throat, her perspiration acrid. She already had her suit on; once she was sealed into her helmet, she'd be alone with the smell of her fear.

So she put the moment off, circulating among the newcomers, making sure Chandra had everything he needed because Chandra's aide, Faragher, hadn't yet showed.

Chandra said, "Are the sunspots going to be a problem?" The yellowish whites of his eyes seemed excessively bloodshot; his pupils were constricted more than the white-room light could account for. "Should we postpone? The radiation hazard—"

"—isn't significant," she finished for him, though she shouldn't have interrupted. The man was irritatingly self-centered. She didn't realize she had her gloved fists balled on her hips as she continued. "Sunspots of this intensity aren't great for communications, especially from the moon to Earth, Dr. Chandra. But sunspots are like rain, a class of phenomena. Unless you intend to go romping around on the surface for any length of time protected only by your suit, you're safe." *As safe as you're going to get up here, Mr. Diplomat.* "Here, let me check that helmet seal."

With a satisfaction she shouldn't have felt and an impulse she shouldn't have indulged, she took Chandra's helmet from unresisting hands and stretched to place it over the Indian's head. Once she had him sealed off from the world, she stood back and mimed him through his com-check procedures, thinking that at last she'd found a way to shut one of these bastards up.

The sunspots Chandra was worried about were more of a problem to the Seal team than to the forming dark-side expedition: communications with Earth were . . . spotty. She grinned inwardly at the pun, letting her mind seize on anything that would distract it from her real concerns.

But the ploy didn't work. Where the hell was Ilya? And Rand? And that witch Faragher? Ilya had wanted very badly to come along and Kate was intuitively afraid for him: if Ilya's desperation wasn't a ruse, this trip could be the most important one he'd make in his life. She wished Rand were here. She needed to clear procedures for Ilya's possible recruitment and/or defection—before the event. If Ilya didn't propose it, she would. And she had to have the authority to follow through.

Normally, she would have. Arguably, she still did have that much authority, Rand or no Rand. He wasn't a diplomatic operative. Yet, while he was here, he outranked her. She needed at least to inform him of her intent to offer asylum to Ilya Palladin—so provocative an act that, to do it, she needed to make sure she could get Ilya off the moon before any such defection was announced.

International protocol might not be sufficient to protect Ilya, otherwise. He was the sort of defector one smuggled out, on Earth, very carefully. Here, where there was no place to hide, a high-ranking defection could begin a series

of events she hesitated to contemplate: demands by Sveboda officials for Palladin's return; coercion by the inevitable Soviet interviewers who'd come demanding to see
him; armed contingents of Soviet moonbase personnel in
Cop One . . . the ramifications were daunting.

She kept asking herself if, had Ilya not been her lover,
she'd be considering such a risk, and the answer kept coming back *yes*.

So her greatest fear was that, somehow, he would be
prevented from making this trip. Her second greatest was
that Rand would refuse to compromise his mission's security by adding Ilya's troubles to their own.

And neither man was present, though it was less than
half an hour to debarkation. She wandered over to the white
benches circling the white walls, and sat down there, eyes
on the door, wishing she had something to drink. But you
drank as little as possible in a spacesuit; the less you put
in your bladder, the better. Once she put on her helmet,
she could sip from her sealed water supply. Until then,
she'd tough it out rather than risk getting out of her suit to
void any water she'd added to her system, she told herself
harshly.

Watching the door, she saw Crane and his ConSecs as
soon as they came in, already suited up, helmets under
their arms and MMUs—Manned Maneuvering Units—on
their backs.

Crane saw her and waved, coming toward her. She realized as she rose to meet him that he was toting a spare
MMU, collapsed on his belt. When he reached her, he held
it out. "Want any help with this, ma'am?"

"Kate," she sighed. "Don't you think those could have
waited?" Chandra was watching. She had no idea what
he'd made of the MMUs. She didn't want to draw attention
to herself in this way. Crane should have known that.

"No, I don't think so. Arms out, okay?" The MMUs
were of the new miniaturized sort. Crane helped her into
the body harness and checked her straps, saying, "Look,

235

ma—Kate . . . we're taking a different flight over: you, Rand, and us. Which means different personal specs.'' He eyed the attaché case on the bench next to her seat. ''If you're taking that, don't sweat the small stuff.''

''I'm taking it,'' she said coldly. ''And Ilya Palladin, even if we have to wait for him. If you see Rand before I do, tell him I've cleared it.''

''Oh yeah?''

She turned around as if checking with Crane about the fit of her straps. ''What's the tone of voice, mister?''

Crane's eyebrow raised. ''I was going to tell you, anyway. We intercepted a weird transmission just before the interference got too bad—bounced from D.C., best we can figure, to Sveboda. Mostly coded, and Marshall hasn't got it broke yet, but it was to Palladin's office—sender ID'd as Khimik. Means 'chemist.' Bet that ain't all it means. You want to tell us anything about this Palladin?''

Kate's mouth dried out so that she was sure that when she parted her lips there would be a sound like separating velcro. Crane was making assumptions about Palladin that she might be able to use. ''Just that we might want to get him off the moon in a hurry—with us.''

''Yes ma'am,'' Crane said, nodding conspiratorially. ''We'll figure something out.'' He gave her harness one final jerk and began telling her about debarkation procedures for their contingent of the travel party.

She hardly listened. She'd just lied by omission to one of the most important players on her team. What the hell was Ilya doing? Who was Khimik? Even in her suit with its determined temperature regulators, she was suddenly and unbearably cold.

''Couple more things, then I've got to go,'' Crane said, easing past her to heft her case as if it were the most natural thing in the world for him to carry it on board, past security, for her. ''You get your Palladin and Rand, and wait around till these have left, then go through the military access; we'll be waiting with the transport. Rand wanted a cross-check on Faragher from Bates. Tell him I couldn't get it—sunspots, I guess.''

''He did?'' Confusion and then a relief she wished she didn't feel. Maybe Rand wasn't screwing up; maybe he was just being Rand—first guy out on the flimsiest limb he could find. ''Thanks, Crane.''

But Crane was already sauntering off, her attaché case in one hand. He stopped when he reached Marshall and Foster, and as they left, each of the other two ConSecs left a mini-MMU on the white room's encircling bench.

Effective, if nothing else, those two. But what it all meant, she wasn't certain: Crane was taking her case because somebody, probably Rand, had demanded a thorough security check of all boarding passengers. It wasn't usual; it wasn't even polite. But it showed a degree of concern that verged on siege mentality. And for the life of her, she couldn't imagine why; no one was going to smuggle weapons aboard the ESA-dedicated flight to Einstein. No one was going to start shooting in a pressurized vehicle. It was just too long a walk back to civilization. And who would benefit if the ESA contingent never reached dark side? Not any of those in this room, she was certain.

Nevertheless, she found herself studying the three women and seven men making the trip with Chandra, looking for the fanatical gleam of terrorist martyrdom among those excited eyes.

God help me, I'm going to be as crazy as Trace when this thing's over. She rubbed her face with gloved hands, and when she took those hands away, there was Tracey Rand, coming toward her with a smooth and springy stride she hadn't seen for far too long. Fully acclimated to moon gravity now, he moved like he once had—like he had before the accident. And she squeezed her eyes shut because, for all his faults and everything her mind held against him, the sight of him made her heart glad.

*Damned fool girl,* she chastised herself. That was what he'd call her, in his derogatory use of the term—a girl.

Like he'd called Crane's team when he'd had dinner with them on LSS.

Behind and off to one side she saw Faragher, orbiting Chandra's party as if she'd always been there. Had Faragher come in with Rand? Or had they decided on a decorous interval between arrivals?

*Cut it out, Kate, it doesn't matter,* she told herself fiercely, and then Trace was upon her. He didn't have his case in hand. No doubt, one of the ConSecs had already appropriated it. It bothered her that he was running all the details of this trip around her; but then, she'd been so busy with Ilya, there'd been no opportunity to include her in any logistical or strategic discussion.

"Hey, Katydid, you look ready to go." Same ingenuous smile; same honest pleasure at seeing her; same reaction from some deeper self, which didn't care that he was an impossible chauvinist.

"Trace, where have you been? I need to talk to you about Ilya. Crane said to tell you that Bates hasn't RSVP'd your check on *her.*" Kate's head flicked to Faragher. "And that we're to hold back at boarding, then meet Crane at the military docking bay."

"I know," he said levelly. "Just relax. Everything's under control."

His voice was down an octave; every fiber of his body told hers that he meant what he said. He reached out to touch her shoulder and she didn't pull away. She felt herself ceding control, because she always had and he'd always been right—until their last mission, when things hadn't been under control at all.

In his face was none of the pallor she'd expected, that she'd seen the last time he'd suited up. She let her eyes lock with his and found no fear there, just flat attention to duty and an overt concern for her welfare that should have been insulting, but wasn't.

She said, "When we're done with this, I'm going to put

in for a lobotomy," under her breath, and he said, "Excuse me?"

"Never." She smiled. "How's Faragher?"

"How's Palladin? You were going to tell me—"

"Ilya ought to be here by now. Unless you've got some damn good reason why not, I'm going to proceed as if he's a Class-A defector candidate."

A shadow slid over his eyes. "No reason but simple survival. We'll talk about it later, okay? We'll have plenty of time on the trip dark side." He was fingering his helmet and she saw, because he hadn't yet put his gloves on, damp prints when he moved his hand away.

"I want him to come with us; I cleared it with Crane."

Rand shifted, choosing that moment to survey the room. Beyond Chandra, blue-and-gray-uniformed men were circulating among the ESA party, checking their equipment and escorting them toward the hatch leading to the docking complex.

"You haven't cleared it with me," came his quiet voice when he turned back. "Kate, we've got too many variables already, without this wild card of yours."

"I couldn't *find* you to clear it, unless I wanted to risk walking in on you and your—"

"Jesus, Katydid, I'm just doing my job. Look, if Palladin shows up too late for the ESA bus, we'll take him. But it's going to put a real crimp in our style." He moved closer and bent his head to her, lowering his voice even more. "Kate, you don't know how something like that might be construed, especially if he's in trouble at Sveboda. I don't mind dying up here, if it comes to that, but I don't want to be the clay pigeon the Soviets decide we owe them for that truckski—or collateral damage incurred in preventing a defection."

He was good, she'd give him that. "Fine, we'll play it your way: if he misses the ESA bus, he comes with us." *And if he doesn't, it'll give me more time to make you realize that you're using so-called security concerns to mask personal ones, that Ilya's too valuable to be lost because of what either of us feels about him.*

"Got to go make nice to my target," he said, neither affirming nor denying her statement. "I'll be right back."

She watched him buttonhole Faragher, averting her eyes when Faragher reached out to him in greeting or farewell. What *was* it about that woman? Kate wasn't normally afflicted with jealousy so badly that it affected her judgment.

Bates had given Faragher a clean bill of health—repeatedly. And all that should matter now was ZR/SEAL and WARLORD. Faragher was just what Rand had called her—his target. It was Kate who was making things worse than they had to be.

Rand wasn't asking that Faragher go dark side in the special, armed and armored transport Crane had arranged for them. Rand wasn't asking for anything more than the room to do his job. She shook her head, irritated at her own poor performance, and told herself that Ilya would either make it in time for the ESA bus, or not.

Just then, the Soviet colonel entered, flanked by two nervous Cop One functionaries who brought him directly to her.

Ilya was wearing his Soviet style spacesuit, and the few remaining heads in the white room—including Robin Faragher's and Tracey Rand's—swiveled at his approach. "You," she said to the first functionary. "Run ahead and confirm that the bus will be four short on debarkation: Colonel Palladin is accompanying the ESA contingent; myself, Dr. Rand, and three of my people will catch up with them at Einstein."

That told Ilya all she dared. He peered after the man loping into the hatchway and then said, "Are you all right, Catherine?"

"I don't know, Ilya. I do know we've got to talk. I think I can help you . . . if you want."

Palladin was paler than usual; his nostrils flared as he

240

said, "I would like to kiss you good-bye, but it is imprudent."

"I'll see you over there," she said again. "Do me a favor?"

"Surely." Palladin's clipped voice and expressionless face were frightening her.

"Ah . . . see if you can shake out that Faragher woman on the ride over."

"Da."

He never slipped into Russian unless he was agitated. "Be careful, okay?"

"It is too late for careful, my dear. But take care."

Damned dour Russians, she told herself: never miss a chance to make a bad situation worse. But his obviously controlled distress had shaken her. As she watched the tall Soviet disappear behind Faragher into the hatchway, she had an awful feeling that she should have asked more questions, been more insistent, acted sooner or in some other fashion.

What did you say to someone who wouldn't tell you what kind of trouble he was in? For all she knew, it was just a ruse. That was what Trace would think, she knew.

When Rand came up to her and said, "You satisfied? Let's go. The fun won't start till we're over there," she replied, "Maybe I should have gone with them, you know? Probably could have learned something."

"You're too valuable to risk where we can't help you if you need it. Anyway, we've got plenty to learn—how to put this sorry excuse for a team back together before we have to put it—and our lives—on the line."

# Chapter 2
# KHIMIK

Khimik had sent an unsolicited message to Palladin and that message had been garbled by solar interference. What Palladin had been able to make of it still troubled him more than anything else as he boarded the insectlike lunar ferry with the rest of its passengers, the ESA contingent.

The ferry was commodious, by Soviet standards. This was probably the best the U.S. had to offer, made to seem standard in order to impress the Europeans, Palladin told himself. In his helmet, a miniaturized motor drive clicked and whirred in response to taps on a button in his belt.

Nice of the Americans to require that suits be worn throughout takeoff. The ferry to Einstein crater, the Americans' dark-side staging area, was a nonscheduled four-hour flight, after which the tour would be bussed in another vehicle the Americans had not yet specified.

Palladin might have been elated by this intelligence coup at any other time—here he was, effortlessly insinuated into the belly of his enemy, off on a guided tour of something called WARLORD.

Kate's admission that the RTI—radio telescope installation—was WARLORD might well have been the truth: she was an American. He had purveyed it as the truth this morning, when Moscow Center had reacted so angrily to Ruskin's execution.

Accustomed to estimating the survivability of embattled assets, Palladin sat quietly during takeoff, estimating his own. The chances that the ferry would explode during its lift sequence were much less than Palladin's chances of self-destructing over the Ruskin incident.

It had not seemed so at the time, and this was troubling. He had had three angry communications from Moscow Center. He had played his cards with the chairman's office and waited. The results had been foreseeable, but surprising, nonetheless. Men had come to his office; security guards he did not recognize were placed at his doors. His assistant was suddenly replaced by someone he did not know.

And he had been officially reprimanded. Only this junket that Kate had proposed had staved off what seemed to be inevitable—demotion, perhaps expulsion to groundside, even incarceration when he got there. He had not thought Ruskin was so well placed. He had assumed that he still had trust where trust mattered—among the highest echelons of Soviet authority.

He had been wrong on some very crucial points. Of course, no one had yet said to him, "Palladin, you are a traitor and a fool. We have been watching you and the Western woman whose pawn you are. Your usefulness is over. You are remanded into custody of such-and-such GRU officer." But it seemed likely that they would.

What made it seem most likely was this final, unsolicited, and partly jammed communication from Khimik, his Western source, warning him of something. The warning was a code word; the appended specifics were too garbled by jamming—or by untimely sunspots (he was willing to credit that supposition)—to tell him anything more.

Khimik had warned Palladin against any further communications. That meant that Palladin was under not just a cloud, but an avalanche of suspicion. Suspicion in KGB was difficult, if not impossible, to recover from. Only some croup that would justify and explain all actions viewed as subversive could save Ilya Palladin now.

Since Kate Brittany was one of the factors in Palladin's fall from grace, he blamed himself. But he also knew a life preserver when one was thrown to him. This WARLORD was of paramount importance. The very word caused a hush and a still and a stay of execution, once Palladin had sent it groundside. They would wait and see what he learned; they would not act precipitately. WARLORD was his salvation, whatever it was.

If it was nothing, then he had only a single chance: defect. Kate had suggested, without using the word, that he consider it. On this trip, he would do nothing but consider it. He had much to offer America, many dreams of the free world. And Kate Brittany was one of those dreams.

As long as he was alive, Ilya Palladin would fight to stay that way. He looked out the window, through quadruple thicknesses of special American-made glass, at the voided surface of the moon below. It was a giant, pockmarked corpse's face that had washed up on some beach of space. It was bereft of any emotion but violence and death. It was more sterile than the Lubyanka's deepest dungeon, colder than Gorki in the dead of winter.

It was one place in the known universe Ilya Palladin did not want to die. He kept thinking of Ruskin, photographed decapitated in the tunnels. He had the swollen whitish finger with its signet ring to prove his order had been obeyed.

And he kept thinking of the flagged reports he'd been given, of the refusal—point-blank and brusque—to inform him of Ruskin's mandate, to let him access Ruskin's files.

The only thing he had learned for certain, backtracking through the tapes of his interview with Ruskin and then using up a favor from a groundside friend to confirm it, was that Moscow had ordered the wetwork on someone called Nathan Davies. This groundside friend of his, too powerful and bold to fear being tainted by Palladin's shaky position, a man from Directorate S in charge of such things as assassination, had confirmed that this was so. ZR/SEAL personnel had short lifespans, the communiqué had said; they were enemies of the State.

And Kate was one. He wished she had come on this ferry with him. It was possible that, even now, his proximity could protect her at least a little longer. ZR/SEAL and WARLORD. WARLORD was like a magic wand from an ancient tale, one that turned on its wielder.

The mere mention of it could protect you; the mere knowledge of it could kill you. If it were no more than the radio telescope installation, Ruskin should not have had to die for it.

Palladin had broken the code on Ruskin's active file and found drone surveillance of the RTI area. He had found comings and goings and notations of nuclear signatures. In some way, WARLORD was nuclear. In some way, this dead man, Davies, a Space Talks negotiator, had been working on WARLORD. How WARLORD interfaced with Davies and his proposal to alter the path of U.S. and Soviet tunneling, Palladin could not determine.

But he had determined enough to know that he must either learn WARLORD's secrets, or flee. Outside, the moon went by, a blur of craters large and small, impacts from thousands upon thousands of years.

The moon was a survivor. Palladin was a survivor. Khimik once had been Palladin's hole card. Now, because of this WARLORD, Khimik had forbidden Palladin to contact him. But now Palladin had Kate.

Kate knew the risks of trying to receive a defector in such a venue as the moon. It warmed his heart that she would allude to it. He did not know if trying was succeeding: if an attempt at defection might turn to suicide. Many things could happen on the moon.

Above his seat, a yellow light went on. He could now take off his helmet, mix with these honored guests of the United States. Among them was the woman named Faragher, whom Kate distrusted. For Kate, Palladin had run a check but turned up nothing on Robin Faragher.

Nothing often meant something: normal KGB procedure would be to have a dossier on anyone of power and influence, especially in such a tight community as those who went to the moon.

Palladin reached up to release his helmet seals and lifted it off his head. Immediately, sounds and smells assailed him. He found them more pleasing than the sour odor of his nervous breath and the hushed rush of his pulse in his ears.

An American in ConSec uniform was offering lozenges on a tray. Conversation around him was excited. People were releasing their safety harnesses and moving around in the ferry's padded gray confines.

Palladin was about to do the same when one of the passengers approached him. "Secretary Palladin, I'm Robin Faragher," said the woman.

"Of course you are," replied Ilya Palladin.

"Thought you'd like a mint." She smiled, perching on the arm of the empty seat beside him.

He took the mint she offered and popped it into his mouth. "Sit down and tell me all about ESA-METALLE," he said wickedly.

"My pleasure," replied the woman who reminded him so much of Alicia Harper.

Beside Palladin's head, out the window, the moon whizzed by a mile beneath. He wished again that Kate were with him, where he could offer her the protection of his person, among these ESA people who were so sure that their noncombatant status would protect them from anything and everything.

# Chapter 3

# SITTING
# DUCKS

"That's what we are, all right—sitting ducks. Or at least that's what *they* are," Crane said, jabbing with a forefinger out the window of the armed-and-armored aerospace plane in which they were shadowing the moon truck full of ESA visitors on their way to Einstein crater and the U.S. staging area there.

"You don't have to sound so happy about it," Kate said. Helmets off, all five of them were strapped into seats on the flight deck. This craft was a smaller, stealthier version of the TAV they'd flown from LSS to Cop One—just one more example of how little she'd really known about America's lunar arsenal.

It was a fighter, there was no doubt about that. All around her was telemetry capable of more than surveillance, although the plane Crane referred to as the ATF (for Advanced Tactical Fighter or Awesome Total Fucker, depending on to whom Crane was speaking) had plenty of "mapping capability."

The plane could tell its pilots how much change Ilya Palladin had in his pocket and how much film was in his camera, Foster had told her proudly, even though the moon truck was shielded against conventional multiband surveillance. Half of its fuselage was taken up with power packs and transformers and fuel for long-distance flight and weaponry. It was technically a CMC3I fighter—Countermeasures, Command, Control, Communications, and Intelligence—and it was all the Seal team needed, Marshall was sure, to put WARLORD on line no matter what the opposition fielded.

It had frozen Kate wordless when she'd realized that someone—Bates, Andresson, perhaps even Harper—had expected trouble all along. You didn't dedicate a juggernaut of destruction like this to a routine mission. And the familiarity the ConSecs displayed with the plane told even her unpracticed eye that these men and this machine were parts of one very deadly whole.

Rand seemed to be taking it all in stride, once he got his helmet off. She kept hoping he was all right, and checking her impulse to ask. He was pale, but the light in here was meant for easy reading of displays, not to flatter the human skin.

On her right, beside what seemed to be a topographical display showing their position and that of the moon-truck ferry containing the ESA personnel, Rand sat quietly, watching the screen and occasionally tapping buttons that caused the display to shift to more distant craters.

"Trace," she said, "this may not be the best of times, but we've got to discuss Ilya before we touch down at Einstein."

"You're right, it's not the best of times." A quirk of his mouth softened it. "Did we tell you that Robin Faragher wants to hire Cislunar? She's security officer for them, or so she's led us to believe."

*We. Us.* Him and Crane's ConSecs. Her spine stiffened. "Did I tell you," she replied, knowing full well that Crane and Marshall, at least, could hear—only Foster had a headset on, "that Harper hit the ceiling about the truckski blowaway, and that you're all in the doghouse as far as he's concerned—negative reporting notations, the whole nine yards?"

248

Crane swiveled his seat, his face sardonic. "We'll be done and gone before old Hysterical Harpy—or his meno-pausal missus—can hurt us. Or at least hurt you guys. As for what he'll try to stuff in our jackets, ma'am—Kate: doing the job we do makes for plenty of abrasive comments from Harper's sort."

"Yes, well, that's fine, then. For all of you." She looked to Rand but he was chewing a stylus, some obscure amuse-ment hiding behind his eyes. Letting her swing. "I'm the one who's promised we'll be responsible. That means, gentlemen, that we get these people back in one piece— with no more untoward incidents."

It sounded faint and foolish, even to her own ears. They knew what she was, and what she was trying to say. "My cover's got to hold," she continued more openly. "Even if none of you cares about that. I intend to continue work-ing up here."

"That so?" Now Rand did take a hand. "After you've boosted Ilya Palladin, a KGB colonel, off the moon from under the multiple eyes of his government? That's what you want to talk about, isn't it? Getting your boyfriend a defector's ride home before his ass goes back to Moscow in a basket?"

*Rand, you bastard. There's no need to play to this crowd.* But he had. "Ilya's important, yes. Do you want me to ask Bates for permission, or a recommendation on how to proceed? Or—"

"Shit no, lady." Marshall joined the conversation. "Let's not ask Bates anything more for a while— not when we can't tell who's intercepting, and we've got these 'sun-spots' to garble whatever we get back."

"Never mind, Marshall, I'll handle it. Help Foster with the over-the-horizon scans." Crane gestured dismissively, and Marshall hunched down over his controls. "Look, is that what you two want to talk about—ways to get a Soviet off the moon before his ticket's punched for internals?"

"Something like that, yeah," Rand said.

She could have kissed him. Her recent fury at him for referring to Ilya as her boyfriend evaporated before the sure knowledge that Trace understood better than she how to deal with men like Crane.

"Not part of our mission description," Crane said, tapping his fingers against one of the padded console bumpers.

"For brownie points and nuisance value," Rand said with a half-taunting, half-conspiratorial nuance in his tone. "Palladin's worth lots if we get him home alive."

"Some authority'd have to clear it," Crane responded ruminatively. "Unless Secretary Brittany and yourself could be considered . . ."

"You're putting your ass on the line for me, Crane— your life, your men—already. I don't need to call home for permission to do anything while I'm up here. Those were the conditions under which I agreed to take this on. I do need to know that you three honestly believe this extra action is worth the risk. I've thought about it and I can tell you I do."

"Yeah, but I dunno. Not that I wouldn't like to help, but it's going to raise one hell of a stink. . . ."

Kate wanted desperately to add how much a man like Ilya was worth when he came willingly into U.S. hands. But she didn't. Rand was plumbing the murky depths of macho mentality and working-group honor. She'd seen it many times, but never understood it. Now she simply made herself small and watched the two men as she might a tennis match.

"It sure will." Rand grinned as if he couldn't think of anything he'd rather do. "Put a big fat burr under more than one saddle—the dip community up here on both sides. God knows they could use shaking up. Might even get Harper fired. But the intelligence boys groundside'll love us forever. A completed return of a high-ranking KGB officer from the moon to Earth . . . the propaganda's value alone probably outweighs this plane we're sitting in."

"But how you going to do it?" Crane's forehead creased.

"If he's in trouble, I mean . . . they're not going to let him go with a— Oh yeah, I see. Keep him with us, you mean? Don't let him go back? But that would mean putting WARLORD on line while all these ESA guys are around."

"I haven't thought about that. Kate and I will try to figure whether, if Ilya goes back to Sveboda, we could get him out again. Well, Katy, what do you say?"

"Jesus, Trace," Kate blurted, startled at being brought in. "If we could keep him with us, under the guise of a special perk—that would work. But only if we could get him off the moon from Einstein or RTI, no going back to Cop One, even . . ."

"What do you think we've got this baby for, ma'am?"

"Crane, if you don't stop calling me ma'am— Look, let's get some contingency planning worked out. I don't even know that Ilya's ready to jump."

"But if he were," Rand insisted with a gleam in his eye, "and we could work up some little glitch to ground the ESA contingent at Einstein or RTI for a while, then that ought to give us all the extra time we need. Otherwise, you've got lots of variables."

*Oh great, a little glitch!* "And we've got lots of time," she said uneasily. "Three hours and change. Let's use it." With an awkward feeling that she was setting all five of them on some irrevocable course and that, no matter how it turned out, everything would be different for her forever after, she leaned forward and began to outline the difficulties she saw in Palladin's proposed defection.

She owed them that much, if they were going to give it a try.

When she'd run dry of words, Trace rubbed his neck and screwed up his face. "Can't risk WARLORD for this, you realize, Kate. Palladin's fine as an add-on. Let Crane and me bounce around just how we might want to do that— add him on. You find out from Mr. KGB if he wants to play rabbit. Because there's no way he'll be anything but."

She leaned back, satisfied, and watched Crane and Rand

huddle. Over the backs of the two Q-leaders, past and present, she saw Marshall watching her with a sardonic gleam in his eye.

Why the hell trying to get Ilya out of Sveboda was any worse than Trace cozying up with Robin Faragher to see what would happen, she couldn't fathom. But there was a difference: nobody was trying to quantify Faragher, the way Kate was going on line for Ilya Palladin.

If Ilya was running a game on her, if he wasn't in any trouble and all this was just a scheme to get a close-up look at WARLORD by a clever KGB man, she was going to kill Ilya herself, very slowly and very painfully. Or maybe she'd just kill herself, because at that point, she'd have ruined not only WARLORD, but the lives of everybody in this spaceplane.

Too late, she regretted broaching the subject of Ilya's defection. She should have realized that Trace wouldn't say no to her. He'd only come to the moon because of her. And because, finally after so many years, he had a chance to prove himself—in both their eyes.

She was still thinking about what a fool she'd been to load him down with more mission objectives despite his very full plate when Foster said, "Got some bandits, drones from their scan—just shadowing, three of them, coming up over the horizon at three to six o'clock."

There was a sudden silence in which all the men swiveled their chairs to their combat stations, and then she heard Trace's voice, saying, "Well, damned if it ain't Soviets. Maybe Faragher's just what she says she is, and nothing to do with our problems. Maybe your friend Palladin's in so much hot water that they're going to come get him out of Einstein—which I don't see that we can prevent."

"Not closing," came Foster's laconic assessment. "Just keeping formation—homing on the truck, not us. They're not even seeing us. Won't unless I want them to. Boss, do I want them to?"

The stealth technology of the little fighter was beyond

Kate's expertise, but not Foster's: in his voice was all the excitement of a competitor; this was what Foster did and he was having the time of his life.

"Not yet," Rand answered.

"Vector up some, don't push it," Crane advised at the same time.

She barely felt the attitude correction as Foster followed orders, whistling gratingly through his teeth.

She'd wondered which man would answer to "boss." Since both of them had, she assumed it wasn't a problem. Then Trace tapped her on the knee and pointed to the screen he'd been watching. "Here they are, see? They're being real obvious, like they want the ferry to know they're there. You ought to think about whether you want to invite them in for tea once we get to Einstein."

"Unless they start shooting first," Crane amended.

No one added to that, and in the confines of the space-plane she could hear every one of them breathing as the telemetry tracked the six approaching blips in silent, urgent red.

# Chapter 4

# EINSTEIN BASE

When the two U.S. vehicles began their final approach to Einstein, the three Soviet follow planes were still with them. Tracey Rand was sure that the Soviet prowlers had sighted the ConSec craft long since, but Crane wasn't and they were arguing procedure.

"Look, Dr. Rand," said Crane, implacable with his arms crossed and matters he considered to be national security resting on his shoulders, "if they haven't seen us— and we can't assume that they have—I'm not giving them a ringside seat at a demo of what the ATF can do. We sit up here, let the ESA moon truck touch down, and wait a decent interval."

Marshall looked over his shoulder, one pad of his headset pushed back behind his ear. "He's right, sir; if the Soviets were going to hit the moon truck, they'd have done it by now. They're just here to make things difficult—escort service. We're still bright side, after all." In Marshall's voice was a plea for understanding that had been missing in Crane's.

"You can't tell"—Rand sighed, watching Kate watch him and feeling like he was in some Red Team/Blue Team exercise from his past—"whether we're not the only thing keeping the Soviets from moving on the truck. They're built for action and speed; the truck can barely handle basic low-altitude maneuvers, loaded down like that. I say we assume we've been spotted and make our own escort mandate clear.''

It was a stalemate that would break in Crane's favor only when it was too late to implement Rand's suggestion—unless he downright ordered Crane to put the ATF on the moon truck's tail.

None of the ConSecs responded to Rand until Crane finally said, ''Okay, guys, drop down and let's get visible,'' with an exaggerated salute aimed his way.

Inwardly, every fiber of Rand's being relaxed: push had just come to shove and the command decision had gone his way. It wasn't fun to shake this sort of thing out, but he'd needed to know that, in a pinch where opinions differed, Cranc would go his way.

Now he could worry about simpler stuff, like whether Ilya Palladin was playing some complex game, shielding Faragher with his presence and just pretending to be on the outs with his team. Just because the Soviet escort was there didn't prove that it was hostile to those on board the U.S. moon truck carrying the ESA reps—and Faragher and Palladin himself. He wished it did. It proved only that the Soviets were determined to show themselves. But Palladin's presence aboard confused any determination that might be made from the follow planes' appearance.

Stealing a glance at Kate who'd forsaken the display monitors for a long-range view of the low-flying craft approaching Einstein's landing strip and the three Soviet followers in its wake, he supposed that she was trying to get things clear in her own mind.

Was Palladin just masking whatever Faragher was up to? Was he really in trouble at home? Would he bite when she offered him a defector's berth? Would it prove anything if he did? Those were the questions all right, and Tracey Rand had to remind himself that the answers didn't really impact his primary mission.

But they impacted Kate, and no matter how he felt about Palladin, he wanted her not to be disappointed. Not in anything. Not in any way. And, most especially, not in him.

He was still letting the data roll in his head without any hint of the mental *click* that occurred as bits and pieces of information collated, when Foster called out, "Buckle up, kids." Then he realized that three things had happened: the moon truck had put down in the landing area in a circle of indicator lights; the Russian escort had spotted that—and/or the ConSec ATF—and peeled off, climbing to hover a mile away and a mile high, just out of territorial range; and Foster was beginning their descent sequence.

The ATF liked having a runway. She was VSTOL—very short takeoff and landing—but she wasn't meant to put down vertically except in combat or hazard conditions. And it was obvious from Crane's choice of landing vectors that the ConSecs were determined that the ATF's touchdown not be turned into a show-and-tell for the opposition.

Below, a strip of level surface was suddenly outlined in red and white stripes of runway lights at the end of which a touchdown *X* flashed prettily until Rand couldn't see it anymore as the ATF rolled to a stop in its center.

Smooth as silk; the ConSecs knew this plane like they knew each other. All of them slid out of their harnesses. As Rand fumbled for his helmet, considering the walk in vacuum he'd have to make before he entered the crude cylinders that were the heart of Einstein base, Kate tugged on his arm.

"Thanks," she said. "For Ilya. For everything."

Her eyes were intrusive. "It's nothing," he answered, not wanting her to be so damned observant when he was about to put his head in his fucking helmet and endure the lurch in his gut that still plagued him whenever he sealed himself off from the world.

He wished she'd let him pretend the problem wasn't there.

But she couldn't, and he nearly shook off her hand, waiting for her to tend to her own business. She ought to know him well enough to realize he'd get through whatever he had to. He always did.

When the ATF's exterior door opened and the ladder came down, he was already alone in his helmet, dealing with his gut fear, so he didn't hear the depressurization bell. But he saw the light. And then he had to follow Kate out and down the ladder and onto the dusty surface of the moon.

Einstein base was a collection of towers and radars and bulldozed flatness with terraced channels whose sides were paneled and smooth. Five Spacehab-type cylinders, each with railed staircases leading up to them, comprised the habitable part of the staging area, each one half dug into the regolith for shelter from radiation. Atop some were small con dishes with their distinctive directional needles; from others, stairs on elevated girders led to pyramidal structures that were part of the solar collecting project. The whole scattered expanse was interlaced with thick cables slung on pylons, at the top of which red lights blinked.

Five years ago, Cop One had been no bigger than Einstein was now. Following the ConSecs up the metal stairway leading into the nearest habitat module, Rand felt a satisfaction that overrode even his physical fear of malfunctioning equipment: this was what it was all about. Digging in for good up here; making it on the moon.

Even if his life-support system gave out now, before the pressure door closed behind him—even if every ounce of liquid in his body burst through his skin before it froze solid to the inside of his helmet, he'd seen it come this far. It was something. It was more than something. In Tracey Rand's terms, it was winning.

It was a clearer case of winning than WARLORD was, in its perverted form. WARLORD was beginning to seem like a child that had gone delinquent: it was his but he didn't recognize it. It was mean and nasty and it didn't want for itself what he'd wanted for it. He hadn't ever wanted children because he knew his expectations were too high and his temper too short for the job. This close to WARLORD, its nuke components were beginning to really bother him.

But it was a long time too late to be worrying about that, especially with all the complications they had at hand.

He followed close behind Kate and the ConSecs, first into a pressurization chamber and then, when the light turned green and the far door opened, into a receiving area where the ESA contingent milled in close quarters, their helmets off.

He had his own off before Kate, so he was the first to notice Palladin, sitting by himself over in a corner, as green as Rand felt, with Faragher bent down, talking to him earnestly.

Now was his chance, he wasn't going to miss it. He moved quickly, trying to ignore the fact that Kate would probably be right behind him.

When he reached Palladin, he said brusquely to Faragher, "If you'll excuse us please, Robin, I've got to talk to the secretary."

Palladin looked up at him blearily. Faragher straightened, her lovely eyes questioning. "Surely, Dr. Rand." All decorum. "But he's not feeling too well."

"I get moon-sick, myself. Why don't you take the tour?" He waved vaguely to where a man with an Einstein mission patch was getting the ESA group together.

Faragher moved away with a slight flush. He'd deal with her later. Palladin was watching him. He bent down and said bluntly, "We've picked up a Soviet escort—three planes. They here to take care of you, or what?"

"I . . . don't know." The Soviet seemed somehow fragile. "I— Did Kate tell you, doctor . . ."

Kate's voice came from over his shoulder. "Trace, please." Then she moved into view, sitting beside Palladin. "Ilya, are you feeling okay?"

"Yes, just . . . nervous." The Soviet forced a self-

deprecating grin. "It's not every day one contemplates . . .
one's life."

"He knows, Ilya. I told him. I had to. We'll try to help
you, if you'll let us. But you have to say so, unequivocally." Kate's breath was coming fast, her words tumbling
out in a rush.

Rand moved one step closer, bending lower. "That's
right, friend. You want to see the promised land, we'll give
it a go. But it's tricky. I need to hear it from you before I
take the risk."

"Risk?" Palladin's eyes roved slightly and Rand wondered if the man was just a piss-poor actor; he'd seen other
defector candidates; Palladin didn't have to put on such a
show for him. "You mean, the follow planes you spoke
of? I—"

"Just say yes or no, Ilya. We've got to get this moving
if we're going to do it."

"You won't be going back with this bunch, is what she
means." Tracey Rand believed fervently in simple declara-
tive statements at times like these.

"Yes, I see." Palladin closed his eyes and leaned his
head back against the wall, swallowing with difficulty twice
before he continued. "Let us try, then. I am in your
hands."

The guy was about to cry, Rand realized with discomfort, not the least of which was from Kate's reaction. He
had to get out of there before she pulled Palladin's head
against her breasts and began cooing to him like a mother
with a kid who'd just had a bad dream.

"That's good enough for me, then. Kate, go do what
you have to do. I'll go tell my guys. Palladin, you separate
yourself from the ESA tour—say you're sick; you look it."

He turned on his heel and walked away, heading for
Foster, who leaned against the far wall, obviously waiting
for him.

Rand's instincts were telling him he'd missed something, but his logical mind knew he was probably missing

plenty: there was too much going on here for him not to be screwing up somewhere.

Foster said, "We've still got company, just out of official complaint range."

"Good enough," Rand replied. "Everybody knows where everybody is. Palladin says they're not here on his orders, or at least implies it, if that's worth anything." It wasn't to him, but it was to Kate. So he'd live with it. For the time being. "Let's find Crane and the others and check out the ESA tour's crawler."

The ESA party would go the rest of the way to RTI by ground conveyance. A crawler was ready and waiting when Foster guided him to the underground garage and Marshall let them in the door.

Crane was just wriggling out from the crawler's gizzards, a circuit board in hand. But for themselves, the bay was empty. Crane, straightening up, grinned at Rand and threw the card in a huge, wheeled tool box, but said nothing.

"Okay," Rand said, "what's up?" He could smell this particular rat a mile away; if there weren't one, some Einstein personnel would have been in here; Marshall wouldn't have been posted at the door like the security type he was.

"Well, sir, we figured that the best way to keep the traffic down was to make sure the crawler doesn't make it to RTI." Crane's eyes were as bleak as the moon's surface. "Nobody'll get hurt. They'll just have to limp back on half power—which keeps the squawk level down. Or else they'll sit out there bitching until somebody from here goes after them."

"Wonderful," Rand said sarcastically. *Who's fucking bright idea was this, buddy? Yours? You on our side, or what?* But he couldn't say that in front of Crane's men. He said, "You talked to groundside?"

"No sir, we're on our own, like you said. Figured that, this way, if you wanted to stash Palladin here for safekeeping, you'd have an easier job of it. Also puts Faragher

260

on ice, which'll ease my work load. I'm not smart enough
for all this cloak-and-dagger. I just want to do what I came
up here to do. And we need your decks cleared so you can
concentrate, sir.''

''Sure you won't get these people into more trouble than
they can get out of?''

''Yes sir, except if Murphy's Law kicks in, which can
happen anytime, anywhere.'' Crane's jaw set when he
stopped talking.

''I'm not arguing with you, Crane. I'd just have preferred you told me first.''

''You were busy,'' Foster put in from behind him, and
Marshall whispered, ''Shut *up*, fool; let the lieutenant handle this.''

Crane ignored them, replying to Rand. ''Sir, the Russian
escort out there, that changes everything. We don't want
these people in jeopardy and we can't say, 'Gee, don't go
out there because we've riled the Bear and maybe they
want to even the score with this guy Palladin enough to
take out your whole damn ESA party to get him.' It's
tempting for the Soviets, and we'd take the blame—the
U.S., I mean—for any fatal 'accident' that happens out
there. So, seems to me, the best thing is they don't go out
there, at least not too far, anyway.'' There wasn't even the
hint of pleading in Crane's tone, but there was a demand
for understanding.

''Okay, Crane; you win. Next time, check with me first.
I'm going back there to tell Kate. We might take Palladin
with us, I can't say.''

*And you're not taking Faragher, whatever she's about,
into consideration. But then, I wouldn't know how to factor
her in myself. Damned fool way to run a mission.*

''Hey sir,'' Foster said as Rand left the crawler's maintenance bay, ''we left the spare MMU for Palladin back at
the debarkation lounge on Cop One. If you didn't pick it
up, we'll have to find him another.''

''You do that—find him another. The more spares we've

got, the better." He brushed by the ConSec sergeant, angry for no more reason than the thought of needing the MMUs: that meant EVAs—Extra Vehicular Activity—in deep space. The thought of it was one he'd been ignoring as long as possible, and as concertedly as possible.

If he hadn't been, he might have picked up the collapsible spare on Cop One. But it didn't matter; Palladin could have his, if the Russian wanted it. Tracey Rand had no intention of EVAing, under any circumstances.

Asking him to do so was about as crazy as bringing Palladin along—a Soviet citizen who could redefect as soon as he'd seen all he wanted of WARLORD—while they put the pieces of the project together.

Determined to tell Kate that Palladin would have to stay here with Faragher and the others, he hurried down the corridor, wishing the thought of MMUs and EVAs didn't make him so goddamned seasick he was looking for a men's room as he went.

# Chapter 5
# SHAKE-OUT

"But Ilya's really sick," Kate protested, huddled with Trace in one corner of Einstein's cramped executive offices, separated from the installation personnel by only a freestanding baffle of fabric and plastic.

He'd found her in the infirmary with Palladin, who had such a case of cold feet he'd developed flu symptoms, even a low-grade fever.

"Well, we're not waiting for him to get better," Rand stated flatly, as if talking to a child. "It suits me; we'll pick him up here when we're done over there. He'll keep. We'll jockey the doctor into holding him here for us, if the ESA tour comes back early."

"Early? Why would they do— Trace, there's something you're not telling me."

"Good girl. One point for your side. Now figure out why not." His head jerked toward the partition, behind which half-a-dozen other people inhabited "offices" like this one. "When you're finished with Palladin, come find me somewhere more private. I've got those Soviet shadowboxers to watch and Faragher to tend to." He turned to leave.

"Trace, I sent Harper word about Ilya. We might need help from Cop—"

*"You what?"* Then he got hold of himself. "Fine, Kate. Any way you want it, as long as I don't have to give him a guided tour of whatever's blackest. Get my drift?" *I don't trust this guy worth a fifty-cent round; I've got enough to worry about without inviting a maybe-defector on board for the most sensitive operation of my goddamned career, no matter how good he is in bed. You read me, Katydid?* He couldn't object that, if her communiqué was intercepted and broken by the Soviets, she might have signed Palladin's death warrant. He didn't care enough to bother on personal grounds, and as long as Palladin wasn't with him and his ConSecs, maybe it would give the Soviets something more to worry about than what ZR/SEAL was doing dark side.

Maybe.

He left her then, with her doubts and her fears. He had plenty of his own. And he had Robin Faragher waiting for him, asking casually, as soon as decorum allowed, about the "rumors that Soviet spaceplanes were following us—still are out there waiting for us. Dr. Rand, are we in danger? Should we cancel our inspection of your RTI? Is there anything we should know?"

Chandra was right behind her, in a gray room overcrowded with the ESA visitors so that there was no privacy to be had. And Chandra was hanging on every word.

"I don't know what you heard, Robin," said Rand, using her first name to try and ease the tension by seeming relaxed, "but it's not that unusual to have Soviets shadow traffic out here—like it's not unusual back home for their planes to have American escorts on the polar route to Cuba. Doesn't mean anything except that it's free space out here. That's what you people want, isn't it? A little replica of Earth, with all the old territorial wrangles and partisan boundary disputes—the same myopic idealism that got us into such a mess down there?"

Faragher blinked in surprise and cast a look over her shoulder at Chandra, who was drawing himself up to his

full height, obviously preparing to give Rand a lecture on
the territorial imperatives of sovereign nations and the international community of interest and whatever the hell else
diplomats talked about when they wanted to say nothing
new or interesting but take a long time and use real fervor
in doing it.

Before the lecture started, Rand held up his hand.
"Sorry, I was out of line. But as far as your security goes,
I don't believe I'm on your payroll yet, so we'll call this a
free consultation." He watched Chandra as he spoke and
he didn't like the snake-eyed Indian any better than he ever
had. "Stay with your group. You're as safe in the U.S.
crawler Einstein's loaning you as you can be on the moon.
Me and mine will be around; you can hail us on your
emergency international distress frequency if you need to;
the Russians still don't let their pilots have that channel
because they think it'll facilitate defection."

Unfortunate to use that word here. "Otherwise, there's
not much that can be done about hostile nations with surveillance craft." Indians who attended Oxford tended to be
pretty far left. Chandra's sympathies would have been a
given, even without the briefing material Rand had read.
"That's the way totalitarian societies stay totalitarian. You
have complaints, make them to the Soviet representative
accompanying your tour. Not me. My specialty is keeping
butts intact, not egos. You think you're too good for low-
intensity harassment, write to Moscow."

He edged away and, to his surprise, Faragher followed.
There wasn't really much of anywhere to go, but he found
a gray filing cabinet to lean on and she was still beside him
when he'd settled back against it to survey the room.

"You're angry," she posited. "Why is this?"

"I hate confined spaces. I don't like dips. I don't like
giving free advice. I'm not a nice person." All of those
were true. He didn't smile when he looked at her.

She did. "I know better. Secretary Palladin is not feeling
well, you know. He has gone to the sickbay."

265

"KGB *Colonel* Palladin has got his own hand to play, Robin, like the rest of us. Like you. Want to tell me what yours is? How you heard about the Soviet prowlers?"

She didn't even twitch. "Everyone has heard. Our pilot spotted them and made us assume emergency positions, in case they acted in a hostile fashion."

"Terrific. A regular thriller weekend, courtesy of the superpowers. As for Palladin, maybe your tour ought to wait for him before you debark. It's only polite. We wouldn't want to give Sveboda the sense that we were trying to hide something."

"Mint?" said Faragher, popping one from a tin into her mouth.

"No thanks, I like tasting my fear. When we get over to RTI, if your boss is still so nervous, I'll finalize arrangements with you, on the terms we discussed, for extra security coverage, starting when we get back to Cop One." Might as well play his role; she was playing hers. If there was someplace to do it, he'd have tried to get her alone to see if, this time, he couldn't get more than laid: he kept thinking she wasn't behaving quite right for a ComBloc player. She'd set him up to give the right explanation to Chandra as if she were on his side.

But he couldn't quite convince himself she was.

Kate was in the com room when Harper's response to her proposed initiation of defection procedures for Ilya Palladin came back: a resounding no.

The communication gave no reason. Harper had sent only, "Negative. Repeat. Negative to query."

Intransigent dip. She couldn't very well argue with him from here. She wondered why she'd bothered to inform him, then admitted it was because Ilya was sick and probably wouldn't make the second leg of the journey to the radio telescope installation.

Damn their luck. Forsaking the com room with its rack mounts and shredders and whirring consoles and blank-eyed terminals, she returned to the sickbay, wrestling with herself. There was no reason to tell Ilya what Harper had said; there was no reason to tell anyone if she played her cards right.

Despite Harper's repeated requests for reports, Rand was his own authority up here. Trace didn't need Harper's permission and neither did she. She'd been a fool to ask for it. She'd do her best to convince Ilya to either make the trip or keep playing sick until she got back.

When she reached the sickbay, she realized that he wasn't playing, and that Palladin couldn't possibly make the trip to RTI, not the way he looked.

"What's wrong with him?" she asked the male nurse on duty.

The man shrugged. "Flu. Germs that came up with the newbies, probably—strains he never was exposed to before. Stuff mutates fast down on Earth. Don't worry, Secretary, he'll be okay in forty-eight hours."

That solved one of her problems: if Ilya had to rest here for forty-eight hours, she wouldn't have to be concerned for his safety or whereabouts.

But he looked positively green. His eyes were sunken and his breathing short and labored. She sat by his bed and said, "How are you feeling?" She took his hand and it was cold; she ran her hand up his arm and that was burning hot. They'd put him in a johnny and into bed and the sight of him that way scared her.

He rolled his head toward her and said, "Kate, I'm sorry. These doctors of yours are worse than our militia. Ordering me about. How goes it?"

"Okay. But you get better, quick. You've just got defector's blues. Cold feet." *Cold hands. Bloodshot eyes. Jesus, Ilya, why'd you have to get sick now, of all times?*

Even in his condition, he scanned the room when he heard her words. "Do not be too cocky, Catherine. Nor too certain of what you must do for me. I'm not certain of anything, right now. The escort . . . Perhaps I should go back to Sveboda. I can ride out this storm. This will be too difficult for you, too dangerous—your friend Rand was right.''

''Hush, Ilya. Don't you dare talk like that. You've just got a damned bug, is all.''

''There are many kinds of bugs, my dear.'' He stopped, swallowed a cough, and raised his head. The breath coming out his mouth was sour and she forced herself not to flinch backward. Just a flu and terrible timing. ''I would kiss you if I could without infecting you,'' he said, and lay back.

''Ilya, I want you to make the ESA tour if you possibly can,'' she said, realizing how much she was asking and how dangerous it was to discuss anything at all with him here and now. ''If you can't, just stay here and get better—*stay until I get back*. Do you understand?''

''I understand,'' he said, and it wheezed out of him. He seemed to be getting worse as she watched. ''I am not sure, however, that I agree.''

''I don't care what you think now. You're sick. You just get better. I'll—''

''Ma'am?'' said the nurse, poking his head around the draped partition between Ilya's bed and the next. ''The doctor wants to examine him again. And you've got somebody waiting for you outside.''

''Thank you,'' she said. Then, rebelliously, she bent down and kissed Ilya Palladin on the cheek before he could turn his head away. ''You take care now,'' she said, trying with her stare to feed energy into his dulled and weakened eyes.

Outside, she found that Trace was the ''somebody'' who was waiting. ''A flu, do you believe it?'' She put her hand to her own forehead, realized what she'd done, and jerked it away as if she'd burned it. ''Of all the luck.''

''Probably good luck, considering. Chandra and Faragher are real wired. I think we ought to just go and let this thing shake out. Go now. So does Crane.''

268

"That's a quorum, isn't it?" she snapped. "Why are you asking me, then? You're telling me we can't wait for Ilya?" Watching Rand, she was trying to decide whether he'd found out, some way, what Harper's reply to her communication had been.

"I'm telling you that forty-eight hours is too long to sit around, and too obvious for us. The tour won't wait, either, and the medic I just spoke to says this guy should be in quarantine for at least that long, or we'll have an epidemic on our hands. The only alternative is to let his Russian escort types pick him up from here and take him straight home to Sveboda—if they'd be willing, seeing that he's infected."

She crossed her arms and stared at him wordlessly.

"I didn't think you'd want that." He watched her levelly for a moment in silence. "Come on, Katydid, you with me? We've got a world to shake. This guy will keep. Won't he?"

And he was asking her more than that. He was asking her to choose, there and then, between personal alternatives. Damned Rand, he'd misconstrued this whole thing in his inimitable way.

"Trace, it isn't like that. It's business with him. Worthwhile business." She didn't know why she said it; until then, she hadn't been sure it was true. She wasn't sure she was certain of it now. But she knew what Rand needed to hear. "What we're doing comes first. Even if there wasn't a mission, it would."

He shook his head at her imperceptibly and let out a long, slow breath. "That's good. I've got a couple things to tell you that you won't like, but what you just said makes it easier."

"Tell me, then." It was Harper, it had to be. Rand was going to withdraw his support for Ilya's defection because of Harper's reaction. And that was all her fault; she shouldn't have told Harper. She'd misjudged Harper and it could cost Ilya his only chance.

Panic-stricken, she was preparing to object when Rand answered, "I can't. It's too sensitive to discuss here. Once we're aloft, we'll talk about it. Until then, you'll have to trust me."

"Have I ever not trusted you?" she said, relief flooding her. If he knew about Harper, he wasn't going to make an issue of it.

And he was right: without any conflicting orders from Rand, the ranking U.S. authority at Einstein while he was here, and at RTI when he got there, Ilya would keep nicely until they got back, right where he was.

She went with him through three connecting locks and found herself among the ConSecs, two of whom were already suited for the moon's surface.

Nobody was chatting; the silence was unnerving. She got into her suit and watched Rand as he double-checked every seal of his.

It was obvious to her what he was doing, now: he'd bumped the mission schedule. They were going to try to outflank the waiting Soviet surveillance craft by leaving before the ESA crawler did.

With any luck, the Soviets would stay with their initial target. She remembered what Crane had called the ESA tour on the first leg of the journey: sitting ducks.

They filed into the lock, waited for the green PROCEED light. Crane hit the lock seals and they stepped out onto the staircase. Through her polarized faceplate, the moon had a silver tinge.

Her feet seemed heavier than the sixth-gravity pull could account for as she left Einstein behind and headed for the tactical fighter crouched in the open on its bull's-eye.

Men scrambled off and away from it; a fuel tanker was resting nearby.

When they'd all climbed aboard and the flight deck was pressurized, they took off their helmets, and the regular, low-level banter of the ConSec team began again.

Rand swiveled his chair toward her and said, "Kate, I'm

going to fill you in on what we've done about the ESA tour bus and you're not going to get upset."

"All right on one condition," she said, making a bargain out of a problem; whatever he wanted to tell her couldn't be any worse than what she had to tell him.

"Which is?" he asked cautiously.

"I'll tell you what Harper said and *you* won't get upset."

"I can guess. Well, it's a deal." Soberly, he began to explain about what Crane had done to the moon crawler earmarked for the ESA tour bus, and she wanted to forbid him to use those people so crassly (even if Faragher was one of the people in question). Not only would they be stranded for a time on the surface of the moon, but there was the Soviet contingent of watchers to consider. She was furious.

But Crane gave a signal and Foster ignited his engines and everything she would have said was drowned out in the ferocious lift-off of the ATF.

The only comfort she could draw from this whole mismanaged venture was that Ilya probably wouldn't be aboard the ESA tour bus when it failed on the surface of the moon.

# Chapter 6

# ACROSS
# THE LINE

Lieutenant Lincoln Crane's total attention was fixed on one thing: the moment when their ATF would cross the dividing line between the near and far sides of the moon. That passage across the demarcation line between what were familiarly called the bright and dark sides was all he could afford to concern himself with: it was the first success on which all later successes, and WARLORD, depended.

He cast a few cursory glances at Rand and Brittany, his oh-so-highly touted passengers, during the initial climb to cruising altitude. After that, seeing nothing untoward in their faces or their attitudes, he ignored them.

Rand and Brittany wouldn't matter again until their special expertise was needed. They were weapons in his arsenal, nothing more, waiting for the proper circumstances in which he'd deploy them.

Now, he had close to ten thousand other problems, nearly half of them unadmitted and thus unquantifiable: every damned nonclassified, classified, and ultra-classified satellite in cislunar space was his enemy until he crossed that demarcation line and had the bulk of the moon between him and nobody-knew-how-many prying eyes.

The stealth capacity of the ATF was helpful, but no panacea. Foster's expertise was more comforting. They were using every counter-countermeasure they had at their disposal, plus a couple more experimental tactics that might or might not work.

The ATF had rockets. Rockets burned. Heat-tracking devices locked on to your burn and learned lots about you from it. In addition to all physical shielding measures possible, Foster was sending a blanketing electronics bath aft of the ATF. The electronics signature was modeled to read like a negative heat signature. Hopefully, the false reading would be accepted by any surveillance equipment slightly before or at exactly the same time as the actual rocket burn itself. Depending on the capabilities of the tracking equipment encountering this mixed signal, the digitized result would be either the difference between the two signals after confused equipment did the math, or the equivalent of a white noise screen if the electronic negative reached the sensors soon enough to fill up every digitized increment with fake readings.

If, however, analogue surveillance was in play, Foster's ploy would be useless. Same result for other types of sensors if their electro-chaff and frequency hoppers and composite skin and related stealthing measures didn't do the trick. There was no way to be certain that any technology was foolproof, ever: whatever man could devise, man could counter. Especially with the amount of espionage in technical fields. If you understood how the other guy's stuff worked, it wasn't hard to construct countering equipment.

And so the game went on. Most times, it didn't bother Crane much. Today, when any piece of uncataloged space junk up there could be an enemy surveillance device trained on him and his spaceplane, it was bothering the hell out of him.

He felt like he was walking naked down Pennsylvania Avenue with a rocket launcher in his hands. He'd spent more time keeping that feeling from spreading among his two subordinates than he had on any other component of this mission: morale was everything when you were going to do what Crane's ConSecs were going to do.

Crane had no political stake in the outcome. He didn't care for WARLORD's objective and he didn't care for Tracey Rand, who (rumor said) had brainstormed the concept. But he did care mightily about the repercussions if WARLORD blew wide open. A baby could see the results of that. They were so negative for man's expansion into space that Crane would have volunteered to ride shotgun on this go if it had been guaranteed he wouldn't come back alive.

So there weren't any second thoughts in his head, beyond operational ones. Marshall had brought Rand's special weapons case aboard and they'd taken a looksee. Pretty standard stuff: steel and tungsten carbide pellet loads in his pistol and sawed-off shotgun—for velocity rather than retained energy, as low-G required. Dial-a-recoil gas systems to minimize the force with which the shooter would be moved backward. None of that was surprising: standard crowd-control and threat stuff, packed by fools groundside who saw everything in John Wayne terms.

There'd also been an experimental plasma rifle in three quick-assembly sections; a multipurpose laser tool that could saw through armor plating or somebody's physiology until its charge ran out; and thallium-shot rounds for maximum prejudice situations—"spook shit," Marshall had called it. What with the emergency electronics and self-destruct boxes nestled beside the ammunition, nobody had argued. But they'd known what Rand was.

Just what this project needed, was what. A guy who was committed beyond normal limits; somebody who identified with WARLORD the way Foster did with his birds or Marshall with keeping Marshall alive and Crane with keeping his jacket clean.

The woman's briefcase was weirder: some of the same hardware, including a hand-held computer with the power of a mainframe and com capabilities for short-term satellite bounce, but also a nasty forty-four magnum that somehow didn't fit with the delicate frame of the short-haired, tall lady who managed to seem so feminine despite everything.

You couldn't underestimate your players, though. If they'd had a mini-railgun in their steel cases, or a grenade-size nuke, Crane wouldn't have been surprised.

If he were as endangered a species as these two remaining ZR/SEAL vets, he'd have wanted to put one big one over the top, for his peace of mind and his dead friends.

But they didn't act like they felt that way. They acted like everything was still within normal parameters. They worried about Palladin like it mattered if they got a Russian defector off the moon. They watched each other like hawks and got their backs up about which of them was sleeping where.

Rand was annotated in Crane's briefing material as left-leaning; he'd moved south of the border when he'd gotten hurt, or sulky, or whatever had happened. That annotation was a warning flag. Crane was here partly because he had enough technical knowledge to be sure that Rand, during calibration and launch procedures, didn't decide that WARLORD ought to miss its target. If that happened, Crane's orders were clear: remove Rand from the field and finish the job himself if possible.

That would be possible only if Rand were sufficiently far along, unless Crane had Brittany's help. She wasn't doubling as the science attaché on Cop One for nothing. But Crane had real doubts that Brittany could or would help him finish WARLORD, if prejudicial action had to be taken against Rand.

So he wasn't worrying much about it yet, just keeping the scenario in the back of his mind. Rand hadn't liked it when Crane had decided to cripple the ESA tour, and that meant Rand wasn't totally with the program. You did what you had to do, to assure the desired results.

One decidedly undesirable result was having those three Soviet surveillance craft follow the ATF dark side. "What think, Marshall? We clean?"

"So far so good, sir," came Marshall's voice, hardly clipping through the super-fast voice-actuation headset Crane had over one ear. They could have done without the com gear if Rand and Brittany hadn't been aboard, but with them here, Crane had felt the extra precautions were necessary.

This way, Rand and Brittany could dither about Ilya Palladin and the Faragher woman all they wanted, without being distracted by little things like the ConSecs running their butts through the surveillance gauntlet to get dark side.

"Great, let's keep it nominal," Crane said, and sat back in his seat, eyes half focused on the heads-up displays it was his job to read for trouble. The computers on the job would goose him as they brought up possible targets, of course, but the quarter-screen systems allowed him to make eye-mind computations on less data than computers needed—something called instinct that any good flight commander couldn't afford to be without.

Listening with his free ear to Rand and Brittany talking spook jargon about the intricacies of their human collection mission—about Faragher and Harper and Palladin and Chandra and Bates and command structures—he realized that they were bound and determined to try and boost the Soviet they had stashed at Einstein off the moon, from under the very noses of Sveboda.

It would be fun, he had to admit, to stick one up the Russians' noses. But it was such a long shot, he couldn't take it seriously. Not yet. Not until WARLORD was on trajectory and it was no longer his responsibility to see that, if anything went wrong, only Crane and his two ConSecs came back alive.

Bates had been real clear about that.

As clear as the visual sighting Crane was getting, on his horizon, of the demarcation line between near and far sides—actually light and dark today, so that he could confirm with his naked eye what the computer monitor outlined in red.

276

"Here we go, folks," he said, palm over his mike so Rand and Brittany could hear. "Once we cross over, it's a whole new ballgame." *No more worrying about all those goddamn satellites; no more sweating what they're thinking on Earth; just you two and us and how the job gets done—the easy way or the hard way.*

Rand and Brittany were watching something else—the rearview over-the-horizon screens.

Marshall's voice came through his headset: "Sir, they're monitoring the ESA crawler; it's picked up its Soviet escort and they're tracking that for the record. I didn't want to bother you with a peripheral."

"You did right, Marshall," Crane said very softly into his mike and then, louder: "Heads up, back there. Let Einstein take care of Einstein's. You're both operational just about . . . *now.*" As he spoke, the ATF flashed over the line into darkness, on its way to the radio telescope installation where WARLORD's nuke drivers were waiting to be boosted into low moon orbit.

And the rest was just about to become history, so far as Crane was concerned.

# Chapter 7

# DEFECTOR'S BLUES

Ilya Palladin lay in the Einstein sickbay, weak and compromised and in American hands. If it had not been for Kate's involvement, he would have been terrified to be here.

As it was, he strove to suppress his fear. Outside, hovering within strike range—or rescue range—were spaceplanes of his government. He could still, if he wished, demand that Einstein's base commander put in a call to Sveboda asking that the planes be instructed to pick up Palladin and return him there, where Soviet doctors could look after him.

It could still work. He could still back down. He had done nothing, said nothing, to anyone at home—at Sveboda or on distant, blue Earth—about defecting. Only Kate made it seem sensible. And Kate was off doing whatever she'd come here to do.

She hadn't even said good-bye. Ilya had found out from the male nurse or orderly . . . or spy. Whatever the man was, he'd blithely told Palladin that "the lady had to go kinda sudden. No, she didn't leave no message."

And what was he to make of that? Had Rand, who in every way made it clear to Palladin that the two of them were enemies, prevailed on Kate to withdraw her offer?

She would have said farewell to him, if she'd been able. One always wondered if, at heart, the U.S. operatives were not much more like their Soviet counterparts than they would admit. Surely, if she had not been ordered to abandon him, Kate would have come back to kiss him one more time. . . .

He tried to remember if she'd said anything he could or should construe as reassurance, but he could remember very little of her visit. It was his fever, which was climbing, making his memory spotty and filling the dark patches with fantasies that seemed like memories. Had she told him to wait here, to play sick? Had she told him to go with the ESA contingent? Or not to go with it?

In his bed, he was sweating and shivering at the same time. The ceiling was covered with pink, moving dots and they were as sharp as the breaths of icy air he struggled to get into his lungs.

Someone came and hovered over his bed, someone with a blue mask on. This might be a doctor or it might be an interrogator who did not want Palladin to remember his face. The Amerikanski started asking Palladin questions about where he had been and who he had seen and many other questions that Palladin could not keep straight.

The order of these questions was important. Interrogators played games. He did not answer any of the questions and the man went away. Then more men came and they took his bed and wheeled it somewhere. The sensation made him want to vomit. He was going to tell them that he needed to vomit but somehow he couldn't find his mouth. And they were sticking needles in his arm.

So he vomited over someone's hand and then he tried to push the hand away because it was so ugly. This ugly hand was trying to inject him with truth drugs, he was sure. Truth drugs made you very sick.

He struggled and heard unintelligible English curses before he heard nothing at all.

When next he knew anything, he knew that he was in a

tent of special devising, an isolation place. His arms and chest were strapped down and there was something over his mouth. His nose and throat were raw and scratched; there was a tube down his throat. There were tubes in his arms. There was a man with a clipboard speaking to him.

He was sure he could not answer with the mask over his mouth and the tube down his throat, but then he heard his own voice, responding in Russian.

And in English he thought he heard, "This isn't right. Let's get this guy a full set of X rays. Look for anything metal—some kind of microscopic ball. I've heard these guys use 'em to dispense poisons. There are some that could account for these symptoms . . . ricin for one."

"But why would his own people—" said another voice.

"How the hell would I know? Short of changing all his blood, I don't know what else to do. His stomach's pumped; we've filled him with enough mycins to sterilize a herd of cattle. I'm down to trying long shots or calling his people to ask them what I ought to do, and I don't think we can get cleared for that in time."

The voice stopped talking and suddenly there were wide eyes close to Palladin's face. Under the eyes was one of those masks and behind the mask, features worked so that the mask moved when the man said, quite slowly and precisely, "Colonel Palladin, can you hear me? If you can hear me, listen very closely: we need to know how to help you. You've got to pay attention. We don't have a Russian speaker here, not until the ESA tour gets back. We—"

Palladin closed his eyes. The man was too large and his face was melting. It was not a kind face; it was a devious face, under the mask. And behind Palladin's lids were soft clouds. Somewhere, among those clouds, Kate was hiding. If he could just find her, he knew everything would turn out fine.

Kate spoke Russian. He said her name and he was shocked to hear it echo in his ears. The sound of speaking aloud was very unpleasant. It made his ears hurt and it made his throat hurt. He would not do that again. Find Kate, and all things topsy-turvy would right themselves. Kate spoke Russian. Find Kate . . . Kate and the America of his dreams, or Kate at the Winter Palace in Leningrad.

Perhaps that was where she was. Perhaps he had been dreaming; perhaps it was Kate who had decided to defect and that was where they were, celebrating the White Nights together. It was like this in Leningrad, full of pale sky and clouds so thick you could think only of how it would feel to lie among them and drift forever with one you loved. . . .

# Chapter 8

# TOURIST TRAP

In the ESA tour's moon crawler, Robin Faragher had not taken off her helmet or her suit's gloves. She sat in the rear of the vehicle, playing with the lap computer she'd brought along.

The computer was very special, and what she typed into it now, in its shielded sending mode, would cut through any interference a conveyance such as this might engender.

She was sending a burst-transmitted report groundside via satellite and the powerful communications package her American spacesuit provided. When she'd finished, she would have to conserve the unit's energy, or plug it into one of the crawler's outlets for resupply. She was trying to decide if she dared do that.

She was a very careful person. Only caution had kept her alive this long. Like the helmet that she still wore, Robin Faragher endured hardship gladly as long as it was hardship that would ensure survival. She was willing to be teased by Chandra and his wife, and even by the Muslim woman who accused her of "longing for purdah, this is proof," as long as she was alive to resent it.

The situation in which she now found herself was complex, but not impossibly so. When she arrived at RTI, she would meet up once more with Tracey Rand and his group.

There she would put a stop to WARLORD, once and for all. Accidents at an installation like RTI were easy to concoct. She had a taser, a projectile gun that shot tiny needles carrying electric charges. The same sort of weapon she'd used on Richelson.

Here, the taser was extremely effective; it did not need its tracks covered by a fall such as Richelson's. The needles would breach her enemies' suits, and death would naturally follow—through depressurization, electrical malfunction . . . The mess left after that would be sufficient to discourage any probe for more obscure causes.

There might be a scandal about the poor quality of American spacesuits. That was a risk one took.

She needed only to arrive at RTI in one piece and reasonably on schedule. This, it seemed, was a certainty.

The three Soviet spaceplanes following the ESA tour's crawler were doing only that: following. A legacy of Ilya Palladin's befuddled operations. Palladin should be dead by now. It would have been better if he'd died sooner, but one did the best one could, when new orders were piled upon old. Improvisation was not Robin's strong suit.

She was methodical, stubborn, and thoroughly committed to her job. She was not, however, a planner. She was merely an expediter.

There were contingency plans, of course, for every eventuality, but so many that she hadn't studied all of them. She was sorry, now. However, the message she was about to send, verifying her position and the plan she was implementing, would bring an answer. A message would be waiting for her at RTI. It would, of course, seem innocuous, but it would have a letter-number designation that would confirm her orders.

Meanwhile, she might as well mingle with the passengers, which meant taking off her helmet and trusting to the crawler's life support. It wasn't something she relished, but as soon as her lap computer's display returned to "ready" mode, she stowed it in her briefcase and began carefully unsealing her left glove at the wrist.

It wouldn't do for Chandra to become suspicious—or for anyone else to look at her askance. Once she had her helmet off and her computer stowed in her carry-on, she could mingle, partake of the refreshments the Einstein crewman was offering. She could even, she decided, risk having a drink. It was a long ride to RTI. . . .

As she went forward, Chandra's face brightened. If she'd planned to stay long on the moon, she'd have discouraged his advances. He was a pest and a bore. But he was convenient and malleable, for her present purposes.

"My dear, come join us. You've decided to trust to this marvelous technology at last? I'm so pleased." His voice had that lilt that made everything he said seem like a humorous American movie, a lilt that not even an Oxford education could completely eradicate. He was as innocent as a newborn babe of anything but socialist naiveté, a product of his teeming culture's revolution, a Hindu who thought technology could make up for what Rama could not make right.

It wasn't so. Neither Chandra nor anyone from his country had the steel to do what was needed to make India great. India was a force, like her neighboring Muslim nations, out of control, a pit of chaos, a fount of cannon fodder and angst that rivaled darkest Africa.

Someone she considered wiser had told her that there was no problem with such nations that proper guidance could not solve—guidance and time. They must be brought forcefully into the modern world, but that force must be their own desire for—

She reached for a drink from the tray Chandra had bidden be brought around again, for her benefit alone. As her fingers closed on the poly container, the moon crawler shuddered and lurched, as if its driver had miscalculated the grade ahead or the best way through it.

Inwardly, she shivered. Outwardly, she smiled sardonically. "You'd think, Dr. Chandra"—she was always very formal, very polite to him when his wife was within earshot—"that the Americans could have lent us a conveyance that didn't have to crawl over every inch of the moon between Einstein and dark side. Do you think it has anything to do with—"

Then the crawler lurched again and one of the women stifled a scream as people staggered for purchase. One of Chandra's aides slipped and careened against the wall.

She looked around quickly, toward the back of the crawler where she'd been sitting, where her computer was. Where her helmet was. Her mind was racing. The cold drink in her hand was burning her, numbing her. She wanted to put it down and rush to the rear of the vehicle, don her gloves and helmet, grab her computer terminal, and message for help. Immediately.

But Chandra was demanding to know what was wrong and those demands were going up toward the cockpit, or whatever one called the pilot and navigator's stations in these things. She had a job to do. As Chandra's executive assistant, she must find out for him what was wrong.

She began shouldering her way through chattering people—less than a dozen of them, but in these distressing circumstances, in so crowded a space, they suddenly seemed packed like sardines in a can.

The Muslim woman was talking about a safe arrival, if Allah willed.

"And if he doesn't?" Robin said sharply to the woman who seemed likely to become hysterical at any moment. "I suggest that we take care of our bodies and our survival, without putting such things in the laps of gods with too much to do." She pushed past the pale-lipped Pakistani woman and toward the Einstein personnel who were all huddled forward.

It wasn't until she had nearly reached them that the crawler lurched one more time and came, abruptly, to a halt.

She heard one man whisper harshly in English, "Fucking stopped dead in our tracks."

She took that opportunity to demand, "What is this? Has this vehicle broken down? Stopped, are we? Why and for how—"

"Lady," said a crew-cut, pale-haired American youth from Einstein. "Go back with the other civilians. You want to help, keep 'em calm back there. This is gonna take how long it takes, and there's not a damn thing you rank-and-privilege types can do about it."

"But what," she asked, not moving from the man's path or allowing his attention to divert from her, "is the problem? Are we truly stuck? And if so—"

The lights flickered. Someone in the passenger compartment screamed. The scream went on too long, and then was muffled, as if someone had put a hand over someone else's mouth.

"Shit, I ain't got time for this, lady," said the American, and turned his back on her, walking forward and slamming a sliding partition shut.

They were, by that action, effectively sealed off from the Americans who were in control of this vehicle. She moved back among the passengers, conscious of the flickering of the lights and of an urgent need to get to her computer terminal.

She had made half the distance when Chandra's hopeful face separated itself from the knot of milling passengers. "So, Robin? What do they say?"

"They say they have a problem: we are 'stuck.'" She shrugged acidly. "Americans. What it means, I don't know. They will not say. They have sealed themselves off up there. I suggest we do the same."

"What? What do you mean?" Chandra couldn't seem to decide how to react. He was either angry or frightened, or some combination of both. Most obviously, he was helpless, perhaps panicked beyond rational thought.

If that was so, he was doing an admirable job of appearing to be the vacant-eyed simpleton of a diplomat she'd occasionally told better men that he was. "Dr. Chandra," she said slowly and very clearly. "Get your people into their suits. Check everyone's seals. Then sit quietly."

She brushed past him. Only seconds later, as she reached her rear seat and her own equipment, the loud speakers in the walls began telling all and sundry to be calm, that the crawler was experiencing a "slight, temporary malfunction. Until we have it fixed, please put on your life-support—"

She stopped listening. The entire ESA tour was being treated like expendables, like cattle in a cattle car. When she returned to civilization, she was going to make whatever waves she could, and urge Chandra to scream in his loudest diplomatic voice for redress.

Yes, that was it: redress. Shivering with adrenaline, she fumbled into her helmet, checked its seals twice because she was so nervous, and then with equally methodical care, donned her gloves.

Once suited up, she put her computer on her lap and began tapping a sequence that allowed her to contact Sveboda.

Just then, every light in the crawler went out. Above her head and to her right, the EMERGENCY EXIT light flickered as it came back on battery power. By it and the light on her terminal's face, she tapped urgent queries into her keyboard.

And waited for a return message.

When she got it, she stared in disbelief at the instructions on her screen. And nodded, finally, in unnecessary agreement. Then once again she tapped: *Will exit vehicle. Have emergency rescue beacon for desired frequency.* She estimated the amount of time she needed, added that, and slowly began packing up her gear.

Not ten feet away from her, people groped in the almost complete darkness of the crawler's midsection. None of them would follow her, she was willing to bet.

The emergency exit lights weren't strong enough to let her see if anyone had failed to put on his helmet or gloves. They were no longer her concern, however. She had new orders.

She put her computer carefully in its case, zipped the case, checked all her seals again, and leaned sideways to pull down on the emergency exit handle.

The door popped from her hands, slamming outward as the air evacuated the crawler.

With her helmet now on Soviet com channels, she couldn't hear screaming if there was any. She was on her feet, jumping out the open door with little care about how far she might have to fall.

Luckily, the crawler was on reasonably level ground. She landed not on her knees but on her feet, flapping her arms for balance.

Then she ran, away from the crawler as fast as she could in long, dangerously high strides. Above her head, the silent shapes of the three Soviet spaceplanes zeroed in on the crawler that they had just received orders to destroy, blanketing the area with surveillance-defeating interference.

It was the only way, Robin Faragher was certain: the Americans would have a terrible disaster, a technical failure to explain to the European Space Agency and the six nations represented in the crawler. And Robin Faragher would not be prevented from carrying out her mission, even though some clever Americans had found a way to prevent her from getting to the radio telescope station in time to stop Tracey Rand from putting WARLORD on line.

The Americans had miscalculated: they had not realized that the ESA personnel in the crawler were expendable—all but Robin Faragher, of course. Nor were they clever enough to realize that she wasn't trapped like those cattle, in any case.

Once the crawler was destroyed, one of the Soviet spaceplanes would simply land and pick her up.

Nevertheless, she dove for cover as the planes assumed

attack formation. Hiding behind the ridge of a low crater, she covered her head with her arms, eyes closed behind her faceplate. She mustn't be blinded by the explosion.

She wouldn't look, no matter how satisfying a sight it might be. She did, however, feel the concussion as the crawler blew apart—a tremor that ran through the rock and up into her bones.

Then she held her breath, praying that no shard of wreckage would find her, piercing her suit and ending her life.

Robin Faragher was not too proud to pray, or to thank whatever God existed when she was still alive after the tremors under her ceased.

Then she sat up and set her beacon, still faced away from the crawler. If anyone was out there, if anyone had survived, the spaceplanes would take care of it. It wasn't her business.

Her business was to survive.

# Chapter 9

# RADIO TELESCOPE INSTALLATION

The radio telescope installation was dug into the very strata of the dark side. From above, it looked like a great bowl with little party flags around it and a single festooned "popper" of silver paper off to one side. That cylinder, which so much reminded Rand of a forgotten party favor, was the RTI's single habitat module. Beyond the telescope array and the maintenance sheds that housed the robotic servomechs to tend it was a typical lunar landing strip: bull's-eye, garage, and short runway.

They'd come the final distance in a radio-silence swath that the ConSecs must have thought was necessary to protect the ATF from the prying eyes of various nations' satellites.

Rand wouldn't have done it that way. The chances of any component of either superpower's precious space-based defense systems being trained on the moon were vanishingly small. Neither the U.S. nor Russia had even bothered to orbit anything more forbidding than lunar service stations around this life-forsaken hunk of rock. And they wouldn't recalibrate just for Rand and his—he hoped—low-profile mission: doing so would leave a hole in the defensive umbrella of any nation foolhardy enough to let its attention be diverted.

So, in Rand's estimation, they had come through undetected. The real danger had been roving Soviet or ESA observers, and Crane had taken care of that when he'd crippled the ESA tour's truck and the Soviets had stayed with the larger target.

Now, coming around for touchdown, the ConSecs were talking to RTI's ground station—although they were expected, it was still nice to tell the guys down there you were who you ought to be.

To Rand, the whole paranoid waltz was wearing thin. He still believed in what he was doing; he still believed that man's only chance was expansion and settlement in space. But he didn't believe that simple colonization was going to fix what was systemically wrong with mankind— not since he'd had his nose rubbed in reality. All colonization could do was provide an escape valve, a less crowded range, while humanity's primitives grew up. There was no technology that could protect a race of raving paranoids from greed, fear, or psychotic hatreds.

And since those were present on the moon in greater— or at least more obvious—measure than even Tracey Rand could have predicted, he wasn't particularly enspirited by what lay ahead.

But then, he'd never thought he had some special mission from God. He'd simply looked pragmatically at population curves and conflict percentages and made the obvious deduction: there'd be less killing if there was more elbow room; there'd be fewer suicidal martyrs with more hope; there'd be real progress, rather than zero-sum management, with somewhere for his manic kin to go *to*.

He still believed it, he told himself. He was just tired and facing a strenuous physical and mental effort. He didn't need lots of high-flown idealistic imperatives to weigh him down right now. If truth be known, he didn't need Kate there like some auditing angel, watching his every move with a critical eye.

He needed a little room to falter, a margin for error, a

sense that he could fail if he had to and she wouldn't be right there, making it worse. But she was there, beside him every step of the way from now on.

She was watching the ConSecs go through their landing procedures like she'd watched the back-scanning radar screens that showed the crawler as long as she could—until interference and Crane's determination to shut down everything but running gear to reduce their electronic signature had intervened.

Then they'd had time to talk, and that was never good, with the two of them. She probed and he backed off; he wasn't about to bare his soul for inspection when he himself had no idea what comprised it. He'd guided her into an operational consideration of the human assets they were dealing with, and that hadn't helped calm either of their nerves.

A whole trip's worth of analysis had brought them to the uncomfortable conclusion that there wasn't a single player involved in this mission whom they could trust any further than they could trust Ilya Palladin. And that included Crane and his boys, so far as Kate was concerned, because of what Crane had done to cripple the crawler.

Rand wasn't good at making excuses. He said, "Well, yeah, I wouldn't have done it that way, but it's their lives too." Crane knew what he was doing, you had to assume, or everything got too damned shaky to contemplate at all.

"I don't like it," she'd replied. "I don't like them. And I don't like the way you're avoiding me whenever I try to talk to you about Ilya."

"Talk to Harper; that's the way you want to play it," he'd said, and she'd bitten her lip.

They'd avoided looking at each other for some time after that. Now, while she was still studying the spaceplane's landing drill like she might have to try it herself someday, he leaned close: "Hey, Katy, let's get our front united, okay? We've got the worst still ahead. I need to know you're firmly in my corner."

292

"If you've got to ask, what's the good of me saying anything?" she retorted as Foster put the nosewheel of the ATF exactly where it ought to be and happy-looking green lights started flashing at the pilotry station.

"Nice job," Crane said approvingly, taking off his headset as Foster cut the engines.

"Nah, ain't nothin', sir," Foster replied. "These fly-by-wire's can beat my time whenever I'm willing to let them." He patted the maze of controls before him.

Rand was sliding out of his seat, reaching for his stowed case and helmet, anxious now to get started.

Kate looked at him questioningly. "Fly-by-wire?"

She should know what that meant, Rand thought as he said, "Remote capability: the computers on board this bird can be controlled by an outside source, from takeoff through military maneuvers to landing—no human factor necessary."

"From *Earth?*" she said disbelievingly.

Then he realized she did know the term; she was gauging emergency procedures. "The delay time in transmission's prohibitive, you're thinking? Yeah, a nanosecond is still longer than eleven inches, and there's a lot of them between us and Earth. But I'd be willing to bet there's remote capability for this sort of craft at Cop One, with redundancy at LSS and LEO: if we had to, we could get this baby home with just a radio, no manual required." He'd lowered his voice so that Crane wouldn't hear.

Was she thinking along preemptive lines? Devising contingency scenarios? Or just not feeling good about Linc Crane and his ConSecs? Kate could get pretty tough when she had to.

So he added, "Let's not worry about last-ditch stuff until we have to. My guess is, we won't have to." *Let me take care of you, remember? I promised I would. I'll get you home in one piece. Maybe I'll still shanghai you down to Puerto Vallarta when this is all over. Deprogram you back into the woman I used to know.*

293

"Yes sir, boss," she said brightly, with only a bit of an edge to her tone. She wanted Palladin and she wasn't going to let him off the hook until he offered his complete and unqualified support, which he wasn't ready to do. First things first: he had WARLORD to run.

They all suited up and checked and rechecked everything on board. Then Crane said, "All clear for deplaning," as he must have done a hundred times, and the five of them moved to the opening door.

As the ladder descended, up came a little moon cart on wheels and the fellow in it waved to them. Marshall went first, down the stairs, and stood by with a rifle as the rest of them descended.

This bunch didn't take chances. The sight of ready armaments at the RTI station made Rand even more nervous. If some Soviet spaceplane came blazing over the horizon now, he couldn't see how Marshall's single rifle was going to save them.

And if anything like that did happen, then it was a function of intelligence failure: Kate's fault, officially. Pumped up the way he was, his mind started sorting projected difficulties based on that assumption. . . .

As he climbed down the ladder, he shook his head viciously, as if he could shake off the train of thought. You couldn't sideline WARLORD now for anything less than a frontal assault, and not even Marshall really expected one.

The ConSecs were just being ConSecs. Once in the jeep-like open cart, the tension in Crane's personnel evaporated, although Marshall still had his rifle handy.

Kate said something about it not being "bear season out here," and Marshall cracked back that, "If I had the kinda arsenal you do, ma'am, it wouldn't matter what season it was."

Through his helmet's com channel Rand could hear her breath suck in, the pause she forced herself to take before she said in her most coldly authoritative tone, "Would you like to explain what you just said, soldier?"

"Easy, Kate," Rand broke in, turning from the waist to reach out over the seat. She should have realized that the ConSecs would find a way to check what they'd brought aboard: it was their plane, their project, their lives, too.

"My people don't do anything they aren't ordered to, ma'am," Crane said stiffly at almost the same time.

And Foster muttered, "Aw shit, Marsh," under his breath.

"Cool it," Rand warned, loud enough that everyone remembered where the command structure topped out. "We haven't got time for this. Let's go open channel, please," and he dialed his com link onto the RTI frequency. To delay doing so any longer was not only impolite to the man driving them, it was tantamount to screaming "intelligence operation in progress." And there was no reason in hell to do that.

The driver was still waiting patiently for a signal that the five of them were ready to go; the open cart hadn't moved an inch. "Okay, we're ready if you are," Rand said on the RTI channel. The driver introduced himself, wheeled the moon cart toward the single habitat module and began asking Crane about the ATF: did he want to leave it out, cover it with cammo netting, put it in the hangar—what?

They'd nearly crossed the mile or so of distance between the strip and the habitat when Crane and the RTI man finished going over details and the fellow said, "You guys hear, yet?"

"Hear what?" Crane and Rand spoke in absolute stereo.

"The crawler—those other guests we were expecting. It blew up out there. A Soviet observer mission called it in . . . some sort of accident. No survivors, they say. No piece big enough to need a flatbed for. Hell of a mess. Going to be a real flap about—"

"Jesus," Rand said.

"Chandra!" Kate whispered.

None of the ConSecs said a damned thing.

Rand shifted until he could see Crane clearly, despite their helmets. The cart was just coming to a stop before a stairway leading up into the cylindrical, forty-foot habitat. Crane met Rand's questioning stare with a calm verging on defiance and deliberately, very slowly, shook his head back and forth.

Rand was realizing that somebody had better say something else, that all of them had better get out of the stopped cart and go on into the habitat when Kate said, "Crane, I want to talk to you as soon as we get inside. Privately. Fara—"

"Kate, let me handle this." Before he said anything else, Rand jacked out of the cart and reached back for his case. Hefting it, he said to the driver, "Secretary Brittany's going to need the best-shielded line you can manage to get her, to Cop One. She had friends on that crawler. And we'd like a conference room, if there's anything like that in there."

"Sure thing, sir, you got it." The driver was trying to be helpful; he had his hand out for Rand's case. Rand didn't give it to him, so the RTI man offered Kate the hand as she started to scramble out of the open moon cart.

Crane's people were already out, their heads together: conduction of sound waves made it possible to hold an immaculately secure conversation in a spacesuit by the simple mechanism of touching helmets and making sure your com systems were off.

As the RTI man led the way up the steps empty-handed, Kate caught up with Rand, motioned him to bend his head to hers. When their helmets came into contact, she said in a rush, "Trace, did Crane do that, do you think? Blow the truck? Was Faragher that much of a threat?"

"If she was, she isn't anymore. We're not going to find out by asking, Katy." He thought about the interference on the rear surveillance screens and Crane's insistence that they turn them off when they had. There would have been some record of what had happened, if Rand hadn't done as Cranc asked. "We'll just not take the ConSecs for granted, okay? You understand?"

"I wasn't, anyway," she said huffily, and he could hear, even through the helmet, that she was near tears. He wanted to get her inside, strip off her suit, and hug her until they both felt better.

There'd be time for that. Before she could pull away, he put an arm around her shoulders. "I know you weren't. I was. I'm sorry. Sorry for Chandra and the others, and the damned mess this is going to cause. That investigation's going to get nasty; I don't want you involved in it. Let Harper take the weight. You and I don't know anything about this. We don't even have relevant tapes aboard the spaceplane."

She didn't pull away, as he'd been afraid she might. She nodded and the motion brought their helmets out of contact. She let him help her up the steps, although he was sure she didn't need any help, and into the lock.

Standing there in close quarters with the ConSecs, including Marshall who still had a ready rifle in his hands, Rand kept wondering why the fuck Crane had done it—if he had. There were cheaper diversions available than blowing the ESA tour's crawler at the cost of better than a dozen lives.

And one more time he wondered who was who in this puzzle of an operation; where Cranc stood was just one more question of an endless list. Even if his assumption was wrong, even if Crane hadn't blown the crawler—if nobody had, if it was just Saint Murphy doing his worst—that didn't change Tracey Rand's determination to trust nobody until this operation was over.

Inside, when they took their helmets off, Kate's face was tear-streaked, her lips swollen. Without apology or excuse, she came into his arms. Somewhere in that interval, before the RTI crew found a place for the five of them to talk privately, Rand decided that he'd been wrong.

He had to trust somebody. Palladin or no Palladin, he

was going to trust Kate. Trust her completely. Nobody as broken up over the crawler's casualties as she was could be faking it.

He kissed salty tears from her lips and offered her coffee that the RTI staffer had brought. "Come on, Katy, stuff happens. Accidents. Casualties. We've got a job to do. *You've* got to call in."

She ran the back of her hand impatiently across her eyes and pulled free of him, taking the coffee. "I must look terrible," she said shakily. Then her chin lifted. "Okay, get me that com channel. I'll call Harper and see what we can find out. Then we'll have that conference we need." Her eyes raked the ConSecs, lounging against the tiny reception area's walls.

"Fine, you do that. But none of this is any of our business," Crane said, and consulted his wristwatch.

Rand didn't say anything to mitigate the exchange. Crane was right. They weren't an investigative agency, they were an operations team, here to boost some contraband nukes into orbit.

The sooner they got started, the better.

# Chapter 10

# FROM RUSSIA WITH LOVE

The sick Russian in the intensive care unit wasn't responding to anything the Einstein medics had tried. They waited for their X rays, and when they got them they pored over the films, looking for microminiaturized delivery systems that might be spewing poison into the patient's system.

The poison would have to be one that imitated a virus; or it could be some biological warfare agent. Or it could be some simple, virulent, mutated but natural virus. Whatever it was, the Einstein medics couldn't find a tiny metal bead in any of Palladin's muscles or a specific the flu-type virus would respond to.

And they had their hands full, on alert in case the disaster out on the surface might yield some casualties they could treat.

The only fully qualified physician at Einstein was going out with the search and rescue teams, and he was taking most of his best equipment with him.

He looked in one final time on the delirious Russian muttering unintelligibly in his mother tongue and told the paramedic he was leaving him in charge, "Don't call Cop One again about this guy until I get back. They've got their hands full and so do we. If the Soviets helping with the search show up, don't let them in here—this guy *might* be contagious. But keep tape rolling; we'll get somebody to translate this garbage he's spouting. Maybe it'll mean something to somebody."

"But sir," protested the paramedic, "if the Soviet teams come back here, I can't keep them from taking this guy . . ."

"That's right, you can't. If they insist. But say what I said, and wait for Cop One's authorization to release him—if anybody pushes. Suits me if he's not on our turf, especially if he dies, but I've got orders too, and those orders said 'wait for further instructions from Mission Director Harper's office.' When the head honcho speaks, us peons, we listen." The physician in charge ducked his head and clapped the paramedic on the back before he picked up his emergency bag and walked away, toward the waiting search and rescue team leaving for the crawler disaster site.

Damned weird that the brass didn't want to get rid of this sick Russian as soon as possible, but the physician had learned not to question. Didn't want to give the Russians an excuse to send extra personnel to Einstein, probably. Or really were worried about an epidemic—not a small consideration, up here.

Content that rolling videotape would be his best defense, the physician forgot about Palladin because there was nothing his expertise could do for the man, and began steeling himself for what promised to be hours of sorting through severed limbs and frozen internal organs.

Ilya Palladin was absolutely certain he was already dead. It felt terrible to be dead. Every limb hurt and whenever he spoke to God, that hurt too. But God was there, big and bold with his flowing beard. Palladin was glad there was a God. He'd always believed in his heart there was a God. A Russian Orthodox God with a snow-white beard and mighty limbs and all the jewels of a czar in his diadem.

God was good, but He wanted to know everything about Palladin's life. He wanted to know about Palladin's sins and about his tragedies. He wanted to know about his mother and his father and his stillborn twin brother, whom mother had always blamed Ilya for outliving.

Ilya had taken the strength of his stillborn brother into himself and lived; this was his first sin. Ilya had lied to his mother and his father and lied to the State. Ilya had denied his faith in God. God did not like to be denied.

This was why Ilya's death was so painful. His limbs felt as if they were molting; his dead lungs kept trying to breathe; his dead tongue kept trying to speak. And the Russian that he spoke was falling on the deaf ears of a God who knew that the State was His enemy.

Ilya Palladin was crying and he knew it. The tears that ran into his mouth were salty but they were wet. His lips were so dry and blistered and cracked that the tears burned him, but they made him realize he was alive. "Water," he croaked. Then, again, louder: "Water."

Someone gave him water, someone with a growly voice he could not understand. But he understood now that he had been given a warning. God had come to him and told him to confess all while he had time. KGB men held so many sins in their hearts that they never could get to heaven. Each sin was a stone weighing him down and those stones would take him straight to hell.

He had glimpsed that hell. It was Bosch's hell. It was Breughel's hell. Ilya Palladin didn't want to go there. He demanded in Russian of the man belonging to the big, red-skinned hand that swam into his vision with a nippled bottle of water, "Stay. You must stay and listen to my confession!"

Since the shape of the man did not disappear, Ilya began at the beginning, the day of his first willful sin: he had taken the neighbor's kitten for a ride on his bicycle, and when the kitten cried and scratched him, he had become furious. He had grabbed the kitten by the tail and pedaled his bike harder and faster, holding the kitten by the tail so it would learn that Ilya could control its destiny, its fate, its life, and its death. He wanted the kitten to love him, to be grateful, to purr in his arms when he pulled it up from where he dangled it, by the hub of his bicycle's wheel.

But the kitten was so frightened that it urinated on him and he dropped it in the street. It had run from him across the street, right into the path of an oncoming car. . . .

This was only the first of many sins that he had to recount.

He told them all, every one he could remember, until he got to the days and years he'd spent in KGB.

Then something cautioned him. He was not to tell these secrets, even to God. And his throat hurt terribly. He was weak and tired. When the hand with the water bottle came again, it seemed to have the wrong number of fingers.

This frightened him and the fear pierced his delirium. He struggled to push himself upright in his sickbed and found that he was bound with straps. He tossed and turned and perhaps he yelled, for a face came close and someone said, slowly and clearly, "Easy, buddy. You're sick but you're safe at America's Einstein base."

And then he remembered everything. Everything but what he might have said, what he might have confessed, while God had been appearing to him.

In slow, halting English, he grated: "I want to write . . . free my hands . . . write a note."

Nearly all his strength was expended in the asking. When the man came back with a clipboard and a pen, Ilya Palladin had nearly forgotten what he wanted it for. But then he remembered. He was in American hands and he was dying and God had given him this last chance to make amends.

With shaking hands he took the clipboard and raised it

close to his face and printed with shaky, laborious movements, the one thing he thought might weigh against his sins in the eyes of God:

*Dear Kate,* he wrote. *I love you. Forgive me. Khimik is Bat-*– He never finished the note. The pen fell from his sweating, nerveless fingers and his head flopped back against the pillow.

# Chapter 11

# BOOST
# PHASE

Kate kept asking herself what she'd really expected as each newly revealed facet of WARLORD startled her more and more.

But, like her unsatisfactory call to Harper's office, which had yielded only the information that "Director Harper is busy in conference, now," everything she saw should have been predictable to someone as space-seasoned as Kate.

Only it hadn't been. She hadn't expected to be driven in an open cart, down into a terrifyingly long and low, badly lit burrow that extended right under RTI itself, with only Rand and the ConSecs for company.

She hadn't expected the exposed wiring and cursory fluorescents that made the place seem like an open mine shaft. She hadn't been expecting to work under such hazardous conditions—staggering under the weight of heavy equipment, bumping up against jagged tunnel sides, sweating in her suit, and all of it without an air lock or even an emergency suit-patch kit.

It was as if the ConSecs had determined by a vote that nothing so untoward as a torn suit would slow them up, and thereby obviated the need to prepare for one. It *was* like an open mine shaft, down there, with girders of punched steel here and there from which hung cabling and lighting fixtures.

In the glow of them, she saw the stashed components of WARLORD for the first time: the long sleek nuke drivers in their rocket-shaped assemblies; the antennae and stabilizers, the calibration equipment in its heavy travel cases.

The men worked in silence and she worked with them, lifting and prodding heavy pieces onto motorized gurneys which rolled on tracks that disappeared down where the tunnel got darker. She didn't ask any questions; it wasn't time and she had neither energy nor wind to spare.

Brute force was in demand here. As she tired, Kate found she was more worried about Rand than about herself. She didn't have a prosthetic hip that might not do well under this sort of strain.

Foster and Marshall seemed to have been assigned the scariest task of all: the two ConSecs did the close-up work with the nuclear drivers. The two men occasionally put their helmets together, but generally worked without a spoken word, climbing over the nukes as if the modern skull-and-crossbones that was the radiation danger symbol wasn't stenciled to their thick, curving sides.

When Foster and Marshall had the drivers on their gurney, the two cylinders took up nearly the entire width of the tunnel. There was barely room enough for Foster to climb over them, disappear beyond, and call back through his com set: "Okay, folks. Meet you up there."

Then, with a vibration she could feel but no noise that her headset picked up, the gurney Foster was driving pulled off slowly into the deepening tunnel.

Kate realized she had no idea where it would come out, or what was supposed to happen next. She paused, holding one end of a thick, reinforced electronics case, and Rand, holding the other side, caught her eye and grinned encouragingly behind his faceplate.

*Okay, buddy, we'll play it your way.* Part of her was

angry: she wasn't a dock worker. This wasn't the sort of thing she was trained for. She wasn't a heavy-lift vehicle; she was a diplomat. If she could, she'd have wiped her forehead with her arm; her suit wasn't handling the sweat of exertion as well as it might.

Even in one-sixth G, the ratio of body weight to dead weight didn't change: The hundred-pound travel case she was wrestling with didn't weigh that, here, but she wasn't any stronger than she'd have been at home.

Suddenly, for the first time in years, she wished she *was* home . . . in Washington; on her porch in Arlington, sipping lemonade and talking over lobbyists' heads with Andresson or Bates.

Desk job on good old Earth, that was what she'd put in for when this was over. And then she admitted that the nukes and the degree of care that had been taken by Consolidated Space Command Security to protect those nukes had unnerved her. Damned tricky, all this up here and she hadn't known a thing about it. There were two more big pieces to go—crates marked only with assembly numbers—and then they'd be done, she thought.

When she and Rand had levered those crates, with the help of a dolly, a few unladylike curses, and the power of prayer, onto the last remaining gurney, she sat on its tailgate and looked back the way they'd come.

And there, emerging out of darkness like Leviathan, was an additional gurney, two lights in the semidark.

"Rand," she said into her com mike.

"Yeah, just Crane with the OMVs; nothing to worry about," he said calmly.

She stared at the approaching gurney and realized that both Crane and Marshall had been gone for some time—perhaps since Foster had disappeared with the nuke drivers. The gurney now pulling to a halt held Orbital Maneuvering Vehicles—OMVs; not the sort of thing you could stick out there in orbit and have nobody wonder why.

The two octagonal constructions were the size of walk-in closets. She had no idea how Crane thought he could get them into the ATF—the spaceplane's cargo bay would be crowded by the nuke drivers—crowded enough that Kate was beginning to wonder about radiation hazard.

But she didn't ask. It was as hopeless as trying to break in on Harper's crisis committee: Harper had a disaster to deal with and nothing Kate could have done would have gotten him to take her call.

She didn't care about Harper; she'd tried, for the record. She was happy enough not to have gotten him, she told herself; Rand was right, she ought to stay as far away as possible from anything to do with the crawler's destruction and the inevitable bloody investigation to follow. Heads would roll; she should keep hers down. If possible, she should keep completely out of sight.

She'd be willing to do that, as soon as they got this project on line and they'd picked up Ilya. Rand knew she was adamant about that. So it was an extra advantage that she hadn't had to lie to Harper by omission. They were going to sneak Ilya Palladin off the moon under the very noses of both superpowers.

Rand had as much as promised her he'd back her. Once they got Palladin out safely, the Soviet would go through a metamorphosis peculiar to her business: he would go from being a liability to being a valuable commodity.

On Earth, Palladin represented an intelligence coup of immense proportions, the kind that got you promotions and citations. It would be good for all of them—Rand, Ilya, and Kate herself—if it worked. But that wasn't why she was doing it. She was doing it for Ilya, and Rand knew that.

She wanted to tell Trace that it was the only way she could clear her conscience. If she and Tracey Rand had any future, she had to do right by Ilya Palladin to make way for it.

She kept reminding herself that her personal reasons only added to, and certainly didn't obscure, her operational concerns in the matter of this particularly valuable defector. It would be the first time that anyone from the Soviets' Anticosmic Defense establishment had come over. It would give their side so much information that whatever waves it caused could be ridden out. . . .

"Kate? You in there?" Rand's voice broke into her reverie. She focused her eyes and saw Crane, who'd climbed to the front of his gurney, gesturing to them.

"Sorry, Trace. I was thinking about something else. Are we ready?"

"Ready as we're going to get. Put your feet up. Hold on. I don't want to lose you now."

She did that, facing forward so that she could see what Rand was doing. He hit toggles on the gurney and, under her, it began to roll forward. She tightened her grip on the guard rail.

As the gurney picked up speed and the tunnel lights began to grow long tails, she had the errant thought that this part of the journey resembled nothing so much as overprivileged boys with a giant set of toy trains.

She looked back, and there was Crane with his heavily loaded gurney, just far enough behind them that if anything fell off theirs, he wouldn't collide with it. Boys with toys. There were certain theorists who said that aggression was "hard-wired": a genetic attribute of human males. If that were true, then not only militarized space, but militaristic behavior was a certainty as long as the human race survived.

She'd argued with someone about it once, and the argument had degenerated into a heated debate. She'd said then that a rational being had options, because that being had self-consciousness as well as consciousness—an alternative to selfishness that was called altruism.

The person with whom she'd argued, who had spent more time reading behavioral genetics than she, had countered that altruism was a self-delusional strategy, just one more weapon in the arsenal of self-interested survivalists.

"If violence and conflict are hard-wired," he'd said, "you've got only two choices: create acceptable venues in which to exercise those imperatives, or wipe out the carriers." He'd grinned. "There's no race without males, and I don't mean feminized males. So we're stuck with giving ourselves the room to be what we are, while trying to get ourselves civilized enough to recognize and sublimate what we don't like about us."

That person she'd argued with had been Tracey Rand. They'd had the discussion before a mission not so unlike this one, in personal terms: a mission on which lives could be lost; a mission on which more could be lost, in geopolitical terms, than a few lives.

They'd completed that mission without loss of life to their side, and they'd ended the argument in agreement that lives, when they're the lives of people you know, weigh differently in any equation than do the lives of strangers. And since she'd conceded that, during the argument, and known it was true, she'd been trapped into admitting that "the hard-wiring for violence and conflict" might not be totally confined to the male of the species.

If she needed further proof of his premise, now, it was the sudden desire to touch her hip and check that the forty-four magnum was still holstered there.

When it came down to personal survival, none of the big words or fancy theories mattered. For all Kate Brittany could tell, the world would end, effectively enough for her at least, when she died—there was no proof to support any conflicting theory.

Moving at autobahn speed down a tunnel that shouldn't have been dug here under an American installation on the dark side of the moon, she suddenly felt that particular imperative quite clearly, felt it in a way that words could not convey, unless those words were short and sweet: she wanted to live through this. She wanted to win. She wanted to survive to find out if she and Trace could make it together.

Maybe they'd go for each other's throats, sequestered at his jungle retreat. Maybe she'd go nuts from boredom. She had a hands-on attitude to life that he'd let her know, long ago, he didn't entirely share.

And yet he was willing to put hands on WARLORD. Because it mattered to him. No matter what he said about coming out here to protect her, it was WARLORD, not Kate Brittany, that had brought Tracey Rand out of retirement.

She didn't blame him for that, but she blamed him for not telling her how extensive the preparations here had been; he must have known. The dark-side tunnels she was now speeding through were a good example of what the security classification referred to as "Sensitive Compartmented Information" was meant to protect. It was why SCI clearances were so sought after by those in Washington who counted clearances as status symbols.

Out here, clearances were more than symbols; out here, information or lack of it could be the difference between life and death. And he'd known so much more than she for so long. . . .

She shook her head, forcing herself back from thoughts of distrust or betrayal. Trace was secretive. So was she. So was Ilya. If he came through for her with Ilya, she'd forgive him for holding back. And if she could bring Ilya home safely, she could retire herself when Ilya's debriefing was done, if she wanted to . . . "How much longer, Trace?" she risked in her phones.

"We're just about there, aren't we, Crane?" came Rand's voice.

Crane cut into their circuit. "Five, six minutes, tops. Foster'll have the ATF fired up, the drivers loaded. Marshall will be bringing up the two moon trucks we're taking. You guys can ride wherever you want, but the best seats are going to be in the ATF with me."

"That's where we want to be then," Trace answered for both of them.

310

She almost told him that she'd make her own decision, but since he'd made the only sensible choice—the one she'd have made if he'd given her time—she shelved it. He was just that way. She'd either get used to it, or not. You couldn't change a man; you either adapted or went on your way.

Adaptation, she was musing dreamily, watching the moon rock blur by under her feet, was like that; you adapted or you died. Then the rock stopped going by quite so rapidly as the gurney slowed.

She scrambled upright as it came out of the tunnel, trying to figure out where she was.

They were in a crater, but most craters weren't particularly distinguishable from one another unless there were human artifacts emplaced nearby. And she saw none of those, except the little ATF and the two moon trucks that Crane had promised would be there.

These moon trucks were the same sort that were used on the lunar oxygen-and-passenger ferry system; they were plenty big enough to accommodate their pilots and the OMVs. They looked like wingless flies with stubby, suction-cupped legs. Toward them, Rand headed the gurney, now running over bare rocks, the tracks in the tunnel left behind.

Crane was right behind them. Ahead, the ATF's lights were blinking, its cargo door closed, its passenger door open. Off to one side was the gurney Foster had loaded with WARLORD's nuke drivers.

A thrill ran through Kate. This was it. This was what it had all been for.

Rand pulled the gurney up to the two moon trucks and Marshall swung out of one to help with the cargo stowage.

They played stevedores for the better part of half an hour, Crane cursing the length of time they were "exposed." Exposed to surveillance, he meant.

But Rand told him what Kate was thinking. "Too late to worry about that, friend."

And it was. When the two moon trucks were loaded with the OMVs and the remaining electronics, Crane spoke to Foster through his com link and the ConSec sergeant swung down from the ATF.

Until that moment, when he deplaned, Kate hadn't realized why Foster wasn't loading cargo: he'd been at the ATF's weapons battery, ready to shoot any interloping observer out of the moon's black sky.

When Foster reached them, he said, "Okay sir, all the jamming measures are still up and running. Shut 'em down when you get aboard." Foster held out a gloved hand somberly. "Good luck, sir. See you up there."

"Luck, Foster, ain't none of what we got to do."

Marshall and Crane put their helmets together and Rand took Kate's arm. "Shall we?" he asked with exaggerated gallantry. "Your carriage awaits, madame."

"Why not," she agreed with a suppressed giggle, and they headed for the ATF waiting, its ladder down, in the desolate crater.

From here on out, there was no time for second thoughts, or anything but WARLORD. She knew it; Rand knew it; Crane knew it.

The lieutenant was right behind them when they climbed the ladder, slapping toggles before they'd slid into their seats and fastened their harnesses. Kate wished, as Crane touched his throttle and the spaceplane's engines burned to life, that she'd called Einstein base to see how Ilya was doing. He could have used some moral support.

But any unnecessary communication might have jeopardized their mission. As it was, there was no certainty that chase planes wouldn't appear behind them, if their security had been blown.

You couldn't tell. You had to wait. Behind her, nestled in the cargo bay, were the nuke drivers for WARLORD. Ahead was the most difficult part of the mission: assembling the components in space and launching them without attracting any attention, so that WARLORD could pass for harmless space junk broken free from an erratic orbit, headed for a crash landing on Mars.

As the moon dwindled below them, Kate Brittany reached out for Rand's hand and, taking it, squeezed.

# Book Five

# WARLORD

# Chapter 1

# ERECTOR
# SET

*God help us, here we go,* ConSec Lieutenant Lincoln Crane heard himself thinking as he cut his engines, putting the ATF into a parking orbit only meters from the space junk that was his objective.

A parking orbit that was going to look real curious if anybody noticed—miles above the moon, next to nothing in particular but the detritus of human space flight, where a billion-dollar spaceplane and two moon trucks had decided to stop for a picnic.

At least it was dark side. There wasn't squat for surveillance back here—not yet. When this mission was over, the superpowers would start taking the moon's backside more seriously: the U.S., because it had pulled off this coup right under the Soviets' pug noses; and the opposition because intelligence leaked.

Nobody back home seriously expected to be able to keep WARLORD secret forever. They only expected Crane to get it up and running and make sure that, once the calibrating and initial course corrections were done, the remote course-correction gear was turned into a one-man dog. And that man was him.

He had a black box under his seat that, when added into the circuitry Rand was here to assemble, would make sure that the U.S. could honestly claim WARLORD was unresponsive to remotely sent abort signals. Once the black box was in place, WARLORD would listen to nothing but its own on-board guidance system.

You couldn't be too careful, when you were changing history. The two passengers he'd ferried up here would be told only that the box was to be put into place—where and how, but not why. Why wasn't their business. Especially when one of them was Tracey Rand.

Crane sat quietly at his helm, waiting for Foster and Marshall in their moon trucks to answer his coded signal by EVAing. That was what the rest of this mission was about: Extra Vehicular Activity.

Until all parties were so engaged, strict radio silence was in effect. When Foster and Marshall had deployed the two OMVs, Rand and Brittany would start earning their keep: remotely piloting the OMVs from the safety of the spaceplane's pressurized cabin to help jockey the large pieces of WARLORD into position. But after that, even Rand would have to get into one of the MMUs and go outside for the final, close work.

That was going to be the really hard part, for Crane. His job was to see that some last-minute wave of left-wing idealism didn't sweep over Rand and cause him to sabotage his own project. Bates had been adamant about that. Crane was to use his own judgment.

Likewise, if the project misfired for any reason, Crane was empowered to terminate all human components he considered liabilities. Crane loved the way the brass got down to the bottom line—with euphemism and averted eyes. But you got the message. Always. Or next time, they used somebody else.

Crane knew almost enough about WARLORD to be able to do what was necessary without Tracey Rand's help. Almost. Some of the computational adjustments weren't the sort Crane could handle without down-links for guidance. Once in a great while, these volatile egghead-operators were worth what they cost the government. This was one of those times. Crane wished it weren't.

Behind his back, the two high-powered operators were talking to each other, watching the monitors that showed the OMVs being off-loaded from the two moon trucks.

"Almost ready, back there?" Crane asked. Brittany was ready for any damn thing, with the forty-four she was carrying. The woman was no lady, but Crane wondered whether, dial-a-recoil or not, she'd shoot that thing out there and risk being propelled with equal and opposite force out of orbit, with only her MMU to get her back. It was a pertinent detail for him to consider: if he had to take out Rand on site, Brittany's hand weapon could be a real problem.

"Ready and waiting, Lieutenant," came Brittany's crisp reply. He risked a backward glance and saw that she was at the remote pilotry console, chewing a stylus, tracking her chosen OMV with a concentration and an energy he could almost feel.

Beside her, swiveled left in his seat, was Rand. Rand had put up a split screen so that he could not only track his OMV, but get long-range views of the entire scattering of project components, which he was checking against a manifest open on his lap.

Crane had managed to "misplace" their weapons cases in back with the nuke drivers, but somehow she'd held on to the piece she was wearing. Annie Oakley in a spacesuit. It was the last thing he needed. When he got home, he was going to bitch like hell that there was no warning of this sort of thing in her psych profile.

Unless, of course, everything went perfectly and Crane didn't have to make the sort of command decisions on site that would cause Brittany to use that weapon.

Crane hated to wait; he did too much waiting. Too many of his decisions were made only after others had made bad ones. His specialty was damage control, but by default. On

WARLORD, he had nearly enough clout to prevent any damage he might later have to control.

That was why he was staying in here with Rand and Brittany instead of manhandling those chunks of WARLORD out there, along with his two mission specialists.

He punched up better telemetry and fiddled with his magnification until he could see Foster, with his MMU deforming his back, pushing one of the expendable launch canisters toward the coordinates that would form the assembly point for WARLORD.

Crane itched to get out there himself. There were forty-two pieces of WARLORD all told. Pieces big and small. Pieces that must be laser-soldered and pieces that must be handled with extreme care, no matter how dented and useless the cosmetic camouflage boys had made them look.

He watched as Foster got the component into position and slapped his retro-rocket pack: putting on the brakes in space wasn't the easiest of tasks. Once Foster got the booster stabilized, he looped cable around it and left it, jetting back toward the general area of his moon truck for another piece. Marshall was doing the same, but more slowly.

As soon as the two operators with Crane in the spaceplane got their OMVs under control and into position, some of the heavy assembly work could be done by the remotely piloted arms of the octagonal orbital maneuvering vehicles.

Crane was concerned most of all with that part of the mission sitting behind him: these two were already behind schedule. He swiveled his seat and said, "Okay, folks. We can use your help out there. You want to get that remote muscle of yours on line so we can haul the goddamned nukes out of our cargo bay?"

They should know what to do without him telling them.

"Easy, Crane, okay?" Rand said absently. "It's my hen house, and I'm still doing my head count."

Antsy beyond his ability to control, Crane tapped the buckle that freed him of his harness and floated out of his seat, reaching as he did so for the stored MMUs. "Hurry up, then, okay? I've still got to get you both space ready before I can get the goddamn nukes out of cargo bay."

"Space ready?" said the woman, craning her neck to look at him.

*Christ, Rand didn't tell her. Why the fuck not?* "Yes ma'am, like it says in our orders: final assembly is all EVA."

"Not for her, it isn't," said Tracey Rand. "I need somebody on board to maintain an overview. Crane, back off, will you? For the next couple of hours, it's my show."

Crane wasn't surprised at Rand. But he was surprised at himself, at the anger that surged through him. "Those are my guys out there, buddy. So part of it's your show—the hardware part. And I don't want to argue with you about the rest. Get suited up, both of you; I've got to depressurize to get out of here. Brittany, you're staying here with the ship, that's fine. Both the OMVs aren't too much for you to handle, are they?"

Kate leaned back in her chair, draped one arm over it, and gazed at him levelly. "What do you think, Lieutenant?"

"I think that, if you get into trouble, you can't call out to us for help. So you'd better be sure." Why was he letting this happen? They were arguing over nothing in particular; he didn't care if the woman decided to ride out the rest of this mission curled up with her teddy bear in the pull-down sleeper aft of the com station.

Except that somebody had to run the OMVs and she was that somebody.

Rand floated out of his seat, muttered, "Ignore this bullshit, Kate. You know what to do," and pushed off toward the storage lockers.

Crane shoved himself irritably after. At least the lady and her goddamn forty-four weren't an immediate part of his workload. One more time, he regretted the security measures that prevented him from contacting Foster and

Marshall until, outside the spaceplane and free of its constraints, he could establish communications with his specialists via their low-power suit radios.

Until then, this damned mission had to run like clockwork; there was no way to improvise anything different without chancing discovery by trying to prevent it. Anything Crane did to mask transmissions from the ATF could draw attention to its position. It wasn't likely, but it was possible—a bounced signal, making its way over the "horizon" that was the bulk of the moon, was all it would take to defeat their security. The only time the spaceplane was really safe up here was when she was in passive mode, with her smart electronics dedicated to keeping transmissions in, not sending them out.

And she had an entire cargo bay full of nuclear material to mask. It was all the plane could be expected to handle; making them invisible hinged on keeping their high-tech spacecraft as quiet as possible. The "space junk" that was WARLORD was unremarkable because it had been there all along; the ATF might hide among that junk if she were passive; the tiny human beings in the MMUs were too small to be noticed by anything but already-alerted highly selective screening and analysis of what was there.

So Crane had no choice about radio silence, like he had no choice about Tracey Rand. Where Marshall and Foster were concerned, he had a lot more faith that his human components wouldn't disappoint him.

As he was helping Rand check his oxygen and fit the MMU in place on his back, Crane reminded himself to make sure that his kinetic-kill pistol was in his tool kit and that Rand never got his hands on one of the attaché cases filled with special weapons that were now stashed in the cargo bay with the nukes.

# Chapter 2
# SWITCH

Foster was ahead of schedule. He'd managed to bring in his share of the perimeter components and now he had two choices: go for one of the remaining large sections that ought to have been handled by one of the two OMVs, which weren't performing up to speed, or use his MMU to float across the entire quadrant to where Marshall was just visible behind a nearly man-size cube that was part of WARLORD's payload.

He decided he'd help Marshall. There was some actual junk up here, too—collected garbage like stuff washed up on a beach. He'd come across three pieces that hadn't a damned thing to do with the project he was assembling: part of a dead telemetry satellite that belonged to some Arab country; an antenna from somebody's exploded target; a piece of salvageable ESA hardware that was probably worth a million or so to its insurers. Stuff got trapped in gravity wells all the time.

There were little pieces, too, over near the moon trucks, but they didn't bother Foster like the extraneous large chunks did. It had confused the hell out of him at first: he'd gone looking for an assembly number and nearly snagged his suit in the process. With no radio contact but what his spacesuit's short range could provide once he hit the relevant switches, he'd probably just have had time to say good-bye to Marshall before he vomited his lungs up.

Damned spooky out here, under these conditions. The MMU he was wearing was the best and newest and he took comfort in its power. Its nitro pack was nearly full; its armrest supports didn't impede his movements. He could run the whole system with the joysticks that the MMU's superstructure put conveniently into his hands: push in for forward, pull out for retro, nudge in any direction you wanted to turn. The old ones had taken two hands to operate; this one weighed half as much and left your right hand completely free.

He was trying to decide whether Crane would consider it a security breach if he jetted right across the nexus of the assembly area—it was the quickest way to Marshall—when he thought he saw a head and arm peek out over the oblong he was approaching.

Marshall, however, was over at one end of the component designated 31A, pushing it slowly toward the center where WARLORD was coming together like something you assembled for your kid on Christmas Eve in the middle of the living-room floor.

So he looked again, blinking, cursing polarization and his nerves. *Wasn't nothin'. Ain't nothin' there. Can't be.* There was nobody else out here.

He fumbled for his joystick, coming to a halt near a separation mechanism with DANGER: EXPLOSIVE stenciled on it, and took his own head count: Marshall, out there where Foster was headed. Crane and some other, probably Rand, screwing around with the nuke drivers in the space-plane's open cargo bay.

That left the last party member—Brittany, if Foster knew his boss—inside handling the OMVs. Which was probably why the OMV part of this wasn't on schedule, he told himself sourly.

But it didn't help the foul taste in his mouth. Okay, he

knew where everybody was, and therefore what he'd seen wasn't real. That was something you didn't want to admit, not when the only thing between you and a very lonely death was what you'd come into this world with: your own self.

*Come on, Foster,* he told himself harshly. *Shape the fuck up.* He pushed down on the joystick under his left palm deliberately. The sensation of motion that was always confusing in weightlessness assailed him, pushing away more peripheral doubts. His body wanted to know how come it was moving under conditions like this, feeling what it was feeling. He concentrated on his own physical reactions, using them to push away others he couldn't afford to have. You couldn't start seeing things. You couldn't hallucinate. You couldn't slip for a second out here, or you were the worst kind of dead, and fast.

He was glad, for a candid instant inside his suit, that he didn't have radio contact: he might have said something about what he'd thought he'd seen. And he hadn't seen it. From this angle, he couldn't even see Marshall. All he could see was the heavy oblong, coming toward him slowly because it was moving toward the central assembly point and so was he.

He kept his hand clenched on the joystick, using his MMU's propulsion pack sparingly for course correction. He was going fast enough, and things were beginning to come together.

Out of the corner of one eye he could see the remotely piloted OMV, like a wheel from a tinker toy kit, nudging the disposable third stage of the package toward the growing aggregate of parts.

This whole mission was something you could probably tell your grandchildren about with pride, if it was declassified before you died. Making the moon safe for humankind—at least, American humankind. He liked that. Foster had always liked space; he loved the velvet black and the diamond stars. He wasn't articulate the way Crane and

325

some of the higher-ups were, but he felt what he felt very deeply. And he felt good about doing something as obviously useful in his terms as helping man get a foothold in space.

And, like Marshall, Foster felt good about anything Crane figured was worth doing. Crane was a good guy, and there weren't many like him up in those ranks. . . .

Again, Foster thought he saw an additional figure—a little stick figure this time, a full human in spacesuit tumbling head over heels. A tiny, receding figure that came and went as if it were tumbling in and out of sunlight, or starlight, or . . .

Foster closed his eyes and counted to ten. When he opened them again, the figure wasn't there. Time for some R&R, if he could get it without admitting why he needed it. He couldn't tell the guys; he'd be ribbed about seeing things for the rest of his natural life.

As his vector and the oblong's showed signs of convergence, Marshall waved. Foster waved back with his right hand. Then he realized that Marshall was pointing toward the spaceplane.

He toggled his joystick and the MMU turned him obediently, a neat about-face.

He saw then that Crane and Rand—had to be: the two suited men were about the same size; Brittany was lots smaller—had both nuke drivers out, lashed together with cable, and were trying to loop the cable over the OMV's extended robot arm.

Good thing there wasn't an open com link, or the curses Crane would be spouting now would have echoed to Sveboda and back.

Without further ado, Foster depressed his joystick and headed over to give them some help.

The impact that killed him wasn't something he felt as pain. It was like a twitch or a thrill as electrical impulses beat depressurization to his nervous system, and his whole body spasmed. His hand on the joystick clenched; jerked.

His vector altered drastically. Already dead, his limbs now still, Foster floated on an elliptical course that would take him past the spaceplane and on, toward the orbit of Venus.

# Chapter 3
# MARTYR

Robin Faragher cleared her weapon and checked her charge as she pushed the oblong component labeled 31A toward WARLORD's assembly point.

She talked to herself occasionally, preparing a burst transmission she'd send to Sveboda in the event of capture or imminent death. All she had to do was push a button on her belt and the data would be on its way.

But it wasn't time yet. She didn't need to send her precious intelligence yet. She was still collecting. And there was a chance she'd be able to deliver this information in person: all that the camera in her American-style helmet was recording; every comment she'd made about the radiation warning symbol in black and yellow on the nuclear missiles that the two Amerikanskis had wrestled out of the spaceplane's cargo bay—everything she'd learned was invaluable.

She fully intended to make a profit on it, of one sort or another, if she survived.

Two down, three to go, if she knew what she was looking at. There must be one of them left in the spaceplane itself. That would be the woman, if she understood American strategic thinking.

And she did. That proclivity of Americans to underestimate females had been her best cover, her most dependable ally. Besides that, she had only the willingness to die in order to win, to win at all costs. It was a sufficient arsenal to triumph over American men.

She'd been trained as a martyr; she would still gladly give her life to stop this, or any other, travesty of American imperialism, against which she warred. She could go home when this was over, go home to fetes and luxury. Or she could rest and prepare to fight again, once WARLORD was destroyed.

If she'd wanted it, she probably could have had Ilya Palladin's residency up here. She had considered it. Because it would be such a coup and because she always considered only what she would do once she'd won, never what she would do if she lost.

There was no use considering losing: if she lost, she died. The Soviet pilots who had dropped her off up here did not understand her. They had been concerned, then confused, then scandalized at her refusal of an escape craft. If she won, she would have the ATF. She didn't need a pickup, or an escape craft. There was no escape. There was only winning.

Marshall had been as easy to kill as Palladin, easier than the Seal men. Foster had been a gift.

Now she was in improvisational mode, pushing her piece of hardware calmly toward its drop-off point, watching through her American-style helmet as Rand and Crane guided their filthy nuclear-tipped drivers toward a rendezvous with fate.

As she pushed her cargo with careful taps on her MMU, she was conscious of many things: the speed of her heartbeat, the exhilaration that killing two targets in close succession produced, the shallowness of her breathing as she prepared to choose her third.

If she must, she had an explosive device on her belt that would make an end to both her enemies at once—and WARLORD. And probably, from electromagnetic pulse

329

and shards of hurtling metal, the ATF as well. But she had been encouraged to acquire the spaceplane. Its technology was worth as much as preempting WARLORD to Khimik and to the others. The Soviet Union would give her anything she asked, for as long as she lived, if she would merely take possession of the ATF and make it theirs.

Closer and closer she pushed her burden, like some old woman on the streets of Pest with a handcart. For all the old women on all the streets of all the cities racked with war because the imperialists' left no other options to the people, she would do this. . . .

She only thought that way when she was frightened. The admission of it startled her. She was going to claim the lives of these Americans, then WARLORD's. Then she would take the spaceplane as her rightful prize, turn it over to the authorities at Sveboda, and leave the moon to accept her kudos.

To disappear, to ready herself to fight again. The fear came only from the vacuum of space all around her, from the sure knowledge that a mistake here would make her a martyr. There was no simple way, as there had been when the crawler stopped in its tracks, to recoup.

She'd refused the escape craft, she admitted to herself as, ever so slowly, she floated toward the congealing and horrible mass of destructive material soon to be aimed at Mars, not because she was brave, but because she was practical.

Very little up here would escape the attention of these planners. It was enough to have maneuvered a hiding place, camouflaged to look like space junk, into orbit. It was enough to have gotten here undetected. There was no acceptable fallback that did not heighten her risk of discovery. Therefore, she had relied on her earliest training and the core of her being. She had killed not to be killed, twice in close succession.

And she would do so again. Because she must, to survive. These simple decisions were those that she preferred.

Within a hundred meters of the assembly point, she

330

cleared her weapon, checked its charge, and began looking for a clear shot at one of the two men floating toward her on tethers, their obscene nukes in between.

One OMV was out of her line of sight; the second was at the rear of the nuke drivers, pushing the load beside which the two men floated.

She decided on the nearer man and sighted down her weapon's ramp, but the distance was still too great.

So she waited, content to propel her piece of WAR-LORD toward the two men guiding theirs ever closer to a resolution neither of them expected.

Robin Faragher always counted on the element of surprise.

Moments later, one of the men seemed to drift farther on his tether than was prudent. Foolish, sloppy behavior on the part of this enemy, for it gave her a nearly perfect target.

Faragher let go of the shielding oblong of metal and, with both hands, took her taser off safe and sighted down its yellow ramp for a perfect shot.

Just as she was squeezing her trigger, the man in her sights seemed to jump backward and downward. Furious and concentrated, she stiffened her arm and tracked him, ready to shoot again.

She was still lining up her ramp on his white chest when the tungsten and steel bullet tore into her stomach. She had only time enough to realize that the recoil from his pistol had been the force that made him jump backward, before she died with her mouth open and a snarl of rage on her lips.

# Chapter 4

# LONG
# SHOT

"Trace, Jesus, Trace! Answer me!" Kate was yelling at the screen before her, her radio dialed to emergency frequency. Fuck the project! Couldn't they see what was happening?

Foster was spinning off into space and she'd already sent one OMV after him. Now Marshall was turning end over end and she didn't have the faintest idea what was going wrong. But something was wrong, very wrong.

Watching the screens dry-eyed, she suddenly stopped trying to make radio contact: Rand and Crane couldn't be unaware that Marshall was in trouble, not from this distance. They were simply ignoring it.

She slapped the radio off and put her chin in her fists, watching. The damned project meant more than Foster or Marshall's lives, was what the screens were telling her. Crane and Tracey Rand were calmly guiding the nukes into place.

When they'd done that, one of them—she couldn't tell which—went after component 31A, which had been Marshall's responsibility. She'd have given anything to talk to them, to yell at them, to find a good reason to cry or quit. But there wasn't one.

She had her own job to do. She punched in automatic vectoring numbers for the remote she was disengaging from the nuke drivers and concentrated her attention on the other one, the one she'd sent after Foster.

It was tough and delicate work, especially when she had to grab Foster's body with the OMV's remote arm. When she'd done that, she sent the OMV after Marshall.

While she worked, Kate was trying to avoid asking the obvious questions about what had happened out there. She'd find out when Rand and Crane got back. *If they get back.*

"Shut up," she muttered to herself, this time out loud. "They'll get back. And I'm going to find out how come it looked like Crane shot Marshall—before I let him in here."

Her weapon was on her hip, that was something. She hadn't let it out of her sight. It wasn't stowed, like Rand's, in the cargo bay. She could have gotten those cases, now, if she thought she could spare the time. But she didn't think it was worth it. If there was any trouble up here that a reasoning attitude and a forty-four magnum couldn't settle, then Kate Brittany couldn't settle it.

She had enough trouble trying to make the remote arm fold in on itself sufficiently to stow Foster's body in the OMV's storage bay so that she could free the arm to pick up Marshall. She didn't trust her ability to grab Marshall without losing Foster. And she knew that retrieval of those bodies was going to be crucial to any ensuing investigation—or preventing one.

So she sweated as she worked, developing cramps in her upper arms and shoulders. Chasing a spinning body on no particular trajectory, even with computer assistance, wasn't easy.

She had no idea how long it had taken when, at last, she extended the robot arm to pincer Marshall around the waist.

Her first try missed the spinning corpse by inches and she bit her lip.

It bled, but she didn't notice. "Damn, you bastard, stay still," she told Marshall's corpse. "Come to Mama." Then she tried again.

This time, she wouldn't be so careful about the force she exerted. Better to break the back of this already-dead man than have to start all over again.

She lined up the robot arm, extended it, and snapped it closed. The pincers of the arm caught Marshall squarely around the waist and her screen went blank.

White. Black. Static. Dead.

She snarled at her equipment and demanded, "How dare you fuck up, camera?" But it didn't answer. It took her only seconds to bring up another camera, from the other OMV at the assembly area.

But she couldn't find the first OMV, or Marshall, at all.

She leaned back in her chair and massaged one shoulder. "Okay, have it your way," she told the equipment she assumed was recalcitrant and, with a savage jab, switched to the spaceplane's surveillance recording system.

It would glitch up the records that the ATF system was keeping, but she had to find out what had happened. She pinpointed the time frame and the camera she wanted, and ran the tape she'd rewound.

There, before her eyes, she saw the explosion take place—an explosion that seemed to start with Marshall's person, as if he were volatile, but instantly engulfed and destroyed the OMV.

*Okay, a little hardball. So what? Marshall was already dead and we've got another OMV.* Now, conscious that anything she said aloud was recorded by the cockpit recorders on board the spaceplane, she kept silent. It was

334

getting nasty out there. And she didn't understand who was doing it, or why.

But she knew what she had to do. She designated one of her cameras to keep close watch on Rand and Crane and sat back, her arms crossed, her head beginning to ache, ready for the worst.

If Lincoln Crane made one false move, he was history. Kate was going to slam him into pieces with the remote arm of her remaining OMV.

# Chapter 5

# PROJECT
# WARLORD

Floating beside component 31A, Tracey Rand was sweating profusely in his spacesuit, one hand on his tether for comfort. In his helmet, Crane's voice sounded tinny, but the fidelity was sufficient to transmit Crane's agitation as the ConSec said, "Well, Rand, it's up to the two of us to finish the job."

Not *Can the two of us finish the job*. Rand was acutely conscious that Crane had used the pistol he was holding. They'd turned on their spacesuit com systems as Marshall headed toward them. Crane had hailed Marshall twice on that shielded frequency, gotten no response, and calmly shot the man. It wasn't really confidence-building behavior in Rand's terms.

"You bet we'll finish it. Fast, before that explosion brings anybody out to investigate." The chances of that were vanishingly slim, but Rand wanted Crane to think about it. And he wanted to get WARLORD together as fast as he could possibly manage so that he could back into the spaceplane before his nerve gave out.

The last thing he needed was a long leisurely interval in which to meditate on Foster spinning off into nothingness or Marshall with his guts blown out—guts like a frozen umbilical cord. . . .

"Look, Rand," came Crane's voice. "That wasn't Marshall—whoever it was didn't know enough to be on the right com channel. And if that's not good enough for you, check the tape when we get back: that helmet didn't have anybody's name stenciled over the faceplate."

"I wasn't asking," Rand said, and pulled himself hand over hand along the tether toward Crane.

But Crane was bound and determined to explain himself. "And whoever that was, was drawing a bead on me the same time I shot . . ."

Rand realized that Crane's voice was choked with emotion and somehow that made him feel better. Crane had lost two good friends out here, somewhere . . . then something occurred to him. "If that wasn't Marshall, where is he?"

"Want to bet he's out there somewhere?" Crane's voice turned cold.

Rand was so close to the ConSec lieutenant now that he fancied he could see taut features behind the polarized faceplate of Crane's suit. *Hope to hell you've got yourself believing what you're telling me, buddy. Especially since you're the only one with a gun out here.*

Guns in space—it had seemed so unnecessary to Rand that he hadn't objected when Crane had stowed his attaché case full of weapons back with the nukes and then, while they were in the cargo bay together, said, "Leave that stuff—you've got enough to do without trying to cover my end of things." Crane's voice had been command-sharp then, and Rand, facing a sojourn into vacuum and zero-G in just his spacesuit, was having enough troubles dealing with his memories.

Now he wished he'd insisted, but realized it was probably a good thing Crane, pumped up beyond what, in any other circumstances, could be considered sane limits, was the only one of them with a weapon.

If Crane got too crazy, there was always the laser torch the ConSec was now handing him. Rand, taking it and the black box Crane was so concerned about, floated free, hanging in space, connected only by his tether to WAR-LORD.

He ought to count his blessings: none of the exploded fragments of the OMV Kate had sent after Foster had come his way. He wasn't decapitated; he wasn't dead in a rent suit. Neither was Crane, for what that was worth. And the ATF hadn't taken any shrapnel. He wanted more than anything to finish this job and get back inside that plane, where he could see to Kate.

She must be frantic, by now. He'd calm her down, they'd run the tapes, figure out why the OMV blew like that. And then, if Crane's version of the shoot turned out to be paranoid delusion, they'd do something about the ConSec. Kate still had her forty-four. But they'd do it after Crane had flown the spaceplane back to Einstein base. . . .

And right now, he had to concentrate. Forget about the hostile vacuum around him, the possibly unbalanced security man watching his every move, the fragile tether that, with the manned maneuvering unit on his back, comprised his only safety net.

He had WARLORD to empower. To enable. To bring to life like he was some Frankenstein . . . or some minor god.

He turned the black box Crane had given him, examining it carefully. Inputs and outputs and not a damned thing to say exactly what it was supposed to do. Probably, from the look of it, it was a destruct module. It was definitely designed to receive a signal and perform a task on receipt of that signal. Its placement in the electronics package was enough to tell him that. It could also be a tamper-prevention device, or a soft bomb to dead-end remotely sent signals. . . .

He stopped worrying about it and began soldering it into place, in the guts of component 31A, where the brain of WARLORD waited to be activated by coupling it to a power source.

Frankenstein, all right. But Tracey Rand was feeling paternal toward his monster. Even if his second thoughts about the wisdom of using nukes to kick up enough dust to begin warming the Martian climate were more grave, the events of the last few days would have overridden them.

Too many had died for WARLORD for Rand to be tempted to let it fail. The very fact that someone was so concertedly trying to *make* it fail convinced him that he had to see it through.

There'd be no need of remote course correction if he did his job right. And he was going to do just that. With his tool box floating beside him and Crane hovering nearby, he began calibrating his equipment.

It was so complex a task and so demanding that he forgot all about the possibly homicidal ConSec at arm's length, except when Crane was needed for muscle. He even forgot about the dangers of life-support failure, about the vacuum beyond and the fragility of his protections.

He thought about Mars, about the red sands and the polar ice caps, about the dust WARLORD would throw up into the Martian atmosphere. He thought about the greenhouse effect he was hoping to catalyze, about the way the pole water would melt, about the chloro-fluoro-carbon carrier canisters that WARLORD would eject onto the Martian surface thousands of miles short of her final, explosive collision with the planet's equator.

And he thought about the Soviet sensor stations on Mars; they'd better be robotic, as the Russians claimed, or else there were going to be casualties.

Finally, he thought about the subsequent, bio-active packages that had already been sent to Mars, the long way. Canisters of biologically engineered "primal soup" were on their way to Mars via Jupiter. Two and a half years to slingshot Jupiter; the soup would arrive on Mars when the time was right, if all went well.

If all didn't go well, there was still time to send a second load of biochemicals. The project was a long-term one.

Tracey Rand had never expected to see it this far; he didn't hold out hope of witnessing the end of it: a warmer Mars with a more oxygenated atmosphere, a Mars more suitable for colonization and eventual habitation than anywhere else in the solar system.

In Rand's mind, destroying the Martian ecology was worth it, if that was what he was doing; altering the Martian ecology to support more life, eventually human life, wasn't any more evil than irrigating a desert or dredging a sea bed. But there'd be plenty of screaming, from all quarters, that the U.S. had taken it upon itself to begin terraforming Mars.

By the time that screaming began, the process would be under way. It wasn't going to be quick, or easy; but once it was started, it wouldn't be easy to stop, either.

Although Rand probably wouldn't live to see the end of it, if he ever had children, they would. And they'd have somewhere to go, if they were restless, if they were adventurous, if they needed breathing room.

It beat the hell out of a lot of lesser objectives he'd risked his life for. Working with his hands and his mind on a tether in a lunar parking orbit, manhandling components into position with Crane, who'd just lost two men to WARLORD, Tracey Rand found that he wasn't laboring under a shadow of a doubt.

He hadn't a single qualm. He hadn't one remaining reservation. He just wanted to light this candle and watch the sucker burn.

Soldering a final joint, he pushed himself back from the single, aggregated mass that was WARLORD and said to Crane through the com link, "Okay, if you want to check my numbers, go ahead. But I think that's got it. We're set for an equatorial hit—Edom crater if Mars doesn't duck out of the way just as WARLORD gets there."

Crane's harsh breathing was all Rand heard for a ten-beat pause. Then the ConSec said, "I've been watching. Looks good to me."

340

"Let's pack it in then," said Rand, pulling himself along his tether, the remote box that would fire up WARLORD's rockets in hand.

When he reached Crane he said, "Here. You do the honors. For Marshall and Foster. They deserve it."

"Yeah," said Crane thickly.

It suited Rand just fine if Crane had something to do with both his hands besides rest one on the butt of the pistol in his work belt. Behind Rand, the spaceplane waited, its cargo-bay door open invitingly.

All he had to do was get from here to there, using his tether and his MMU, without tearing his suit or making some fool mistake. Now that he had nothing else to worry about, the specter of life-support trouble from his spacesuit was beginning to bother him more.

All he wanted out of life was to get inside that spaceplane before the fear he'd been suppressing broke loose and froze him cold.

He started pulling himself, hand over hand, along the tether. Eventually, he had to unfasten it and rely on his MMU. Every time he looked around, Crane was right beside him like a pale shadow in the endless dark.

He could hear the other man's heavy breathing through his com set and it made him even more nervous. The joystick under his hand would have slipped in his grasp if his suit gloves hadn't been so well constructed.

But they were, and eventually that interminable distance was crossed and he floated, one hand on the thick composite hatch of the ATF, with Crane beside him.

Looking back at WARLORD one more time. "Okay, Crane," Rand prodded. "Let 'er rip."

The ConSec pushed the remote ignition device and Rand slitted his eyes as WARLORD came to life, shook itself all over, and blazed away, headed for a tiny red light in the sky that men called Mars.

# Chapter 6

# AFTERMATH

When Rand and Crane came aboard, Kate was standing behind the hatch, her face unreadable in her helmet, her forty-four trained steadily on the men coming forward from the cargo bay.

"Hold it right there, guys. Trace, take Crane's gun and move away from him. Crane, if I didn't need you to fly us back to—"

"Kate," came Rand's voice in her ear, through the suit's com channel, "it's okay, he's not—"

"I'll be the judge of that." Without taking her eyes from Crane, who'd put up his gloved hands to signal his lack of resistance, Kate punched the repressurization button.

Rand had Crane's gun now. Both men were staring at her silently, looking like aliens in their helmets.

"Kate," Rand said again, "if this is about Foster and Marshall, you're jumping to con—"

"What else would it be—oh." Suddenly she realized that her actions might have been misconstrued. "Even if Crane doesn't, you should have better sense than to think I'm part of any plot to . . . to . . ." She broke off, bit her lip again, and winced because she'd already bitten it once until it bled. Then she straightened because her gun had wavered and Crane's hands had started to come down: "Tell me about Foster and Marshall, Crane. Tell me how you didn't shoot Marshall. I've got it on tape."

Now, for the first time, Crane spoke. And just before he did there was an audible sigh of relief that must have come from him, because Rand was imploring her to "relax, okay?"

But she wasn't about to relax. She didn't dare. She had no idea what had gone on out there.

And Crane was saying, ". . . wasn't Marshall. The ATF tape will back me up, if you go on high magnification and look for helmet ID. Can we do that, ma'am?"

Not until Rand had booted up the surveillance tapes with computer enhancement did she allow Crane to so much as take off his helmet. Then she slumped, still spacesuited, the gun limp in her hand. "But then, where's Marshall?" she heard herself say shakily.

"Don't you think you owe Lieutenant Crane an apology?" Tracey prompted gently.

"I—"

"Nah, she doesn't, Rand. Would have done the same myself, most likely. Good instincts, ma'am," said Crane too lightly.

"Kate, I keep telling you." She took off her helmet, her sidearm once again in its holster, and began sheepishly to help Rand scan for anything that might be the real Marshall's body.

She was so busy doing that, she didn't realize Crane was taking the ATF out of its parking orbit until he called out, "Okay, folks, forget it. The haystack's too big for a needle Marshall's size. Strap in. Next stop, Einstein."

"But . . . Marshall. What if he's out there somewhere, alive?"

"He's not," said Crane flatly, and fired his engines, so that she didn't have time to answer.

The way Crane had said it, so coldly, bothered her.

343

When the initial acceleration let up, Rand leaned toward her and whispered, "Those were *his* men we lost. Marshall would have broken radio silence and screamed his head off if he could."

"But the body . . . we've got to search for—"

Trace was looking at her like she should know better. A top-secret mission. With casualties. Nobody would look for Marshall, she realized. Like the moon trucks, programmed to crash on the dark side over the next few hours, Marshall and Foster's deaths would be chalked up to inexplicable accidents, if they had to be chalked up to anything. The term "Missing in Action" took on a whole new meaning up here, especially when the action was so classified that it hadn't officially taken place at all.

And then, on the way to Einstein, it occurred to her. "Trace, Crane—if that wasn't Marshall whose body exploded . . . who *was it?*"

"Bad guy," said Crane. "Take a look at your tapes again—I shot in self-defense."

"I don't know," Trace said at the same time. "And I'm not sure I want to know. Or that, even if I did, we'll ever find out."

Which made her ask, "What do you guys mean—that you think the operation's been blown? That it was the Soviets? An interdiction? That they knew all along?" She was appalled.

"If they did," said Rand, "they'll keep their mouths shut. And it beats the other contenders." Rand looked at Crane, who said nothing, busy flying the spaceplane.

And Kate looked at Tracey Rand, who'd just completed the most important single mission of his life but seemed not to give a damn.

Then she realized what must be bothering Trace: they were going back to Einstein—at Einstein, Ilya was waiting.

All this time to think, and she hadn't come up with a

single suggestion as to how they could smuggle Ilya Palladin to Earth, where they could announce his defection. She didn't even know how sick he was, if he was capable of making the trip.

But she had to start thinking about it. Now. There wasn't a moment to lose.

# Chapter 7

# EINSTEIN REVISITED

Einstein base was crawling with investigators when they got there, which made problems for Linc Crane because of the classified nature of the spaceplane he was flying. There were only two ways out of the mess he was in: put the ATF down brazenly where every intelligence professional posted to the moon under diplomatic cover could see it, along with military attachés from half-a-dozen armies, or take Brittany and Rand on a nonscheduled tour of the Consolidated Space Command's covert basing procedures.

In for a penny, in for a pound, he'd thought, and decided on the latter. Brittany and Rand knew enough about him now that he might as well treat them as if they were on his side. Which was, as far as he was concerned, the truth. You don't go through what Crane had with the two ZR/SEAL specialists and not forge an operational bond. A bond thicker than the sheaves of papers he'd found in the attaché/weapons cases he returned to them when they deplaned in an underground garage three-quarters of a mile south of Einstein.

On the way to the habitat, in a ConSec crawler kept at the security hangar for such emergencies, he tried to broach the subject uppermost in his mind. "Look, you two, I've been talking to my people, off and on during approach and landing. And I want to clear something up.''

Kate Brittany hadn't said one word to him since he'd pulled the ATF out of its parking orbit. Like Crane didn't care more about Marshall than she did. Like he'd leave his second-in-command out there to suffocate in a spacesuit if there was the slimmest chance that Marshall'd survived. . . .

So he was defensive, despite his best efforts not to be. And he was holding back about as much grief as he was capable of feeling, trying to transmute it into something useful: rage, investigative drive, even raw energy. But he wasn't having much luck. And Brittany wasn't helping, with her eyes boring into his back so that he could feel them through his suit.

He resented the hell out of these Agency types sometimes. They thought they were better than their military counterparts. They were more privileged, was all. They went to schools with crests and ties and they could handle more forks at dinner. Maybe they didn't need the money from their paychecks. Their entry-level jobs all had at least captain's ratings. But it didn't make them any better than men like Crane, just snootier. And sometimes that made them less fit to do their jobs.

Ms. Snoot-Brittany and her blueblood boyfriend were having their noses rubbed in the real world up here—for better or worse. The only thing Crane regretted was that it had taken the loss of Marshall and Foster to shake things out. But because it had, Crane wanted to make a clean sweep of things.

So when Rand finally replied, after too long a silence in which he waited for Brittany's ice to melt, ''Go ahead, Crane. What were you going to say?'' the ConSec took a deep breath.

And said: ''Look, my guys say that the odds are seventy/thirty against the ESA tour's crawler having exploded by accident. And I don't mean what we did to it, either.

There's some surveillance we shouldn't have that shows pretty clearly that the Soviet escort fired on that vehicle. But since we shouldn't be able to cut through their jamming, we can't show the evidence. You read me?''

He had more to tell them. He'd expected to get on to the rest of what he had to say.

But Brittany entered the conversation, her feathers all ruffled and her upper-class umbrage waving like an American flag in a high wind, wanting to know just what Consolidated Security had, and whether Crane's superiors had consulted with her superiors in order to find a way to at least leak the incriminating evidence.

When she was done with what amounted to a tirade against the paranoia endemic to ''myopic military security types'' who ''neuter whatever effectiveness services like ConSec might have,'' Crane didn't feel like talking anymore.

But he did answer her, saying: ''Your Director Harper's been told and his reading is that it ain't worth informing the Russians about what we can really do, not just to start a flap that'll only raise U.S./Soviet tension levels—nothin's gonna bring those dead Europeans back.'' He stressed the last few words, reminding her that the United States hadn't lost anybody aboard that crawler but the poor bastards chauffeuring those dips around.

And nobody cared about those non-coms but guys like Crane, who'd worked with them, who knew the names of their wives and kids. Foster had had kids. . . . Brittany was going to have other things to think about soon enough; he ought to let her stew, he'd thought as he parked the crawler next to a lift station and shepherded his charges out, and into the lift that would take them into Einstein by a rear door.

He'd given them their damned weapons back, and Rand, at least, understood what that meant: Linc Crane was willing to trust them with not only all that firepower, but the briefing materials on WARLORD—no small thing.

They rode the lift in silence, and when it had pressurized and the door opened, Brittany took off her helmet, looked Crane squarely in the eye, and said, "I'm sorry about your friends—our friends . . . Foster and Marshall. When I get Ilya back home, I'll be able to do something for their families. . . ."

Power and privilege. These types couldn't help but flaunt it. Sometimes Crane wondered if this woman had any brains whatsoever; other times he thought she was smarter than he was. He flicked a glance at Rand, still struggling out of his helmet.

Rand said, "Crane—Linc, Kate's trying to say that neither of us harbors any suspicions that you might have had a hand in the crawler's 'accident.' "

Rand had a real knack for hitting the nail on the head. Bates had been way off base about him. Crane let his face soften, and said, "Yeah, I wanted to hear that. And . . . whatever you can do for my guys' dependents, I'll be real thankful." Because they could, and he couldn't; he couldn't get his casualties any more than letters from a grateful government. These two could probably get their grades—and pensions—upped posthumously.

"My word, we'll give it priority," said Rand quickly, obviously uncomfortable with the woman's behavior. Well, that made two of them. But she was about to get hers, and Crane figured that would even the score.

Out in the corridor, she strode ahead, making a beeline for the sickbay, where she was about to find out what Crane had learned an hour ago. Rand held back, saying softly, "Look, we'll go with her on this one. Whatever she decides. You know Harper won't clear this if we ask, so I'll take the responsibility—if you'll just tell me the ATF can get us down to Washington with a minimum of stopovers where we might have to argue with the dip core—ours, or theirs."

Rand was asking him to smuggle the Soviet out and groundside. Since it wasn't going to happen and Crane needed to count on Rand's good will, the ConSec answered, "Langley Field, or Andrews, is as close as I could get you. With no stops. That's the only way—no LSS, no LEO—just coast on down." Technically, he could do that if he wanted to, on Rand's authority, or on his own.

He thought again how wrong Bates had been, all but ordering him to take out Rand. Bates had expected him to do that—had expected Rand to balk, to screw up, to blow WARLORD and his own life in the process. Funny, Bates didn't usually make that kind of mistake. But, mistake or not, Rand had operational jurisdiction, since he was alive. If these two wanted to go home, instead of back over to Cop One where Harper was going to give them one ace of a hard time, that was fine with Crane.

Preferable, in fact, to having Rand and Brittany decide that Harper was trustworthy enough to know what Crane had done to the crawler, or what Crane's own sources said about the reasons for the crawler's destruction. The contingency plan for a successful mission had been pretty openended. Rand might not know it, but he had as close to carte blanche as you could get in this business. And if Crane had had that much clout, he wouldn't be in any hurry to hunker down with Director Harper and start fielding requests for explanations that security considerations precluded him giving.

Crane stopped at the reception desk outside the sickbay and asked for a line to his control section. "I'll wait here, Rand. You two see what you've got to see and then tell me how you want to jump. I'll be ready."

Might as well get the ATF turned around—fueled up and checked out. Even if these two decided they were going to join the investigatory body, wrestle protocol at Cop One, and generally behave like the dip-hybrids they were, Crane was going to need the spaceplane. He couldn't afford to get entangled in the crawler investigation. The best thing for him to do was shoot down to D.C. and give Bates his report verbally.

Which might not be necessary for reasons of security, but was necessary on other grounds—Crane's peace of mind. He didn't want Marshall's live-in lover and Foster's family to see ominous uniformed strangers waiting on their doorsteps. It was such an impersonal way to get this kind of news—the worst kind.

Crane's mother had gotten word about his dad that way, years ago. It sucked. Crane always made it a point to do the dirtiest of all his jobs personally. On whatever excuse, he'd get down there in time to tell the families himself.

It was the only honorable thing to do, and Foster and Marshall deserved at least that. Anything else they got, they'd get under the auspices of the two ZR/SEAL operators disappearing down a white corridor toward a room they didn't yet know was empty.

"Dead? Ilya's dead?" quavered Kate, as if she didn't believe the green-smocked physician standing before the intensive care unit, his hairy arms crossed over his chest.

Rand already had one arm around her. He'd half expected her to shake it off.

The medic was saying, "Secretary Brittany, we did everything we could. We think it was some bio-engineered virus . . . or poison, if you like. It was too fast, too lethal, and not at all contagious. But we couldn't do an autopsy. The Soviet doctor who took charge—the man that came in with the investigating party—had total control over one of his own citizens. . . ." The man uncrossed his arms and spread them. "I'm sorry. I've prepared a full report and sent it to Director Harper's office, but I can give you a copy, if you like."

Kate was quite still against him, not even leaning on him. She didn't answer the doctor for some time.

Into an uncomfortable silence, the man said, "If you'd like a sedative, Secretary Brittany. . . . ?"

"No."

"Well, then, if there's nothing more I can do, and you don't want to see the tapes, I'll be—"

"Tapes?" Rand said because he was afraid Kate wouldn't.

"You bet," said the pleasant-faced doctor with the five-o'clock shadow and matching circles under his eyes that testified to how much the ongoing investigation was taking out of him. "When I got called to the crash site, I had the paramedic tape Palladin, nonstop. So I've got a couple of cassettes' worth of what went on—up through when the Soviets realized we were taping, but by then Palladin was dead. . . ."

"Good man," Rand said. "We'd like to see them— somewhere I can computer-scan for movement, if you can arrange it."

As he was asking, Kate suddenly slumped against him. He thought he heard her whisper, "No, Rand, I can't take that."

But he ignored it. She had to deal with this. Cry. Yell. Throw things. Anything that proved she'd registered the data. She wasn't reacting the way she should.

The physician got him the room and the computer-scanning monitor, and he called Crane from there, telling the ConSec what he'd found and what he was going to do, and inviting Crane to join them. It might have been more politic to tell Crane in person, but he didn't want to leave Kate alone until he was satisfied that she wasn't blaming herself for what had happened to Palladin.

There wasn't any reason for her to do that—people died. People like Palladin were expert at estimating the risks they took. But Rand knew what it was like to lose somebody you were pushing the way she'd been pushing Palladin— not just to defect, but to share information and confidences. Those two had been making their own rules. It had been going badly enough, in the wake of the chances they'd taken, that Palladin had been considering defection. There was no way that Kate Brittany wasn't thinking what a case officer always thought in these circumstances: that it was her fault, that Ilya would still be alive if she hadn't brought him under the shadow of suspicion.

If Rand had had the slightest inkling of what the physician was going to say, he'd have tried to get the man to lie to her. But then, they wouldn't have been able to go over the tapes like this.

The room was light green and the computer equipment was on a wheeled dolly. The walls were windowless and soundproofed with thick, textured foam. They pulled up two of the four chairs and Rand brought her some burned coffee from a hot-plate system. She took the poly container from him with shaking hands.

Her lips were blue and her skin had become waxily transparent. He could see her pulse bumping through the veins at her temples; another, in her forehead, was engorged so that it seemed like a scar down the center of her brow. "Thanks, Trace," she said.

"You want me to watch this alone, I will," he offered, suddenly uncertain whether he was prescribing the right cure for what ailed her.

"No, let's get it over with. I need to know—to see it, I mean."

He started fiddling with the equipment, setting the computer-governor to give him any frames where movement exceeded minimal parameters he decreed. When he was done with that, the tape would stop wherever Palladin's lips moved enough to produce sound, or his limbs thrashed, or he sat up in bed or drank water or somebody came into the room who exhibited normal "waking" behavior.

By the time Crane arrived, Rand was zeroed on a particular piece of footage and about to call the chief physician to find out if the paramedic on the tape had kept the clipboard visible on the screen.

On that clipboard, just before Palladin sank into a coma from which he was never to emerge, the Soviet had written something.

The only trouble was, the camera hadn't picked up what Palladin had written.

"Look at this," said Rand to Crane, and the ConSec whistled through his teeth. Rand, glancing away from the screen for the first time since he'd come upon the intriguing piece of footage, saw Kate's face: it was puffy and streaked with tears.

He got up and Crane took his seat. Walking over to Kate, he stood behind her chair and said, "You're doing great. Let's see if Ilya left us something that might make his dying worth it."

Then she started to cry in earnest and he backed off. You never knew how hard to push with this sort of emotional stuff. But you knew that pushing was better than not pushing. He didn't want any more on his own conscience than was absolutely necessary. He especially didn't want Kate to curl up in some nice, impenetrable shell. Not Kate.

It took a while for them to get the paramedic into the room, and the man knew just what they wanted. "Yeah, I saved it for her. I mean, for her if she's 'Kate'?"

Rand let out a long-held breath and the paramedic, with puppylike pride, pulled out a carefully folded piece of paper. Then he handed it to her, and Rand didn't understand the tenderness in the young paramedic's face until Kate said, "Damn, oh damn."

She was still holding the piece of paper. He leaned down and took it from her. It said, *Dear Kate. I love you. Forgive me. Khimik is Bat—*

"Crane," Rand said sharply. "Take a look at this." And, to the paramedic: "Okay, thanks. We need to be alone now."

"What the fuck does Khimik mean?" Crane asked.

"Chemist," said Kate.

"You ever heard that before, from Ilya?" Rand wanted to know. None of them was asking questions about the other word, the one that came after the verb. This wasn't the place. There was only one place that Rand could think of that was secure enough for the rest of the questions he wanted to ask.

Crane beat him to the punch. "Listen up, you two. What say we burn our tails out of here? Dinner at the American Cafe in Tyson's Corners Friday night, on me, if we hurry. You can continue my Russian lessons on the way."

Rand wanted to get out of there so much it was a physical sensation; he wanted to get back into the ATF as much now as he had when he'd been floating on that tether, with WARLORD by his side.

But he leaned down and caught Kate's eye and, very softly, very calmly, said, "Okay with you, Katydid? Can you handle it?"

A fire lit somewhere in eyes too dull for too long. She said, "Of course, Trace. Get those tapes and let's be on our way. And our cases, don't forget the attaché cases."

He didn't like the manic edge to her tone, but she was right: wouldn't do to leave anything incriminating, anything that had to do with WARLORD, behind.

Like it wouldn't do to let anyone, most especially Harper, know where they were going, or how, or why.

# Chapter 8
# LAST LEG

Kate sat in the ATF, immune to all normal emotions. She wasn't impressed by the advanced tactical fighter's quick turnaround time, its nonstop-to-Earth capability, or its pilot's matching skills: Linc Crane had promised them that nobody but ConSec's closemouthed mission control personnel would know they were headed for Washington—until and unless Rand wanted it otherwise.

Trace was like a dog with a bone, worrying the ramifications of the note Ilya had left her, talking it through out loud, every watt of his intellect engaged to their mutual benefit.

Somehow, it was all happening somewhere else. It was as if there was a Brittany-shaped wall of glass between her and the world. Ilya had been killed by his own people. It scared her to death.

It wasn't the delivery system, although that was treacherous—a virus tailored to kill. It wasn't that it was her fault, although that could be argued: Ilya had told her how much trouble he was in, or at least hinted at it; she should have acted, somehow, to prevent his death. But even the guilt didn't penetrate behind her personal wall of glass, where the two words *Khimik* and *Bat* were etched before her eyes. Bat could mean batch file (a computer notation) or it could mean what Rand was assuming it meant.

Bates.

Rand had asked, "Can we defeat the cockpit recorder in here, Crane?" shortly after lift-off.

"Already did that, sir," Crane had replied absently. And then the two of them had started comparing notes.

Crane had offered laconically, "You can guess what the orders from Bates's office were, if you went left or screwed up."

"Now that I know you had your own orders from Bates's office, yeah, I can. Do you want to talk about this with us?"

Crane had cocked his head; Kate would have given anything to see his face. But she couldn't. She heard only his reply: "I lost two guys back there. I heard you guys lost some—Richelson, Davies, that bunch."

"That's right," Kate had said, surprised at herself. "And now we've got extensive documentation on a project that doesn't exist."

"Easy, Katydid," Rand had warned, turning toward her. "What she means is, Linc, we've got to find the right authority to take this to."

"If," said Crane, "our assumption is correct, the closest I'd want to get would be Bud Andresson's office."

"It's correct," Kate had told them bluntly. "I know who Khimik was . . . is."

"Yeah?" said Crane as, beyond his head, out the windscreen, the blue ball of Earth came into view.

"Khimik was Ilya's . . . Ilya's 'Western source,' as he said."

"Jesus God," said Rand, and the rest of the discussion became tactical.

# Chapter 9

# SHUTDOWN

Rand had still been worried that General Thaddeus (Bud) Andresson was part of their problem, not the solution, when Crane pulled their rented sedan right into the Pentagon's high-security underground garage. Then, flashing his Con-Sec credentials, Crane led the way through reams of red tape until the three of them were ushered into Andresson's fourth-floor office.

The flight home had been uneventful—if you were hardened enough not to feel something when you set foot on solid ground after so long in space. Rand wasn't, he'd found out. The fabled impulse to kiss the ground under your feet was one he'd never had before, and the strength of it had startled him.

But with Kate to look after, he couldn't show the slightest weakness—she was too far off center. Oh, she was controlling it, but he knew her well enough to know that everything he was being shown was only that: a mask over what she really felt. In there, somewhere, behind her facade, the woman was hurting like he'd never expected to see her hurt.

If he hadn't felt so helpless, if he hadn't felt some modicum of responsibility for her distress, he'd have been glad to see it. It made him know she was in possession of a full deck. But the ability to feel deeply, in someone who commonly suppressed it, could be a debit in circumstances like these.

Every time he'd tried to talk to her about Ilya—about the man, not the operator—she backed him off abruptly.

The one relevant thing she'd said, when Crane was taxiing the ATF down its Langley runway, wasn't comforting: "If Ilya were still alive, if he was with us . . . we'd have no trouble pinning Bates to the wall."

Crane had shaken his head minutely, even though he'd been pretty busy making sure the ATF was well away from prying eyes as he taxied her toward a high-security hangar.

Kate was sure about Bates—sure beyond what the evidence substantiated. She'd made up her mind. Maybe if Palladin had been alive, she'd have been able to support her conclusions. A defector of Palladin's stature could have pointed a finger at the man he'd known as Khimik, and CIA security would have taken it from there.

But Palladin was dead, and after more than twenty-four hours of comparing notes, the three of them had come up with nothing solid to corroborate Kate's reading of Ilya's note.

Now, in Andresson's office, waiting for the big, white-haired, horse-jawed general to join them, Rand was steeling himself for the inevitable result of this meeting: Andresson would listen to what they had to say, put some internal security people on the matter, and tell them that they'd be advised of any results from the ensuing, very low-profile investigation. That response was a given.

What bothered Crane almost as much as it did Rand was the chance that, for any of a dozen reasons, Andresson was in this up to his four stars, too. If that was so—if Andresson was on Bates's team, and that team was responsible for the ZR/SEAL casualties and the leaks to the Soviets that had almost scuttled WARLORD, and gotten Marshall and Foster killed—then their lives weren't going to be worth a damn once they left this office. If they did.

Which was why they'd stopped at three randomly chosen District banks and stashed three photocopies Kate had made of the WARLORD briefing material while both men waited in the car. The whole maneuver made Rand feel like he was in some B-movie, but Crane was right: if they were going to make waves, they'd better have life preservers. Each of them had a key to one of the safe-deposit boxes, and Kate had already mailed hers to her parents' address. It wasn't much, but it was something.

Now that they were sitting here, before the mahogany desk flanked by an American flag draped with battle standards and a Defense Security Agency seal, Rand was filled with doubts. You couldn't muscle the U.S. government. If Andresson leaned across that desk and told him that, for national security reasons, Bates had been acting under orders and his actions could not be scrutinized, let alone questioned, Rand was going to have to accept it.

You didn't make policy. You didn't blow an operation like WARLORD to the adversarial American press, no matter how many casualties were sustained during its run. It would make Rand part of the enemy. It would make all those deaths, all that work, all the sacrifice, useless.

He knew then that he'd never do anything with the documentation he'd copied. But he wasn't willing to lay odds that Kate Brittany felt the same. He cast a sidelong glance at Crane, who couldn't stay seated, but kept getting up, going to the window overlooking the parking lot, and standing there spread-legged, his hands clasped behind his back, before beginning another circuit of Andresson's office that inevitably ended with Crane trying once more to get comfortable in one of the leather-upholstered chairs.

Rand didn't blame Crane for being nervous. What they'd done with the photocopies was as close to treason as you could come and still be able to step back over the line. The only excuse for it was how pumped up they'd gotten over the lives lost to WARLORD. At that moment, Rand would have been willing to bet his life that neither he nor Crane would ever surface those documents, no matter the provocation.

He wouldn't bet a nickel on Kate's falling into line with them, though. She sat perfectly still, her hands folded over the attaché case in her lap. Inside it were the original documents and the weapons they'd taken into space but never used.

Armed and dangerous in the Pentagon—they'd never have gotten that stuff by the hand-search guards on the bottom floor except for Crane.

The ConSec at the window had been adamant about retaining the hardware. "If Kate's right," he said with a grim smile, "you'll want to keep that stuff for the next few months—next to your bed or on your person."

So nobody was underestimating the danger they were in if their own government had been the instigator of the repeated attempts to derail WARLORD. And Crane had thrown in his lot with them, as of this visit, because of losing Foster and Marshall.

"Are you sure?" Rand had asked Crane, just before they'd come up here, down in the garage, which somehow seemed comforting because you couldn't see the open sky and it reminded him of the lunar bases he'd just left. "We could do this alone. Somebody on the outside might be—"

"You wouldn't get ten feet, with those cases. Even without them, Andresson's not going to take you seriously if I'm not there."

He'd been right, so Rand hadn't argued. And Kate wasn't talking today. She just followed along, as if her soul were still up beyond the clouds. Rand had a scheme in mind to shake her out of it, a proposal to make to Andresson that ought to bring her to her senses, if they could get through this without starting an internal brouhaha that she couldn't survive, professionally. . . .

The door behind the mahogany desk opened and Andresson came in, flashing his congressional smile of welcome. Tall and ramrod straight in an immaculate blue suit, he boomed, "Madam, gentlemen—a triumphant return, I hope?" as he settled behind his desk.

Bright, intelligent blue eyes in a perpetually tanned face gave no sign of what Andresson was expecting.

Crane had turned from the window. Now he sat as Rand said, "Yes and no, sir. That's what we'd like to talk to you about."

Beside him, Kate was still absolutely motionless, her hands folded demurely on the case in her lap. Damn, Rand wished she'd move—throw something, yell at Andresson. Anything.

But she didn't. And Andresson, the chief security officer of the United States government, the interrogator's interrogator, didn't say anything, either. He knew better. Not a single question, or even a prompt, came from Andresson's lips. He just fixed his eyes on them and waited.

Crane shifted in his seat and muttered, "Damn, Rand, let's get it over with." Then he shot Rand an almost pleading look.

"Okay, here goes." Rand met Andresson's gaze. "We haven't checked in with Bates, or written our reports yet. We wanted to talk to you first. Confidentially. Off the record."

"You got it," said Andresson, steepling his fingers. "Shoot."

Rand said, "We had hoped to bring down a Soviet defector—Ilya Palladin, KGB station chief at Sveboda, but he died myster—"

"Excuse me," Kate muttered, rising suddenly. "I have to find the ladies' room." Fumbling with the case she held, she hurried out the office door.

When it shut behind her, Crane let out a sigh of relief, looked at Andresson who still watched with keen, silent attention, and said, "Maybe I better just lay this out quick and dirty, sir, while she's gone. The collateral damage on this project was real high—ESA tour included. You know that. And you know about the ZR/SEAL attrition rate. I lost my two mission specialists; we were attacked up there, during the assembly phase. This Russian that Brittany was running, he was going to come over. He implicated Bates as his agent. We've got a note to that effect.'' Crane paused.

Rand held his breath. Now was the time for Andresson to tell them they were stepping into quicksand, that their clearances didn't extend as far as Bates's operational goals . . . in short, to back the hell off while they still could.

But Andresson only nodded and said, ''Go on, Lieutenant. That's what you're here for.''

Rand's head started to spin as Crane lay out the multitude of tiny irregularities he'd collated from his part of WARLORD: the top-secret order to terminate Rand's team on site if WARLORD misfired or Rand seemed in any way out of order; the attempted sabotage of the TAV that took them from LEO to LSS; the Soviet drone that had managed to lock onto Crane's delivery truck while it was dark side; the repeated clear checks on Faragher, who was obviously somebody's player from the way she'd acted toward Tracey Rand; the Soviet takeout of the ESA tour bus; the murder of Ilya Palladin by his own side once Palladin started considering defection. . . .

''Any one or two of those screw-ups could be bad luck or bad planning, sir,'' said Crane with a tinge of desperation in his voice and a sheen of sweat on his upper lip. ''But not all that. Somebody was leaking data to the other side. Somebody who'd have sacrificed even Director Harper and his wife to get Rand, here, out of commission. Somebody who had enough connections in the Soviet system to put Ilya Palladin, Brittany's agent, on the sidelines and then smoke him when the time was right. Somebody who was able to put an agent with termination orders at the goddamn *coordinates* where WARLORD was being assembled—right place, right time, right American-style spacesuit. . . . Just luck we got through that one with anybody left to push WARLORD's buttons. And it had to be done with inside help. Only my guys and Bates knew WARLORD's exact coordinates—we did all the freight runs ourselves.''

Crane sat back in his chair, slumped from the effort the long speech had taken. He wiped his upper lip with the back of his hand and said in little more than a whisper, "So we're wondering if it's just Bates, running with the opposition, or if it's something else. . . .''

"Something else?" Andresson scowled. "What are you implying, Lieutenant?''

"He wants to know whether this government really intended WARLORD to go on line," said Rand with all the brutality he could muster. "There was a black box— a soft bomb, is my guess, that Bates gave Crane, with orders to make sure I included it in the package at the last minute.''

"Did you?" said Andresson sharply.

"Hell, yeah. I'd be dead if I hadn't. But I didn't trip its dip switches—WARLORD's my baby, remember? I know her specs like I know my own. Now, is that add-on something this government okayed, or not?''

Andresson didn't even blink. "Not to my knowledge. All right, we'll look into it.''

"That's not good enough," Rand said as Crane stood up, anxious to be out of here. "I want a clear answer—yes or no: was the opposition to WARLORD internal? Did you have us going through some very expensive motions? Are you and Bates in this together? Because I've got to report to that bastard in the next few hours, and I want to know what I'm walking into.''

"Oh, Christ," Rand heard Crane whisper to himself.

Andresson stood up too, his face reddening. "I'll try to ignore your lack of tact, doctor. You've been through a rough time and there *have* been an inordinate number of problems—and casualties—during WARLORD's run. The answer, doctor, is no. A resounding and across-the-board no. As far as I'm aware, the only opposition to WAR-LORD in this government is in Congress—and they don't play this kind of hardball.''

Crane was moving around, near the door, off to one side. Suddenly, with Andresson's bald denial of complicity, a weight lifted from Tracey Rand. And yet he was still uneasy. He stood, too. "So, what do we do? How do you want to play it?''

" 'We' don't do anything out of the ordinary," Andresson said. "You two report to Bates, leaving out your conjectures. We'll undertake an investigation, but these things take time. I'll need to see Palladin's report to Brittany—''

"Note. Deathbed note," Crane corrected sourly.

"It's enough to start with," Rand put in. "Look, while I've got your ear, General . . .''

"Go ahead, this is no time to stand on ceremony," said the general, whose face was still flushed.

"Davies is dead, and whoever you've got in mind to replace him probably doesn't have Secretary Brittany's firsthand experience in lunar affairs. Also, she's pretty well blown where she was: the Soviets are on to her, or Palladin wouldn't have been taken out of play. Palladin told her that KGB took out Davies because he was going to propose a two-degree shift outward in both superpowers' tunnel projects and . . . God, Kate! Where is she?''

He whirled and felt acutely the sluggishness of his muscles in full Earth gravity. Crane was standing beside the door, his hands on his hips. The ConSec said, "It took you long enough to start worrying.''

Not only had Kate failed to return from the bathroom, she'd taken that damned attaché case with her. In it was enough firepower to alter Bates's future drastically. Rand was already running clumsily for the door when he told Crane, "Get with the general on what kind of help we can get her. If she's not in the ladies' room, meet me at Langley, ASAP.''

''Shit no.'' Crane had the door open. ''I'm coming with you. General, get me some backup—*just* backup. The last thing we want is to get the lady killed.''

Rand was already too far down the hall to hear Andresson's reply.

# Chapter 10

# EXACTION

Langley had never looked more forbidding. Kate flashed her credentials to the guard and parked in front of an AU-THORIZED PERSONNEL ONLY sign. Then she walked in the front door, carrying her attaché case, its manacle snug around her wrist.

She handed her card to the woman at the desk, who slid it into a computer's slot and handed it back with a cheery, "Good afternoon, ma'am."

Then she walked down to the elevators and waited. They'd changed the artwork again, she thought, but modern canvases looked so much alike . . . Waiting for the elevator, her nose decided to clog up: her sinuses had had about all they could take, confused by the unfiltered air of Earth after so long in space; the climate-controlled filtering system at CIA headquarters caused them to tangibly palpitate.

The crying hadn't helped. She hated it when she cried. She'd almost started again, in Andresson's office, when Ilya's name had come up. It was no use trying to get Bates through channels. Not when those channels could be compromised; not when Andresson himself could be involved.

She saw complicity everywhere she looked. The proof of it was in Crane's disclosures: Crane had seemed to be fully on their side, but had had orders all along to kill Rand—and then herself, no doubt, because she'd have been a material witness—if any little thing went wrong.

Or went right. She knew what Bates was doing. Ilya had told her enough, and she'd guessed the rest: Bates was playing both sides against the middle—working for the Soviets in an attempt to stop WARLORD at any cost but that of his position in CIA's Staff D.

Part of Staff D's responsibility was *exaction*—extortion, enforcement, tasking in extreme situations. Exaction could also mean forcing obedience, or execution. Revenge.

It was the right office to be going to, for what she had in mind. She pushed the proper button when the elevator came and held her case before her demurely, both hands around its handle, its comforting weight resting against her knees.

You couldn't expect the system to be perfect. You couldn't expect, when you were dealing with a professional's professional like Bates, to find something he'd overlooked—some loose end, some incriminating factor, some unswept corner where dust had been allowed to gather. Men like Bates were good housekeepers. They cleaned up after themselves. In this case, what Bates was cleaning up was a certain human untidiness—lives.

Blake. Kendall. Frank. Richelson. Davies. The entire ESA tour—Chandra, Faragher, the lot. Foster. Marshall. Ilya.

Trace and Crane would be next, once she was gone. If it was allowed to continue. Nobody who'd been involved with WARLORD would be left alive.

Somehow, she didn't mind that she was already dead—one way or the other. You couldn't do what she was going to do and survive it. But maybe she could stop Bates. No one else could, that was sure.

If Andresson was a co-conspirator, nothing would happen to Bates at all . . . they'd been foolish to go there. If

Andresson was spotlessly clean, he'd mount an investigation.

And that investigation wouldn't alter Trace's fate, or Crane's—unless to hurry it. Bates would get wind of any attempt to flush him, and do one of two things: ride it out and come through smelling like a rose; or jump for ComBloc, where he'd receive a hero's welcome.

The elevator stopped; it wasn't her floor. Two men with credentials hanging around their necks on chains got in, ceasing their conversation because they didn't know her. All three of them stared at the indicator lights above the elevator's door as it continued climbing.

If Bates, by some unlikely chance, was arrested before he could break for Moscow, his trip east would only be delayed. There was no way the U.S. could try the man openly, because of WARLORD. They could jail him after a series of closed hearings, even convict him of espionage, but that meant nothing—he'd be traded east inside three years.

No, there was no way to put Ilya's soul to rest except her way. Then it didn't matter if she was wrong about Bates's motives. Then it didn't matter that he could claim, even if he were selling his expertise to the Soviets, that he was just doubling, really a patriotic American doing provocation duty for the U.S. government. It wouldn't matter even if it turned out that her own government had sanctioned Bates's activities—if the U.S. had wanted WARLORD to fail, but must pretend to try to launch in order to get a neat shutdown.

Because Bates would be dead. And Ilya had weighed all the data he'd had and chosen to send her after Bates. Bates was Khimik. Khimik had been Ilya's Western contact, who'd deserted Ilya Palladin in his hour of need, who'd refused to help him once WARLORD went on line, who'd sentenced him to death by inaction if not by direct action. . . .

She didn't want to start crying again with the two men

watching her. She gritted her teeth because she didn't want to bite her lip. The elevator stopped and all three of them got out.

She walked down to the proper reception desk, conscious that the two men in suits were right behind her.

When she reached the desk, she said to the man there, "Will you tell Mr. Bates that Secretary Brittany's here on emergency business?"

Bates was Staff D's ranking officer; he'd been in charge of protecting the lives of ZR/SEAL personnel, like he'd been in charge of WARLORD's security; you couldn't do that bad a job without trying.

The two men behind her had taken seats in the reception area. They must be here to see Bates, too. Only they'd had an appointment. . . .

She didn't want to wait. She couldn't bear to wait. She was afraid she'd lose her nerve, or Trace would call her. If he realized where she was and what she was doing, he'd call her and then she might not be able to follow through. And she had to, because, like WARLORD, Bates was worth whatever it cost.

Only, she thought dreamily, with WARLORD you wanted to enable; with Bates, to disable.

The man at the desk was talking to her: "Madam Secretary? You can go right in."

She had only the blurriest memory of his face as she moved past him, taking one clammy hand away from the handle on her case to open the door with Bates's name on it.

Bates was alone in his office, looking exactly the way he had when she'd last seen him: same salt-and-pepper hair cut exactly one-half inch from his scalp; same moon face, now breaking into a polite smile.

A stiff smile. He was disappointed she'd survived. He was probably wondering where the others were. He was—

"This is a surprise, Secretary Brittany. I wasn't expecting you for another—"

She walked past him to the coffee table before his office's black leather couch and balanced her case there, keyed the locks, slipped the manacle from her wrist, and opened it. "For another what, few hours? Days?" She was just chatting, getting out the forty-four magnum under the cover of pulling a report folio from the case's organizer.

"Ah, is something wrong?" Bates asked. "You said this was an emergency. What are you doing on Earth? I received a message that WARLORD was go, but it's too soon for you to be—"

She let the report folder fall away from the gun.

Across the coffee table from her, Bates was very large, standing there. She was thinking, *You'd better shoot him before you lose your nerve,* but her mouth was already moving: "Something's wrong, all right. Ilya Palladin's dead. Do you remember him, Khimik?"

"I . . ." Bates took a step backward.

She said, "Don't," very sharply, and disengaged the safety. It clicked. Bates winced.

"Look, Kate," said Bates, "you've misunderstood what you think you've learned. Palladin was good, he had you fooled. He was the one sabotaging WARLORD. He was using you. His Directorate S buddies killed your Seal personnel to stop the project from going operational. Put that away and we'll talk about—"

"No, I'm not putting this away." Beside and a little bit behind her, the door opened very slowly.

But she saw it, out of the corner of her eye. "Come on, Bates, admit it: *you've* been sabotaging this project all along. How else could you know about the Directorate S hit on Davies—"

"Kate," came Tracey Rand's voice from the doorway. "I'm coming in there, with Crane. Don't shoot Bates, for God's sake. Thanks to you, we've got him dead to rights. Don't throw your life away over this bastard. . . ."

With every word, Rand's voice was coming closer. She knew she ought to shoot Bates. She knew there was no other way. The U.S. had no death penalty for espionage. She *had* to. . . .

Trace's hand came down over hers, on the gun. "Come on, Katydid, would I lie to you? We'll get the bastard— for murder. Andresson sent guys with us to arrest him. They're right outside. Don't do this to us, please."

His voice was thick, choked. Her eyes started to fill with tears. But she could still shoot Bates. Rand knew that, too. His hand on hers, curled around the gun, was exerting no pressure.

*Don't do this to us.* It echoed in her head. At least he hadn't told her not to do it because Ilya wouldn't have wanted it. Ilya would. But Ilya was dead and Trace was here and she was so tired.

She really didn't want to look at Rand, but she did. A quick glance, not long enough away from her target for Trace to make a move or Bates to get away.

Behind Trace was Linc Crane.

Crane said, "This guy ain't worth the death penalty to any more of us, ma'am—Kate. Let us handle it, okay?"

She looked back at Bates, who was standing quite still, except for a tremor she could see even from this distance. He was sweating so that his moon face shone.

He really did look a lot like the man in the moon.

"Trace . . ." Her hand loosed around the gun and somehow she let Rand take it. But that was all right, because he was there to hold her and Crane had his own gun, pointing at Bates.

It wasn't until Rand took her out of there, into the hall, that she realized how terrible she must look. Everyone was staring at them.

Even Andresson, who somehow wasn't angry at her. Andresson came up to them and asked Trace, as if it was nothing out of the ordinary for there to be brandished handguns and a woman crying hysterically on the fifth floor at Langley, "Did you tell her yet?"

And Rand said, "No, I didn't need to mention it—she'll be all right, just give her a little time."

Kate had no idea what they were talking about. It didn't matter. She was holding on to Tracey Rand for all she was worth, and the stupid tears streaming down her face were beginning to ebb.

# EPILOGUE

The Mexican moon was full and Rand was down on the beach, alone, in the surf up to his knees. America was cooking dinner and he could smell the spices, mixing with the salt air.

Candles flickered on the veranda and he knew that, any minute, America was going to call him up to the house to eat. He was almost done, anyway.

The surf around him was littered with shredded WAR-LORD photocopies, strands like seaweed decomposing before his eyes. When he looked up at the moon now, it wasn't the same for him.

He'd been there. He'd done his stint. His memories of it were still fresh, but they would fade. He couldn't see Mars tonight with his unaided eye. He'd never see WAR-LORD that way. If he'd known what it would cost, at the beginning, would he have done it?

Probably.

Would it ever be worth the price they'd paid? That one, he couldn't answer. He never felt good coming off a mission, and this one lingered. Because of Kate—seeing her again. And not seeing her, once it was done.

Three months after the incident at Langley, and he still thought about her too much. Especially tonight.

He heard the chopper long before he saw its running lights. When they were nearly overhead, he started walking quickly down the beach.

At least he had his Earth legs back. It had been weird to feel so heavy, so clumsy; it had reminded him of learning to walk all over again once his prosthetic hip had been emplaced.

Now he could run if he wanted. He did.

When the chopper door opened, he helped her out of it, taking her by the hand and ducking with her under the rushing rotors.

When they had made a safe distance, the chopper lifted. Its wash blew her white skirt and her hair, grown longer, around her face.

He put his arms around her and hugged her until she gasped, "Trace, you'll crush me."

Then he arched back to look at her and said, "Well, how're the Space Talks coming?"

Kate Brittany-Rand screwed up her face in a parody of disgust and said, "Ditsy bunch of dips. They need this week's recess to figure out what it was they said last week."

He chuckled and she pouted. "It's not funny. You did this to me—forced this miserable job on me so you could have America all to yourself."

"You bet." He chuckled as America called from the veranda that dinner was ready. Then he kissed his wife and, arm around her waist, escorted her up to the house.

# FREE!!
# BOOKS BY MAIL
# CATALOGUE

BOOKS BY MAIL will share with you our current bestselling books as well as hard to find specialty titles in areas that will match your interests. You will be updated on what's new from Pocket Books at no cost to you. Just fill in the coupon below and discover the convenience of having books delivered to your home. Please add $1.00 to cover the cost of postage and handling.

------------------------------------

**BOOKS BY MAIL**

320 Steelcase Road E.,
Markham, Ontario L3R 2M1

Please send Books By Mail catalogue to:

Name_____
(please print)

Address_____

City_____

Prov._____ Postal Code _____

(BBM2)